DEBT OF LOYALTY

Professionally Published Books by Christopher G. Nuttall

The Embers of War

Debt of Honor

Angel in the Whirlwind

The Oncoming Storm
Falcone Strike
Cursed Command
Desperate Fire

The Hyperspace Trap

ELSEWHEN PRESS

The Royal Sorceress

The Royal Sorceress (Book I)
The Great Game (Book II)
Necropolis (Book III)
Sons of Liberty (Book IV)

Bookworm

Bookworm
Bookworm II: The Very Ugly Duckling
Bookworm III: The Best Laid Plans
Bookworm IV: Full Circle

Inverse Shadows

Sufficiently Advanced Technology

Stand-Alone

A Life Less Ordinary

The Mind's Eye

TWILIGHT TIMES BOOKS

Schooled in Magic

Schooled in Magic (Book I)

Lessons in Etiquette (Book II)

Study in Slaughter (Book III)

Work Experience (Book IV)

The School of Hard Knocks (Book V)

Love's Labor's Won (Book VI)

Trial By Fire (Book VII)

Wedding Hells (Book VIII)

Infinite Regress (Book IX)

Past Tense (Book X)

The Sergeant's Apprentice (Book XI)

Fists of Justice (Book XII)

The Gordian Knot (Book XIII)

Graduation Day (Book XIV)

The Princess in the Tower (Book XV)

The Broken Throne (Book XVI)

Cursed (Book XVII)

Mirror Image (Book XVIII)

The Decline and Fall of the Galactic Empire

Barbarians at the Gates (Book I)

The Shadow of Cincinnatus (Book II)

The Barbarian Bride (Book III)

HENCHMEN PRESS

First Strike

DEBT OF LOYALTY

CHRISTOPHER G. NUTTALL

This is a work of fiction. Names, characters, organizations, places, events, and incidents are either products of the author's imagination or are used fictitiously. Any resemblance to actual persons, living or dead, or actual events is purely coincidental.

Published by 47North, Seattle

www.apub.com

ISBN-13: 9781542019545
ISBN-10: 1542019540

Cover design by Mike Heath | Magnus Creative

Printed in the United States of America

DEBT OF LOYALTY

PROLOGUE

There was blood on the captain's chair.

Lieutenant Commander Sarah Henderson tried not to think about Captain Saul as she took his seat. Saul had been a decent old man, for all that he'd been a dyed-in-the-wool reactionary who'd been reluctant to promote colonials when he could promote a Tyrian instead. She'd learned a great deal from the older man, from starship tactics to how to manipulate the system . . . and, perhaps unintentionally, just how badly slanted the system was against colonials. She'd thought, when she'd joined the navy, that there would be room for promotion, that she might climb to a command chair of her own. Instead, she'd discovered that most command chairs were reserved for Tyrians. She'd been lucky to be allowed to stay in the navy after the war had come to an end. She wasn't blind to the simple fact that most of the officers who'd been placed on half pay, transferred to the naval reserve, or simply let go had been colonials. The old resentment had curdled long before the civil war had broken out. She was good enough to fight, to risk her life, but not good enough to be promoted into a command chair of her own.

She took a long breath as she studied *Merlin*'s display. The mutiny hadn't been planned, not really. Sure, there had been times when she'd *thought* about taking the ship for herself, but it had been little more than an idle fantasy. Where would she go? A *Warlock*-class heavy cruiser was designed for long-duration missions, but *Merlin* would need a refit sooner or later. And what would she do? She hated pirates too much to become one, and there was little else she could do. But now . . .

It had happened so quickly, so quickly that part of her still couldn't believe that it *had* happened. It had been sheer goddamned luck that she'd been manning the communications console when the message came in, sheer goddamned luck that she'd been able to copy the message to a datapad and erase all traces from the message stream before Captain Saul or his XO had been able to see it. The orders had been clear—and devastating. All colonials, all naval personnel who weren't from Tyre itself, were to be rounded up and held prisoner until they could be transferred to holding facilities on a penal world. Sarah had no idea what had prompted the message, not then, but she'd seen an awful truth in the cold, hard words. She could fight, she could take control of the ship . . . or she could go tamely to her fate.

And my ancestors didn't tame their new home by being tame, she thought. She'd linked up with a dozen others, put together a plan at desperate speed, and taken the ship. The remainder of the crew—Tyrians, or colonials she couldn't vet personally—had been put into lockdown, where they would stay until . . . She didn't know. She honestly had no idea where to take her ship, not now. *If I go home, what happens then?*

She felt a worm gnawing at her heart as she paged through the starcharts. They were committed now. They had been committed from the moment the mutiny stopped being a theoretical exercise and turned deadly. There would be no mercy if the navy caught them. They'd be lucky if they were merely dumped on a penal colony, with a handful of supplies; they'd be more likely to be put in front of a firing squad and shot, their bodies unceremoniously cremated and the ashes dumped in the nearest sea. She knew they were committed . . . and yet, what were they to *do*?

A hundred ideas ran through her head. She could take the ship to *her* homeworld, but what then? The planetary government wouldn't be pleased to see them. They'd have no choice but to hand Sarah and her comrades over to Tyre for trial and execution. And even if that hadn't been a concern, the only thing that linked her and her comrades together was that they were all colonials. They came from a dozen different homeworlds. In hindsight, she wondered if that had been deliberate. The navy might have intended to spread its colonial recruits out as thinly as possible, just to keep them from developing any sort of planetary camaraderie. They were united by their dislike and resentment of the Tyrians, but disunited by everything else. No one would agree on where to take the ship if she put it to a vote.

And we shot the command structure to hell when we launched our mutiny. Her lips twitched in bitter amusement. *Who would back me if I tried to impose my authority by force?*

Sarah gazed around the bridge. There were only four officers on duty, three men and a woman she'd known for the last two years . . . but how far could she trust them? Really? She hadn't been the only officer to want to climb the ranks, no matter how hard the authorities tried to keep her down. She was only the *nominal* commanding officer, even though she'd planned and executed the mutiny. She'd set more than enough precedent for her mutineers to mutiny against *her* . . .

Lieutenant Olaf, the communications officer, glanced back at her. "Captain, we're picking up a push message from the local StarCom."

Sarah felt her expression harden. "Another one?"

"Yes, Captain," Olaf said. "It's being pushed out *everywhere*."

"Show me." Sarah let out a breath. It had been a push message that had started the whole goddamned affair in the first place. "We may as well hear the bad news directly."

King Hadrian's face appeared on the display. Sarah watched, feeling a multitude of emotions. The king had been the strongest supporter of the Commonwealth, before and during the war; he'd been the only one fighting for the Commonwealth on Tyre while the dukes and duchesses had been trying to draw back as much as possible. Sarah knew—it had been on all the newscasts—that the king had been pushing for more integration, for more investment . . . for everything that would make the Commonwealth *work*. And yet, he'd lost more than he'd won. The House of Lords had been steadily cutting the Commonwealth's budget. The cornucopia of resources and investment that had been offered to the colonials during the war had dried up almost as soon as the war had come to an end. Sarah had heard the news from home. Jobs had been lost, businesses were failing, banks were collapsing . . . They'd thought the good times would never end.

But they did, Sarah thought. *We really should have known better.*

She listened to the king's message with a growing sense of disbelief. The king had been forced to flee his homeworld? The king had been declared an outlaw? The king had led his loyalists to Caledonia, where they had established a government-in-exile . . . a government that claimed to be the legitimate government? And hundreds of ships, hundreds of thousands of loyalists, were rushing to join him, to fight for their rights against the cabal that had captured Tyre? It was madness . . .

But she'd heard the rumors. She'd seen the signs that all was not well. Perhaps, just perhaps, the outbreak of civil war was a matter of time.

Had been a matter of time, she corrected herself. The message ended with an appeal to loyalists, inviting them to join him. *The civil war is already here.*

She supposed that explained the message, the one that had sparked the mutiny. The king's loyalists must have been seizing ships, if they hadn't been in command already. His enemies would have moved to stop him . . . She had a vision, suddenly, of superdreadnought bridges being torn apart by gunfire as loyalists battled for control of their vessels. *Merlin* wouldn't be the only ship that had been taken by mutineers. There would be others. She hoped there would be others.

"We have to go," Lieutenant Vaclav said. "Where else *can* we go?"

Sarah contemplated her options carefully. They were painfully few. She couldn't surrender, not now. She couldn't take her ship to her homeworld, not without risking a mutiny or being arrested as soon as she arrived. She couldn't abandon the ship without risking being caught the moment she passed through a bioscanner. She couldn't become a pirate or mercenary or anything else without . . . She looked down at the uniform she wore. She liked to think it still meant something, even though it was splattered with blood. The king wasn't just their *best* option. He was their only *realistic* option.

There was nowhere else to go.

"Nowhere," she said. She straightened up in the command chair. "Set course for Caledonia."

"Aye, Captain," Vaclav said.

And hope to hell we don't get intercepted along the way, Sarah thought as she felt her ship thrumming to life. *They could have set up a blockade by now if they had time to get organized.*

She kept her face impassive, keeping her doubts to herself. The StarCom network wasn't known as the net of a trillion lies for nothing. Even with the latest advancements in interstellar FTL communications, with messages relayed through a dozen nodes rather than simply radiating out of Tyre, it was still possible for *someone* to take control of the network . . . or simply use it to spread lies. There was no way to tell the difference between truth and lies, not from a distance. They were possibly flying straight into a trap.

But we have nowhere else to go, she thought. *We'll just have to do our best to avoid contact until we reach Caledonia.*

CHAPTER ONE

CALEDONIA

"Transit complete, Admiral," Lieutenant Kitty Patterson said. "We have reached Caledonia."

"Transmit our IFF codes," Admiral Lady Katherine Falcone ordered. She felt numb, too tired and worn to be relieved that they'd finally reached their destination. "And keep the vortex generator in readiness."

"Aye, Admiral," Kitty said.

Kat sat back in her chair, one hand brushing blonde hair out of her face. It had been a nightmarish voyage, even though the task force had avoided enemy contact . . . *enemy* contact, damn it. Thinking of her comrades as enemies hurt deeply. She knew there would be ships and crews that had remained loyal to the House of Lords, commanding officers who owed their positions to patronage or crews that simply didn't understand what was at stake . . . She knew it was only a matter of time before fighting broke out in earnest. The brief exchange of missiles at Tyre had made it clear, brutally, that the time for talking was over. The dispute could be settled only by war.

She forced herself to watch the display as more and more icons flashed to life, heedless of her churning thoughts. Everything had happened so *quickly*. She'd known trouble was brewing, everyone had known trouble was brewing, but she hadn't expected a descent into violence and civil war. She hadn't expected to have to make a choice between supporting her king or her family. She hadn't expected . . .

None of us expected this, she thought. *And perhaps, if we'd taken the possibility of war more seriously, this would never have happened.*

She gritted her teeth as her sensors picked out massive orbital fortresses, each one packing enough firepower to give a superdreadnought a very bad day. The king had been confident that Caledonia would side with him—he'd been pouring resources and investment into the colony world for years—but Kat didn't dare take it for granted. If Caledonia sided with the House of Lords instead . . . She shook her head. She wasn't blind to just how badly the colonials had been treated, even during the war. It was unlikely that anyone on Caledonia would feel any real allegiance to the House of Lords, whatever they felt for the king. She knew many of them would want to sit on the sidelines and do as little as possible for either side.

"They're hailing us," Kitty said. "They're requesting permission to speak to the king."

"Relay the message to him," Kat ordered curtly. "And order the fleet to hold position here."

"Aye, Admiral."

This would never have happened if my father had survived, Kat thought glumly. Lucas Falcone had been a stiff-necked old bastard, but he'd been a *man.* He'd understood the importance of winning the peace as well as the war, the dangers of constantly slashing budgets and cutting spending when people were desperate. He'd understood that desperation could lead to war. *And he would never have pulled ships out of the occupied zone until peace was firmly established.*

She let out a breath, feeling sweat prickling down her back. If there was one thing that had angered her, just one thing, it was how the House of Lords had played politics while the occupied zone had burned. She'd watched helplessly as chaos had swept across the region, planets collapsing into civil war or being raided by pirates or simply being hit with genocidal attacks by the remnants of the Theocracy. The war had been won—she'd emerged triumphant from the deciding battle—but the peace had been constantly on the verge of being lost without a trace. Every starship that had been pulled from her command, every marine regiment that had been sent back home . . . Everything she'd lost had meant more dead people, more destroyed lives, more hopelessness and desperation and . . .

We promised those people that we'd protect them, she told herself again and again. *And then we abandoned them.*

She felt a surge of bitter anger. She'd never got on with her oldest brother, but she'd thought better of him. He'd been an adult when she'd been born, a young man who had acted more like a third parent when he'd had time for her at all. She'd never realized that he would abandon the people the Commonwealth had promised to help. He'd sat in his chair, in their *father's* chair, and pronounced a death sentence for hundreds of thousands of people he'd never met and never would. And he'd done it because of politics. He hadn't had any personal hatred for the dead. They'd simply been collateral damage.

Her console chimed. The king's face appeared in front of her. "Admiral?"

"Your Majesty," Kat said stiffly.

"We're welcome here," he said. His handsome face betrayed no trace of the concern he must have felt. "Take the fleet into orbit, then join us for a planning session."

"Yes, Your Majesty," Kat said.

The king smiled, warmly. He didn't look *that* put out, for someone who'd been forced to flee his homeworld at very short notice. He looked every inch a monarch, from his handsome face to a perfectly tailored naval uniform. But then, Kat supposed he found the outbreak of civil war to be something of a relief. The endless circle of politics, the endless debates over the same issue, time and time again with no resolution in sight . . . over. He didn't have to argue for hours over the slightest concession, over something that could be withdrawn at a moment's notice. He could finally command his own ship.

"You've done well, Kat," he said. "Thanks to you, we will thrive."

"Thank you, Your Majesty," Kat said. "I have a small matter to attend to first."

She couldn't help feeling conflicted as the king's image vanished from the display. The war wouldn't just be waged against the House of Lords. It would be waged against her family, against men and women she'd known since she was a little girl . . . She wouldn't be the only one, she was sure, torn in two. How many people would be asking themselves which side they should take? And how many would try to steer a course between the two until neutrality was no longer an option?

And how many will be laying contingency plans for defeat as well as victory? The thought mocked her. She knew her fellows too well to have doubts. *The loudest among them, baying for the king's blood, will be planning how best to surrender if he wins the war.*

She stood. "Order the fleet to enter orbit, as planned," she said. "And then . . . order all off-duty personnel to assemble in the shuttlebay."

"Aye, Admiral," Kitty said.

Kat took one last look at the display—the orbital fortresses were sweeping space with powerful active sensors, but weren't charging their weapons or launching missiles—and strode through the hatch into her ready room. *Her* private space, perhaps the only truly private space on the ship. Everyone else was sharing quarters, doubling or tripling up as the king's staffers and allies crowded onto the ship. Even the king himself was sharing quarters with his fiancée, Princess Drusilla. Kat felt her lips twitch sourly. She didn't *like* the princess—her instincts told her Drusilla was trouble, but the king evidently disagreed.

She put the thought aside as she splashed water on her face, changed into a clean uniform, and studied herself in the mirror. The uniform was pristine, her face was clear . . . but her hair was unkempt, her eyes tired.

She ran her fingers through her hair. She'd allowed it to grow out over the last few months, when she'd been stationed in the occupied zone, but she'd get a cut close to her scalp as soon as possible. She couldn't allow herself to grow lax. She'd done too much of that over the last six months.

And we were the most well-drilled unit in the postwar navy, she thought. *The rest of the fleet must be much worse.*

She scowled, feeling a pang of loss. It was terrifying how quickly standards had fallen once the war had been won. She'd seen too many officers neglect their duties, forsaking drills that taught their crews vital skills; too many experienced officers and crewmen had been pushed out of the service while inexperienced officers with the right connections had been allowed to keep their ranks. Kat had done what she could to arrest that trend during her last deployment. She dreaded to think how badly the other peacetime deployments had neglected the fundamentals. They'd been more concerned with saving money than saving lives.

Maybe William was right to get out when he did, she thought. *Leave on a high note.*

She wondered, as she walked through the hatch and down the corridor, just what had happened to her former XO. She'd taken him back to Tyre, but . . . He hadn't rejoined the fleet in time to leave the system. Where was he? Had he been sent back to Asher Dales? Or was he under arrest? William was, technically, her family's client. What would Duke Peter Falcone, Kat's oldest brother, have made of him? A hero? A traitor? Or someone who had merely been in the wrong place at the wrong time? Kat wished, in hindsight, that she'd kept William on her ship. It would have been good to have his support over the last two weeks.

A handful of crewmen were hurrying into the giant shuttlebay as she approached, their faces pale. There had been all sorts of rumors flying through the ship, even though there hadn't been any official announcement of . . . well, *anything*. A couple of the king's staffers had complained about the rumors; they'd even demanded she shut the rumormongers down, but Kat had merely shrugged. One could no more stop rumors than one could stop the tide by shouting at it. Sure, she could put a handful of loudmouths in the brig . . . but what then? That would simply suggest—to anyone who cared to look—that the worst of the rumors were true.

"Admiral." Captain Akbar Rosslyn was standing by the hatch, looking grim. "They're ready for you."

Kat nodded her thanks and stepped past him, into the shuttlebay. The giant deck had been cleared, the shuttles and landing craft pushed against the far bulkhead so the crew could gather as a body. Chatter hummed through the air as Kat took the makeshift stand and looked down at the gathered crew. There were hundreds of warm bodies in the shuttlebay, only a fraction of the superdreadnought's entire crew. The remainder would be on duty or listening in from the other shuttlebays. It took more than three thousand officers and crewmen to operate a superdreadnought.

Although we could do the job with fewer people if we didn't mind losing efficiency, she reminded herself. A marine sergeant bellowed for silence. *A small crew couldn't fight the ship once she started taking damage.*

She waited for quiet, studying the crew. It was strange to realize that the chain of command had been badly weakened over the last two weeks, even though there hadn't been any serious incidents. She'd studied history. Civil wars weakened the bonds between people, fragmenting society into smaller groups . . . She frowned inwardly. The only thing linking the various colonies together was the Commonwealth itself. If the Commonwealth fell, the colonials would fragment. A chilling thought. The association of worlds she'd sworn to serve was, in many ways, a victim of its own success.

"Two weeks ago, civil war broke out." Kat kept her voice calm, even though she knew she was giving voice to the worst of the rumors. "The dispute between the House of Lords and King Hadrian turned violent.

It is unlikely that the crisis can now be settled by anything but force of arms. I, and this ship, have joined the king."

She paused, choosing her next words carefully. Some of her crew would fight for *her*. Others, colonials all, would fight for the man they saw as their ally and protector. Still others would do their jobs without thinking about the wider implications. And others . . . They wouldn't fight for the king, not against their own people. Or they wouldn't share the grievances that had kick-started the civil war.

"If you want to join us, to fight for the king, you are welcome. I won't attempt to influence your choice. You should choose your side for whatever reason makes sense to you. If you *don't* want to fight for the king, you can either go into an internment camp on the planet's surface or travel straight back to Tyre. We will make transport arrangements as soon as possible. You have my word that no one will be hindered if they want to return to Tyre."

A low rustle ran through the gathered crowd. She didn't give it time to build.

"Make your choice, whichever one you want to make," she said. "But whatever choice you make, stick with it. I won't fault anyone who wants to leave now. Afterwards . . . I need the crew to be united. There will be no chance to switch sides later, once the fighting begins in earnest."

And anyone who tries to switch sides later will be seen as a traitor, she mused as she surveyed the crowd. *And he'll be lucky if he only spends the rest of his life in the brig.*

"If you want to leave, let your section chief know and report to Shuttlebay A by 2100," she concluded. "The marines will transport you somewhere safe, at least until we can arrange transport. If you want to stay, just remain in your place and resume your normal duties. I will be happy to have you."

She stepped down and headed for the hatch, ignoring the chatter behind her. She'd meant what she'd said. She wasn't going to try to influence them, even though she knew she *could*. The Royal Navy had been an all-volunteer force from day one, when there had been only a handful of destroyers to protect Tyre, and that wasn't about to change now. Besides, trying to run a navy with conscripts was difficult and dangerous. The Theocrats had found that out the hard way.

And our crewmen are far from ignorant, she reminded herself. *A handful of resentful crewers could do a great deal of damage if they decided to rebel instead of submit.*

She winced at the thought. She'd never understood how the Theocratic navy had managed to function. There were limits to how far one could brutalize one's crews before the starships started to fall apart, if the crew didn't mutiny first. The Royal Navy had never made that mistake, thankfully. Tyre trusted its crewmen. But it also meant the crewmen couldn't be press-ganged into fighting for either side. Better to lose half her crew than risk having a mutiny at the worst possible moment.

General Timothy Winters met her outside the shuttlebay. "Admiral, we've borrowed a colonist-carrier from Caledonia for the . . . ah . . . *dissenters*," he said. "They should have no trouble getting home."

"Good," Kat said. A colonist-carrier had the great advantage of looking harmless. The defenders of Tyre might be jumpy after everything that had happened, but they were unlikely to slam an antimatter missile into a colonist-carrier, particularly one that was careful not to violate the planetary defense perimeter. "And your men?"

Winters looked impassive. His voice was disapproving. "We had a few desertions, Admiral. But most of my troops chose to remain."

"It's important they have a free choice, General," Kat said, although she knew saying it would be pointless. She'd done her best to keep her thumb off the scales, but she was uneasily aware that there would be people who would feel pressured into making a choice that didn't sit well with them. "We . . . This isn't what we signed up for, when we took the oath."

"No," Winters said. "But that doesn't mean we can change our minds when the shit hits the fan."

Kat shrugged. The Theocracy had been a serious threat when she'd joined up. Everyone—at least, everyone with a gram of sense—had known that war was coming. But no one had seriously expected a civil war, not back then. It was unreasonable to expect everyone to be *happy* with the prospect of firing on their own people. She would have been seriously worried about anyone who *was*.

"Don't pressure anyone," she said. "Just . . . give them the same chance."

She nodded, then walked down the corridor. The next few days were going to be very busy. She would have to reorganize everything from crew rotas to squadron formations, transferring officers and crewmen all over the fleet to fill the gaps in her roster. It was going to be a nightmare, even if she could pass most of the work to her subordinates. She wondered, sourly, what she'd do if her staffers chose to go home. She'd never really understood how important staff officers were until she'd been promoted. *Someone* had to turn the commanding officer's orders into reality.

Two of the king's personal guardsmen were on duty outside the VIP section. They checked her identity and scanned her for concealed weapons, then waved her through the hatch. Kat snorted at their paranoia, although she understood their concern. The superdreadnought was an alien environment, manned by crewmen who hadn't been thoroughly vetted. Who knew how many crewmen might try to end the civil war by murdering the king?

"Admiral," a quiet voice said as she passed through. A short man was standing by the king's cabin, waiting for her. "We need to talk."

CHAPTER TWO

CALEDONIA

Kat didn't know Sir Grantham that well.

He was one of the king's privy councilors, one of his foremost advisers, but he and Kat had hardly shared the same social circles. He'd been knighted at some point, suggesting that he'd done the kingdom some service, yet the act hadn't made the news. Kat knew there was a lot that *didn't* make the news, of course, but she should have heard whispers if it was something classified. The fact she hadn't heard anything meant . . . *what*? She didn't know.

And she didn't really like him. She wasn't sure why. He was handsome, in a bland way that suggested he'd had cosmetic surgery rather than having his genetics engineered or relying on blind chance. His brown hair and wry smile made him look warm and friendly, although there was an edge to his posture that suggested it was an act. Maybe she was bothered by the hints of sycophancy, of a social climber trying to make his way to the top through any means necessary. God knew she'd met enough social climbers in her early life. She could have surrounded herself with a small army of sycophants from birth if she'd wished.

But he is completely dependent on the king, Kat reminded herself, as she allowed Sir Grantham to lead her into a small conference room. *He has no independent power base or wealth of his own.*

The thought stung, more than she'd expected. *She* didn't have an independent power base now, insofar as she'd ever had. She'd been her father's client, for all intents and purposes; now, technically, she'd betrayed her family by siding with the king. Her trust fund had probably been confiscated, at least until she gave a full accounting of herself and sought her family's forgiveness. The thought made her snort. Her brother had never liked her. He'd sooner see her starve than forgive her . . .

She rested her hands on her hips as she turned to face Sir Grantham. "What do you want?"

Sir Grantham looked, just for a second, unsure of himself. "We have to talk," he said finally. The hatch hissed closed behind them. "We . . ."

"Then *talk*," Kat said. She had too much to do. The fleet had to be reorganized, the crews had to be shunted around . . . She simply didn't have *time* for a long and pointless chat. She'd never liked high society's habit of using ten words when only one would do, and she had no intention of embracing it now. "What do you want?"

"You're sending half your crew back home," Sir Grantham said. "Back to the *enemy*."

The enemy, Kat thought. A month ago, everyone had been on the same side. It was hard to believe that the Commonwealth was now irreparably split in two, that they were about to start shooting at each other. *We're already thinking of them as the enemy?*

She kept her face carefully blank. "Yes. So?"

Sir Grantham flushed. "You're giving aid and comfort to the enemy!"

Kat took a long breath. "Would you rather I kept unwilling crewmen on this ship?"

"You shouldn't have sent them back to Tyre," Sir Grantham said. "I . . ."

"Let me put it to you as simply as I can." Kat met his eyes, silently daring him to look away. "Spacers, soldiers, marines . . . They're not *machines*. None of them signed up to fight their former comrades. None of them. They joined to defend the Commonwealth or fight the Theocracy or simply because they wanted adventure and excitement . . . They didn't join up to fight a civil war. And we dragged hundreds of thousands of crewmen all the way to Caledonia without so much as *asking* if they want to join us."

"They should follow orders," Sir Grantham insisted. "They're paid to—"

"*Legitimate* orders." Kat cut him off. "There's no provision in the Articles of War for *civil* war. They didn't know they would be fighting their former comrades when they joined up."

"And so you want to send them back home?" Sir Grantham sounded astonished. "You should keep them here . . ."

"And then what?" Kat held his gaze. "There will be—there *are*—crewmen in this fleet who don't support the king. What am I meant to do with them? Hold mass executions? Throw them out the airlock? Dump them on a penal world? You know what? I don't even know which members of my crew might support the king! Perhaps I should just start shooting crewmen at random."

Sir Grantham flushed. "You know what I mean."

"I *don't* know what you mean," Kat corrected, coldly. "Please. Enlighten me."

"The crewmen you're sending home will join the enemy," Sir Grantham said. "You're *helping* them to . . ."

Kat let out a long breath. "First, it probably doesn't matter. The House of Lords is not short of manpower. We're not going to be sending entire squadrons of superdreadnoughts into their welcoming arms. They will have no trouble mustering a fleet, if we give them time, with or without the crewmen we're sending back. It simply does not matter.

"Second, and I want you to think carefully about this, what sort of message do you think it sends to everyone, the people on both sides, if we *don't* let our crews vote their conscience?"

She didn't give him a chance to answer. "I'll tell you what sort of message it sends. It suggests that we don't give a damn about the people who fight for us, that we are willing to press-gang crewmen into fighting for us . . . that we are dragging people who have nothing to do with our fight—who don't *want* anything to do with our fight, who don't give a damn who comes out on top—*into* our fight. That we are *forcing* them to fight for us. Do you really want a mutiny? Or someone trying to sabotage the ship?"

"They'll follow orders," Sir Grantham insisted.

"It only takes one person to cause a great deal of trouble," Kat said. "If we force people to fight for us, they will resent it. They will see us as the enemy even if they see our cause as *right*. The ones who don't really care about our cause will sympathize with the ones who see *us* as the enemy, because we press-ganged them into fighting for us. We cannot afford to treat our crew as *slaves*. Slaves can revolt."

She sighed inwardly, knowing he wouldn't understand. He'd probably grown up among the lesser aristocracy, at a guess, the ones who obsessed over status and social precedence, the ones who snapped and snarled whenever someone of lesser birth threatened to climb past them . . . the ones who clung to their social pretensions because they simply didn't have anything else. To them, the servants—their butlers, their maids, even their bodyguards—were just tools. The idea that they might have thoughts and feelings of their own was alien to them.

"I did what I had to do," she said, firmly. "This way, we know that the people who fight for us genuinely *want* to fight for us. And the remainder of the crew will know it too. It will be harder, much harder, for any dissenters to plot a mutiny or sabotage the ship."

"You weakened us," Sir Grantham protested.

Kat allowed her gaze to sharpen. "I would sooner take an undermanned ship into battle than risk having my crew turn on me," she said firmly. "And I will *not* betray my crewmen by forcing them into a war they didn't volunteer to fight."

"We have to win," Sir Grantham said. "And that means . . ."

". . . Not doing things that might cost us the war?" Kat strode past him. "I am in command of this fleet. If you have a complaint about the way I do things, take it to His Majesty. He can tell me what he thinks of your complaints."

She stopped by the hatch, slowly turning to face him. "And if you try to interfere with the off-loading, I will break you."

Sir Grantham purpled. Kat was sure he was trying to think of a response, of a crushing remark that would send her to her knees, but she didn't give him time. Instead, she turned back to the hatch and walked through. The hatch hissed closed behind her, leaving him in the conference room. She wasn't really surprised he hadn't tried to follow her. She'd put him in his place.

I sounded just like my cousin, Kat thought sourly. She'd never really *liked* Cousin Olivia, who'd married well and didn't let anyone forget it. *And she would have been a great deal nastier as she cut him off at the knees.*

Her lips twitched as she made her way down the corridor, passing a handful of open cabins where the king's staffers and closest supporters, the ones who couldn't remain on Tyre without being arrested or forced into exile, were making their preparations to disembark. Kat's crew would be glad to see the last of them. The superdreadnought was no *Supreme*, no interstellar liner with gold-plated bulkheads and staffers willing to do anything, anything at all, for a hefty tip. Kat had had to put one of the aristocrats in the brig for harassing a young crewman. The dumb bastard hadn't realized, somehow, that he wasn't in his estate any longer. Or, for that matter, that no one had to put up with his conduct. He'd been lucky not to have his lights punched out.

A pair of servants hurried past her, carrying a large trunk. Kat wondered idly what its owner had packed, then decided it probably didn't matter. The king himself had packed well—he'd been one of the few people to realize he might have to leave Tyre—but the others hadn't had much time to think about such eventualities. Kat had read the security reports. Some of the aristocrats had brought clothes and money, in a number of interstellar denominations; others, less practical or simply caught on the hop, had brought everything from shooting gear, as if they were going on safari, to works of art and other absurd comforts. She found it hard to believe that anyone could be so stupid.

But I suppose they could sell the paintings, if they desperately needed money, she reflected as she reached the final cabin. *They'd just have to find a buyer . . .*

She pressed her hand against the scanner and waited. The king's guardsmen had been horrified when it had dawned on them that it was difficult, very difficult, to keep the superdreadnought's crew out of Officer Country. The superdreadnought was no luxury liner, with firm lines between first-, second-, and steerage-class passengers. The guardsmen had wanted to seal off the whole section, but the king had overruled them. Kat rather suspected her old friend was enjoying his freedom, such as it was. He'd never sailed on a superdreadnought before.

The hatch hissed open, allowing her to step inside. The quarters, designed for an admiral, were palatial by naval standards, which hadn't stopped some of the aristocrats from openly wondering if they'd been dumped in *midshipman* cabins. Kat honestly hadn't known if she should laugh or cry when she'd heard the complaints. Midshipmen, even *aristocratic* midshipmen, could only dream of having a boxy compartment to themselves. They simply didn't have enough room to swing a cat.

And they have to share it with a handful of others, Kat reflected. She'd enjoyed her first cruise, but the lack of privacy had grated on her. *They would kill just to have the compartment to themselves.*

She looked around the compartment, feeling an odd twinge of discomfort. The quarters had been hers a couple of weeks ago. She'd moved into her ready room to provide space for the king, his princess, and his attendants. They hadn't changed the compartment much, she noted, save for the handful of boxes stacked awkwardly against the far bulkhead. The portrait of her father she'd hung on one bulkhead hadn't been removed. She wondered, grimly, what her father would have thought of the civil war. It was hard to believe that the situation would have spun so badly out of control if her father hadn't been assassinated at the end of the war.

The last *war*, she reminded herself. She'd never really been at peace, even after the formal end of the Theocratic War. *How quickly we forget.*

A hatch opened. She straightened to attention as the king stepped out of the bedroom, wearing his carefully tailored naval uniform. He looked good in it, Kat had to admit, although he'd never served a day in his life. His advisers hadn't either, she guessed; he might not know it, but he didn't *hold* himself like a naval officer. His posture was a little *too* sharp, his bearing a little *too* authoritative. But he'd look good on the holovid, she supposed, and that was all that mattered.

"Kat," the king said. "Thank you for coming."

"Your Majesty," Kat said.

She bobbed her head. They'd known each other since childhood, although the demands of their respective social classes had kept them from being too close. And she was a privy councilor in her own right. She had the right to call him by his first name, if she wished. But she knew better. They *had* to tend to the formalities, now that the established order was starting to fracture. They had to keep telling themselves that very little had changed. Who knew? Perhaps the pretense would be enough to make it so.

The king grinned. He'd always been handsome, with dark hair, dark eyes, and a roguish look that had melted more than one heart. Kat had heard the rumors about the king's girlfriends, although none of them had ever been confirmed. It was hard to take them on faith when she knew the rumors that the king had engaged in an affair with her were complete fabrications. Her lips twitched at the absurd thought. An affair with the king? She was sure she would have noticed if she'd had an affair with the king. She liked and respected him—not least because he was the only one who'd fought for colonial rights—but they'd never been more than friends and allies.

"I hear that you're disembarking some of your crew," the king said. He gave her a reassuring smile. "I *quite* understand."

"Thank you, Your Majesty." Kat kept her face impassive. "Sir Grantham has already tried to tell me off for it."

The king shrugged. "Some of my advisers feel that it is a mistake."

"Keeping them would be an even *greater* mistake," Kat pointed out, again. "We don't want people who haven't committed themselves to our cause."

She shook her head in irritation. She had little patience for politics, for endless debates over pettifogging issues when there were *real* problems on the horizon. Politicians seemed to produce nothing these days but hot air . . . while *real* people were robbed, raped, and murdered. Her father, at least, had been an exception. She wondered, bitterly, why he hadn't taught his oldest son the difference between important matters and petty politics before it was too late. The king might have been inexperienced, at least before the Theocratic War, but at least he had a good head on his shoulders. He knew not to waste time with nonsense.

"Quite," the king said. "There will be others who will join us, of course."

"Of course," Kat echoed. The Commonwealth had been fracturing into two camps well before the shooting had actually begun. Now . . . Everyone who wanted to fight would be heading to Caledonia. "Why do you keep him around?"

The king blinked. "I beg your pardon?"

"Sir Grantham," Kat said. She knew why most of the privy councilors had been chosen, but Sir Grantham was a mystery. "Why is he on the privy council?"

"He's a fixer," the king said, simply. "He gets things done for me."

"Ah," Kat said.

The king's smile grew wider. "I'll be transferring myself to Caledonia this afternoon," he told her. "The people down there"—he jabbed a finger at the deck—"have already laid on a reception, after which we will discuss reclaiming Tyre before our enemies rally their troops and prepare for war. You'll be joining us?"

"Of course," Kat said. "It would be my pleasure."

That was a lie. She would have preferred to remain on her flagship, but she knew it wasn't really a request. Besides, she would have to ensure that the king and his councilors didn't come up with a plan that looked good on paper but would fail spectacularly the moment someone tried to put it into practice. She'd seen enough problems caused by armchair admirals not to want to let the councilors dictate the course of the war. They were good people, in their way, but they were not experienced military officers. She shuddered to think how many lives had been lost, during the *last* war, because too many officers had never fought a real war.

"Very good," the king said. "I'm sure you'll enjoy it."

"We'll see," Kat said. She was pretty sure that was a lie too. "But I don't have much time to waste. I'll be needed back aboard ship fairly soon."

"We have time," the king said. He sounded confident, for someone who had never witnessed combat from the flag deck. "It will take them weeks, perhaps months, to organize themselves for war."

"Yes," Kat said. True, as far as it went. But her duty consisted of pouring cold water on his thoughts. "And it will take us a long time too."

CHAPTER THREE

CALEDONIA

Caledonia, Kat recalled, had been a surprisingly well-developed world when the Commonwealth's expanding border had washed through its system. Indeed, in many ways, Caledonia had been an *ideal* candidate for membership. The system had a small but growing industrial base, a thriving educational base, and a handful of freighters plying the spacel-anes, helping to reinvigorate interstellar trade. But Caledonia had been hampered by the Commonwealth itself. Tyre had seen Caledonia as a rival, a potential threat; Tyre had manipulated the Commonwealth's structure to ensure that Caledonia would always be second-best. Kat rather suspected the move had been nothing more than petty, pointless evil. In the short term, it had worked; in the long term, an entire planet had become enraged and united against Tyre.

And the king was able to position himself as the protector of the small, Kat thought, as they finally, *finally*, headed for the royal residence. *The entire planet loves him.*

She didn't blame the planet for welcoming the king, their savior. It had been the king who'd insisted on establishing shipyards and industrial nodes at Caledonia, the king who'd invested *trillions* of crowns in the planet's infrastructure . . . the king who'd argued for the planet to be heavily defended, who'd pushed for defending *every* planet in the

Commonwealth even though such measures prolonged the war. The contradiction amused her more than she cared to admit. Caledonia loathed Tyre but adored Tyre's king. He could literally get away with murder, as far as the locals were concerned. He'd worked hard to earn their goodwill.

Kat felt tired, a deep, aching tiredness that pervaded every inch of her body. She detested formalities, but ever since the shuttle had landed, there'd been nothing but formalities. An endless series of speeches from local dignitaries, all of which had blurred together in her mind, followed by a long parade, where everyone on the planet seemed to want to shake the king's hand or meet his eyes. She hadn't been the only one, surely, who worried about what a lone gunman could do when the king was in the open. A sniper could have put a bullet through the king's head with ease if he'd had the chance. The security cordon had been almost pitifully weak. She was relieved when they finally entered the palace, leaving the crowds behind. And yet, part of her wanted only to return to the ship. The latest set of updates had suggested she'd lost a third of her crew.

It could have been worse, she told herself as the staff showed them into the conference chamber. *We could have been stuck with all officers and no crewmen.*

She looked around the chamber, not bothering to disguise her interest. The space was quite efficiently designed, certainly in comparison to the conference rooms back home. The walls were paneled with dark wood, and a painting of the *previous* king hung on the far wall, but otherwise the chamber was strikingly modern. There had been no attempt to hide the holoprojector or the drinks cabinet, no attempt to pretend that the chamber dated back to a bygone age. Kat had always found the pretensions amusing, when they hadn't been awkward. There wasn't a person alive who remembered the days before FTL travel and high technology. She didn't think there was anyone on Tyre who'd been born on Old Earth.

A serving girl wearing a strikingly conservative uniform offered her a mug of coffee. Kat took it gratefully, nodding her thanks. The servants looked pleased to be fawning on the king—although, the cynical part of her mind noted, their fawning wasn't quite up to Tyrian standards. She wondered, as the servants were shooed out of the chamber, just how they'd cope with the king and his court. Too many people in his retinue were used to taking their servants for granted.

And he'll have to deal with it, somehow, she thought. The king might be popular and lauded, but that wouldn't last. If he wore out his welcome, the planet might turn on him and his followers. Kat had no illusions. Caledonia's orbital fortresses could blow the hell out of her fleet if they opened fire at point-blank range. *We'll have to do whatever it takes to keep them onside.*

Sir Grantham rose. "Ladies and gentlemen, the king!"

Hadrian waved for his councilors to remain in their seats, then leaned forward. "We are at war," he said. "The time for talking is over. The issues between us, between the Monarchy and the House of Lords, can only be settled by violence."

He lowered his voice. "The universe does not *care* who is in the right, my friends. The universe doesn't give a damn if our cause is just, if we are righteous souls; we do not have the strength of ten because our hearts are pure. There is no time, now, for debating the rights and wrongs of the situation. The time for talking is over. This is the time of war. Might may not make right, as many have argued; might determines what happens. The winners of this war will be the ones who determine what is *right*."

Kat shivered, despite herself. She knew he was right.

"There is no room for compromise," the king continued, coolly. "We cannot come to terms we, or they, would find acceptable. Either we win and impose our will on them, or they win and crush us. There is no middle ground. We will not negotiate with them on major issues, because there is no way to come to terms. We will discuss minor issues with them, such as trading our loyalists for theirs, but nothing else. I want everyone to be absolutely clear on this. We are at war. There is no room for half measures."

There was a long, chilling pause. Lord Gleneden spoke first.

"Your Majesty," he said. "Are you proposing that we fight an *uncivilized* war?"

Kat winced. Lord Gleneden had always struck her as being conservative, so conservative that she was surprised he'd remained on the privy council, but his expertise as an economist was unmatched. He'd worked closely with Kat's father when they'd prepared the Commonwealth for war. And he'd served the *king's* father, practically from birth. He might be conservative, but he wasn't disloyal.

Hadrian looked annoyed. "No. I am making it clear that we cannot reach a compromise that both sides can accept."

"And how far are we prepared to go?" Lord Gleneden pressed, sharply. "Because we may have an edge in the short term, Your Majesty, but *they* have the long-term advantage."

"Then we take advantage of what we have." Earl Antony thumped the table with one meaty fist. "We move now to retake Tyre and crush our enemies!"

Kat felt a flash of irritation. Earl Antony genuinely *did* have military experience, but it had been in the planetary militia. He'd never seen real action. And, like all people who didn't have experience, he underestimated just how difficult it could be in wartime to get the slightest thing done. He'd never had to worry about moving troops from one place to another, making sure they arrived on time and armed . . . He'd never had to actually *fight*, outside training exercises. He'd done well on the tests, Kat had to admit, but exercises always left out the *real* emergency. A platoon of Royal Marines would have wiped out a militia regiment before its commanders even realized they were under attack.

"We will fight according to the Articles of War," she said firmly. "It is important, particularly now, that we honor the rules. This war could easily spin out of control if we don't."

"The Theocracy didn't give a *damn* about the Articles of War," Earl Antony snapped. "You should have nuked Ahura Mazda to retaliate for what they did to Hebrides!"

Kat cocked her head. "And how many *billions* of innocent civilians would have died, if I had?"

"They were enemies," Earl Antony hissed. "They had no right—"

"I was there." Kat cut him off, her voice as sharp as a knife. "The average person on Ahura Mazda—male, female, whatever—had *no* power. They could no more have stopped the war and brought their leaders to heel than I could repeal the law of gravity! And they didn't deserve to be slaughtered simply because their leaders were utter bastards!"

She met the king's eyes, willing him to understand. "This is a civil war. The people we will be facing—the people we will be trying to kill, the people who will be trying to kill *us*—are our people, our friends and families and countrymen. We will have to live with them after the war comes to an end, whoever wins. We cannot hope to win by turning the homeworld, *our* homeworld, to glass. We have to put limits on what we are prepared to do to win.

"If nothing else"—she allowed her eyes to sweep around the table, silently gauging their reactions—"we have to convince them that they *can* surrender. That we *will* treat them with honor, if they come to terms with us. That there *is* a future with us . . .

"If we don't, they'll fight to the last. And they might win."

Another pause grew and lengthened.

"Anyone who fights for the House of Lords, against the king, is committing treason," Earl Antony growled finally.

"Technically, perhaps," Kat said. It might be true, but the issue would be decided by whoever won the war. "But if we start refusing to accept surrenders, or mistreating people who do surrender, they won't surrender. Why should they?"

The king nodded slowly. "We will fight according to the Articles of War," he said. "And yes, we will accept surrenders."

Kat allowed herself a moment of relief. Attitudes would harden, she knew. The war would make sure of it. Earl Antony wasn't the only one to argue that the Commonwealth should have repaid mass slaughter and genocide in kind, even though it would have been futile. She doubted the Theocracy's leaders would have cared if a handful of colony worlds had been glassed, scorched free of life; she knew, deep inside, that she would have refused to carry out such orders if they'd been issued. Perhaps she would have been relieved of command, with her successor carrying out the genocide, but . . . At least her conscience would have been clear. She couldn't have lived with herself if she'd wiped out billions upon billions of innocents whose only crime had been to be born on the wrong planet.

"And that means sending the guilty parties into exile, rather than putting them on trial and executing them," Earl Antony grumbled. "They . . ."

"If it ends the war sooner, with us victorious, it is a small price to pay," King Hadrian said. "And Admiral Falcone is right. We have to live with them afterwards." His smile thinned. "Lord Snow, where do we stand?"

Lord Snow took control of the display and projected a holographic starchart above the table. Kat leaned forward, studying it thoughtfully. Thirty-seven stars were blinking green, suggesting their planets had joined the king; twenty-two stars were red, indicating that they were either hostile or occupied by enemy forces. A handful of stars were blue, suggesting that they had declared neutrality and refused to join either side, but none of those were particularly significant. They were on the edge of the Commonwealth, too poor and primitive to tip the balance. Kat guessed their rulers were secretly hoping they'd have a chance to join the winning side, once the outcome became clear. Their allegiance probably wouldn't make any difference.

"We've been exchanging diplomatic notes ever since the shooting started," Lord Snow said, calmly. The king's diplomat seemed unconcerned by the prospect of all-out war. "A number of worlds have declared for us, although their ability to support our ships and troops is limited. We believe that Boskone and Yale *would* declare for us, given half a chance, but the House of Lords controls the naval bases in their systems. It might be . . . *dangerous* . . . for them to come over to our side."

"Probably," Kat said. "The House of Lords wouldn't have to occupy the planets to render them harmless."

Lord Snow nodded. "The majority of our *enemies* have strong ties to the House of Lords," he added, "and have no particular interest in switching sides at the moment. We're still exchanging messages, of course, but I feel we're unlikely to get anywhere, at least until we produce victories. Right now, Your Majesty, that means that a sizable chunk of the Commonwealth's industrial base is under enemy control."

"Then we have to take it off them," Earl Antony snapped.

"If we can," Lord Snow said. "I've sent missives to foreign governments, declaring the existence of a government-in-exile, but so far there haven't been any replies. I suspect that any formal recognition of our existence, either as a government-in-exile or the legitimate government of Tyre and the Commonwealth, will have to wait until we show that we can and do exercise power. Right now, foreigners have nothing to gain and a great deal to lose by offering recognition. Whatever our legal status, on paper, it is a simple fact that our enemies are in control of Tyre."

"The government rests in *me*," the king said, sharply. "I *am* the government."

"With all due respect, Your Majesty, that isn't true." Lord Snow took off his glasses and cleaned them with a small cloth. "Your person is *part* of the government, true. But, even in the best of cases, you are not *all* the government. Nor do you exercise effective control over Tyre.

The post-Breakdown standard is to recognize governments that exercise control. You, we, do not."

And that means, sometimes, that we have to recognize governments we dislike, Kat reflected sourly. There were some planetary governments that deserved to be unceremoniously crushed, their armies disbanded and their leaders hanged. And yet, they had to be recognized. It was *they* who were in complete control. Nothing short of an invasion would remove them from power. *Right now, we're a motley band of refugees.*

The king's face darkened. "Do we *need* their recognition?"

"Not now, Your Majesty," Lord Snow said. "And, once you retake Tyre, you will have it by default."

"Good," the king said. "Are we ready for war?"

Lord Gleneden spoke first, snapping out points as if he expected to be silenced at any moment. "They control roughly two-thirds of the Commonwealth's industrial base, Your Majesty. There were . . . *difficulties* . . . caused by the postwar drawdown, as you are aware, but the House of Lords should have no real difficulties in getting the industrial base back online. In most cases, it will merely be a matter of switching back to military production. They will need some time to deal with bumps along the way, I suspect, but by raw numbers alone they will outproduce us by a fairly considerable margin."

"And parts of their tech base will be more advanced too," Lord Snow injected.

"Quite." Lord Gleneden glanced at Kat, his face unreadable. "If we don't win the war soon, Your Majesty, we will lose. The skill of our commanding officers and the valor of our fighting men will not matter in the face of overwhelming force. We will be crushed."

"We'll be in the same boat as the Theocracy," Kat said.

"Then we will take the offensive as soon as possible," the king said. "Can we strike Tyre? Now?"

"Not yet," Kat said. "We will need time to reorganize, to compensate for the crew who've left us and integrate newcomers from all over the Commonwealth. We do have an edge—my fleet was the largest single unit outside Home Fleet itself—but we will need time to gather ourselves before we can take full advantage of it. Right now, any attack on Tyre will be, at best, extremely costly."

"And if we lose the fleet, we might lose the war," the king mused.

"There's no *might* about it," Lord Gleneden said. "Without the fleet, we will lose."

"Quite," Lord Snow agreed. "Let us have no illusions. Our supporters will start edging away the moment it looks like we're losing. They will want to come to terms with our enemies, just to save their skins."

"Then we should gamble everything on one strike," Earl Antony said. "If we will lose if we do nothing, then we should take the risk."

"It would end badly," Kat told him. "Tyre is heavily defended. There's no way we can take and hold the high orbitals without losing much of our fleet. We would have to lay siege to the planet, which would give them time to recall their fleets to dislodge us."

Earl Antony glared. "So you're saying it's hopeless?"

"No," Kat said. "I'm just pointing out that we have to lay the groundwork *properly* before we gamble everything on one throw of the dice. We have a great deal of work to do before we can launch *any* offensive."

"Indeed," the king said. His voice was very calm. "What do you have in mind?"

"I have half an idea," Kat said. She did, although she knew she would have to consider the strategy carefully before she took it to the king. "But our first priority has to be to ready the fleet."

"And call for others to rally to our banner," Lord Snow said. "We *might* have more allies than we think. We've already had a couple of ships report for duty, after their crews rose up in the king's name. There will be others."

"Yeah," Earl Antony said. "And how many of them will turn out to be fair-weather friends?"

CHAPTER FOUR

TYRE

From a distance, the city looked peaceful.

Duke Peter Falcone stood at his window and gazed over Tyre City. It was hard to believe that the city teemed with unrest, that there had been riots and bloodshed on the streets only two short weeks ago. The police, army, and militiamen were clearly in evidence, patrolling thoroughly in hopes of nipping any trouble in the bud before it turned into another bloody riot. *Who would have thought*, he asked himself grimly, *that so many people would put their lives on the line for the king?*

But they only heard one side of the story, he reminded himself tartly. The opinion pollsters had been wrong. No, perhaps they'd told their patrons what they thought their patrons had wanted to hear. *They never heard the other side.*

He shook his head slowly. King Hadrian had been on the verge of being impeached. He'd known it too. In hindsight, they should have expected a violent reaction. The king had fought tooth and nail for his pet causes, ever since he'd gained the throne. And yet . . . None of them had expected the king to start a goddamned civil war. They hadn't even expected him to send troops to the Houses of Parliament, to seize the aristocrats and MPs and . . . and what? Peter didn't know what Hadrian had in mind, but he was sure the king had intended to do *something*. A man with as little regard for the niceties as the king wouldn't hesitate to force the aristocrats to surrender their power. Or merely execute them on the spot for getting in his way. Peter knew he'd been lucky to survive. Others had been gunned down before they'd realized that all the old rules had been thrown out the airlock.

And now we're at war, Peter thought. *And we have to win.*

He winced. The endless stream of reports from all over the Commonwealth had made it clear that the king commanded a great deal of support. Planets, asteroids . . . even starships . . . He supposed he shouldn't have been surprised. The king had positioned himself as the protector of the colonials, shielding them from the greed of the planetary elite. And the gesture had paid off. A dozen starships had reported mutinies, their colonial crewers rising up in support of the king. Peter wondered, grimly, just how many ships that had dropped out of contact had gone to Hadrian. Hundreds of starships were unaccounted for, seemingly lost forever. Some of them would be in transit, he thought, but others . . . They might have gone to the king.

A flyer zoomed overhead, approaching the palace. A team of dedicated researchers was digging through the king's files now, what was left of them. The king had planned to abandon his homeworld, they claimed. A number of files had simply been wiped, purged from datacores that had been physically destroyed afterwards. Peter rather suspected they were right. The king had clearly had a contingency plan to flee if the shit hit the fan. If he'd stayed and fought . . .

We underestimated him. It had been easy to forget that the king controlled a corporation *and* the navy. He had hundreds of thousands, perhaps millions, of people who would do his bidding. Peter ruled a corporation himself, but even *he* couldn't quite grasp the combination of power and influence Hadrian had wielded. *Even when we thought we had him on the ropes, he came up swinging.*

He heard the door open behind him, but he didn't turn. Only a couple of people could enter his office without permission, particularly now. The tower was heavily guarded, the rest of the district evacuated. If the king's loyalists thought they could attack him in the seat of his power, they were in for a nasty shock. His guards had authority to open fire if they thought they were under attack, *without* waiting for the prospective terrorist to open fire first.

"Your Grace," Yasmeena Delacroix said. "The holoconference is about to begin."

Yet another thing to blame on the king, Peter thought. Traditionally, meetings were always face-to-face. Now the government was meeting in holoconference, as if they feared being attacked if they clustered in one place. *And the hell of it is that we* are *afraid.*

"Thank you," he said tiredly. "I'm on my way."

"Yes, Your Grace," Yasmeena said. "Would you like me to bring you coffee? Or tea?"

"I've probably had too much coffee," Peter said. He rather suspected he was going to have to cut the meeting short. All the jokes about corporate executives who prospered because they had large bladders had stopped being funny the moment he'd had to start spending most of his time in meetings. "Bring me some tea, if you please."

"Yes, Your Grace."

Peter turned to watch her go, then walked through the door into the conference room. A handful of holoimages were already in place, moving with a faint stiffness that suggested they weren't synchronized perfectly with their subject. Peter wasn't too surprised. Formal etiquette insisted that people at *their* exalted level didn't have to worry about precedence—they could enter the room in whatever order they pleased, without upsetting the social order—but it wasn't fun to wait while the rest of the participants assembled. They were probably reading books or studying their datapads or doing *something* while they waited.

Yasmeena brought him a cup of tea, placing it neatly on the table. Peter nodded curtly as the holoimages rapidly synchronized, their eyes darting around like a sleeper who wanted to claim that he'd merely been resting his eyes. Thankfully, just about everyone invited to attend the conference was senior or experienced enough not to make an issue of it. The world had turned upside down only two short weeks ago. They didn't have time to worry about formalities.

He glanced from face to face as the war cabinet assembled. Israel Harrison, now technically the prime minister; Duke Rudbek, Duchess Zangaria, Duke Tolliver, Duchess Turin . . . the men and women who'd set out to limit the king's power, before realizing just how far he was prepared to go to retain it. And, at the back, Grand Admiral Victor Rudbek, the new First Space Lord. He'd been a compromise candidate—normally, the king chose the First Space Lord—and not everyone was happy with his selection. They feared it gave the Rudbek family too much power.

And we don't have time to worry about that either, Peter told himself as Harrison called the meeting to order. *Right now, we have to stop the king.*

Israel Harrison looked grim. Peter wasn't surprised. The prime minister had been one of the king's strongest opponents on the benches, resolutely arguing against the king's bid for more power and patronage. It hadn't made the man popular—he'd only retained his position as Leader of the Opposition through patronage—but it *had* given him prestige. Being the only one who'd been warning everyone about the king, right from the start, had done wonders for his electability. Besides, the war cabinet needed someone to serve as its public face. Harrison had been the natural choice.

"We've just had confirmation from one of our agents on Caledonia," Harrison said without preamble. "The king has established himself there."

Duke Tolliver snorted. "We have more industrial nodes here, orbiting this planet alone, than there are in the entire Caledonia System."

"That doesn't make their industrial nodes useless," Peter said. He made a mental note to reward his analysts. They'd predicted that the king would head directly to Caledonia. "And the king does have a great deal of support there."

"We can trash the system in an afternoon," Tolliver snapped. "Tell them, Prime Minister. Tell them that we will take out their entire system if they don't hand over the king."

"We can try," Harrison said, "but they would refuse."

"Then we carry out our threat," Tolliver said. "Grand Admiral? Can Caledonia stop us from blasting the hell out of their system?"

Grand Admiral Rudbek didn't look at his uncle, Duke Rudbek, as he spoke. "Right now, Your Grace, our navy is in disarray. Our units are scattered . . . some damaged and requiring immediate repair. Our loyalists are doing what they can, but the king's clients were scattered through the entire fleet. It will take weeks, perhaps months, to put a task force together . . ."

Tolliver was not impressed. "We have the most powerful fleet in the *galaxy*!"

"Had," Grand Admiral Rudbek corrected. "And whatever task force we sent would be facing more than *just* the planetary defenses. Admiral Falcone's fleet would presumably defend the planet. We would need to concentrate a sizable fleet to guarantee victory."

He let out a long breath. "The blunt truth is that the fleet is heavily disorganized. It will take quite some time to recall the reservists, assign them to ships, and take the offensive. We have a great deal of work to do. And then . . ."

His eyes flickered to Peter. "Admiral Falcone's fleet might well be in better condition than anything at our *immediate* disposal. She is a good officer, Your Grace, and her fleet was effectively at war for the last year. She has experienced officers and well-drilled men under her command. She presumably *also* has access to war stockpiles on the other side of the Gap."

"She would have to move through *our* space to *reach* the Gap," Duchess Turin mused.

"So you're saying it's hopeless?" Duke Tolliver sounded as if he couldn't believe his ears. "That we can do nothing but wait for Duke Falcone's treacherous sister to bomb our planet into submission . . . ?"

Peter felt himself flush. He didn't understand why Kat had sided with the king, but . . . He controlled his temper with an effort. There would be time to decide if his sister really was a traitor later, once the war was under control. She'd betrayed the family, that was a given, but had she betrayed the planet? He didn't intend to waste time worrying about it now.

"No," Grand Admiral Rudbek said. "The situation is not hopeless."

"Oh, *goody*," Tolliver said, sarcastically. "I was just a *little* depressed there."

Duke Rudbek cleared his throat. "Perhaps you could let him finish . . . ?"

"Tyre itself is secure," Grand Admiral Rudbek said. "The planetary and system defenses are firmly under our control. The king's forces may raid the system—they have enough firepower to do a considerable amount of damage—but they will be unable to take the system, at least with the forces currently under the king's command. They will presumably need to concentrate their remaining forces and switch their industry to a war footing before they can take the offensive. Even if we assume that every missing ship went to the king, they would still need time to reorganize before they launched an attack.

"That gives us time, time enough to reorganize the fleet and switch our own industry to war production. Given a couple of months, we should have enough mobile firepower to give Caledonia a very hard day; given a year, we should have enough to crush the king's forces and reassert control over the rebel worlds. The precise question of what we should do with them, afterwards, is a *political* issue, but from a military point of view we should be able to render most of them harmless fairly quickly."

Tolliver frowned. "So you're saying we're certain to win?"

"Nothing is certain in war," Grand Admiral Rudbek cautioned. "We cannot underestimate the resources under the king's control or, for that matter, his appeal to the discontented across the Commonwealth. He was quite successful in patronizing excellent officers who repaid him with loyalty. Nor should we forget that the navy has a long tradition of loyalty to the king. There are a great many problems we will have to overcome before we can declare victory, from the shortage of experienced officers and crew to the hulls that were placed in long-term storage after the war. But yes, if we survive the next six months, we should win."

"They said that during the Theocratic War," Duchess Zangaria noted.

"And we won," Peter reminded her. "If the odds are in our favor . . ."

"If we survive the next six months, they will be in our favor." The grand admiral nodded to the starchart. "However, they are perfectly capable of making the same calculations themselves. There's also the potential problems caused by the king's control over the Next-Gen Weapons Program. There *may* have been something that will tip the balance firmly in their favor."

Peter frowned. "May?"

"May," Grand Admiral Rudbek said. "I don't believe so, Your Grace, but it is something to bear in mind."

"Quite," Harrison said. "Grand Admiral, how do you propose we win the war?"

Grand Admiral Rudbek didn't hesitate. "Stand on the defensive while we reorganize and rebuild our fleets, then stab straight at Caledonia and win the war in a single engagement."

"They won't let us do that unmolested," Duke Tolliver murmured.

"No," Grand Admiral Rudbek agreed. "I think we'll find this system under attack fairly soon. The king will have no choice."

"Depending on who's calling the shots," Peter agreed. He made a mental note to review the files. Which of the king's councilors would have his ear? Kat? Or someone more inclined to be careful? "But you're right. We have to be ready."

"Yes," Duke Rudbek said. "And that leads to another issue. Do we try to negotiate?"

"No," Harrison said. "The king cannot be trusted."

"He's still *the king*," Tolliver countered. "We cannot simply dethrone him . . ."

"Of course we can," Duke Rudbek growled. "He has thoroughly disgraced himself, has he not? Let us declare him dethroned and select someone more . . . pliable as his successor."

"A difficult task," Peter pointed out. "We couldn't risk giving the newcomer any power, could we? And who would want the job *without* power?"

"There's always someone willing to whore himself for a fancy title and fancier robes," Duchess Zangaria snapped. "You know that as well as I do."

"And then the balance between the king and . . . us . . . is shattered," Peter said. "Do we *really* want to tear the whole system down? Where do we stop?"

"The blunt truth is that we are in serious trouble," Duke Rudbek said. "We need to exercise more control, not less. And if there's a way we can end this war without fighting, we need to take it."

Harrison cleared his throat. "What do you believe we can offer, reasonably, that the king will *accept*?"

There was an awkward silence. Peter felt a twinge of sympathy for Duke Rudbek. The king had definitely disgraced himself, no doubt of it, but the blunt truth was that the war was going to be terrifyingly destructive. Tyre had been on the verge of a full-blooded recession before the civil war had broken out, shattering the fragile political consensus into fragments of smashed glass. If the war could be ended without serious bloodshed . . . He shook his head. Harrison was right. There was little they could reasonably offer the king and be offered in return that would be accepted.

Which probably won't stop some of us from trying to keep the communication channels open, he mused as the discussion raged back and forth. *If the war does go against us . . . Well, we put survival ahead of principle.*

He sighed inwardly. The hell of it was that he was in a good position to come to terms with the king. His *sister* was on the king's privy council. He wouldn't be too surprised if some of his fellows on the war cabinet expected him to be opening communications with Kat, if not the king. The family came first, after all. But there was no way the king would leave the Falcone Corporation alone, not if he won the war. He'd want to bring the entire planet firmly under his control.

"We can stall for time," he said simply. "We can offer talks, and talks about talks, but we will have to accept, right from the start, that we will not be able to talk him into submission. He's gone too far. We have to prepare for war."

"Quite," Harrison said. "And we have much to do."

"We have a plan, at least," Grand Admiral Rudbek said. "We just need time to execute it."

"Or be executed ourselves," Tolliver punned. He cleared his throat when the joke fell flat. "We can reach out to the rebel worlds, if we must. Perhaps we can lure them away from the king."

"At what price?" Duchess Zangaria leaned forward. "They don't trust us, with reason."

"They can talk to us at least," Peter said. His datapad bleeped. He glanced at the message, then frowned. "I have something to attend to, if you don't mind. We'll talk again tomorrow."

"We'll speak tomorrow," Harrison agreed.

Peter nodded, then dismissed the holoimages. The illusion of sharing a table with his fellows vanished, leaving him alone. It was hard to believe, at times, that the holoimages weren't *real.* He felt his stomach twist as he contemplated what he'd been told. They could lose the war. He was the youngest of them all, yet he felt old. He wondered, morbidly, if Kat felt the same way.

Yasmeena stepped into the room. "Your interviewee is here, sir."

"I'll see him in the office," Peter said. "And then"—he shrugged—"and then I guess I'll know what to do with him."

CHAPTER FIVE

Tyre

They weren't precisely in prison.

Commodore Sir William McElney wasn't precisely sure *where* he was or, for that matter, on what grounds he and Tanya Barrington were being held. They'd been plucked out of space, after the brief and violent exchange of fire between the planetary defenses and Kat Falcone's ships, and rapidly transferred to a suite that was a holding cell in all but name. A luxury hotel, he supposed, except the door was firmly locked.

He'd searched the suite the moment they'd been left alone. It hadn't taken him long to find the pickups. It was easy to build and conceal devices so tiny he couldn't have seen them with the naked eye, devices so tiny that they were literally undetectable without specialized equipment. Whoever had designed the suite wanted them to know they were being watched. They spoke in hushed voices, turned out the lights whenever they showered, and waited. It was hard to tell how long they'd been kept in the suite. The people who brought them their food, changed the beds, and emptied the bins said nothing. William was starting to wonder if he and Tanya would ever see daylight again.

We're pretty low on the priority list, he thought as he paced the living room. *Someone wants us kept out of the way until they can decide what to do with us.*

He glanced up sharply as he heard the outer door open. Someone was coming . . . He stood and waited, feeling a thrill running down his back. Their caretakers had visited only a few short hours ago, bringing food and drink. Their routine had been broken, and that meant . . . what? He tensed as a man in a dark suit, someone who could easily have passed for an office worker, stepped into the lounge. His face was so bland that William found it hard to pick up any details. The man could vanish in a crowd.

"Sir William?" The man's voice was very calm, betraying no trace of emotion. "If you'll come with me . . . ?"

William glanced at the door to Tanya's bedroom, feeling a twinge of guilt. He'd dragged her into this, although he wasn't really sure what *this* was. A war? A dispute between the king and his fellow aristocrats? Or something else, something unprecedented. He looked back at the man and frowned. The odds were good that their visitor had no authority whatsoever.

He met the man's eyes. "Both of us, or just me?"

"Just you," the man said. "Please."

He inclined a hand towards the door. William hesitated, then allowed himself to be ushered into the hallway and out into the complex beyond. It looked and felt like a hotel, although *he'd* never stayed in a hotel where the staff were allowed to spy on their customers. A monitor had been placed next to the door, showing the live feed from the pickups. Tanya was lying in her bed, sleeping. William understood. She'd been bored stiff ever since they'd been marched into the suite and told to wait. The suite had everything they could reasonably want, except freedom.

And I don't know if we'll ever be free again, William thought. Technically, it was illegal to detain someone without charge, but he had a feeling that the wartime Emergency Powers legislation was back in force. The government could hold them indefinitely, if it wished, without having to listen to complaints. *If no one knows we're being held here, no one is going to be making a fuss about it.*

The man led him to an elevator, which glided upwards. William tried to count the floors but rapidly lost count. The building had to be huge, then. Perhaps one of the megascrapers that dominated Tyre City. He'd visited one, back during his first visit to Tyre, a structure so big that a person could spend his entire life inside without ever needing to come out. He'd never liked them. He preferred the open air and a life that wasn't entirely grounded in high technology.

Then perhaps you shouldn't have joined the navy, he thought, laughing inwardly at himself. *Try living on a starship without technology.*

The doors hummed open, revealing a pair of guards. William's eyes swept over them, noting the Falcone insignia on their shirts. Kat's family? He'd heard that Kat didn't get along with her family now that her father was dead. He wondered, as the guards scanned and searched him, just why he'd been held by the Falcone family. He was, technically, one of their clients. What did they want with him?

A tall, dark-skinned woman entered the chamber as the guards stepped back. "Sir William," she said. "If you'll come with me . . ."

William nodded and followed her down the corridor. She held herself with a poise that suggested she had power, although there was something a little *too* sharp about her dress and appearance that argued otherwise. Someone highly placed, he guessed, but perhaps someone without the power and position that would allow her to relax, just a little. She wore her dark hair in a long braid, but it was just *too* perfect. A corporate assistant? A secretary, in all but name? Or something else?

A door hissed open, revealing a massive office. William was impressed despite himself. The room was elegant, in an understated way that spoke of old money. The furnishings were wood, all neatly embedded within the walls; a single portrait of Kat's father hung on one of the walls, glowering disapprovingly as William entered the room. The rear wall was a giant screen . . . no, a window, overlooking the city. A large desk sat in front of it. And, sitting behind the desk, Kat's oldest brother.

William blinked in surprise. Duke Peter looked to have aged decades overnight.

And we're the same age, roughly speaking, William thought. It was hard to believe that Duke Peter was Kat's *brother*. There wouldn't have been such a big age gap between oldest brother and youngest sister on William's homeworld. *No wonder she didn't get on well with him.*

He remembered his manners. "Your Grace?"

"We can skip the formalities," Duke Peter said. "Please. Take a seat."

William obeyed, studying the duke without making it obvious. The man's voice was harsh, suggesting he was tired and cross. It didn't seem to be directed at William personally, but he took warning anyway. Someone in his position could be a very dangerous enemy, even if William *hadn't* been a prisoner. He wondered, sourly, just why he'd been held in the first place, then dismissed the thought. There was no point in worrying about that when everything rested on *this* meeting. He had to keep his mind on the job.

And he definitely looks to have aged, William thought. The duke's body looked young, as if he was barely entering his thirties, but there was something about the way he held himself that suggested he was much older. His hair was blond, like Kat's, and his face was unlined . . . And yet, he looked old. *He's trying to take his father's place.*

The duke leaned forward. "Do you know why you are here?"

"No, Your Grace," William said. "The guards didn't give us an explanation."

"No," the duke echoed. "The Commonwealth has split in two. Civil war has broken out."

William sucked in his breath. He'd seen the shooting, he'd seen the planetary defenses firing on starships, but he hadn't wanted to believe it. The Commonwealth had been a *thing* for most of his adult life. He'd been a child when his homeworld had joined the Commonwealth . . .

He knew there were problems, had faced them himself, but he found it hard to believe that they'd degenerated into a shooting war.

"The king has fled this world," Duke Peter said. "And sworn to return."

". . . Shit," William said.

"Quite," the duke said. His lips curved into a humorless smile. "Listen."

William listened in growing disbelief, mingled with horror, as the duke outlined everything that had happened in the last two weeks. Naval mutinies, uprisings . . . entire *planets* declaring for one side or the other . . . It was like a nightmare. But it was true. He didn't doubt a single word. He'd seen too much. He'd seen the stresses threatening to rip the Commonwealth apart, all the little problems that had been allowed to fester because the war had demanded their attention . . . all the resentments and hatreds that had simmered under the surface, ignored by those in power. And he knew the king. He could easily see Hadrian taking advantage of the situation to push his own agenda . . .

"So I suppose I need to ask you," Duke Peter said, "which side are you on?"

William blinked in surprise. "Does it matter?"

"You're a client of my family," Duke Peter said. "Yes, it *does*."

William felt an itch at the back of his head. They were alone, but that didn't mean they were unobserved. And that meant . . . if he gave the wrong answer, or if he threw himself at the duke, he could be blasted down in a moment. And yet . . . Kat had never thrown a fit, or threatened him with serious consequences if he gave her bad news. He found it hard to believe that her brother was any different. God knew their *father* had been one of the most realistic—and hardheaded—men William had ever met. In a different world, perhaps they could have been friends.

He considered the problem for a long moment. His homeworld was gone for all intents and purposes. His people didn't want him. He'd tried to join them, after the war, but they'd rejected him. And while he had found a job on Asher Dales, it wasn't *home*. His home had been the navy, and he'd foolishly retired, thinking he'd be kicked out during the postwar drawdown. He didn't really have anywhere he *wanted* to go . . .

His heart sank. He'd met King Hadrian, dealt with him. His first impression had been unpromising and never really improved. The king had felt like a newly minted officer, too far out of his depth and too foolish to admit it and ask for help. The king had smiled too much, he'd thought, something he'd seen too often among the aristocrats, the ones who'd thought William was foolish for being both a commoner and a colonial. The smart ones learned better, either from their parents or from experience. The king might have wielded vast power during the war, but he'd never been in a position where failure would have disastrous personal consequences.

And William was morbidly sure that it had been the *king*, or someone from his faction, who'd supplied the Theocrats with weapons and a base. He had no proof. He doubted there would ever *be* proof. But the king had been the only one to benefit, at the cost of millions of lives . . .

He shuddered. Kat had joined the king, if her brother was to be believed. William wasn't surprised, even though he was disappointed. The king had spent years cultivating her as a potential ally, making a show of being on Kat's side when so many others had been trying to cut the ground from under her feet. And the ploy had worked. The part of William's mind that was loyal to Kat personally wanted to go to her, to join her; the part of his mind that regarded the king with suspicion and dislike thought otherwise. The king's house of cards would come crashing down, sooner or later. It would end badly.

And it will end badly for everyone else, if he wins, William thought. No one, no matter how clever or capable, could hope to wield unlimited power. The greatest minds humanity had produced could not take everything into account when they made their decisions. *The Commonwealth will be destroyed.*

A grim thought. He wasn't blind to the *failings* of the Commonwealth, nor to how the Theocratic War had made the government worse. All the plans for steady integration, for uplifting the colony worlds that had been cut off from the galactic mainstream by the Breakdown, had been shattered by the demands of the war. He knew *he* was the highest-ranking colonial officer in the Royal Navy, or had been until his resignation, and it had taken him *decades* to gain the command he'd earned years ago. He still resented, at times, how he'd been forced to watch less capable officers with better connections, even something as simple as being born on Tyre, being promoted past him while his career had seemingly stalled . . .

And yet, the Commonwealth had won the war.

He sighed, inwardly. The king could not be allowed to gain supreme power. William had no doubt the king would abuse it, if he did. And even if he didn't *intend* to abuse it, the results of gaining the power and then trying to satisfy his supporters would be disastrous. It was easy to see what would happen, if the king tried. The entire edifice would come crashing down in short order. It would be the end.

"I cannot support the king," he said flatly. "And doing nothing isn't an option either."

He wasn't entirely sure that was true. He *could* go back to Asher Dales. He could go elsewhere . . . to his brother the smuggler, perhaps. But he couldn't do nothing. The king had to be stopped. William couldn't sit back and let someone else do the work while he sat and watched from the sidelines. He had to do *something*.

"I'm on your side," he said. "Does *that* answer your question?"

Duke Peter studied him for a long moment. William wondered, coolly, what the duke saw. A client? A loyalist? Or a colonial who simply couldn't be trusted? God knew there had been enough distrust of colonial officers, long before the mutiny on *Uncanny*. William wouldn't be surprised if Duke Peter told him to go. It wasn't as if the Royal Navy *needed* him to win. There was no shortage of commanding officers who *didn't* have embarrassing ties to the other side . . .

His lips quirked in wry amusement. There probably wasn't an aristocrat on Tyre who *didn't* have embarrassing ties to the other side. Civil wars tended to split communities right down the middle. He had no idea who was next in the line of succession, he'd never cared enough to look up who had the best claim to the throne when the king died, but there was a good chance that whoever it was might be on Tyre. *That* would be awkward for the king's followers if Hadrian died. Really, William's ties to Kat were minor. Her *brother* had a far closer tie.

"Yes," Duke Peter said. "We're recalling everyone we can to the colors. Are you interested in returning?"

"The king has to be stopped," William said. He'd never really been happy outside the Royal Navy. The chance to return was not one to turn down, even if there was a civil war on. "Yes. I do want to return."

"Very good," Duke Peter said. "I'll arrange transport to the fleet. Admiral Kalian will be pleased to see you . . ."

William held up a hand. "I have a condition."

"Really?" Duke Peter looked surprised. "And that would be . . . what?"

"Two things, really." William met the duke's eyes. "First, I want Tanya released and returned to her homeworld. She didn't do anything wrong and doesn't deserve to be held without trial. She's certainly *not* on the king's side."

"She was going to be released fairly quickly anyway," Duke Peter commented. "We simply didn't have time to evaluate everyone . . ." He shrugged. "And the other condition?"

"I'll be resigning from the Asher Dales Naval Service," William said. "If you should happen to have a replacement, someone who might hesitate to fight in a civil war, please can you forward him to Asher Dales too?"

"If we can, we will," Duke Peter said. He smiled, rather tiredly. "But right now our resources are a little tied up. We can't supply more ships."

"I understand," William said. If the navy was desperate for ships, outdated hulls with no place in the modern line of battle would be pressed into service. "And I don't fault you for it."

"Yasmeena will make the travel arrangements, for both of you," Duke Peter said. He paused, lowering his voice. "Why do you think Kat sided with *him*? Against *me*?"

William hesitated. He wasn't sure he wanted to try to answer that question, even though he thought he knew the answer. He was pretty certain Duke Peter didn't want to hear it.

"I think she thought you were ignoring the important issues," he said finally. He didn't want to get into a discussion about how an overbearing older sibling could push a younger one into rebellion. There were only ten years between William and his brother, and God knew they'd sometimes fought like cats and dogs. "And the king was the only one to take them seriously."

Duke Peter frowned. "But I had other important issues to handle . . ."

"She didn't see them," William pointed out. Kat's brother had worried about an economic crash that threatened to ruin the family corporation, while Kat had been trying to catch the remnants of the Theocracy before they slaughtered their way through the entire sector. "Your issues were relatively minor. Hers, a matter of life and death."

And perhaps you should have talked more, he added, in the privacy of his own head. *But neither of you were prepared to meet the other halfway.*

CHAPTER SIX

CALEDONIA

"That's the revised crew roster, Admiral," Lieutenant Kitty Patterson said as she held out a datapad. "We have more on the way, apparently, but we won't try to slot them in until they actually arrive."

Kat nodded, taking the datapad without reading it. There was no point in allowing herself to get bogged down in the little details. That way led to madness and micromanagement. She trusted her staff to handle the little details, while *she* concentrated on the bigger picture. Kat knew of no contingency plans for civil war, nothing she could take off the shelf, dust off, and put to work. She had to devise her operational plans from scratch.

"Very good," she said. "How many have we *lost*?"

Kitty looked pained. "About a third of the crew," she said. "Mostly crewmen, Admiral, but we lost several dozen officers too. Captains Rogers and Danton were the highest ranking . . ."

"I'm not surprised," Kat said sourly. The majority of her officers were Tyrians. Some of them were loyal to the king, but others . . . They had stronger ties to the House of Lords. She supposed she should be grateful that they were leaving, even if they *did* leave headaches in their wake. Better to get rid of them now rather than have them turn on her in the midst of battle. "And their XOs?"

"Commander McDougal has taken Captain Danton's chair," Kitty said. "Commander Artfield, on the other hand, also insisted on returning to Tyre. *Headstrong* is currently under her tactical officer's command. We may need to transfer someone from one of the other ships to take command . . ."

"Which may cause problems later on," Kat said. She shook her head. "The lower decks?"

"We're going to be shorthanded at least until the newcomers arrive and get slotted into the ships," Kitty said. "But we don't have any serious problems."

"Good," Kat said. She studied the display. Five more starships had arrived over the last five days, one so badly damaged by internal fighting that she'd need weeks of repair work before she could return to the line of battle. Kat was impressed the surviving crew had managed to get her to Caledonia at all. "And our supply lines?"

"Shot to hell," Kitty said flatly. "We're drawing supplies from the depots here, of course, and the other allied worlds, but . . . it will take time for the local industrial base to start churning out what we need in sufficient quantities. We probably don't want to get drawn into a long, indecisive engagement."

"No," Kat agreed, dryly. "We don't."

She stood. "Inform me if there are any further changes. I'll be in my ready room."

"Aye, Admiral."

Kat nodded, then turned and walked through the hatch, into the ready room. The hatch hissed closed behind her as she took a cup of coffee from the dispenser and sat at her desk, trying to avoid looking at the latest reports. Paperwork had always been the bane of her existence, even when she'd had a full-sized staff to intercept the reports and decide what she really needed to see. She knew she shouldn't be annoyed, when her staff had erred on the side of caution, but . . . She shook her head as she brought up the starchart. Paperwork could wait. She had a tactical problem to solve.

And nothing being decided planet-side will matter if we don't win the war, she thought. The king had been joined by representatives from every rebel faction, and a few fence-sitters—all of whom wanted their concerns to be heard before they did anything else. Kat didn't blame them for making sure that they were heard, but . . . Victory came first. There was no point in dividing up the spoils before they were even won. *What's going to happen if we have a falling-out over our war aims?*

She put the thought out of her head—that was the king's problem, not hers—and studied the starchart carefully. She felt oddly frustrated to realize that there was nearly six weeks' travel time between Caledonia and the Gap, let alone the supply depots at Ahura Mazda. She'd sent orders to the naval crewmen to pack up everything they could and ship it to Caledonia, but there was no guarantee it would actually *arrive*. She couldn't count on anything. The naval crew might be loyal to her personally—and that couldn't be taken for granted, not in the middle of a civil war—but the House of Lords would have ample time to set up a blockade. Or try to convince the naval crewmen to join them instead. Who knew which way they'd jump?

The problem is simple, she told herself. *We have to win the war before they can gather their forces and bring superior power to bear against us.*

She contemplated the problem thoughtfully. It was difficult to be sure, as her estimates were little more than informed guesswork, but she thought it would take the House of Lords somewhere around six months to repair the damage to their fleets. And then they'd have to produce new ships . . . Two years, perhaps, to rebuild after the postwar drawdown and start churning out construction. They probably wouldn't have any serious manpower problems, whatever the optimists on Caledonia claimed. There were hundreds of thousands of reservists—and retired naval crewmen—on Tyre. By the time they started producing new ships, they'd have the crew to man them.

And the king is determined not to lay waste to the system, she thought. She understood his logic—she would have hesitated to fire on her family's industrial nodes, even though they were serving the enemy—but it caused all sorts of tactical headaches. The only real way to win was to win quickly, to strike directly at Tyre itself. And yet, the system was heavily defended. They could lose. *And if we lose the fleet, we lose everything.*

The mantra ran through her head, again and again. They weren't allowed to do anything that might significantly weaken the enemy, at least for the moment. And yet, refusing to weaken the enemy meant eventual defeat . . . unless they won quickly. She wondered, tiredly, how long it would be before the colonial representatives started pushing for strikes on Tyre's industry, *whatever* the king had to say about it. They couldn't be blind to the dangers of having the planet under the king's control, no matter how much they liked him. Tyre's political predominance stemmed from its industrial base. Weakening Tyre might be seen as a good result in the long run.

But then we will be prey to any other threat that happens to come along, Kat told herself stiffly. *The Theocracy would have won the war if we hadn't had the industrial base to absorb our early losses and keep fighting.*

She took a sip of her coffee and contemplated her options. There weren't many. A direct attack on Tyre was out of the question, at least for the moment. And yet, few other options were available. Targeting the loyalist worlds would be—at best—pointless spite. At worst, it would give the king and his provisional government the impression they were doing something *effective*. Kat knew better. They could take out every world but Tyre and still lose. No, they had to find a way to lure the enemy fleet into an engagement away from the planetary defenses. It might be their only hope.

And Shallot might be our best bet, she thought. *If nothing else, it will force the House of Lords to do something, anything, immediately, rather than waiting for reinforcements.*

Her lips twitched. On paper, Shallot was useless. The system sat roughly midway between Caledonia and Tyre, but it had never been of any real value. The only interesting thing about the system was that it had been turned into a naval base years before the Theocracy had started pressing against the Commonwealth's borders. Kat rather suspected that *someone* thought the system had long-term value, although she had no idea what that might be. There were no advantages, as far as she could tell, to positioning a naval base at Shallot. And the disadvantages were really quite striking . . .

She scrolled through the file, studying the naval base. There hadn't been any real push to modernize, even after the looming threat of war had forced the Commonwealth to start taking its defenses seriously. The Theocrats would have had to blast their way through Tyre to get to Shallot, and by then the war would have been lost anyway. Even the king's massive infrastructure program had given the system a miss. She was surprised the naval base hadn't been shut down after the war. The personnel who manned the installations could have been better used elsewhere.

It is *on one of the better-used hyper-routes*, she mused. *And if a threat had developed from the far side of the Commonwealth, Shallot might have been in a good position to intercept it before the enemy reached Tyre.*

The naval base was useless, as far as she could tell. The House of Lords had no real reason to defend the base or to mourn its loss. But the system might serve a greater purpose if she took it. The base wouldn't give her anything, beyond a handful of small industrial nodes and some outdated fleet-support facilities, yet it might *just* convince the fence-sitters that the king was steamrolling towards victory. The House of Lords would have to redeploy their ships to kick Kat *out* of Shallot, even though the system was useless. They couldn't afford to have their own people questioning their ultimate victory. Who knew how many people would switch sides if defeat looked certain?

My family will probably be drawing up contingency plans for surrender, if there is a reasonable chance that they will lose, Kat thought.

Her father had insisted that there should be a plan for everything, even outright disaster. The survival of the family came first. She dreaded to think what they might have done if the Theocracy had won the war. *We need to push them into putting those plans into action.*

It wasn't much, she admitted privately. A great deal would depend on factors outside her control. A smart commanding officer, or an experienced corporate CEO, like her father, would realize that there was nothing to be gained by fighting for Shallot. But whoever was in command back on Tyre might not be given a choice. Truth, objective truth, sometimes didn't matter as much as *perception.* If the other side thought they were going to lose, they might not put it to the test by trying to win.

And it will give us a chance to shake the fleet down, she thought. Her crew rosters had been rearranged on short notice. The crew would need time to fit into their new roles, time she wasn't sure she had. *And a taste of victory will do wonders for morale.*

She keyed her terminal. "Kitty, please establish a secure line to His Majesty."

"Aye, Admiral," Kitty said. "I'll get right on it."

Kat waited, sipping her coffee. Almost ten minutes passed before the king responded, something that worried her more than she cared to admit. Her call wasn't *urgent*, this time, but she feared what might happen if the situation genuinely *was* urgent. The delay might prove fatal. But then, the king had too much to do too. Kat knew she should be grateful that he was giving her a free hand in orbit. She'd had enough political interference to last a lifetime.

The king's image appeared in front of her. "Kat. It's good to see you again."

Kat nodded, keeping her expression under tight control. The king looked exhausted and frustrated, reminding her of her childhood. She'd had all the luxury a kid could want, enough to spoil her rotten if her parents hadn't taken care to keep her grounded, but she'd also faced hundreds of written and unwritten rules, all incomprehensible to a young mind, that governed how she had to behave. The king had spent the last few days with the representatives from a dozen rebel worlds. His countenance looked as if he would have preferred to spend them haggling with his enemies.

"Thank you, Your Majesty," she said. "I hope things are going well . . ."

The king's expression darkened. "There are too many pettifogging objections to everything I want to do," he said. "And too many people making demands for the same fucking things."

"Ouch," Kat said. There were hundreds of issues the Commonwealth had never bothered to settle—or had settled with blatant unfairness in Tyre's interest. Solving them would take time, diplomacy, and the patience of a saint. "Can you not shuffle the demands onto your staff? Let them take time to explore all the aspects of the problems before you make a final decision?"

"Stall for time, you mean?" The king smiled faintly. "They want decisions a bit sooner than the next millennium."

Kat winced in sympathy. Her father had said, more than once, that the best way to deal with an intractable problem was to turn it over to a board of inquiry. By the time the board had assessed the situation and produced its recommendations, everyone involved in the issue would be safely dead. A good way to look as if the government was doing something without actually taking a side. But the colonials wouldn't be fobbed off with a handful of weak excuses. They'd want action. And they'd want public declarations that couldn't be walked back if they proved inconvenient. The king was caught in a bind.

"You can't do *anything* before the war is over, whatever you decide to do," she pointed out instead. "Can you not make that clear to them?"

"But then they wouldn't have so much bargaining power," the king countered. "And they know it too, worse luck."

"I suppose," Kat said. She'd never paid *much* attention to interstellar economics. "I didn't call you out of the meeting for nothing, Your Majesty."

The king's face was somber. "Right now, I'd be quite happy if you called me to laugh at me."

"That bad?" Kat tried for a sympathetic look. "I have been considering how best to win the war for you."

"Action?" The king perked up. "That *would* be good."

"Quite," Kat agreed. She briefly outlined her plan. "I think it should work, Your Majesty."

The king frowned. "And if we lose?"

"We won't lose unless they've somehow concealed a dozen superdreadnought squadrons in the system," Kat said. "And if they had a dozen superdreadnought squadrons on hand, they'd be knocking at our door. They wouldn't waste time messing about if they could win the war in a single stroke."

"Neither would we, of course," the king said. "But you intend to lure their fleet into attacking you."

"That's one option," Kat said. "The other option is using Shallot as a springboard to attack Tyre itself. Or even just to snap and snarl at them while finding other ways to weaken their positions. It's better to have them reacting to us instead of being forced to react to them."

The king nodded. "The sooner we win, the better."

Kat held up a warning hand. "We haven't won yet, Your Majesty. The fleet will not be ready to depart for at least a week. We're still in the middle of reorganizing, distributing—"

"I understand." The king cut her off. "Just get the operation underway as soon as possible. I need to convince the doubters that we're moving towards victory."

"Don't tell them the target," Kat warned. "We don't want the enemy to be forewarned and forearmed."

She glanced up at the starchart. They'd placed filters on the StarCom in hopes of keeping enemy spies from signaling home, but she rather suspected they were wasting their time. An encrypted message would be caught, she was sure—a message that appeared, on the surface, to be completely innocuous would go through without question. A handful of code words, sent to the right people, might convey a great deal of information. She didn't dare assume that the House of Lords hadn't had time to set up a spy network. They'd been spying on the Commonwealth for years.

"Of course," the king said. "Perhaps we should tell them we're heading for Tyre instead."

"Or somewhere on the other side of the Commonwealth." Kat shook her head. "There aren't *many* plausible targets."

"There might be," the king said. "Some of the representatives want us to liberate Gamma Orion. They say the only thing keeping that system from joining us is a large garrison and a powerful naval base."

"But we'd pay a high price for taking the system, without gaining anything in return," Kat countered. The enemy would be *delighted* if the king attacked a heavily defended system . . . as long as it wasn't Tyre. Whatever happened, they couldn't possibly lose. "If we thought they'd come to terms . . ."

She shook her head. The war wasn't a straight fight for independence, a struggle to liberate worlds from an occupying power. It was far more complex. And if they allowed themselves to be diverted, to take their eyes off the prize, they would lose.

And if we give them time to build up, they'll crush us, she thought, once again. She'd heard too many people arguing that Tyre wouldn't fight, or that the Tyrians were too soft to fight a *real* war. It was stupid, particularly after Tyre had crushed the Theocracy. *We have to win this war before they build up the firepower to crush us and bring the rest of the Commonwealth to heel.*

"Quite." The king's expression became mulish. "Recovering my throne, my homeworld, is the first priority. Everything else comes second."

Kat nodded shortly.

CHAPTER SEVEN

Caledonia

"Admiral," Kitty said. "*Laura Wilder* is leaving orbit."

Kat nodded, glancing at the display as the massive colonist-carrier staggered out of orbit and crawled towards the emergence zone. The immense starship gave the impression of *lumbering*, as if it was too heavy to move fast. An illusion, she knew, but she couldn't shake it. The ship was carrying more than one hundred thousand officers, crewmen, and civilians who didn't want to fight for the king. She hoped they'd get home safely. The diplomats had sent messages, informing the House of Lords that the dissidents were on the way, but no reply had come. Kat tried to tell herself that wasn't a bad sign.

They're probably still trying to sort out who's in charge, she thought as two destroyers moved out of orbit and fell into escort position. *The government isn't designed to make decisions in a hurry.*

She shook her head. The intelligence staff had been studying the broadcasts from Tyre, from the newscasts to blog posts and datanet articles, but they hadn't been able to put together a coherent picture of what was actually going on. There were so many contradictions and presumably outright lies coming out of Tyre that Kat rather suspected that *no one* knew what was *really* going on. Israel Harrison was prime minister, apparently, but who was *really* calling the shots? The ducal families? Would they be able to work together long enough to win the war?

Harrison might be able to keep them together, she mused. *He's smart enough to make sure they all go in the same direction.*

Kitty cleared her throat. "They're opening a vortex now," she said. On the display, the three ships lumbered into the vortex and vanished. "They're gone."

"And let us hope they'll get a warm reception," Kat said.

She kept her expression under tight control as she turned back to her console. She'd vetoed the suggestion of sending spies and infiltrators back with the dissidents, but she was grimly aware that the security forces on Tyre wouldn't take that for granted. The dissidents might be placed in holding camps for a time, at least until one side emerged as the clear winner. She'd done her best to warn the dissidents, but they'd been determined to go home. She just hoped they didn't come to regret it. There were people on the king's staff who'd been doing their best to make *her* regret it.

Sending them home was the right thing to do, she told herself, firmly. *And there's nothing that can be done about it now.*

She brought up the latest set of reports and skimmed them rapidly. She'd done her best to leave minor matters in the hands of her staff, but dozens of issues still popped up that she had to review. Most of them were petty and pointless . . . She was tempted to send them back to her staff with a sharp comment attached about wasting her time. But it would be a dreadful mistake to have her staffers thinking she would penalize them for being reluctant to step on her toes. Or, for that matter, to encourage them to make decisions for her. The buck stopped with her.

Kitty cleared her throat again. "Admiral?"

Kat glanced up. "Yes?"

"There's a dispute over who should command *Harrington*," Kitty said. "Captain Davis and Captain Eland both want the battlecruiser."

"I'm not surprised," Kat muttered. Battlecruiser commands were every officer's dream. She'd always wanted to command one herself. She'd just never had the chance before she'd been promoted to flag rank. Now . . . One way or the other, she would never hold independent command again. "Which one has seniority?"

Kitty paled. She looked, just for a moment, like a wild animal staring at an onrushing tank, knowing she would be crushed under its treads and yet unable to turn and run.

"Ah . . . Captain Davis has seniority, Admiral," she said. "But Captain Eland has more experience. He actually fought in the war. Captain Davis spent most of his career chasing pirates or escorting convoys."

"I see." Kat considered the dilemma. There was nothing wrong with chasing pirates and escorting convoys—she'd done both herself—but they weren't *that* dangerous, certainly not when compared to standing in the line of battle. Any naval officer should be capable of taking out a pirate ship, even if he were a dunce. "And where did Captain Eland serve?"

"He was at Cadiz, Admiral," Kitty said. "And then he held three other commands between the opening battle and the final engagement of the war."

And he never got promoted into flag rank, Kat mused. She had a theory . . . She tapped her console, bringing up Eland's file. He'd been born on Tyre, to commoner parents. He hadn't enjoyed any patronage when he'd started his climb up the ladder to command rank. No one had been interested in pushing him further up the ladder when he'd had little to offer prospective patrons. *No wonder he sided with the king.*

She shook her head. "Give *Harrington* to Eland," she ordered. Davis might be a good officer—she hadn't met either of them—but Eland had more experience where it counted. "And inform Davis that we will find a place for him as soon as possible."

"Yes, Admiral," Kitty said. "We do have a handful of destroyers that need commanding officers."

"Offer him one of those, if he's interested," Kat said.

She turned back to her work, skimming through the files and prospective attack plans. Her tactical staff had taken her concept and turned it into a detailed operational plan, although they'd been at pains to point out that, for once, they knew more about the enemy forces than they did about their allies. Kat's lips twitched. Both sides in the *last* war had been forced to rely on educated guesswork about their enemies. This time, at least for the foreseeable future, both sides knew practically *everything* about their enemies. Her lips thinned as she realized the implications. The enemy analysts would be studying her engagements as soon as they learned she was in command. They'd be looking for weaknesses and blind spots, planning their attacks to take advantage of her failings. She'd seen it done before, back during the annual fleet war games. Here and now, there would be far more at risk than bickering over who bought the drinks after each exercise. Lives were at stake.

Perhaps I should study my own campaigns, she mused. *And see if I can figure out how they might tailor their attacks against me.*

Kitty broke into her thoughts. "Admiral, I have a priority call from Sir Grantham. He wishes to speak with you. Urgently."

"Sir Grantham?" Kat was surprised. She hadn't spoken to the king's fixer since the first meeting on the planet's surface. Their respective spheres of responsibility didn't overlap. "What does he want?"

"I don't know, Admiral," Kitty said. "But he's requesting a private conversation."

Kat frowned. "Is he now?"

She briefly considered taking the call in the CIC anyway, then shrugged and stood. "Patch it through to my ready room. I'll pick it up in a moment."

"Aye, Admiral."

Kat felt her frown deepen as she strode into the ready room, the hatch hissing closed behind her. What did Sir Grantham *want*? She wasn't in his chain of command. She reported directly to the king. She talked to Lord Gleneden and even to Earl Antony, but Sir Grantham? He had no reason to be talking to her.

She sat down and keyed the terminal. "Sir Grantham," she said. His face appeared in front of her. "What can I do for you?"

"Lady Falcone," Sir Grantham said. "You can put Captain Davis in command of his ship."

Kat blinked, honestly surprised. "What?"

Her thoughts caught up with her a second later. *Oh, right.* Captain Davis had wanted command of *Harrington*. And she'd given the position to Captain Eland instead. That had only been half an hour ago, hadn't it?

"Captain Davis," Sir Grantham repeated. "I need you to put him in command of his ship."

Kat felt a flash of hot anger. No one, absolutely no one, had talked to her like that in her entire life. Even her *father*—or her brother, come to think of it—had never spoken to her in a manner that suggested he thought she was a complete idiot. How *dare* he? She was an experienced naval officer, the commander of the king's fleet . . . Hell, she took *social* precedence as well! How *dare* he speak to her like she was a little girl?

"I suggest you review the assignment and overrule whoever made the decision," Sir Grantham continued. "And you should speak quite sharply to . . ."

"I suppose I *could* speak quite sharply to myself," Kat snapped. "*I* made the decision. Me. Do you have a problem with it?"

Sir Grantham looked taken aback, as if she'd slapped him. Kat wished, with a sudden burst of fury, that he *was* within arm's reach. She was hardly an unarmed combat expert; she'd never had the time to become a martial artist, but she knew a few things. Pat had taught her enough to give an unwary attacker a very bad day. She wondered, wryly, what the king would do if she knocked his fixer out. He'd certainly have some problems deciding if he could, and should, punish her.

And to suggest I should throw one of my subordinates under the aircar, she thought, with another flash of anger. She'd never punished her subordinates for following orders, and she was damned if she was about to start now. *Who the hell does he think he is?*

Sir Grantham found his voice. "With the greatest of respect," he said carefully, "I think you should reconsider."

"Reconsider," Kat repeated. Her voice turned icy. "And why do you *think* I should reconsider?"

"Captain Davis has *connections,*" Sir Grantham said, after a moment. He looked worried. "I promised him a command myself . . ."

"A promise you had no right to make," Kat said. "I am in command of the fleet!"

"The Admiralty does not have the sole voice in promotions," Sir Grantham countered. He sounded as if he thought he was on firmer ground. "And you need to take political considerations into account when you promote officers to higher rank . . ."

Kat took a breath. "We are at war," she said. How did so many people fail to grasp that simple truth? "*Winning* the war is not just our *first* concern, it is our *only* concern. If we lose, we are thoroughly screwed. It will be the end."

"But . . ."

"But nothing." Kat overrode him effortlessly. "I'm sure Captain Davis is an excellent officer, a great wit, a trencherman and a shooter and everything else that might be important outside wartime, but *we are at war.* I chose to put the most experienced officer at my disposal in that command chair, because I *need* the most experienced officers in command. I will not, I *cannot,* promote someone because of political expediency."

She felt a stab of unexpected sympathy for Captain Davis. She didn't know if he'd asked Sir Grantham to browbeat her into giving him the command. It was quite possible that he hadn't realized that the king's fixer would try to throw his weight around, that he would try to do something that would permanently cost his client *any* hope of promotion . . . Kat winced inwardly. She was damned if she was promoting Captain Davis now, at least until he proved himself. He could have the destroyer or be benched permanently.

"There are people who will be very unhappy about your decision," Sir Grantham warned, ominously. "They will complain to the king."

"Those people will be hanged if the war is lost," Kat said. The king might be left alive, if only so he could be forced to abdicate before he was sent into a comfortable retirement . . . Everyone else? She rather suspected that everyone who didn't have *very* strong connections to the other side would be hanged, dropped on a penal colony, or simply sent into exile somewhere on the other side of human space. "They should let the prospect of being hanged concentrate their minds."

She took a breath. "And if the king is unhappy," she added, "he can tell me himself."

Sir Grantham looked thoroughly displeased, although he was trying his best to hide it. Kat would have been fooled if she hadn't had so much experience with officers, servants, and wretched sycophants who'd spent too much time telling her what they thought she wanted to hear. Sir Grantham was unlikely to bother the king with such a minor matter. And, even if he did, the king was unlikely to overrule his old friend. Kat wasn't sure what she'd do if he *did.* She wondered, privately, if she'd be willing to threaten her resignation and go through with it if he tried to call her bluff. She wasn't sure if she *would* be bluffing.

"I shall raise the matter with His Majesty personally," Sir Grantham said. His voice was cold, hard. "I believe, however, that you should reconsider."

"The answer is no." Kat leaned forward, meeting his eyes. She wanted, needed, him to understand that *this* was the end of the matter. "The military logic should be obvious. The personnel logic too should be quite understandable. And that is the end of the matter."

She tapped her terminal, cutting the connection. Sir Grantham's face froze, then vanished into nothingness. Kat shook her head in angry disbelief. Cutting someone off like that was rude. Her mother would have had a lot of sharp things to say about it, when Kat had been a child, but . . . *Goddamn it.* Sir Grantham had been rude too. And insanely stupid, to think he could browbeat an admiral into *reconsidering* her decision. She smiled, thinly, at the thought. Sure, she *could* reconsider the decision. But the answer would still be the same.

Kat bit her lip as she read through Captain Davis's file. He was minor nobility—surprise, surprise—with connections to the Cavendish family. *That* was odd. The Cavendish Corporation had been on the verge of collapse, the last she'd heard; its patriarch and his presumed successor had vanished under mysterious circumstances. They'd been on *Supreme*, if she recalled correctly. No one knew what had happened to the missing liner. The cynic in her knew that the media had been more concerned about the ship and her passengers than the steadily deteriorating situation in the Occupied Zone.

And Davis didn't benefit that much from their patronage, she mused. The file was curiously bland, really little more than a handful of command postings and notes. All the personnel evaluations dated back to the days before Davis had been promoted to command rank. *Did something happen that got covered up?*

She skimmed Davis's service record quickly. His rise had been swift, although not as meteoric as her own. He'd commanded a destroyer, then a light cruiser; he'd been assigned to convoy and escort duties for most of the war. He had seen action, she supposed, but only against pirates. His ship had never been in any real danger. That was odd. He'd seen service for most of the war.

A lack of moral fiber, she asked herself, *or simple bad luck?*

She shook her head. It didn't matter. She wasn't about to change her mind, if only because it would set a bad precedent. God knew the prewar Admiralty had been bullied into promoting a *lot* of unsuitable officers with powerful connections. Admiral Morrison, damn the man, had come very close to losing the entire war during the first engagement. There were still people who believed he'd been an enemy sleeper agent. At times Kat had been inclined to agree.

Her intercom bleeped. "Admiral, Captain Eland is requesting permission to take command of his ship," Kitty said. She sounded bemused. "Apparently, someone placed a hold on the transfer order."

Kat ground her teeth. "Inform Captain Eland that he is to take command of *Harrington* as soon as possible," she said. Normally, there would be a prolonged period for the new CO to put his affairs in order and transfer himself and his kit to his new station, but they were at war. No time for the niceties. "And find out who placed the hold order and refer them to me personally."

"Yes, Admiral," Kitty said.

Kat sat back in her chair. Sir Grantham wouldn't have dared to pressure one of her staffers *after* speaking to her. He must have done it beforehand, secure in the belief he could force her to do his bidding. Some poor unfortunate in the makeshift personnel department had probably bent the knee to him, unwilling to take the risk of getting involved in the affairs of the great and powerful. Kat wouldn't be too surprised. Normally, any outside interference would be reported up the chain. Now, with the fleet's organizational structure a total mess, it wasn't so easy to make *any* formal reports . . .

"And the sooner we're on our way to Shallot, the better," she muttered. She made a mental note to keep an eye on Captain Davis. If he showed any hints of problems, anything that suggested he'd fly his ship into disaster, she'd relieve him on the spot. "We need to start the ball rolling before it's too late."

CHAPTER EIGHT

Shallot

"Well, Captain," Lieutenant Surber said as the cloaked *Pinafore* sneaked through the enemy system. "The system appears to be completely empty."

Captain Horace Thecae resisted the urge to make a sarcastic remark about the system being crammed with pieces of space junk, from hundreds of asteroids to three rocky planets and a single large gas giant. Shallot was not prime real estate, he had to admit, but *something* could be made of it if *someone* was prepared to make the investment. The asteroids alone could support a fairly large settlement if the inhabitants didn't mind not living on a planet.

"There's a midsized naval base orbiting the largest planet," he said instead. "Can't you see it on your display?"

He shook his head in annoyance. Half of his original crew had been reassigned, sent to fill gaps on other starships. There had only been a handful of replacements, most of which had either come from the reserves or transferred from the merchant marine. He understood—a lowly destroyer was quite far down the list for replacement crewmen—but it was still irritating. Of course it was. He'd had a couple of weeks to prepare for the mission, but he'd really needed months. The crew hadn't gelled and probably wouldn't for quite some time.

The naval base itself looked smaller than he'd expected; a handful of orbital facilities, a single giant industrial node, a cloudscoop, a slipway that looked to have been powered down and placed in long-term storage, and a handful of free-floating weapons platforms protecting the base from all comers. It said something about just how little interest the Commonwealth had shown in Shallot, he reflected, that the industrial node hadn't been put to work turning the system into something *useful*. The base had probably been intended to keep an eye on the colonies, a forward node that wouldn't allow its personnel to mingle with outsiders, but had never really been developed. The looming threat from the other side of the Commonwealth had absorbed the navy's attention.

And it was harder to justify any expenditures here when the base could have only one realistic purpose, he thought grimly. *The only people it could have defended, or threatened, were the colonials.*

He shrugged, dismissing the thought as he studied the sensor feed. The naval base had powered up. The industrial node looked to be working overtime, but there were no warships in attendance, nothing that might suggest the base could put up a real fight. He wondered, as data continued to flow into the sensor display, just what the enemy CO was thinking. Did he expect his base to survive long enough to serve its original purpose? Or had he powered up the industrial node on his own, without orders from home? Shallot didn't loom large in *anyone's* calculations. The base could have already been forgotten or written off.

"We'll finish the sweep, then make our way back to the RV point," he said. It was galling to have to sneak in and out of the system instead of merely opening a vortex and vanishing into hyperspace, but his orders had been clear. "And if there's anything here that might pose a threat, we'll find it."

"Aye, Captain."

♦ ♦ ♦

Kat stood in the CIC, hands clasped behind her back, and watched as the display rapidly updated. *Pinafore* had done well, surveying the system for potential threats. Every energy source had been logged, tracked, and identified. Nothing could be done about ships that might be lurking under cloak or simply powered down so completely that they emitted no betraying radiation, but she would have been astonished to run into an ambush. Shallot was so unimportant, in the grand scheme of things, that no responsible admiral would commit starships to its defense. The handful of orbital weapons platforms was enough to stand off a pirate ship but not a naval vessel.

And we have to hope that they take the defeat a little more seriously than they should, she mused. *And that whoever is calling the shots on Tyre is* not *a responsible admiral.*

She turned to Kitty. "Is the fleet ready to move?"

"Yes, Admiral." Kitty didn't bother to point out that the fleet had been at combat stations for the last four hours. "We're ready to move."

Kat nodded, shortly. It was unlikely that someone would see her starships as they lurked in hyperspace and waited for *Pinafore* to return, but she saw no point in taking chances. Besides, her crews needed the experience. Five days in transit had highlighted a number of issues that might have cost lives and ships if she'd taken her fleet into battle against a real foe. Better to have the problems ironed out before she picked on someone her own size. She felt vaguely dirty as she contemplated just how much firepower she'd brought to Shallot—she might as well have used a nuke to crack open a nut—but she couldn't afford a defeat. A defeat or even a stalemated engagement might cause potential supporters to edge away . . .

"Take us out, as planned," she ordered. "And transmit a demand for surrender as soon as we leave the vortex."

The deck shivered under her feet, and her stomach twisted painfully as *Violence* slipped out of the vortex. The display flickered, then updated rapidly. Shallot-IV—no one had bothered to name the gas giant—appeared in front of her, a handful of icons representing the fleet base and its satellite installations. The base really was quite small. Her display flickered with red icons as the base's defenses went live—they would have had to be blind to miss her fleet coming out of hyperspace—although they didn't lock on to her forces. Someone on the other side had to be desperately hoping she was friendly. Shallot had a StarCom. They had to know there was a war on.

Pity, that, she thought as more icons appeared in front of her. *We might have simply walked in and taken the base without a fight.*

"The surrender demand is being transmitted now," Kitty said. "All ships are falling into attack vector. Missiles locked on target, ready to engage; plasma weapons primed, ready to engage. Gunboats ready to launch, on your command."

"Launch gunboats," Kat ordered quietly. She doubted they were necessary, but it would give their crews more practice. The colonials had always made up the majority of gunboat crews, and hundreds of squadrons had come over to the king without prompting, yet she'd had to reshuffle their squadrons on short notice. "Order them to prepare to engage."

"Aye, Admiral."

Kat watched the timer, silently counting down the seconds. The enemy CO, whoever he was, had to know he was badly outmatched. Resistance would only get him and his crew killed, for nothing. They wouldn't even scratch her paint! But what would he do? Kat knew, beyond a shadow of a doubt, that an effective and competent officer wouldn't have been assigned to Shallot. The simple lack of any expansion over the last five years suggested that the CO had been shuffled to where his lack of competence couldn't do any real harm. No one had seriously expected *Shallot* to be important.

The console bleeped. "I'm picking up targeting sensors," Kitty said. "They're locking on to our ships."

Idiots, Kat thought. She wasn't trying to hide. There was no need to use tactical sensors to aim weapons at her ships. She wondered, sourly, what the enemy CO was thinking. Was he trying to warn her off? Unlikely. Locking active targeting sensors on someone's hull was generally taken as a hostile act. *Do you think you can threaten us into running away?*

Her imagination provided a number of scenarios, all bad. The enemy CO might be too stupid to realize just how badly he was outmatched. Or he might have orders to fight to the last, even though it would be pointless. Or . . . He might be scared of the consequences if he surrendered, of being turned into a scapegoat for a defeat he couldn't possibly have avoided. Kat privately admitted that the latter was the most likely. The House of Lords was probably already searching for scapegoats . . .

"Repeat our surrender demand," she ordered. The range was closing rapidly. She'd have to open fire soon unless she wanted to bring her ships into energy weapons range. "And remind them that . . ."

"Missile separation!" Kitty's voice rose as red icons flared to life on the display. "Multiple missile separation!"

"We'll go with Fire Plan Alpha," Kat said calmly. She didn't panic. It was hardly the first time she'd had missiles fired at her ships. "Order the lead ships to engage."

"Aye, Admiral," Kitty said. "Missiles launching . . . now!"

Kat leaned forward, watching as her ships spat a cloud of missiles towards the enemy weapons platforms. The enemy had gone to rapid fire, relying on her ships to close the range still further before the missile drives burned themselves out and the missiles went ballistic. Not a bad tactic on the surface, she had to admit, but utterly pointless against the sheer weight of fire she'd brought to the battle. She'd worked her point defense crews hard over the last few days and doubted a single missile would reach her ships.

Older missiles too, she mused. Clearly no one had bothered to update the base's defenses since the Battle of Cadiz. The missiles were still superior to anything the Theocracy had produced since the first engagements, but no match for the latest Commonwealth designs. *They're relying on sheer numbers to punch a hole through our defenses.*

She smiled, grimly, as the enemy missiles began to vanish, their icons blinking out one by one. They didn't stand a chance. She told herself sharply not to take it for granted, not to assume she would always have an edge. The defenses around Tyre or any first-class naval base would be a great deal stronger. The only upside, as far as she could tell, was that her forces wouldn't have to tangle with the defenses near the Gap. There would be no need to fight their way across the Commonwealth . . .

"Our missiles are entering engagement range," Kitty commented. "The enemy point defense is engaging . . ."

"They didn't upgrade the point defense either," Kat guessed.

"Yes, Admiral," Kitty said. "Preliminary analysis suggests that they didn't even update their targeting protocols."

Kat felt a flicker of excitement, despite herself, as the engagement developed. A handful of her missiles were picked off, more through luck than judgment, but the remainder made it through the enemy defenses and slammed into their targets. The weapons platforms weren't that tough. Their shields flickered, then failed. A moment later, there was nothing left of them but expanding clouds of plasma. The enemy missiles slacked off, their fire coming to an end. The base was defenseless.

We mustn't get complacent, she reminded herself sharply. *The next engagement will be a great deal harder.*

"Contact the enemy CO," she ordered. No point in wasting any more time. "Tell him to surrender. And tell him that if he doesn't surrender, I'll blow his facilities into rubble."

"Aye, Admiral," Kitty said.

Kat gritted her teeth. She *knew* it was important to accept surrenders, even after the enemy CO had fired a handful of shots for the honor of the flag. The war would be a great deal easier to win if the enemy side knew they *could* surrender. She wasn't sure what they'd do with the prisoners, if they'd be traded back to the enemy or simply held in detention camps until the end of the war, but they wouldn't be killed out of hand. The Theocracy had lost a handful of battles it should have won because it had refused to accept surrenders.

And yet, this idiot nearly got himself and his men killed, she thought icily. She understood the urge to fight to the last, to refuse to surrender when she could still hurt the enemy, but there were limits. *I'd be doing the universe a favor if I put him out of their misery.*

She angrily dismissed the thought as the seconds ticked away. She *could* send her marines to board the naval base, to take it by force, but someone could easily rig the self-destruct mechanism to catch her marines as well as the base's personnel. The thought crossed her mind, just for a second, that the base could have been evacuated weeks ago, with the defenses set on autofire, before she decided it wasn't too likely. Setting the defenses on automatic, when they might fire on anything that entered range, was against the Articles of War. She didn't think the House of Lords was *that* desperate.

"Admiral, we're picking up a signal," Kitty said. "The enemy CO wants to talk to you."

"Put him through," Kat ordered.

A face appeared in front of her. "Admiral Falcone," a man said. He looked as if he hadn't been bothering to take care of himself, his uniform grimy, his cheeks unshaven. "I am Commodore Morris and I . . ."

"My terms are quite simple," Kat said. "You will power down all nonessential equipment, assemble your crews, and prepare to be boarded. My people will land and assume full control of the base. You will hand over all command codes as well as military supplies; you will make no attempt to render the base useless by wiping the datacores or damaging any of the facilities. If you comply with these terms, your crews will be held until they can be traded back to the other side or the end of the war. If you refuse . . ."

Commodore Morris blanched. "Admiral, I can't hand over an entire base . . ."

"Yes, you can," Kat said. A moment's rational thought would have suggested that there was little to be gained by rendering the base useless. But she was damned if she was letting him assert himself. "You have one minute to decide. Comply or be blown into dust."

The enemy CO's mouth worked soundlessly for a long moment. Kat would have pitied him—he'd been in an impossible situation from the moment her fleet had arrived—if he hadn't been doing his damnedest to get his subordinates killed.

"I'll surrender," Morris said finally, looking as if he'd bitten into a lemon. Even without being turned into a scapegoat, even without a general court-martial for gross incompetence in the face of the enemy, his career was over. There was no way anyone would put him in command of a mining station, let alone a fleet base. "But I will require guarantees . . ."

"You can trust that *we* have plenty of incentive to honor our promises," Kat said. If she started refusing surrenders, the other side would soon start refusing surrenders too. And then the war would turn merciless. "Now, power down your facilities and prepare to be boarded. As long as you do not resist, you will be fine."

She turned to Kitty as Morris's face vanished from the display. "Dispatch two companies of marines to take control of the station," she ordered. "Transfer the prisoners to the MEU, then ready the fleet for departure. We'll set course back to Caledonia later today, once we've evaluated everything in their datacores."

"Aye, Admiral," Kitty said. She paused. "They might have had time to alert Tyre . . ."

"That's why we don't want to be here for long," Kat said dryly.

She switched the display back to the starchart as the marines rocketed towards the naval base, ready for anything. They weren't *that* far from Tyre. It was too much to hope that Morris hadn't informed the Admiralty he was under attack before the brief engagement had begun, or that he was going to surrender. Someone daring might just grab whatever ships he could and launch a raid on the system, trying to either smash her fleet or simply drive her back out of the system. Even a handful of minor engagements would drain her strength, winning time for the House of Lords to steady itself, switch its industrial nodes back to war production, and go on the offensive. No, better to abandon the system at a time of her choosing than risk having her ships pinned down trying to defend it.

"And congratulate the crews," she added, after a moment. "Tell them . . . *well done.*"

"Aye, Admiral," Kitty said.

And hope they know that the next *engagement will be a great deal harder*, Kat thought as she sat back in her chair. Her crews would know that. And yet, it was easy, very easy, to catch victory disease. She'd have to warn her crew to keep focused without, somehow, damaging their morale.

The House of Lords won't give us another free shot at them.

CHAPTER NINE

TYRE

"Your Grace?" A voice, a female voice. "Your Grace? Wake up!"

Peter started, unsure just for a second of where he actually was. He was in his tower, in an empty bed. He felt an odd pang, wishing his wife was beside him. Their marriage had been arranged, of course, but he'd grown to love her. They still slept together from time to time. He even took some pride in not having a mistress, like so many other men and women of his rank.

He sat upright as the lights came on. Yasmeena was standing by the foot of his bed, wearing a long white nightgown and holding a datapad in one hand. The windows were dark, suggesting it was the middle of the night. Peter blinked, blearily. A flash of panic shot through him as he realized that his aide wouldn't have woken him unless it was urgent. What had gone wrong now? Was the system under attack?

"What?" It was hard to speak clearly. "What's happening?"

"The war has begun," Yasmeena said. "Admiral Rudbek has called an emergency conference."

"*. . . Fuck,*" Peter managed. The war had begun? It had begun *weeks* ago. But that had been a phony war . . . Had the *real* fighting begun? Or what? "Is this system under attack?"

"No," Yasmeena said. "Or at least no planetary alert has been declared."

Peter rubbed his eyes. "What *time* is it?"

"Four in the morning." Yasmeena sounded apologetic. "I wouldn't have woken you if the admiral hadn't insisted."

"I know," Peter said.

A maid entered, carrying a tray of coffee. Her face was very pale. She looked unwilling to meet his eyes as she placed the tray on his bedside table, then retreated as quickly as she'd arrived. Peter felt a stab of sympathy, mingled with an odd kind of envy. The maid might be *terrified* of being sacked for entering his room in the dead of night, but at the same time she didn't have to worry about making a decision that could cost thousands of lives if it turned out to be wrong. Or even if it turned out to be right. Peter didn't know how his father had ruled the corporation for so long. His body might be youthful, but he felt old. And his father . . .

My father was old enough to be my father, he thought. *He had to be tired.* The pathetic joke was almost *funny*. Almost. *I don't know how he did it.*

He sipped his coffee quickly, then reached for a robe and pulled it over his nightshirt. He was tempted to go back to bed, to say—if anyone asked—that there was no point in making an immediate decision about anything, but people would start to talk. Too many people were already worrying about the war, wondering openly if they should enter into communications with the king. It wasn't as if they could be prosecuted for sedition, damn them. Too many were from wealthy and powerful families.

"I'll be there in a moment," he said as he clambered out of bed. "You can go back to bed, if you like. I'll see you at a more civilized hour."

"I won't go back to sleep," Yasmeena said. "I'll get dressed, then carry on with the paperwork."

Peter had to smile, although his amusement was mingled with sympathy. Yasmeena had worked for him for nearly twenty years, from the day he'd first been appointed to head one of his family's innumerable businesses. If she had any interests beyond being his assistant, the one who translated his orders into actions, he didn't know it. She had no social life, nothing outside the tower . . . She was saving money, according to the security review, probably with the intention of enjoying the rest of her life after she finally handed in her notice. The corporation would happily pay for a full rejuvenation for her. God knew she'd earned a great deal more.

Kat is lucky to avoid all this, Peter admitted as he left his chambers and walked down the corridor. *The price for being part of the family is having to work for the family. And we can't ever* stop *working*.

The tower felt weirdly quiet in the dead of night, even though he knew the lower levels never slept. *Something* was always going on. And yet . . . He saw no one as he walked through the secure door and into the conference chamber. A couple of holographic images were already waiting for him. Grand Admiral Rudbek looked disgustingly fresh for someone who'd presumably been woken only a few minutes ago himself; beside him, his uncle looked tired and worn. Peter allowed himself a flicker of vindictive amusement. He might be the oldest of his siblings, but he was the youngest person on the war cabinet. Even Duchess Zangaria was old enough to be his mother.

And I still feel tired, he thought as the remainder of the holograms flickered into existence. *The others have to be feeling worse*.

"Admiral," Israel Harrison said. The prime minister sounded irked. "What's happening?"

"Thirty-seven minutes ago, we received a FLASH message from the Shallot StarCom," Grand Admiral Rudbek said. His voice was preternaturally calm. "The system was under attack. We lost contact shortly afterwards."

Duke Tolliver frowned. "The StarCom was destroyed?"

"The last status update suggested that it was powering down," Grand Admiral Rudbek said, grimly. "Commodore Morris's final message stated that the situation was hopeless and that he intended to surrender. Since then . . . nothing."

"He *surrendered*?" Duchess Turin was furious. "Why the hell did he surrender?"

"His report made it clear that he was faced with overwhelming force," Grand Admiral Rudbek explained. "He put up a very brief fight, but it was futile. I don't believe he had a choice."

"And people will think we're going to lose the war," Duchess Turin hissed. "I want Commodore Morris put on trial for treason!"

"Agreed," Duke Tolliver said. "I . . ."

Peter cleared his throat before the debate could get out of hand. "I agree that we lost the engagement," he said. "But just how *badly* did we lose?"

Grand Admiral Rudbek looked oddly relieved. "Tactically, it was a complete loss. We did not, as far as we can tell from the reports, inflict any damage on their ships. Strategically, however, we lost very little. The naval base was outdated. We don't know if Commodore Morris had time to wipe the datacores and do a handful of other things that would render the base useless, at least without a great deal of work, but even if they captured it without a hitch, the base still wouldn't offer them very much. We lost a percentage point of a percentage point . . ."

"But the loss still *looks* bad," Duke Tolliver said.

"Perhaps," Peter said. "Where *is* Shallot?"

A starchart appeared in front of him, a handful of stars blinking red, green, and blue. Peter frowned. He wasn't a naval officer, understanding very little about the practicalities of naval combat, but he knew how to read a starchart. If someone drew a line between Tyre and Caledonia, Shallot would be somewhere around the midpoint. It looked as if the king's forces were advancing on Tyre.

"The king could be here at any minute," Duchess Turin breathed.

"No," Grand Admiral Rudbek said. "We know where his ships are, or where they *were*, thirty minutes ago. It will take them at least five days to reach Tyre from Shallot, assuming they set out immediately and redline their drives. Our long-range sensors and watchtower stations remain undisturbed. We will have plenty of warning if they *do* decide to drive on Tyre."

"So you got us out of bed for nothing," Duchess Zangaria grumbled.

"Commodore Morris must be put on trial," Duke Tolliver snapped. "If he survived . . ."

"Your Grace, he didn't have a choice," Grand Admiral Rudbek said. "He . . ."

"Committed treason," Duke Tolliver said. "I demand that he be put in front of a special inquest and found guilty of . . ."

Peter leaned forward. "How exactly do you intend to run an inquest with the outcome ordained before the inquest even *begins*?"

"We need to make it clear that cowardice in the face of the enemy will not be tolerated," Duke Tolliver hissed. "If Commodore Morris is allowed to get away with it, who will surrender next?"

Grand Admiral Rudbek looked grim. "My staff has only just begun analyzing the reports from Shallot," he said. "However, it seems fairly clear to me that Commodore Morris was *badly* outgunned. There was no hope of victory from the moment the enemy fleet dropped out of hyperspace and opened fire. He did what he could, Your Grace. It just wasn't enough to do more than scratch their paint. Any halfway competent naval officer would recognize the truth the moment they saw the recordings."

"We still need to take a stand against defeatism," Duke Tolliver growled.

"It's only been thirty minutes," Peter said reasonably. "Does the general public even know there's *been* an engagement?"

"No, Your Grace." Harrison met Peter's eyes. "But that won't last."

Of course not, Peter thought. *We can clamp down hard on newscasts and censor the datanet, but it won't be long before word starts to spread anyway.*

"There won't be any defeatism," he said. "Right now, no one knows there's anything to be defeatist *about*. We can't hide the engagement, not for long, but we can present it to the public as a minor issue, a battle that will be pointless in the grand state of affairs. There's no shortage of retired naval personnel who can go on the holovid and explain to the public that we lost nothing, save for a largely worthless star and an outdated naval base."

"The base wasn't *that* outdated," Duke Rudbek said. "It *was* established to keep an eye on the colonials."

Which probably didn't do wonders for social harmony, Peter thought. *The colonials guessed what we were doing from the start.*

He sighed, inwardly. If only they hadn't had to fight the war! If only . . . It would have been so much easier to turn the Commonwealth into a going concern if they hadn't had to throw their long-term plans out the airlock. They could have ensured a slow but steady economic growth that would have kept everyone happy. Instead, they'd had to prepare for war, costing them far too much. Even if they won, how could the Commonwealth be rebuilt? It might be better to come to terms with the colonials.

Except the king won't go for it, he reminded himself. *He has no interest in ending the war without securing his position first.*

Peter dragged his attention back to the debate. "We don't have to go into details," he said. "There's ample precedent for not releasing anything of military significance, no matter how much leaks out. We just downplay the engagement as much as possible. Morris's fate can be settled after the war."

"That won't let us make a point about defeatism," Duke Tolliver warned.

Peter shrugged. "He can't defend himself when he's in a detention camp," he pointed out dryly. "And a conviction *in absentia* is of questionable legal value."

"He might refuse to come home," Duchess Zangaria said.

Duke Rudbek snorted. "Do you blame him?"

"We don't have to lie to make it clear that the king had overwhelming force on his side," Peter said. "It doesn't say anything *bad* about us, or our prospects for victory, if the king won a pointless victory. Does it? A millionaire might as well cry and moan about being outbid by a billionaire. We can play up that angle as much as possible."

He leaned back in his chair. "And if we start penalizing officers for losing hopeless battles," he added, "what will that do to our morale?"

"Nothing good, Your Grace," Grand Admiral Rudbek said.

"Then we play down the defeat as much as possible," Peter said. "Anyone against?"

"This leads to another point," Harrison said, when the vote had been taken. "What do we do with the . . . ah . . . loyalists from the king's fleet?"

"They should have stayed and sabotaged the fleet," Duke Tolliver said. "Instead, they fled . . ."

"They chose not to fight for the king," Duke Rudbek said. "We shouldn't let such loyalty go to waste."

"But they might not fight for us," Duchess Turin said. "What do we *do* with them?"

Peter winced. His staff had produced all sorts of position papers, digging back into Earth's long history for precedents that *might* be applicable to their situation. Civil wars were always nasty, they'd argued; fathers against sons, brothers against brothers . . . brother against sister, Peter had reflected after he'd scanned a handful of papers. He couldn't disagree with their conclusions. The issue had to be handled carefully, or it would cause all sorts of problems, some of which might prove fatal. It was hard to remember, sometimes, that the aristocracy weren't the *only* people who counted. Where would they be if no one chose to fight for them?

"They took a considerable risk when they told the king they wanted to go home," Peter said calmly. "And they could easily have been thrown out the airlock instead."

"Or put on a ship with a bomb," Duke Tolliver said. "They haven't got here yet, have they?"

"No," Grand Admiral Rudbek said. "But the king would hardly have told us they were on their way if he intended them to meet an unfortunate accident somewhere along the way. His own people would rise in revolt if they even suspected that he'd killed the loyalists."

Perhaps, Peter thought. The king had hundreds of thousands of people under his command, even now. Some of them would be ruthless, black-ops specialists willing to do anything for their master. His father had told him, more than once, that the king had a whole army of intelligence operatives at his disposal. *If the king wanted to ensure the loyalists never got home, he could make it happen. And none of his people would ever suspect the truth.*

Duke Rudbek coughed. "We cannot refuse to take the loyalists, when they arrive," he said. "If they want to fight for us, they can be vetted; if they want to go home, we can hold them in pleasant surroundings until the end of the war."

"A simple lie detector test would be more than sufficient," his nephew agreed.

"I was under the impression that there were ways to defeat a lie detector," Duke Tolliver said, suspiciously. "A person could be conditioned . . ."

"We've considered the possibility," Grand Admiral Rudbek conceded. "Yes, it *is* possible to turn someone into an unwitting spy, someone who will pass a lie detector test because they don't *know* they're lying. But there's no way to handle the process *quickly*, no way to get it done without raising questions. We will go through everyone who is returned to us, poking and prodding at their stories and watching carefully for discrepancies. Anyone who causes alarm, even a *hint* of alarm, will be vetted more thoroughly. No conditioning can stand up to focused scrutiny."

"And if you're wrong?" Duke Tolliver pressed. "A single person in the wrong place could cause a great deal of damage."

"We believe we can prevent it," Grand Admiral Rudbek said. "There's no way they could have conditioned *everyone* they're sending back to us."

"But they could have influenced one or two," Duke Tolliver said. "I . . . I think we should detain them until the end of the war."

"Sir . . ." Grand Admiral Rudbek looked irked. "We need them."

"We don't need to take the risk," Duchess Turin said. "We can detain them without hurting them."

"Quite," Tolliver said.

Duke Rudbek made a rude noise. "And what message does that send to the universe?"

"That we're being careful," Duke Tolliver snapped.

Peter held up a hand. "We're getting bogged down," he said. "For the moment, let us content ourselves with informing the king, and the rest of the Commonwealth, that we will take the loyalists back. That we *won't* punish them for being on the wrong ship when the shit hit the fan. That we will conduct ourselves with some degree of honor, despite everything that has happened. That even if we have to detain them, we won't *mistreat* them."

Duke Rudbek gave him a droll smile. "Did you learn that at your father's knee?"

"Father always said that it was better to deal fairly with people, even if you held the whip hand," Peter said. He felt a sudden pang. He'd enjoyed his father's favor from birth. His father had taught him everything he knew, and he missed the old man. "In the long run, people remember fair dealing. And they hate it when they get screwed, even if they can't retaliate."

"You must never do someone a small injury," Duchess Zangaria said.

"Father said you never knew which ugly duckling would become a swan," Peter said. "But yes, the principle is the same."

"Then that's settled," Duke Rudbek said. He glanced at his nephew. "Is there any point in trying to recover Shallot?"

"I intend to divert a destroyer squadron to perform a fly-through," Grand Admiral Rudbek said. "If the system is deserted, they'll reclaim it for us. But really . . . Shallot might change hands a dozen times before the war comes to an end. The planet isn't *that* important."

"No," Duke Tolliver said. "But the public will *make* it important."

"Right now, that doesn't matter." Duke Rudbek made a show of looking at his watch. "And, now everything is settled, I think we should all go back to bed."

Peter sighed. He knew he wouldn't be getting any more sleep. Not now.

CHAPTER TEN

Tyre

There was a certain irony, William decided, in the flagship being HMS *King Travis*. King Travis, the *original* King Travis, had fathered King Hadrian. Now, for better or worse, the superdreadnought that bore his name was in the vanguard of the fleet that intended to bring his son to heel. William wondered, idly, why no one had bothered to change the ship's name or even suggest that the admiral move his flag to a different ship, then decided it probably didn't matter. The House of Lords had every interest in pretending that nothing was going to change, even though obviously *nothing* would stay the same. King Hadrian's successor, whoever he happened to be, wouldn't have any real power at all.

Assuming we win the war, William thought. *If we lose, the king will claim all power.*

He settled back in his chair, watching as the shuttle made her final approach to the giant superdreadnought. He was quite looking forward to returning to naval service, even though he'd had to make his goodbyes to Tanya and then pass a security check before the Royal Navy finally issued him a uniform and marching orders. His rank was a mess and didn't look as if it would be sorted anytime soon. He'd be happy being demoted, technically speaking, as long as it didn't come with a cut in pay. The only real disappointment was that he hadn't been given a command of his own.

A dull shudder ran through the shuttle as she docked. William stood, picked up his carryall, and headed to the hatch. A handful of other passengers—officers and crew—followed him, their faces showing the combination of excitement and nervousness common to anyone transferring to a new starship. Two of the midshipmen, both clearly recent graduates, barely looked old enough to shave. William felt a pang of envy, mingled with a wry awareness that the newbies were going to be learning on the job. He hoped their supervisors were feeling generous. It was a great deal harder to turn mistakes into learning experiences when lives were at stake.

And they may not survive their mistakes, he thought as the hatch hissed open. *Space is a very unforgiving environment.*

He pushed the thought aside as he entered the superdreadnought and saluted the colors draped on the nearest bulkhead. There was no formal reception party, thankfully. He hadn't really expected one. He stepped past the crew chiefs and section heads who'd come to meet their subordinates, a tradition that had been old when he'd been a very junior crewman, and headed down to the CIC. His orders had been clear. He was to report to his commanding officer as soon as he arrived. William didn't fault Admiral Greg Kalian for being reluctant to tear himself away from whatever he was doing. There was simply too much to do. And besides, William had never really cared about formalities for the sake of formalities.

The CIC was larger than he remembered, suggesting that the ship had undergone a refit after the war. Dozens of consoles, each one manned by a staffer; dozens of staffers, speaking rapidly into mouthpieces as they worked their way through an endless series of tasks. The chamber looked busy but disorganized. A large holographic starchart floated in the center, red stars glowing like monstrous eyes. No one challenged him as he stepped inside and looked for the admiral. No one seemed to care that he had casually walked into the fleet's command center. William felt a twinge of unease. He wouldn't have been able to board the shuttle without passing through a series of security checks, but the lack of attention to detail still felt wrong.

He hoped it wasn't a bad sign. His experience suggested otherwise.

He caught a young midshipwoman's eye. "Where is Admiral Kalian?"

The young woman flushed, started to answer, remembered she was supposed to salute, and started to answer again. William kept his face impassive, although he suspected this was another bad sign. The young woman's uniform was impeccable, but her conduct left much to be desired. Better to answer a question first rather than worry about showing proper respect. The next time, he might be demanding answers while missiles were roaring towards his ship's hull.

"He's in his ready room, sir," the young woman managed, finally. "Do you need an escort?"

"I know where it is, thank you," William said, a little sharper than he'd intended. "I can make my own way there."

He strode past the midshipwoman without looking back and paced through the chamber until he was standing in front of the admiral's hatch. His instincts were screaming at him to run, as if he wouldn't like what he'd see on the far side. He told himself not to be silly as he pressed his fingertips against the buzzer. The hatch hissed open, revealing a brightly lit chamber. He stepped inside, his eyes searching for the admiral.

Greg Kalian was sitting at his desk, poring over a datapad. A dozen others lay on the desk beside him, bleeping loudly and urgently. William's first impression was that the admiral was a little overwhelmed.

He pulled himself to attention. "Commodore Sir William McElney, reporting for duty."

Admiral Kalian put the datapad to one side and stood. He was a tall man, with blond hair that was several inches longer than regulation.

Handsome enough, William supposed, but he didn't give off the *vibes* of a combat veteran. Odd. William had read Admiral Kalian's file—the public sections, at least—and discovered that he *was* a combat veteran. He hadn't climbed the ranks as fast as Kat, and he hadn't fought in the same battles, but his career wasn't anything to sneer at. The war had turned a lot of inexperienced young fools into combat veterans very quickly.

"Commodore." Admiral Kalian had an upper-class accent, something else he had in common with Kat. The style of speech no longer grated on William's ears. "Welcome aboard."

"Thank you, sir," William said. He shook the admiral's hand firmly. "It is a pleasure."

Admiral Kalian's face twitched. "You may feel differently, when you take a look at these," he said. He indicated the datapads. "You're jumping right into the deep end."

No one's shooting at me, William thought dryly. *This isn't the* deep *end.*

"You probably didn't get a briefing before you boarded the shuttle," Admiral Kalian continued. "You may not have realized that you *didn't* because no one has time to put one together. There are holes in our roster from the very highest ranks to the lowest. My staff—Home Fleet's staff—has been splintered. The king's clients either fled or decided to do what they could to sabotage things before they could be rounded up. We're still trying to sort out the mess."

And you're trying to do too much on your own, William thought. That explained the chaos in the CIC, he supposed. The navy's contingency's plans didn't include civil war. Or, for that matter, mutinies on so large a scale. *You don't even have an effective staff.*

"And we have orders to take the offensive as soon as possible," Admiral Kalian added. "The king took Shallot only a few hours ago."

"Did he?" William was unimpressed. "Do we have orders to retake the system?"

"As soon as possible," Admiral Kalian confirmed. "And we are nowhere near ready to go."

"Yes, sir," William said. Shallot was unimportant, and its loss was a minor pinprick, but he could understand the admiral's political supervisors breathing down his neck and demanding an immediate offensive. "We have a great deal of work to do."

Admiral Kalian nodded, as if William had made a breakthrough that had been baffling everyone for years. "Yes. Your task, your *first* task, will be to batter this mess"—he sat down, pushing the datapads towards William—"into something resembling order. And then I want you to take the lead in reorganizing the fleet."

William took one of the datapads and glanced at it. A squadron readiness report. Interesting, and very heavily detailed, but not something that should be forwarded to the fleet's commanding officer. Admiral Kalian didn't need to scan through page after page detailing missile stockpiles, crew head counts, and other details that were best left in the hands of the squadron's junior officers. William paged his way through the report, comprehension starting to dawn. The admiral was out of his depth and, in his desperate bid to convince everyone, including himself, that he was in charge, he was demanding reports that took his officers away from actually doing their jobs.

William winced, feeling a twinge of sympathy. Kat had been lucky to escape the same trap when *she'd* been an admiral. But she'd been lucky enough to inherit a fully functional staff machine from her predecessor.

And here, half the staff have buggered off, he thought sourly. *And half the ones who stayed behind are still needed elsewhere.*

"I'd have to make a few minor changes," he said, picking his words very carefully. "And I might have to reorganize the fleet's reporting structure. We're not making the best use of it."

"Do whatever you see fit," Admiral Kalian said. "I have a meeting in an hour with the grand admiral himself. He appointed me to this post."

Political connections, William thought. He should have expected it. The House of Lords would have plumbed for connections and reliability over competence. No doubt Grand Admiral Rudbek had taken the opportunity to engage in a little empire building of his own. Who cared about a civil war? There were more important things to do, like establishing a bigger and better patronage network. *And you never had the chance to learn the skills you needed before it was too late.*

"I'll dump my carryall in my cabin, then take control," William assured him. "I'm sure we can get this mess sorted out with a little effort."

Admiral Kalian nodded. "And then we can plan how best to go on the offensive," he said. "The prime minister wants action."

"The fleet has to be readied first, sir," William said. "With your permission, I will begin at once."

He saluted, then left the ready room and found his cabin. He supposed he should be glad he *had* a cabin. The system was breaking down, but it wasn't broken. Not yet. Shaking his head, he dumped his carryall on the bed, answered the call of nature, and headed back to the CIC. The massive compartment seemed to be crammed with officers trying to work. Two-thirds of them seemed to be doing busywork.

William took a console and brought up a roster. Had Admiral Kalian indulged in some empire building of his own? No, it was too random, too slapdash for *proper* empire building. The files were vague, but it looked as if the admiral had summoned staff officers from all over the system without any clear idea how best to use them. William snorted, although he rather suspected the admiral hadn't had much choice. It would have been better to take over a preestablished staff machine, but it looked as if one didn't exist. The admiral had been right. There were gaping holes throughout Home Fleet's command roster.

Too many officers were loyal to the king, William thought. *And too many spacers on the lower decks turned against the House of Lords.*

He shook his head, then started to work. No point in having squadron commanders, who already had too much to worry about, send daily reports to the fleet commander. They didn't have time to write them, and the admiral didn't have time to read them. He canceled the orders, telling the squadron commanders to handle their own problems. They were the men on the spot. They should damn well know what needed to be done and do it without involving their senior officers. And the admiral shouldn't be looking over their shoulders either.

A couple of protests popped up in his inbox. He ignored them as he studied the staff officer roster with a jaundiced eye, looking for people who could be assigned elsewhere. Too many people were on the admiral's staff, too many people who didn't have clear duties . . . He knew some of them would regard being sent elsewhere as a demotion, even if it gave them more responsibility, but he didn't care. They were in the navy, and they could suck it up or hand in their resignations. He would probably receive complaints from the aristocracy—no one reached high rank without political patrons—but he found it hard to care about that too. It would be interesting to see if Admiral Kalian defended him. Technically, he *was* carrying out the admiral's orders.

Technically, he reminded himself. He sent a handful of staff officers to the tactical department, where they could devise plans for winning the war, and went through the list again. Admiral Kalian didn't need a small army of staffers. He needed a competent group who could turn his orders into reality. *If Kat were here . . .*

The thought cost him a pang. He looked down at the console, gritting his teeth. Kat would have understood. She would have backed him to the hilt. But she'd sided with the king. Her decision hurt, even though he understood. And there was a very good chance that they'd be shooting at each other within the next few months . . .

He forced himself to push on, burying himself in work. The personnel department was a mess, trying to accomplish too much too quickly. He spoke to the CO, ordering him to take a more rational approach to the problem of manpower. There was no point in recalling the reserves when no shuttles were on hand to take them to their duty stations nor training officers to bring them up to speed. Someone had tried to implement an emergency mobilization plan, he guessed as he worked his way through the files. Like all such plans, it had left out the emergency. He didn't think anyone had actually tested the plan, except perhaps on paper. No wonder it was already falling apart.

It'll take us weeks to get organized at this rate, he thought. *But at least we've made a start.*

His stomach growled, loudly. He sat back from his console and glanced at the chronometer. It was 1900. He'd been working for hours. The CIC was still busy, but half the consoles had been abandoned. He hoped that meant their operators had gone elsewhere, following his orders.

A steward appeared beside him. William tried not to jump. Stewards had better stealth than Royal Marines on infiltration missions. The man wasn't a regular naval steward, his fancy uniform made *that* clear, but he was still quite furtive. No doubt he'd learned his trade in some noble household where the servants were meant to be neither seen nor heard.

"Commodore," the steward said with a half bow. "Admiral Kalian requests the pleasure of your company for dinner."

And if that's a request, William thought, *I'm the Galactic Overlord.*

He locked the console, then stood. His bones felt as if they were creaking, a droll reminder that he was no longer young. The navy had taken good care of him, over the years, but there were limits. He'd need a full rejuvenation if he wanted to feel young again, and that was well beyond his meager savings. He sighed as he followed the steward towards the admiral's cabin. It was just something else that couldn't be helped.

Admiral Kalian was sitting at a large white table when William was shown into the compartment. "Ah, Commodore," he said. "You've made a good start."

"Well begun is half-done, sir," William quoted. His father used to say that, before his early death. "We have a lot of work to do."

"I can tell." Admiral Kalian's smile grew wider, but there was an edge to it William didn't like. "Do you know how many complaints I've had? People who objected to having their clients reassigned after all the strings they pulled to get them in their slots?"

"No, sir," William said. He could guess. Hundreds. Thousands, perhaps. "It has to be done."

Admiral Kalian looked pained. "Even if it impedes support for the war?"

Kat would tell him to go to hell, William thought. *But Kat has—had—the connections to make his opinion irrelevant.*

"The entire command and control network has been shot to hell," he said instead. "We have too many people in some departments and too few in others"—he shrugged, expressively—"and too much to do to worry about people being where they *want* to be. Right now, it's better to have someone doing a different job than not having that job done at all. We can rebuild the command and control network and put the clients where their patrons want afterwards, when the fleet is ready to depart. Right now . . . the sole priority is getting the fleet ready for battle."

"People will complain," Admiral Kalian observed.

"They would complain more if they lost the war, sir," William countered. "If, of course, they're still alive to complain. The king might simply put them up against the nearest wall and have them shot."

"A valid point," Admiral Kalian agreed. "I will bring it up the next time they ask me to do something. And now"—he smiled as a steward wheeled in a trolley laden with food—"we can talk about something else."

"Yes, sir," William said. "It will be my pleasure."

CHAPTER ELEVEN

Caledonia

Kat wasn't sure what to expect as the fleet passed though the vortex and emerged into the Caledonia System. She had no reason to *believe* that the House of Lords might have dispatched a fleet to crush the king's supporters while she was elsewhere, but she hadn't been quite able to rid herself of the nagging fear that something, somewhere, might have gone spectacularly wrong while she was capturing Shallot. The messages she'd picked up before departure, with the king's supporters gloating over their great victory, hadn't helped her mood. She knew they hadn't won a great victory. She might as well have stamped on an ant and called it a fantastic feat of arms.

"We've exchanged IFF signals with the defenders," Kitty reported. "They've welcomed us home."

"Take us into orbit," Kat ordered. "And tell the shuttlebay crew to prepare my shuttle."

"Aye, Admiral," Kitty said.

Kat nodded, studying the display. It *looked* as if more ships had come in, from mutinous naval vessels to armed freighters, smugglers, and mercenaries. She hoped more crewmen had come in too. The cruise had highlighted a number of problems, almost all of which could be traced to low staffing or officers and crewmen having to learn on the job. She was silently relieved that they hadn't run into any real opposition. Her fleet might have been cut to ribbons.

The House of Lords is probably having the same problems, she told herself. *Too many officers and crew were either colonials or loyal to the king.*

She put the thought aside as she skimmed through the updates. The fleet command structure was a tangled mess, one that her handful of staff officers hadn't even begun to fix. There were too many gaping holes, too many issues that needed her personal attention . . . She cursed under her breath at just how many problems had been left for her to resolve. They were going to have to build a whole new command and control system, a whole new Admiralty, from scratch . . . and they were going to have to do it in the middle of a war. The House of Lords wouldn't have so many problems doing *that*. They'd inherited the Admiralty by default.

And most of the officers who kept the navy running, she thought as the fleet entered orbit. *It won't take them long to fill the gaps in* their *roster.*

"Admiral," Kitty said. "Commodore Yelling sends his compliments and asks if you'd like to arrange shore leave for your crews."

Kat bit down the sharp response that came to mind. On one hand, they didn't really have time to send her crews on shore leave. But, on the other hand, she'd worked her crews hard over the past month. They needed a break before tiredness started to set in, before they started to make mistakes through inattention. And some of those mistakes would be lethal. She knew through bitter experience just how easy it was to make a deadly mistake . . .

"Organize a brief shore leave rota," she said. "But only a day or so for each group."

"Aye, Admiral," Kitty said.

Kat felt a pang of guilt as she stood and headed to the shuttlebay. She was going down to the surface now, even though her crews would be getting their own shore leave in a day or two. She'd never liked officers who abused their positions and effectively deserted their posts—she hadn't forgotten how Admiral Morrison had practically *invited* the Theocrats to attack Cadiz—and she couldn't help feeling as though she was doing the same, even though she knew it was a business trip. She had to report to the king personally.

Her wristcom bleeped as she boarded the shuttle. "Admiral, the planetary coordinator is offering to put on a parade for you," Kitty informed her. "Do you wish to . . ."

"No," Kat said, more sharply than she'd intended. She took a breath. "I don't have time. Tell them I'll land directly at the palace."

They don't need me to throw a parade, she thought. If there was one advantage to being the youngest child of Duke Lucas Falcone, it was that she wasn't expected to be the public face of the corporation. She didn't have to attend a hundred balls a year for fear of snubbing someone important. *And it isn't as if we've done anything worth celebrating.*

She worked on her datapad as the shuttle entered the planetary atmosphere and flew towards the palace. They should have enough crewmen now, she told herself firmly, although most of them would need a little training before they could be trusted to learn on the job. The House of Lords had the training infrastructure too, she reflected. Caledonia's self-defense force was tiny, compared to the Royal Navy. The planet simply didn't have the infrastructure to give even brief refresher courses to hundreds of thousands of recruits. She had the feeling that they were going to be struggling with the issue for months to come.

But the reservists aren't that out of date, she reminded herself. *They should be able to catch up fairly quickly.*

The shuttle landed with a bump. Kat stood, brushed herself down, and headed for the hatch as it hissed open. A faint smell of *something*—the planetary scent, something she couldn't place—greeted her as she stepped through, nodding politely to the guardsmen outside. They scanned her carefully, their faces expressionless. Were they expecting trouble? Kat wondered, morbidly, just how many death threats had been sent to the king. It was unlikely that everyone on Caledonia was squarely behind him.

And it will be astonishing how many people will swear blind they never supported him if the House of Lords wins the war, she thought, cynically. *They'll do everything in their power to avoid admitting they made a mistake.*

Sir Grantham was waiting, just past the guards. "Lady Falcone."

Kat kept her expression blank, somehow. "Sir Grantham."

"I've been asked to escort you to the ballroom," Sir Grantham said. His face was as composed as Kat's own. She doubted he was happy to be escorting her. "If you'll come with me . . . ?"

"It will be my pleasure," Kat lied. Trusted servant of the king or not, she just didn't like Sir Grantham. "I trust I can speak to the king as quickly as possible?"

"The king is currently in a meeting," Sir Grantham said. "But if you'll come with me . . ."

Kat walked beside him as they stepped through a door and down a long flight of stairs. The palace reminded her of her family's mansion, although there was something oddly impersonal about the place that nagged at her mind. It might have been intended for the king, when he chose to visit Caledonia, but the palace wasn't his permanent residence. There were no touches that suggested someone actually lived in the building, nothing particularly individual. Both luxurious and barren, not really a home away from home. It felt more like a luxury hotel.

"We've had more people come in over the last couple of weeks," Sir Grantham said as they reached the bottom of the stairs. "Some of them are quite high-ranking officers. Others are colonials."

"Indeed," Kat said. If there was a point to his comment, and she had a feeling she knew where it was going, he could make it himself. She didn't have the patience for hours upon hours of conversational dueling, where everyone danced around the real issue. "That is good news, is it not?"

"Perhaps," Sir Grantham said. "But they do want important positions in the king's fleet."

Kat glanced at him sharply. "Haven't we had this discussion once already?"

Sir Grantham flushed. "Please, could I finish, Admiral?"

"If you must." Kat wondered, suddenly, if he was leading her in circles. The palace was easily large enough for him to pick and choose his route, taking the long way without ever making it obvious. "What do you have to say?"

"There are politics involved," Sir Grantham said, bluntly. "The officers who sided with the king expect to be rewarded for their stance. The colonials likewise. And if they are not rewarded, it may cause problems further down the line."

So you can *get to the point.* Kat was almost impressed. She reminded herself, sharply, that Sir Grantham had made his career by manipulating people. He'd survived and prospered by making himself useful to the king. He might have figured out how to appeal to her since their last conversation. *And the hell of it is that you do have a point.*

"I'm not prepared to compromise the fleet's efficiency to satisfy demands for rewards," she said stiffly. "Right now, we're shorthanded almost everywhere."

"Then you should be able to slot the newcomers into place," Sir Grantham said. "And satisfy both requirements at the same time."

"Perhaps," Kat said. She had to smile at the thought of a captain doing grunt work. "But you do realize that there aren't many command slots in the fleet?"

"It's a political issue," Sir Grantham said. "The king's supporters have to be rewarded."

And people like you can only prosper by making sure the rewards are distributed evenly, Kat thought. *And you want to get a fair share yourself.*

"I see," she said neutrally.

"And there are other issues," Sir Grantham added. "The colonials want solid proof of the king's commitment to their cause. Giving them a handful of fleet command slots would . . ."

"Be disastrous, if their nominees aren't up to the task." Kat cut him off. "I won't put an untested officer in a command slot."

Sir Grantham gave her a sidelong look. "Are you saying that colonials cannot be commanding officers?"

Kat felt her cheeks heat. William had been a colonial—and a commanding officer. He'd lost a ship—two ships, really—but those losses hadn't been his fault. There was no way that anyone, least of all her, could argue that colonials couldn't be commanding officers. It was absurd.

She glowered at him. "Did you learn to debate on the datanet?"

Sir Grantham ignored the jab. "So you'll be promoting colonials?"

Kat sighed. "I have ships that are technically under colonial command, in the sense that their commanding officers are colonials," she said. "And do you know how they got the posts? They mutinied for the king!"

"For which they should be rewarded," Sir Grantham said.

"Yes," Kat agreed. "But are they up to the task?"

She rubbed her eyes. She was a naval officer. The thought of rewarding mutineers was anathema to her, even if they *had* brought their ships to join her forces. She didn't like the idea of leaving the mutineers in command, of suggesting that command could be taken by force . . . And yet, she had little choice. What sort of message would it send if she removed the mutineers from their posts? It would be hypocritical in the extreme to refuse to accept them in their new roles . . . And yet, *could* a former gunnery officer command a starship?

"It is important we keep everyone onside," Sir Grantham said. "And if that means promoting people for political connections, rather than competence . . ."

"Then we lose," Kat said flatly. She took a breath. *God!* She hated politics. "I'll take the issue into consideration, when the time comes to discuss promotions."

Sir Grantham nodded. He didn't push the issue any further. Instead, he turned the corner and led her into a giant ballroom. The scene before her, as they walked down the stairs, was so familiar that she almost felt homesick. Hundreds of people in fancy clothes milled about, chattering like mad; servants glided from group to group, keeping them supplied with food, drink, and cigars. She was mildly surprised that there were so many smokers in the crowd—public smoking was regarded as dreadfully rude on Tyre—but she supposed it didn't matter.

Her eyes narrowed. She'd never *liked* balls, particularly not the great gatherings where she was supposed to be nice to people who hated her family with a white-hot passion, but she knew how to read one. Several clusters of people had formed around noblemen from Tyre, their clothing marking them as minor aristocracy; others, somewhat less coherent, appeared to be forming around colonial representatives. A number of *them* wore outfits that appeared to be mass-produced, rather than the handmade outfits that had been in vogue on Tyre. She rather suspected that such a choice was deliberate. Their wearers wanted to make it clear that they weren't noblemen.

Curious, she thought as she passed a pair of naval officers in dress uniforms. *How much of the real work is going to be done here?*

Sir Grantham stayed beside her as she walked across the floor, quietly pointing out the genuinely important guests. Kat was amused to hear that the aristocrats were among the least important, no matter what airs and graces they put on. The king had almost no supporters from the higher aristocracy, save perhaps for Kat herself. The Cavendish family had been the only ducal family to consider declaring for the king, and even *they* were torn in two, fighting their own little civil war as the greater conflict raged. Whoever won the latter would win the former.

The right side, as always, was the one that won.

A naval officer in dress whites saluted her. "Admiral," he said. "I am in need of a ship!"

Kat gritted her teeth. The officer was dressed as an admiral, but she didn't know him. That wasn't a good sign. She knew all the competent and experienced admirals, even if she hadn't met them personally. She wondered, as the man gazed at her expectantly, if he was a poser, or someone who'd granted himself a promotion. It seemed unlikely. She had copies of the navy's personnel files. She would *know* if someone was trying to snowball her.

"All such issues are handled through my staff," she said firmly. An admiral who wanted a ship? She supposed it wasn't *that* unlikely. She would like a command of her own too. "Give them your details, and they will consider it."

"But I have rank," the admiral claimed. He'd been drinking, heavily. "And precedence. And seniority . . ."

"And I have a war to fight," Kat snapped. "Contact my staff. They will handle the matter."

She kept her face expressionless as she turned and made her way through the crowds. *That* was going to be another headache. An officer who had seniority, time in grade, would resent watching others being promoted over his head, particularly if he didn't have the competence or experience to get promoted himself. An old story. One couldn't get promoted without experience, and one couldn't get experience without being promoted. Kat understood, all too well, how that could rankle. But she couldn't do anything about it either.

A dozen other supplicants assailed her as she made her way through the ballroom. A colonial politician, determined to make sure that his people wouldn't be denied promotions and postings just because they didn't come from Tyre. Another, more focused on his own homeworld than the colonial cause in general. Senior aristocrats who seemed to expect plum postings to fall into their laps, junior aristocrats who wanted to jump up before the war came to an end . . . The list seemed endless. Kat had no idea how the king coped with so many competing demands. She was tempted to turn around and simply leave . . .

And all of them, she noted, seemed convinced that the war was already won. She could hear them dividing up the spoils, spoils that had yet to be claimed. Black sheep—disgraced scions of families that paid them to stay away from Tyre—were talking about what they'd do when they returned home, how they would avenge themselves on their tormenters and reshape their families to suit themselves. Naval officers, some of whom had clearly been on half pay for good reason, were bragging about battles they'd won, about missiles they'd seen with the naked eye . . . Kat *knew* they were lying. Anyone who saw a missile coming at them with the naked eye wouldn't have survived the experience. She felt her stomach twist as she saw an elderly man pawing a servant girl. She wasn't naive enough to think the servants on Tyre weren't abused, but at least there was a sense of decorum. The king's supporters seemed to have thrown decorum out the airlock.

Sir Grantham materialized at her shoulder. She was almost pleased to see him.

"The war council is about to begin," he said calmly. "The king requests your presence."

"Good," Kat said. She saw another sloshed officer coming towards her to beg or demand a posting. She glared at him until he took the hint and turned away. "You weren't kidding, were you?"

"No," Sir Grantham said. "And we must satisfy their demands as best as we can."

"I knew a girl who had parents who tried to satisfy her every demand," Kat commented as they headed towards the door. "And do you know what it got them? More demands!"

"Quite," Sir Grantham said. He lowered his voice. "But the king needs everyone here, Admiral. And that means he has to try to satisfy them."

Kat winced. Sir Grantham was right, damn him. Everything had changed. The prewar structure had been smashed to pieces. Now . . . On one hand, there was a chance for real and lasting change. But, on the other, the demands for change could not be allowed to supersede the need to win the war. And yet . . . It would be a great deal harder for anyone to demand change after the war was won. The fluidity that allowed a mutineer to remain in command of a starship would be gone.

We have to win the war first, she thought coldly. *And then we can worry about the world after the war.*

CHAPTER TWELVE

Tyre

"Did you hear?" Commander Gwynn Casters smiled as William stepped into the CIC, her blue eyes alight with mischief. "The loyalists returned home last night!"

"And were promptly detained," William commented. "That might have been a mistake."

An unpleasant thought. He understood the problem. He understood that the loyalists couldn't be trusted, at least until they were vetted, but he couldn't help feeling that it was a mistake. Detainment sent precisely the wrong message to any loyalists who might have remained with the king. But now, after the king's loyalists had been offered a chance to go home, it was hard to argue that his loyalists weren't *loyal*. They'd made a very deliberate decision to stay with their master.

"But at least they're home," Gwynn insisted. "We won't be shooting at our *friends* any longer."

William shrugged. Gwynn was too young, really. She'd been a staff officer for most of her career. She was good at her job—William would have insisted on sending her elsewhere if she'd turned into a liability—but she didn't really understand war. She didn't understand that the issues in the files, the figures and tables that passed through her terminal on their way to her superiors, represented living, breathing people. She was detached in a way William knew he could never be.

"We shall see," he said.

He sat at his console and brought up the latest set of reports. He'd quickly improved efficiency, once he'd started to devolve authority as well as responsibility. Hundreds of issues still needed to be solved, along with a whole string of kinks that could be ironed out only through constant exercises, but the fleet was well on the way to being prepared for deployment. His lips curved into a faint smile. The latest reservists were already on their way to their new postings. It was astonishing how well the system could work when half the bureaucrats were ordered to ply their trade elsewhere.

And just how much rot sank into the system over the last year or so, William thought. The great RIF had been an utter disaster, as far as efficiency had been concerned. Kat's fleet, the one that had gone over to the king, had been the most effective formation in the Royal Navy. *We really have too many problems . . .*

He sat back and sighed. In raw numbers, the House of Lords had more than enough ships to counter the king. It wasn't clear just how many of the missing ships had mutinied successfully, their crews flying to Caledonia to join the king, and how many had been lost somewhere in interstellar space; but, even assuming the worst, the numbers should be fairly even. But there were all kinds of gaps in his roster that were making it hard to crew the fleet. Too many senior officers had deserted, heading straight for Caledonia; too many crewmen had tried to mutiny or had simply been taken into custody. William cursed under his breath. Those damnable mutineers on *Uncanny* had done far more damage to the navy than they'd realized.

Bastards, he thought coldly. *What the hell were they thinking?*

He shook his head. He'd done his best to follow the debates on the datanet, in the few minutes he'd been able to snatch for himself. Plenty of colonials didn't trust the king or feared that the king wouldn't be able to win the war, but . . . They had little love for the Commonwealth too. And who could blame them? William wasn't blind to the simple fact that there *was* a great deal of truth in the charges leveled against the Commonwealth. It was a mistake to trust the king, he had no doubt, but the king was the only game in town.

And colonial crewmen who might have remained loyal, if they'd been treated with respect, won't be loyal any longer, William thought. *Who can remain loyal after they're detained on suspicion of disloyalty?*

He told himself to stop brooding and get back to work. The situation was improving, almost despite itself. Home Fleet might have terrible gaps in its roster—he'd been blocked from transferring officers and crew from Planetary Defense—but it was slowly recovering from its nadir. A number of ships were already exercising, fighting their way through simulated engagements with enemy vessels. The only real advantage of fighting a civil war, he supposed, was that they knew everything about the other side. It would take time, perhaps more time than they had, for the two sides to diverge to the point where one of them could surprise the other.

And we have much of the navy's infrastructure under our control, he reminded himself. *They don't have anything like enough time to build supporting elements from scratch.*

Gwynn caught his attention. "Sir . . . Vice Admiral Tomsk's staff say they need more personnel to get the superdreadnoughts up and running."

"Noted," William said. "Can we draw them from anywhere?"

"I don't know," Gwynn said. "No one who has a manpower reserve wants to let go of it."

William rubbed his forehead. Admiral Kalian might not have realized it, but he'd done a lot of damage to the fleet's command structure. It wasn't *just* too large and unwieldy. The different squadrons weren't working together, not as a single body; they were competing with their fellows for access to everything from crewmen to spare parts and weapons loads. The navy had always encouraged a degree of friendly rivalry, but this was absurd. Their sole priority was getting ready for war.

And staving off demands for immediate action, William thought. He'd seen some of the proposals. The politicians kept putting forward suggestions that made no sense on paper, let alone in the real world. Some wanted to recall every ship in the Royal Navy so they could stand together in defense of the homeworld; others wanted to launch an immediate attack on Caledonia, trusting in superior numbers and firepower to win the day. *We're simply not ready to do anything.*

He cursed, again. If he'd known how much needed to be done . . .

You'd have taken the job anyway, he reminded himself. *The king needs to be stopped.*

He worked his way through the files, looking for a manpower reserve he could borrow. But there wasn't one, not one that could be shifted to another squadron without causing major problems. The next class of reservists wouldn't be ready for another week, at best; the merchant marine personnel needed refresher classes before they could go to work. And pulling people from other systems . . .

A thought struck him. It might work. It *should* work. But only if he could get the admiral to agree.

He stood. "I'm going to see the admiral," he said. "Tell everyone else I'll call them back."

"Aye, sir," Gwynn said.

William brushed down his uniform and headed for the hatch. Admiral Kalian had rebuked a couple of junior officers for not keeping their uniforms in perfect condition, something that bothered William more than he cared to admit. Unnecessary nitpicking was almost always a sign of a poor or overwhelmed leader. And Admiral Kalian certainly had good reason to be overwhelmed. He was caught between two different political factions, neither of which would allow him a completely free hand. William felt sorry for the poor bastard.

He smiled, thinly, as he pressed the buzzer. There was a pause, just long enough for him to wonder if the admiral was taking a nap, then the hatch hissed open. Admiral Kalian was standing in front of a starchart, studying it so intensely that William was sure he was putting on a show. There was nothing to be gained by staring at the display, as if hidden secrets would only reveal themselves if the holograms were scrutinized minutely.

"Commodore," Admiral Kalian said. He turned away from the hologram. "What do you have for me?"

"A staffing problem," William said. "We're short of experienced crewmen we can redeploy on short notice."

"Train more," Admiral Kalian said. "I thought we had vast numbers of reservists flocking to the colors."

"We do," William said. "But Admiral . . . the reservists are out of date. It takes time to give them refresher courses. And without the refresher courses, we can't trust them on starships."

The admiral's frown deepened. "I assume you wouldn't have come to me if you didn't have a solution," he said sharply. "What do you have in mind?"

"I do, sir," William said. Senior officers didn't like juniors who whined whenever there was a problem. An attempt to solve it, or at least to propose a prospective solution, would always go down well. "I propose that we put the loyalists to work. The ones who . . ."

"The ones the king sent home," Admiral Kalian said. "Out of the question."

"They *were* loyal," William said. "They could have stayed on Caledonia if they'd wanted to fight for the king or simply stay out of the fighting altogether."

"They can't be trusted." Admiral Kalian looked William in the eye. "Can you *guarantee* that none of those men are traitors, willing or not?"

William took a moment to put his argument together. "First, a willing traitor couldn't fool a lie detector," he said. "The king would be foolish to assume that we *wouldn't* test the loyalists before letting them go to work for us. Second, we can and we will keep an eye on them. If one does happen to be conditioned, and he slips through a security web, we *will* catch him before he can do any real damage."

"You can't guarantee that he won't do any real damage," Admiral Kalian said stiffly. "Can you?"

"No," William admitted. "But I *can* guarantee that we need them. We are desperately short on crewmen, Admiral, and those men are among the most experienced personnel at our disposal."

"I know," Admiral Kalian said. "How did we get into this mess?" He made a face. "Don't answer that," he added before William could put together a reply. "Just make damn sure that none of them causes any trouble."

"I'll do my best," William assured him. It was enough. The admiral had already given him a free hand. "We can take basic precautions, right from the start. And as we bring more of our manpower reserves online, we can migrate the risk of any damage . . ."

"Good, good." Admiral Kalian cut him off. "Have you heard the latest plan from the Strategy Board?"

"No, sir," William said.

"They want to dispatch a couple of destroyer squadrons to Caledonia, to spy on the king," Admiral Kalian said. "And they think they can keep track of the king's ships when he finally starts his offensive."

William glanced up, sharply. "Have our spies reported anything?"

"Not as yet, if intelligence is to be believed," Admiral Kalian said. "But it's only a matter of time." He shrugged. "Do you think it's a workable idea?"

"Perhaps," William said. "But the destroyers would have problems tracking the ships *and* alerting their destination. The king might set out for one world, then change course midway to hit another."

And it won't be the king in tactical command, he added silently. *Kat will be directing the fleet.*

"We can certainly monitor the king's ships from a distance," William said slowly. "The problem will be getting word back home."

"They think they can slip a message into the StarCom," Admiral Kalian said. "They swear blind it will pass through whatever filters they use . . ."

William had his doubts. The StarCom network had been designed to survive a war, with so many redundancies worked into the system that they could lose half the nodes and keep going, but no one had anticipated a *civil* war. He was mildly surprised that one side or the other hadn't tried to shut down the entire network. But . . . They both used it. He wouldn't be shocked to discover that secret talks were being held between the king and his sworn enemies. Both sides had a certain interest in ending the war without fighting.

But they can't come to an agreement both sides can accept, he mused. *Either the king takes supreme power, which would upset the House of Lords, or the king gives up his power and becomes a figurehead. And that would upset him.*

"It might work," William said. "I take it we don't have a direct line into the king's court?"

"Not yet, not as far as I know," Admiral Kalian said. There was a hint of bitterness in his voice. "They don't tell me everything."

What you don't know you can't tell, William thought. The aristocracy spied on each other. If Kat was to be believed, they spent more effort spying on their fellows than on their outside enemies. But the aristocracy's spies hadn't realized that the king was preparing a bid for supreme power. If they had . . . The whole plot might have been headed off at the pass. *We don't have a spy close to the king. But if we did, we'd have to do everything in our power to keep him safe.*

"It doesn't matter." William didn't need the Strategy Board to tell him the king had only a handful of options. "Sooner or later, he *will* be coming here."

"Sooner rather than later," Admiral Kalian said. "I'll be meeting with the war cabinet later in the week, William. Your presence would be welcome."

"Yes, sir." William felt a twinge of dismay. "It might be better to have the meeting after we hold a series of war games. We won't know just how many problems remain to be solved until then . . ."

"We might not have time," Admiral Kalian said. "The war cabinet wants results."

"Yes, sir," William said. "But it would be better to know what the problems are before we go into battle."

"I know." Admiral Kalian sounded waspish. And frustrated. "But everyone else is breathing down my neck."

"I understand," William said.

He kept his expression blank. There was no *need* for him to attend a war cabinet meeting, but he saw no point in arguing about it. Admiral Kalian probably wanted some support from his staffers, even though the gesture would be worthless. If Kalian was too low-ranking for the great and the good to take into account, what did that say about his staffers? William rather suspected he was too far down the organizational chart for most of the aristocrats to know his name.

Duke Peter knows my name, he reminded himself. *And he might listen to you . . .*

"I'll make arrangements for the loyalists to start going through lie detector tests now," he said, changing the subject. "Hopefully, they should be on their new ships within a couple of days."

"Unless Intelligence wants a word with them first," Admiral Kalian said. "They *were* on the rebel ships."

"I doubt they know anything useful," William said. Only a couple of Kat's senior officers had returned to Tyre. The remainder had either decided to fight for the king or gone into a detention camp. "No one was *planning* a civil war."

"Apart from the king," Admiral Kalian reminded him. "In hindsight, he clearly had a plan for war . . ."

"One that went off the rails," William said.

He kept his face impassive, somehow. He had yet another reason to dislike the king. His plan had been too big, too complex, to have a hope of working. *Kat* would have told him to stick to the KISS principle—Keep It Simple, Stupid—rather than simply hoping for the best. And yet, it had come far too close to outright success . . . There was no justice. He wondered, sourly, just what lessons the king had drawn from the whole affair. Perhaps he'd learned some of the right ones . . .

At an immense cost to everyone around him, William mused. *Win or lose, the Commonwealth is never going to be the same again.*

"He presumably has a plan—had a plan—for what to do if something went wrong," Admiral Kalian said. "How long did he have to think about it?"

"He couldn't have predicted what was going to happen," William said reassuringly. "Any contingency plans he had would be very general, very vague. It will take time to turn them into something actionable."

"I hope so." Admiral Kalian let out an odd little laugh. "It's taking *me* time to turn concepts into something actionable."

"Get your staff to work on it, sir," William said.

Admiral Kalian smiled. "Aren't *you* my staff?"

"Yes, sir," William said. "And when the fleet is ready to go, we can go."

"Quite," Admiral Kalian said. "When do you think we'll be ready to go?"

William hesitated. He was fairly sure he knew the right answer, or at least, what his commander wanted to hear. But he had never lied to a commanding officer before, and he wasn't about to start now. He'd spent too much of his career propping up officers who'd been promoted over his head . . .

"I'd say somewhere between two weeks and a month," he said. "But, realistically, it might take longer."

"I'll hold you to that," Admiral Kalian said. "And the war cabinet will hold *me* to it."

William felt a twinge of sympathy. "There's no way we can be sure, sir," he said. He was uneasily aware that the king had an edge. His fleet was structurally intact, even if it was lacking in infrastructure. "The whole situation is unprecedented."

"Yes," Admiral Kalian said sardonically. He sounded as if he were debating with himself rather than snapping at his subordinate. "Perhaps we should have had an earlier civil war to help us prepare for *this* one."

He turned his attention back to the chart. "Dismissed."

William saluted, then left the cabin.

CHAPTER THIRTEEN

Caledonia

Kat lifted her eyebrows as she followed Sir Grantham into the council chambers. Two new faces were at the table, a colonial representative and an aristocrat she didn't recognize. And, sitting beside her fiancé, Princess Drusilla. Kat felt a twinge of unease as she took her chair. Princess Drusilla might be a genuine heroine—she'd escaped the Theocracy, bringing with her a warning of the impending invasion—but Kat had never really liked her. The mere prospect of her marrying the king had played a major role in starting the civil war.

Particularly as the king couldn't be allowed to choose his own wife, she thought. The cynical part of her mind noted that the House of Lords would have been fine with the king keeping Princess Drusilla as a mistress. *He was meant to marry someone who strengthened the throne, not marry for love.*

Kat kept her face expressionless, though she was annoyed with herself. *She* had planned to marry for love before her lover had died. She still missed Pat . . . if he'd survived, she would have left the navy with him. But she was her father's youngest daughter. No one—no one *important*, anyway—cared whom she married. The only people who cared were gossipmongers who would point and laugh at the girl who married a commoner . . .

She angrily pushed that thought out of her head. She'd never cared about their approval before, and was damned if she was caring now.

"Welcome home, Admiral," the king said. "And thank you, from all of us, for your victory."

"It wasn't much of a victory," Kat said, firmly. "We must bear that in mind at all times."

The king seemed unconcerned. "I believe you know Lord Streford," he said, introducing the aristocrat. "And Governor Rogan, de facto leader of the Colonial Alliance."

"Spokesperson," Governor Rogan said. He had a gravelly voice that reminded Kat of William's older brother. "I can only speak for them. I do not lead."

Kat nodded politely. She'd heard of Governor Rogan of Allophone, although they'd never met in person. He'd been one of the loudest voices demanding more local control, if not outright independence, for the colonies, which was probably why he'd never won election to the House of Commons. There had been accusations, if she recalled correctly, that the vote had been rigged. She wouldn't have been surprised to discover that they were true. A man like Rogan could easily become a liability for his allies as well as his enemies.

"I understand," she said. Rogan would have some freedom of action, but not enough to count himself a true leader. She wondered, absently, where the lines were drawn. "It's good to meet you finally."

The king nodded. "The question before us is how to capitalize on our victory," he said. "My spies report that there's discontent and unrest on Tyre."

Which may or may not be true, Kat mused. The king had had ample time to set up a spy network on his homeworld, but the StarComs were in enemy hands. *We have no independent confirmation.*

She cleared her throat. "The fact remains that Tyre is still heavily defended," she said. "And we didn't do any *real* damage when we took Shallot."

The king smiled. "But we did upset them. They're thinking that we're winning the war."

"An illusion that will be lost the moment we suffer a reverse," Lord Gleneden stated. "They still have might on their side."

"We need more victories," the king agreed. "We must strike directly at Tyre."

"Or hit the naval base at Roland," Governor Rogan said. "If it were to be removed, Your Majesty, a number of other worlds would switch sides."

"Perhaps," Kat said. "But the attack would be a serious diversion of our forces."

"And if we won the battle for Tyre," Earl Antony said, "we would win the war in a single stroke."

Kat resisted the urge to rub her forehead as the argument went around and around. The war council had only been in existence for a month and was already starting to fracture. The hawks wanted to press the war, the doves wanted to push for peace, and the colonials wanted to destroy the naval bases and ships that were keeping their fellows under control. She felt a headache forming at the back of her skull as the argument just wouldn't *stop*. They'd hashed it out already, time and time again. There was no point in repeating the old arguments now.

"You just want to accept the best terms you can," Earl Antony said. He glared at Lord Gleneden. "You don't want to *win*."

"I want a peace we can all live with," Lord Gleneden snapped back. "Right now, we're in a good position to dictate terms. That will change . . ."

"It will change when they build up their forces to crush us," Earl Antony thundered. "We have to move now or . . . or it will be the end. You'd have them stalling us while they build up their fleets and crush us like ants!"

"That's why we need to put forward serious proposals now," Lord Gleneden said. "We have to appeal to the moderates . . ."

"Harrison is no *moderate*." Earl Antony thumped the table. "He won't be happy until all of us are stripped of our nobility."

"But he's not the one calling the shots," Lord Gleneden pointed out. "I . . ."

"His allies have every reason to want to crush us," Earl Antony said. "They *hate* us!"

The king cleared his throat. "We can certainly try to put forward peace feelers," he said calmly. "But we can't even agree on what *we* would like to propose. How could we possibly agree to accept whatever they propose?"

"They're not going to give us what we want," Earl Antony said. "The best we can hope for is a pause in the storm."

"None of the issues underlying the war will go away," Governor Rogan added. "There'll be a resumption in hostilities within five years."

"Can we win?" Lord Gleneden looked at Kat. "If we attack Tyre, can we win?"

Kat kept her face under tight control. "It will be chancy," she admitted. "Home Fleet was badly damaged"—*if the reports are accurate*, she added silently—"but they've had a month to get reorganized, repair the damage, and get themselves combat ready. Planetary Defense, of course, was untouched. We would be facing both of them, in an environment that wouldn't allow either of us to be particularly clever. Going for Tyre would be *very* chancy."

"But it could be done," the king said.

"Yes," Kat said. "We do have some advantages . . ."

"Our cause is *right*," Earl Antony said, before she could elaborate. "They'll surrender the moment they see us coming."

"I doubt it," Kat warned. She had no idea who'd taken command of Home Fleet, but the House of Lords wouldn't have picked a quitter. She considered a handful of possible choices, then shrugged. She'd find out when she caught up with the intelligence reports. "I expect they'd want to fight it out."

"Even if we offer decent terms?" Lord Gleneden leaned forward. "We could try to talk them out of fighting."

"They will not give us what we want, not willingly," the king said. "And we cannot give them what they want. They must surrender to us, or we must surrender to them. There is no middle ground."

Probably not, Kat thought. Her lips twitched humorlessly. *A truce is just a period of cheating between wars.*

She felt an odd little pang as the argument restarted. Her father had said that, back when some people had argued for a truce between the Commonwealth and the Theocracy. There couldn't be a long-lasting peace, he'd pointed out, not when the two sides couldn't coexist indefinitely. The king had to keep his power or lose everything; the House of Lords had to strip the king of his power or lose everything. And yet . . . She couldn't help thinking that her father would have found middle ground. This wasn't a war of extermination.

"It doesn't matter if we destroy Tyre's industry," Governor Rogan said. "Would it not tilt the balance of power in our favor?"

"And then it would have to be rebuilt, after the war," Lord Gleneden pointed out. "That wouldn't be easy."

"Such an act would also be butchery," the king said. "I will not slaughter millions of my own subjects."

Kat sighed as the argument continued. The colonials might have a great deal to gain if Tyre's industrial base were destroyed, but it would also start off an economic crisis that would make the last one look pathetic. She could see the Commonwealth collapsing into ruins if the economy fell completely, everything they'd built over the last century smashed beyond repair. The Commonwealth hadn't been an unmixed blessing, she admitted that much, but it hadn't been a complete disaster either. How many worlds would have been ravaged by pirates, terrorists, and religious maniacs if the Royal Navy *hadn't* protected them?

"We move now, or we surrender on the best terms we can get," Earl Antony said, summing up the debate. "And there is no fucking way we can *enforce* those terms afterwards."

And Peter won't hesitate to put the boot in if he has a chance, Kat thought. She knew her brother. He wasn't stupid, but he didn't have the long view either. He might not understand the importance of keeping his word, even to people like Earl Antony. *People won't surrender if they think they'll be killed anyway.*

The king nodded slowly. "Admiral Falcone. Do you have a plan to take Tyre?"

"Yes, Your Majesty," Kat said equally formally. "I have a basic plan that can be fleshed out while we're underway."

And well away from this den of vipers, she thought. She liked the king, but some of his supporters were starting to get on her nerves. *The sooner we win the war, the better.*

"It could cost us everything," Governor Rogan said. "If we lose . . . what then?"

"We won't lose," Earl Antony snapped.

"Really?" Governor Rogan gave him a thin smile. "Can you *guarantee* a victory?"

"No one can guarantee a victory," Kat said, as Earl Antony started to splutter. "But I can guarantee that we won't win if we don't launch the operation."

"Yes," Earl Antony said. "We can stay here, and sit on our asses, until they gather their fleets and crush us."

"And if we lose, we lose everything," Governor Rogan said. "The liberated worlds will be crushed. Again."

"They weren't *crushed*," Lord Gleneden protested.

"Forty years ago, there was a dispute between my homeworld, Allophone, and the Falcone Corporation," Governor Rogan said. He shot Kat a nasty look. His voice was very cold. "There was a rights grab that was nothing more than barefaced theft. The Commonwealth passed special legislation to retroactively legalize everything the corporation did . . . and dump a hefty penalty on us into the bargain. And when we couldn't pay, they seized our orbitals and enacted tariffs to extract the money by force. We had right on our side."

His eyes swept the table. "We had right, but we didn't have *might*. And that made all the difference."

Kat swallowed. It couldn't be true, could it? She hadn't even been born at the time. Her father had been CEO . . . He'd been a hard bastard, at times, but he wouldn't have crushed a planet over a minor dispute . . . Would he? She wasn't sure she wanted to know. Her father had always had a ruthless streak. She hated to admit it, but it was possible. And yet, why hadn't she heard of the incident before? Someone would have thrown it in her face, surely. She made a mental note to look the details up as soon as possible.

But there's nothing I can do about it, she thought grimly. *Peter's the one holding the purse strings now.*

"If the war continues, we will lose," Earl Antony said. "And then yes, your world will be crushed."

"We must put all disputes aside until we win the war," Princess Drusilla said. Her soft voice hung in the air. "Or else we will all be slaughtered when *they* win the war."

"Quite," the king said. "Does anyone have any further objections?"

There was a long pause. "We should at least *try* to keep communications open," Lord Gleneden said. "If nothing else, we might be able to talk them into offering better terms."

"I doubt it," the king said. "Admiral Falcone, prepare your fleet. Your orders are to take Tyre and win this damn war."

"Yes, Your Majesty." Kat felt torn between excitement and a grim unease. It would be a great battle, fought for a cause; it would also be bloody, forcing her to kill men and women who, only a few short months ago, had been on her side. And the winner, whoever it happened to be, would be badly weakened. "I'll make the preparations at once."

"Keep us informed," Earl Antony said. "We might want to add refinements . . ."

"We must keep our objective a secret," Kat said. She doubted anyone on Tyre would be fooled, as there was a shortage of realistic targets for the king's fleet, but it was worth a try. "No one must know the details . . ."

"There will be no betrayal," Governor Rogan snapped. "We are committed."

"It only takes one spy in the right place to catch a secret and pass it on to his superiors," Kat said. "Do you know how many times the enemy was ready for us, during the last war, because their spies discovered what we were doing?"

"Not here," Governor Rogan insisted.

Kat shook her head. "The Theocracy was brutal, right from the start," she said. "It didn't commit genocide until the end of the war, Governor, but it raped and slaughtered its way through a dozen planetary populations. This was no secret, yet . . . People kept spying for them, right up until the end. The Commonwealth, for all its faults, is no Theocracy. There will be people who will be reporting to Tyre, even now. And we have no way of stopping them."

"Shut down the StarCom," Lord Streford suggested. "The treacherous bastards can't hurt us if they can't get any messages back home."

"We need it," Lord Gleneden said. "*Our* treacherous bastards won't be able to get their messages to us without the StarCom."

The king chuckled. "We will keep the decision to ourselves," he said. "And do what we can to pretend we're not doing anything."

"We can just sit on our asses and do nothing." Lord Gleneden smirked at Earl Antony. "A fine suggestion, may I say?"

Earl Antony started to say something cutting, but the king spoke over him. "I think we have argued enough for one day," he said. "Admiral Falcone, please will you join me in my office in twenty minutes?"

"Yes, Your Majesty," Kat said. She was relieved, despite her growing headache. A chance to speak to the king alone was worth any discomfort. "I'll be there."

"Then I think we can consider this meeting over," the king said. He stood. "Go back to the party, if you wish."

Kat caught Governor Rogan's eye as the room emptied. "I'm sorry about what happened to your world," she said, carefully. "It was before my time."

"But not before your father's time," Governor Rogan pointed out. "It happened in living memory."

"I know," Kat said. "And I am sorry."

Governor Rogan cocked his head. "What can you do about it?"

Kat blinked. "Pardon?"

"What can you do about it?" Governor Rogan shrugged. "Can you go back in time and talk sense into your father? Can you undo what his army of lawyers, accountants, tax collectors, and creatures from the black latrine did to my people? Can you even offer recompense? Can you direct the Falcone Corporation to pay back what it owes, with interest? Can you stop it from happening again?"

"No," Kat said. She saw no point in lying. "I don't control the corporation."

"Not now," Governor Rogan said. "Will you control it if the king wins?"

Kat hesitated. "I don't know."

"I imagine you will," Governor Rogan said. "But that's something to think about in the future."

He met her eyes. "Understand this, if you don't understand anything else. We won't let ourselves be rendered helpless again. We'll fight for the king, as long as he fights for us; we won't betray him, as long as he doesn't betray us. But if he does . . ."

"You'll fight him," Kat finished.

"And we expect to be treated as equals," Governor Rogan said. "No more rules blocking us from serving on starships, from *commanding* starships. We want a share of everything. We want . . . We won't ever be weak again."

"Because you don't trust anyone else to protect you," Kat said.

"No," Governor Rogan agreed. He lowered his voice. "We understand, you know, that the Commonwealth might be bad, but the Theocracy was hell incarnate. We understand . . . Yes, we do. But the Commonwealth's protection turned into domination . . . We want to protect ourselves, to make it impossible for someone to dominate us again. And for that, we want equality."

He waved a hand at the door. "Tell the king that, Admiral. And tell the fops he has around him. Maybe they won't listen, but . . . at least you can *try*."

"I do understand," Kat said. She remembered William and felt a twinge of pain. And guilt. He should have been *her* commanding officer, when they'd first met. "I won't let you down."

"That's the point," Governor Rogan said. He turned and headed for the door. "We don't want anyone to be in a position to let us down again."

CHAPTER FOURTEEN

CALEDONIA

Kat wasn't entirely surprised—not remotely surprised, if she was honest with herself—to discover Sir Grantham lurking outside the door. He shouldn't have been able to hear anything, not through the privacy field that surrounded the conference chamber, but still . . . She quietly ignored his attempts at conversation as he led her through a pair of metal doors, past a guardpost where she was scanned for concealed weapons, and finally into the king's living room. The king himself was seated in a comfortable armchair, a glass of brandy in his hand. He looked older, as if he'd aged two decades in the space of a few minutes.

He gave her a tired smile. "Close the door behind you," he said. "Sir Grantham can wait outside."

Like a dog waiting for his master, Kat thought unkindly. *It isn't as if he has anywhere else to go.*

She closed the door and sat down, studying the king warily. He definitely looked older, as if the stresses and strains of running a government-in-exile were wearing him down. She could imagine the problems, even though she'd been occupied with reorganizing the fleet for offensive operations. Sir Grantham had made it clear that hundreds of high-ranking supporters had arrived at Caledonia, all expecting the king to grant them posts in his new administration. And probably underwrite their losses too, if their property back home was seized. Kat rather suspected that sorting out the mess, whoever won the war, was going to take years.

"Your Majesty," she said, formally. "You wanted to see me?"

"It's good to talk to someone who doesn't *want* something." The king's smile turned crooked. "Everyone wants something these days."

"Quite," Kat agreed. "It's been a while since we had a chance to just sit and talk, hasn't it?"

The king took a sip from his glass. "Years, perhaps?"

Kat nodded. She'd been a privy councilor, but her duties had kept her away from Tyre. In theory, she'd had access to the king's chambers whenever she wanted; in practice, it had been pretty much impossible for her to have a private conversation with Hadrian. She wondered, morbidly, just how much had passed her by over the last year or so. She hadn't had any real inclination to use her post to distribute patronage and largesse, building a power base of her own, but she knew others would have felt different. They'd needed to strengthen their own positions for the inevitable day they lost their place on the council.

The king waved a languid hand at the drinks tray. "Help yourself. The local brandy is to die for."

"Not literally, one hopes." Kat had never liked drinking, and she'd never had the inclination to develop any wine snobbery, but she poured herself a small glass anyway, just to be sociable. "Your council seems rather divided."

"You noticed," the king said. It sounded like a joke, but she wasn't sure. "There are people on the council who would stick a knife in my back, if they thought it would get them safe passage back home."

Kat nodded, saying nothing.

"I thought I could nip everything in the bud," the king said. "I thought . . ." He shook his head, heavily. "I thought I could keep matters from spiraling out of control. I was wrong."

"Very few plans survive contact with the enemy," Kat observed. She sniffed her brandy. It smelled sweet, strong. "And you managed to escape the chaos when things went to hell."

"I knew they were going to try to ram impeachment through the House of Lords," the king said. He sounded as if he hadn't heard a word she'd said. "I knew . . . they were so determined to have their way that they were going to ride roughshod over the law, over years of precedent. I knew . . . I should have known just how far they intended to go."

He took another sip. "The Commonwealth had to be preserved. Couldn't they see that?"

"I agree," Kat said. "But others . . ."

"Self-interested twats," the king said. He smiled, but the smile didn't touch his eyes. "They didn't see the bigger picture. They were so interested in retrenching, in putting Tyre ahead of everyone else . . . No, they couldn't even do *that.* They were interested merely in themselves. And they would have dragged everyone else down too, if I'd given them the chance."

Kat frowned. The king had been drinking . . . How *much* had he been drinking? He had the best gene engineering money could buy, his body engineered to resist drugs and alcohol, but there were limits. A few glasses of brandy shouldn't be enough to do more than make him mildly tipsy, yet . . . How much *had* he drunk? It wasn't as if anyone would have stopped him from drinking his way through the wine cellar. He was the king!

Hadrian coughed into his drink. "I did what I had to do," he said. "And it's all exploding in my face."

"You haven't lost," Kat said bluntly.

"No," the king said. "But . . ." He shook his head. "You have to win the battle, Kat," he said. "The *coming* battle. It has to be the last one."

"I wish I could promise you a victory," Kat said quietly. "But I can't."

"Yeah," the king said. He put his drink to one side and sat upright. "Admiral Vaughn hasn't joined us. I don't know if he was caught while trying to leave Tyre or . . . or if he decided he wanted to stay home. He was talking about retiring before the shit hit the fan."

And he might have decided to bow out gracefully, Kat thought. She didn't think Vaughn would have a peaceful retirement, if that was what he'd decided to do. The House of Lords would have a great many questions for him, questions he would be forced to answer. *It might be better for him if he'd been caught or killed while trying to flee the planet.*

The king met her eyes. "Admiral Lord Garstang will be taking over as fleet administrator, freeing you up for offensive operations. He has considerable experience in the Admiralty, which makes him ideally qualified for the role. I trust that pleases you?"

Kat took a moment to think. She couldn't recall ever *meeting* Admiral Lord Garstang. The name meant nothing to her. If he'd been in the Admiralty . . . She made a mental note to download his file and read it as soon as possible. He could be the answer to her prayers, if she could leave fleet administration in a pair of capable hands . . . or he could turn into a nightmare, if he didn't have the common sense that came with actually commanding starships in battle. He might just have reached flag rank before the Theocratic War had actually begun . . .

No point in worrying about it now. "I'm sure he'll do a good job," she said. It was one weight off her mind . . . or it would be, as soon as she *knew* he was a competent officer. "I do need someone to handle the paperwork."

The king didn't smile. "I've also appointed Commodore Henri Ruben as your second," he added. "It was a political decision."

Kat blinked. "I already have a second," she said stiffly. "I . . ."

"I need to shore up my support among some of my followers," the king said. His voice was flat. "And I have to make it clear that there will be patronage."

"And patronizing," Kat muttered. It had been one of her father's favorite puns, even though it had lost any humor long ago. "Your Majesty . . ."

"There's no choice," the king said flatly.

"You told me that *I* was in command of the fleet," Kat said. "And that includes command assignments."

The king's face flushed. "You're *still* in command of the fleet."

"But you are assigning people to positions within the fleet." Kat allowed her voice to harden. "It will not be easy to alter the fleet command structure on short notice."

"It was designed to be adaptable," the king pointed out. "And you yourself stated . . ." He cleared his throat. "There are too many factions that need to be satisfied," he said tiredly. "You saw them at the ball."

"I saw people dividing up the spoils before we even won the war," Kat said, bluntly. "Why do we have to listen to them?"

"You were never one for politics, were you?" The king gave her an odd little smile. "I always liked that in you."

Kat met his eyes, putting her untouched drink on the table and crossing her arms. "Why?"

"I have three groups of supporters," the king said. He picked up his drink and took a long sip. "One group is loyal to me personally, like you. A second has nowhere else to go, at least for the moment. And a third thinks I am their best hope of achieving *their* ambitions. They'll support me as long as they think I can help them."

"Like the colonials," Kat said. Was Ruben a colonial? It seemed unlikely. The highest-ranking colonial in naval service had been a captain. "Do you think they'll stick with you because you put one of them in a high place?"

"They'll see it as a sign of things to come," the king said. He sighed, heavily. "This coalition is very fragile, Kat. The political sphere doesn't operate with naval efficiency. Too many people think they might be able to go back home, to come to terms with the House of Lords and . . ."

"They don't have anything to bargain with," Kat said.

"They think they do," the king countered. "And that is all that matters."

He ran his hands through his dark hair. "And so I have to make a show of rewarding my supporters," he added. "Do you have any *good* reasons for rejecting my picks?"

Kat took a moment to gather her thoughts. "I don't *know* Commodore Ruben," she said finally. "He might be a good and experienced officer, or he might be a complete disaster, someone better at playing political games than actually commanding starships in battle. And I don't want to find out the hard way."

"I understand," the king said. "But I need to satisfy my supporters."

"So you said," Kat said, biting down a sharp remark about satisfying his supporters at the cost of losing the war. "Why not appoint a colonial officer?"

"There isn't one," the king said. "Your old war buddy betrayed us. Do you know Governor Rogan and his people want to put McElney on trial for treason? They think he should have come over to us the moment the shooting started."

Kat felt a flash of annoyance. "He didn't have a chance . . ."

"And now he's working for the enemy," the king said. "That's pretty damned embarrassing for the colonials. They think they would have the edge if your friend was on the right side."

"Cotton, slaves, and arrogance," Kat muttered.

The king frowned. "I beg your pardon?"

Kat shrugged. There was no point in trying to explain the reference. She knew there were colonials who thought they were tougher than the average Tyrian, on the grounds that their homeworlds were generally poorer and harsher than Tyre, but she'd never known anyone in the navy who took it seriously. Tyre had the ships, the shipyards, the training establishments . . . everything necessary to produce and maintain a huge fleet. Maybe one colonial was tougher, more resilient, than a dozen Tyrians. God was still on the side of the people with bigger guns and more of them.

And yet . . . She shook her head. She did wish William had joined her, if only because they'd worked together long enough for each of them to know what the other was thinking. She didn't really understand why William had joined the House of Lords . . . She thought she knew, but she didn't understand. William had never liked the king. He'd believed the suggestions that it had been the king, not a rogue faction, who'd shipped weapons to the Theocracy. And if he believed that to be true, he'd believe the king had to be stopped.

"I don't think they can try him for anything," she said. "Hebrides is a radioactive wasteland. His people have been scattered. There's no one who speaks for them any longer . . . The remnants of his people are so small that they simply don't matter. Have they even declared their support for us? Would it matter if they had?"

"It might matter a great deal, if the House of Lords turns your friend into the poster child for collaboration," the king pointed out. "What will you say then?"

Kat didn't have to think about it. "Nothing."

The king took another sip of his drink. "I'm asking you, as a personal favor, to accept Ruben as your second. I believe he will handle the post with a . . ."

"Fine." Kat cut him off. "But if he turns into a problem, I won't hesitate to relieve him of his post."

"Please don't," the king said. "That would cause more problems back here."

Kat rubbed her forehead. She understood the king's problem, but . . . *Damn it.* He didn't *need* to worry about the good opinions of a load of wastrels and hangers-on. If his supporters had had real power, there would have been no risk of impeachment and no descent into violence. Maybe they *could* go home. Maybe they would be warmly welcomed by their families. It wouldn't make any real difference to the final outcome.

But it would damage the king's prospects if he *didn't* reward his followers. Kat had no illusions about the aristocracy. The House of Lords and the ducal families were committed, but the remainder would be trying to keep their options open. Some would consider jumping ship, if they thought there would be a soft landing. If the king suggested there *would* be a place for anyone who joined his side . . .

And there will be people in my family who will be considering ways to join the king if he wins the war, Kat thought. She'd expected a formal letter of disownment from her brother, if he could convince the family council to go along with it, but none had arrived. They presumably thought she'd speak for them if the family had to come to terms with the king. *The trick will be switching sides when they still have something to offer.*

The king coughed, putting his empty glass on the table. "You do understand, don't you?"

"Yes," Kat said. She made a mental note to keep a sharp eye on the newcomer. "I do understand the stakes."

The king relaxed, slightly. "Once we win, things will be different. Do you want the Grand Admiralty? Or the Falcone Corporation?"

"I don't know *what* I want," Kat admitted.

"Let me know, and I'll make sure you get it," the king promised. "When I am restored, when I have my power, I *will* reward my supporters."

"We have to win first," Kat said. The king's supporters couldn't hope for anything better than being sent into exile if they lost the war. Some of them would probably be charged with high treason and executed. "Victory first, dividing up the spoils later."

She glanced up, sharply, as a door opened. Princess Drusilla stepped into the room, wearing a long white dress that covered everything below her neck and yet left very little to the imagination. Kat felt an flush of dislike, mingled with an odd sense that she and Drusilla had a great deal in common. They'd both left their families to fight for what was right.

And she's all natural, Kat thought wryly.

Her lips twitched in sardonic amusement. There was no shortage of beautiful people on Tyre—even the poorest could afford a basic bodysculpt, if they didn't like what nature and genetic engineering had given them—but Princess Drusilla had grown up on Ahura Mazda. Her olive skin; dark, doe-like eyes; and brilliant smile were natural. It was easy to see why the king was so smitten. Princess Drusilla's looks were exotic compared to the fashionable girls on Tyre. She was outstanding.

"It's been a long day," Princess Drusilla said as she stood behind the king and started to massage his shoulders. Her voice was exotic too, her accent delightfully foreign. "Are you coming to bed?"

Kat felt her eyes narrow, despite herself. She had no reason to worry, she told herself, and yet . . . She just didn't *like* Princess Drusilla. It wasn't her good looks, she thought; it wasn't her accent, which brought back bitter memories of Ahura Mazda. It was . . . She wasn't sure *what* it was. Cold logic told her that Princess Drusilla was a heroine, a woman who had risked life, limb, and freedom to warn the Commonwealth of the oncoming storm. And yet . . . and yet . . .

The king smiled up at his lover, his face softening. "I'm coming . . ."

Kat rose, trying to conceal her embarrassment. "I'll speak with you before we depart," she said. "And I will do my best to integrate the newcomers."

"Please," the king said. He relaxed into Princess Drusilla's touch. "It would be very helpful."

Drusilla shot Kat an unreadable look. Kat looked back, wondering what had disturbed the princess. Kat and the king, alone together? It would never have happened on Ahura Mazda. But then, Kat wouldn't have had a career on Ahura Mazda. She couldn't blame Princess Drusilla for running away. Indeed, she'd often wondered if *she* would be able to pluck up the courage to escape if she'd spent her entire life in such a nightmare. She wouldn't even know for sure there was anywhere to go.

And someone who grew up in such an environment could be a little twisted, she thought. The occupation had been a nightmare. *Who knows what she will do to survive?*

CHAPTER FIFTEEN

Caledonia

The ship is mine, Captain Sarah Henderson thought.

She sat in her command chair and studied her displays, trying not to think about the blood she'd cleaned off the chair only six weeks ago. The flight to Caledonia had been nerve-racking, even though she'd been careful to avoid contact with potential enemy ships. She hadn't even been sure how to announce herself when she'd arrived. Indeed, she'd been mildly surprised that the king and his new administration had welcomed her and her crew without question. They hadn't cared that she'd shot her former CO. They'd even confirmed Sarah as the new captain before she could work up the nerve to ask.

Yet it didn't stop them from taking a third of my crew, she thought without heat. *And dumping a bunch of unprepared trainees on me.*

She felt a twinge of resentment, although she knew she was being selfish. The king's fleet was a hodgepodge of ships, officers, and crewmen. There were hundreds of gaps in their roster, with personnel gluts in some categories and only a handful of qualified personnel in others. She knew they needed to share, if only to ensure that every starship had a core of qualified and experienced personnel, but it still rankled. She was grimly aware that she didn't have anything like the command experience of Captain Saul. She'd never been an XO. She'd never had the chance to shadow a captain and learn what to do . . .

And what not to do, she thought. She knew from grim experience that senior officers often knew things that were never written down, things they considered so obvious they didn't *need* to be written down. What had Captain Saul known about his ship and command that she didn't know? *I don't know what I don't know.*

She sighed as she glanced at the datapad. Fleet Administration was a joke, even though Admiral Lord Garstang had taken command and started to sort out the mess. He was doing a good job for a dyed-in-the-wool aristocrat, she conceded, but it would take months to smooth out the problems. Logistics were an utter headache. Supply lines were a joke. She had a full load of missiles, thankfully, but her ship had a number of other shortages . . . There would be trouble, she thought, if they had to make repairs while underway. And *Merlin* was one of the lucky ships. A handful of patrol vessels had arrived, armed with nothing more dangerous than a pair of popguns. They wouldn't last five seconds against a destroyer, let alone a superdreadnought.

The only upside to the chaos, as far as she could tell, was that no one was singling her out for special attention. *Merlin* was hardly the only ship having problems. The entire *fleet* was having problems, including the ships that had been on active duty in the occupation zone when the shit hit the fan. Even *they* were having problems. Their rosters had been raided for experienced officers too. Technically, it should take months, or even years, to get the fleet ready to depart. They'd been told to get ready to leave in less than a week.

I suppose we don't have to worry about paperwork any longer, she thought as a newly minted midshipman passed her a datapad and then stood at her shoulder like a waiter expecting a tip. *But even that's a headache.*

Her lips twitched at the thought. She'd learned to hate paperwork from the moment she'd realized how much of her time would be wasted filling out useless forms. But now . . . The fleet was so disorganized that it was hard to get anything done. They'd effectively thrown the baby out with the bathwater. They couldn't get supplies to where they were needed if they didn't know what supplies were on hand.

She glanced at the report. Her tactical staff, what was left of it, had held a gunnery training exercise. Simulated only, of course. There was no time for live-fire exercises in the middle of the greatest mobilization in the navy's history, but the practice was still useful. The results were about what she'd expected. The newcomers were keen to learn and determined to get stuck into the enemy, but they had a long way to go. Thankfully, there didn't seem to be any discipline problems. It helped, she supposed, that most of the newcomers were reservists or merchant marine crewers. They might be rough around the edges, with little or no experience with cutting-edge hardware, but at least they understood the value of discipline.

And we have an edge, she thought. The king might be fighting for his throne, and his aristocratic supporters might want their titles, but the colonials were fighting for equality, which was all they'd ever wanted. They had a cause and they would fight for it and . . . It was hard to believe the Tyrians could muster the will to stop them. *We're fighting for something we desperately need. They're not even sure what they're fighting for.*

She nodded to the midshipman, who took the pad and hurried away. He was so young, she reflected, that she couldn't help wondering if he'd lied about his age. The navy refused to take anyone under eighteen, but record-keeping was so poor on some of the more primitive colonies that it would be easy for a youngster to claim he was of legal age. No one would ask too many questions. The navy had been desperate for manpower during the last war. She reflected, sourly, that it was desperate for manpower again.

Not that it matters, she told herself. *The war will be over, one way or the other, before we can start recruiting and training new crewmen.*

An officer waved for her attention. She put her thoughts aside and went back to work.

♦ ♦ ♦

Kat studied the latest set of results and frowned. The exercise hadn't been as bad as she'd feared—this time, at least, no simulated superdreadnoughts had collided in the middle of a simple maneuver—but the smooth perfection of the later war years was gone. Her formation was a joke, barely held together by spit and baling wire. She'd done everything she could to smooth out the flaws, to get her crews to work together, but they needed actual combat experience before they were truly ready. And some of them might not survive long enough to make use of it.

At least Commodore Ruben isn't a serious problem, she thought. Ruben had caused her some embarrassment when she'd explained to Commodore Fran Higgins that she was no longer the fleet's second-in-command, but he was starting to shape up. *And Admiral Garstang is doing an excellent job of organizing the logistics.*

She frowned, again. The fleet was readying itself to depart at breakneck speed. She'd put out a story that the fleet would be attacking Durian, a fleet base only four light years from Tyre, but she rather suspected it hadn't fooled anyone. There simply weren't many targets, short of Tyre itself, that demanded the attention of the entire fleet. And yet . . . Kat was uneasily aware of just how exposed they were. If someone on the other side decided to gamble, he could attack Caledonia while Kat was attacking Tyre. The move would be risky as hell; she rather suspected that no sane admiral would authorize the plan, but if it worked, the war would be won in a single stroke. Nothing would be gained by capturing Tyre if Caledonia, and the king, fell into enemy hands.

Her terminal chimed. She glanced at it. Commodore Ruben was calling.

"Commodore," she said curtly. "What can I do for you?"

"I wanted to discuss the operational plan," Ruben said. He looked young, although he was actually five years older than Kat. His patrons—the king himself, and some of his close supporters—had done their best, but his career hadn't been nearly as meteoric as hers. "I was wondering . . ."

"There's no room for being clever," Kat said. She'd spent *days* looking for a way to take Tyre rapidly and cheaply by outmaneuvering Home Fleet, but as far as she could tell it simply couldn't be done. The battle was going to be a slugging match, calling for her to try to pin the enemy's mobile units against the planet itself. "Even making a feint isn't likely to work."

"But we could try," Ruben said. "If we could convince them to detach a single superdreadnought squadron . . ."

Kat raised her voice, just enough to make her feelings clear. "The enemy is *not* stupid," she said sharply. "If they were, they would have been dispatching ships to all the worlds that declared for the king, trying to bring them to heel. Instead, they are building up their fleet at Tyre. They know, as well as we do, that Tyre is both the one place they cannot afford to lose and the place we must take if we want to win the war. There's no room to be clever."

Ruben leaned forward. "But Admiral . . ."

"We simply cannot bait them out of position," Kat said. "What could we possibly offer them, Commodore, that would be worth the risk of leaving Tyre exposed?"

She waited, but it was clear that Ruben had no answer. "No," she said. "I couldn't think of anything either."

Ruben changed tack with remarkable speed. "Admiral . . . if we take the high orbitals and they refuse to surrender, what then?"

Kat kept her face impassive with an effort. She'd been trying not to think about it. The laws of war stipulated that worlds *should* surrender when they lost control of the high orbitals, but the laws of war had been written by people with no experience in either naval operations or politics. Tyre's ground-based defenses were formidable, easily the toughest in known space. Caledonia's were flimsy by comparison. If the House of Lords refused to surrender . . . She sucked in her breath. A full-fledged invasion would devastate the planet, killing millions of innocent civilians as well as soldiers and marines. She hoped, she prayed, it wouldn't come to that. Surely, the House of Lords would see sense.

"If they refuse to surrender, we will secure the remainder of the system's industrial base," she said. "The decision about what to do with Tyre itself will be a political one."

Ruben looked dissatisfied. "What if they continue to fight?"

Kat lifted her eyebrows in mock surprise. She'd heard colonials suggesting that Tyre should be brought to heel, whatever the cost, but she'd expected better from an aristocrat who'd been born on Tyre. But then, Ruben had had very little beyond a title. She supposed that might have embittered him. Better not to have the title rather than have the title and lack the funds to support it. She'd known a handful of naval officers who'd prayed desperately for prize money to reinvigorate their estates.

And they might have been kicked off the rolls altogether if they hadn't been able to fund themselves properly, she reflected. *And it would be seen as a disgrace even if it actually worked in their favor.*

She allowed her voice to harden. "The king can make that decision," she said. "We will leave it in his hands."

Ruben looked down. "Yes, Admiral."

"We will keep the fleet out of range of the groundside defenses," Kat added. "The worst they can do is devastate the orbital industries, Commodore, and they'll need them for bargaining chips."

Unless they bring in reinforcements, like the Theocracy tried to do, she reminded herself, slowly. She didn't think the House of Lords could bring the reserve fleet online so quickly, although it was something to bear in mind. *But even if they do, the entire system would be devastated.*

She dismissed the point. "I expect your squadron to be ready to depart on command," she added. "We have a departure date to meet."

"Yes, Admiral," Ruben said. "We'll be ready."

"Good," Kat said. "We'll be leaving in two days."

And if you're not ready to go, she thought as she closed the connection, *I'll leave you behind.*

She glanced at the starchart, feeling an odd little pit in her stomach. She knew she was being unfair to Ruben, that he had a difficult job to do that hadn't been made any easier by his impromptu promotion, but she couldn't help herself. It was hardly the first time she'd gone to war, yet . . . Never had so much rested on a single battle. She was the only person who could win or lose the war in a single day.

Her terminal bleeped, informing her that another set of reports had arrived. The king and his staff hadn't *stopped* meddling, damn them. Garstang and Ruben weren't bad choices, she conceded, but others . . . There were too many names being put forward for too few places. She cursed under her breath. The sooner the fleet was gone, the better.

Two days, she told herself. *And then we'll be on our way.*

♦ ♦ ♦

"It's a strange way to go to war, sir," Lieutenant Archie Clancy said, cheerfully. "They shouldn't be letting us anywhere near so close to their homeworld."

Captain Hugh Jorgen shrugged. HMS *Thumbelina* was as close to undetectable as any scout ship could be, as long as she didn't try to cross a laser web or emit a pulse of betraying radiation too close to an enemy sensor platform for comfort. And yet, he had to admit that Clancy had a point. Hugh was an old hand at sneaking into hostile star systems, but Caledonia had been friendly only a couple of months ago. The web of scansats watching for the slightest *hint* of cloaked or stealthed starships in the vicinity was as advanced as the scansats protecting Tyre itself. He was all too aware that they might already have been detected, with a cloaked starship sneaking towards them from the rear. They might be blown apart before they even knew they were under attack.

"They *do* have a lot of crap in their system," he said instead. "They might not be keeping a record of what's actually going on."

He smiled at the thought. Caledonia didn't have one or two giant corporations mining the asteroid and gas giants. The belts were being exploited by local companies and independent asteroid miners, the latter practically free of *any* government oversight. It would be tricky for the locals to spot his scout ship if they didn't know what should and what shouldn't be moving through their system. It was an oddity, in a developed system . . . He dismissed the thought. He didn't care why they were being so lax. All that mattered was that he was in a perfect spot to watch the enemy fleet assemble.

He felt an odd little pang as his ship inched closer. The fleet gathering near the planet had been friendly too, once upon a time. There were people on the fleet who had fought beside him, during the last war. Now, they were enemies. *Thumbelina* had picked up news reports suggesting that there were people on both sides who wanted peace, but they were the minority. It was hard to compromise when neither side could put forward a deal the other side would accept. And that meant war . . . He wondered, bitterly, just how many of his friends were about to die. He was almost glad he'd accepted the scout ship command, even though it might be career death. At least he wouldn't be killing any of his former friends.

Just setting them up to die, he thought bitterly. *How many of them will never see their homes again because of me?*

Too many, his own thoughts answered. It was easy to forget that the king, whatever else could be said about him, had let anyone who didn't want to *fight* for him bow out. *But they made their choice.*

He watched the data piling up in front of him. A picture was slowly starting to take shape, a picture that made a frightening amount of sense. The enemy fleet was slipping out of orbit, readying itself to depart. It wouldn't be long before the fleet opened a vortex and vanished into hyperspace. And then . . . if the communications intercepts were to be believed, the fleet was going to head straight for Durian. Hugh winced. He knew people there.

"Vortex opening, sir," Clancy said. On the display, the enemy ships slid into the vortex and vanished. The vortex spun for a second afterwards, then snapped out of existence. "They're gone."

"Yes," Hugh said. He let out a breath. They weren't out of the woods yet. "Compose the alert message, then send it to their StarCom."

"Aye, sir," Clancy said.

"And ready our generator," Hugh added. The rebels hadn't turned off their StarComs. It wasn't clear if they *could* turn them off, at least without shutting them down permanently. But they might place a hold on all outgoing messages until the fleet reached its target. "If we can't get a message out, we'll have to run."

"Aye, sir." Clancy laughed. "You'd think they'd do *something* to keep messages from getting out of the system."

"They'd have to shut down their own communications as well, if they wanted to be sure," Hugh pointed out. His briefers had stated that an obviously encrypted message would be blocked, naturally, but how could even the most advanced filters catch something that looked harmless? A love letter from an asteroid miner to his mistress might hide a double meaning. "And that would cripple them."

He smiled as the message went through. Clancy was right.

It was an odd way to fight a war.

CHAPTER SIXTEEN

Tyre

". . . And so we come to the final aspects of this preliminary statement, Your Grace," Alexander Masterly informed him. "The economic aspects . . ."

Peter held up a hand. "I don't have time for a long lecture," he said curtly, resisting the urge to point out that Alexander and Clive Masterly had been lecturing him for the last hour. "And I don't need more economic technobabble. Cut to the chase."

Alexander and Clive Masterly exchanged glances. "The Emergency Spending Bill has reinvigorated parts of the corporate environment, Your Grace," Clive Masterly said, carefully. "However, aspects of the economy remain weak. Labor unrest is growing, particularly in areas we cannot *afford* labor unrest. Laid-off workers are sometimes reluctant to return to work . . ."

"I see," Peter said. "How bad is it going to be? For us? For Tyre? For the Commonwealth?"

"It depends on the outcome of the war, Your Grace," Alexander Masterly said. "A short war would mean a handful of minor hiccups, but . . . The economy was in a downturn well before the war actually began. A longer war would give us a chance to stabilize the economy, allowing us to compensate for the downswing and . . . Assuming we win, of course."

"Of course," Peter echoed. He looked from one to the other. "We have the ships, the shipyards, and the industrial nodes. Are you telling me that we might be unable to turn our advantage into something *decisive*?"

Alexander Masterly made a face. "With all due respect, Your Grace, we are in uncharted waters. Our best estimates are often nothing more than guesswork. The corporation took a major hit after the end of the *last* war, doing serious damage to our reputation as a caring, considerate, and reliable employer. The workers who were laid off are not . . . shall we say *enthusiastic*? We may have to make a number of structural changes to satisfy them. And those would be political headaches . . ."

There was a knock at the door. Peter looked up. "Come!"

Yasmeena stepped inside, looking as composed as ever. "Your Grace, Grand Admiral Rudbek has called an emergency meeting of the war cabinet," she said. "Your presence is requested."

A very mixed blessing, Peter thought. On one hand, it would get him out of *this* meeting. But, on the other hand, it meant something had gone wrong, something that might render all his concerns about the economy completely irrelevant. *What's happened now?*

He stood. "Gentlemen, I'm afraid we will have to continue this discussion later," he said. "My staff will show you out."

"A pleasure, as always," Alexander Masterly said as he rose. His husband echoed him a second later. "We can arrange another appointment later in the week."

Peter nodded as he hurried through the door, Yasmeena following him. "Do we have anyone reliable who can take over running the corporation?"

"I couldn't say, Your Grace," Yasmeena said. "Your current position is based, at least in part, on your role in the corporation."

"So I can only concentrate on one job by getting rid of the second, but by getting rid of the second I make myself unqualified for the first?" Peter shook his head. "There must be *someone* who can be trusted."

"Your best choice would probably be Ashley," Yasmeena said. "But she married into another family and . . ."

"Maybe I should talk it over with Candy," Peter said. His younger sister was a playgirl who spent most of her time holding morale-boosting parties, but she was also a keen observer of human nature. And she had her finger on rumor and gossip. "She might have some idea of who could be trusted."

He stopped outside the door. "Bring me some coffee," he said. "I have a feeling I'm going to need it."

Yasmeena gave him a sympathetic look. "Yes, Your Grace."

Peter stepped into the room. A handful of holoimages were waiting for him, three more popping into existence as he took his seat. Grand Admiral Rudbek had brought Admiral Kalian and, surprisingly, Commodore McElney, the latter looking as if he would sooner be somewhere, anywhere, else. Peter didn't blame him. It couldn't be easy to be the highest-ranking colonial officer on the fleet, torn between loyalty to one's navy and one's people. Peter's security staff had warned him that Commodore McElney had received more death threats than anyone else, save for Israel Harrison himself.

And I'd be happy to be somewhere else too, Peter thought. He nodded his thanks as Yasmeena brought him a tray of coffee and sandwiches, enough to keep him going until lunch . . . if he had time to have lunch. *An afternoon spent fishing sounds about right, just now.*

"Three hours ago, relative time, the king's fleet departed Caledonia," Grand Admiral Rudbek said. "We don't have any real-time data, not yet, but the preliminary sighting report indicated that nearly every capital and escort ship under his command was attached to the fleet. This is not a minor raid, sirs. Our communications intercepts indicate that they intend to hit Durian."

He paused. "My intelligence analysts believe that they intend to use Durian as a feint. Their real target is Tyre."

Peter had expected it, right from the start. The words still sent a shiver down his spine.

"Assuming they proceed on a least-time course, they will reach Durian in fifteen days," Grand Admiral Rudbek said. "They could be here, at Tyre, a day or two afterwards."

"And then the matter will be decided," Harrison said quietly.

"Indeed," Duchess Zangaria said. She looked straight at Grand Admiral Rudbek. "Can we win?"

"As commander of our mobile forces, Admiral Kalian will address the issue," Grand Admiral Rudbek said. "He has been planning our offensive and defensive operations for the last month."

And are you allowing him to brief us because he's the best person to answer our questions, Peter asked himself, *or because you want a scapegoat if the shit hits the fan? Again?*

Admiral Kalian cleared his throat. "Your Graces," he said. "My staffers have been considering how the enemy might engage us, or be engaged *by* us, over the past few weeks. We believe the enemy intends to take Durian as part of a long-term plan to draw Home Fleet out of position before attacking Tyre itself. Therefore, we have devised a plan to counter his offensive without risking damage to the home system . . ."

Peter saw William shift, uncomfortably. *Interesting* . . .

"Our scouts should provide us with warning when the enemy fleet makes its approach to Durian," Admiral Kalian continued. "I intend to take two-thirds of Home Fleet and ambush them, pinning them against the naval base's defenses. Depending on the timing, we *may* be able to take up position within the system itself; if not, we can rush to intercept once we *know* the enemy is proceeding to Durian. Either way, their fleet will be attacked and destroyed. The king, lacking any means to immediately replace his lost ships, will then have no choice but to surrender or go on the run. The war will be won at Durian."

"Clever," Duke Rudbek said. "Are you *sure* it will work?"

"Yes, Your Grace," Admiral Kalian said. "The enemy *must* attack Durian for their plan to succeed. We will have a chance to intercept them. If things should go badly, we can fall back on Tyre. They have no such option."

Peter looked at Commodore McElney. He was hiding it well, but . . . McElney clearly didn't believe what his superior was saying. Odd. Peter wouldn't have brought a subordinate who disagreed with him into a meeting, not when it would have undermined his position. It simply didn't make sense.

He cleared his throat. "Commodore McElney," he said. "Do you agree with Admiral Kalian?"

There was a long pause. Peter kept his face impassive, waiting. He'd placed the commodore in a terrible spot, forcing him to defy either his patron or his superior officer. Peter promised himself that he would make it up to the other man, even if it meant accepting his resignation and buying him passage back to Asher Dales. He felt guilty, but he also had to know the truth. And Commodore McElney had more naval experience than either of his superiors.

"No, Your Grace," Commodore McElney said. "I do not."

Peter felt another flicker of sympathy at the flash of betrayal that crossed Admiral Kalian's face. But he had no time to care. "Explain."

"Durian is larger than Shallot, sir, and possesses a far more modern naval base," Commodore McElney said, carefully. "It is also heavily defended, ensuring that the enemy will pay a price for taking it. However, in the strategic sense, the base is actually worthless. If Tyre falls, Durian will fall into the king's hands like ripe . . . durian. If Tyre stands, victory or defeat at Durian will be meaningless."

"It will certainly make the king's cause *stink*," Duke Tolliver joked.

"The king himself is in overall command of his military, if our agents are to be believed," Commodore McElney said. There was a faint hitch in his voice. "However, fleet command—tactical command—has been placed in Admiral Falcone's hands. I know her. I served under her. And I believe she will not waste any time trying to take Durian. She will know, better than anyone else, that Durian offers the king nothing. Either he gets it by default by winning the war, or it becomes a ball and chain around his war effort."

"I see your point," Peter said. He ignored the sharp look Duke Rudbek threw him. "What do you think she'll do?"

"I think she'll come here," Commodore McElney said. "And she will try to take Tyre."

Peter leaned forward. "And Admiral Kalian's plan?"

Commodore McElney looked, just for a second, like a man on the verge of throwing everything away. "Your Grace, I believe his plan will fail."

Admiral Kalian's face reddened. "My plan is to destroy the enemy fleet! I will not . . ."

Duchess Zangaria held up a hand. "Commodore. Explain."

"Yes, Your Grace," McElney said. "Admiral Kalian is partly correct. In most wars, the destruction of the enemy's fleet is a very clear objective. However, this war is different. If the king succeeds in capturing the high orbitals over your heads"—he jabbed a finger upwards—"he can force you to surrender. You will, as part of the terms, have to hand over your fleet. The king does not *need* to destroy your fleet to win the war. He just needs to force you to surrender."

"We control the planet," Duke Tolliver blustered. "The king could not land his forces . . ."

"With control of the high orbitals, the king could land his forces anywhere he chose," Commodore McElney said. "The Planetary Defense Centers have force fields, true, but they don't cover *everywhere*. And they can be battered down with sufficient force. Or simply outflanked."

"The king would not use weapons of mass destruction on a planetary surface," Duchess Turin said. "He's not a *Theocrat*."

"He could still batter the planet into submission," Commodore McElney said. "How long would the population support you if their entire world was being smashed to rubble?"

"Ahura Mazda held out," Duke Tolliver thundered.

"I was there," Commodore McElney said. "We could have battered down the force field protecting the Tabernacle. A handful of antimatter missiles would have sufficed. But that would have done *immense* damage to the planetary biosphere. We would have doomed almost everyone on the surface to a slow and thoroughly unpleasant death. The Theocrats were not just protected by their force field, Your Grace. They were protected by millions of human shields."

"By our own good nature," Duke Tolliver sneered.

"Forgive me for wanting to be on the side that *doesn't* commit atrocities and crimes against humanity," Duke Rudbek commented.

"If they held out, we can hold out," Duke Tolliver insisted.

Commodore McElney sighed, noticeably. "The average citizen of Ahura Mazda, save for the people at the very top, lived a very deprived life. Their food rations, even before the war, were pitifully small. They knew very little of the world outside their enclaves, still less of the greater universe beyond the upper atmosphere. They were used to being short of food, drink, and medicine for years before we invaded. And they knew . . . believe me, they knew . . . that any attempt to question their masters would be met by immense force. You cannot imagine the horrors routinely meted out to the handful of people who dared say no. It wasn't until the government collapsed completely that all the deep-rooted hatred burst out, ripping the remnants of their society apart.

"Tyre, on the other hand, has a population that *hasn't* been battered into submission, a population that is very aware of the outside universe, a population that happily debates the issue of who is really in the right . . . a population unaccustomed to deprivation in any form. There isn't a single person on Tyre who doesn't have enough to eat and drink, who doesn't have access to medical care and education and . . . There isn't a single person who is too scared to lift his head and demand answers. And they have weapons. They will not tolerate their lives becoming miserable. They will rise up in support of the king if he takes the high orbitals."

"We're the legitimate rulers of the planet," Duke Tolliver said.

"Who has the guns makes the rules," Commodore McElney countered. "And even if you're right, even if the population will join you in defiance, there won't be much of a planet left when matters come to an end."

"Of course not," Peter murmured.

Duke Rudbek and Grand Admiral Rudbek had been having a quiet chat. Now Duke Rudbek leaned forward. "We're getting off topic," he said. "What do you propose we do?"

"We defend Tyre," Commodore McElney said simply. "For us, the destruction of the king's fleet *is* an important war aim. And we know their target."

"If you're right," Duke Tolliver said.

"There is nowhere else to go," Commodore McElney said. "Yes, they can attack the handful of worlds that have remained loyal. They can. But what will it gain them? More enemies . . . While we spend the time building up our fleets, readying ourselves to punch out Caledonia and bring the king to justice. Tyre is the only logical target."

"I see," Duke Rudbek said. "Grand Admiral, can you hold Tyre?"

"I believe so," Grand Admiral Rudbek said.

You wouldn't have said anything else, Peter reflected. *You would have been urging us to make peace, even on unfavorable terms, if you thought you couldn't hold the planet.*

"They may still attack Durian," Grand Admiral Rudbek added. "And that will be a black eye, politically speaking."

"Yes, but survivable," Duchess Zangaria said. "Is there any *strong* push for peace among the commons?"

"Not yet," Peter said. His clients had made that clear. The House of Commons, so far, seemed inclined to refrain from rocking the boat. "But that may change if things go badly."

"If things go badly, we will be in no state to care." Duke Rudbek snorted, loudly. "There is a time for listening to people and a time for ignoring them."

The duke looked from face to face. "I propose we prepare our defenses here, to protect the homeworld," he said. "And Durian can take its chances."

"We may wish to take the time to evacuate Durian," Duchess Turin said. "There are lives at stake. We cannot afford to throw them away,"

"Already underway," Admiral Kalian said. He sounded calm, but Peter could hear an undercurrent of fury. Commodore McElney was for the high jump. Hopefully, only metaphorically. "The trained and experienced personnel are already being evacuated. If the facilities are destroyed, they'll be reassigned elsewhere."

"Then I agree," Duchess Turin said. She nodded at the starchart. "We defend ourselves first."

Peter watched, casting his own vote when the time came. No one dissented.

"If we win, we can rebuild," he said. He thought about the economic briefing and smiled, even though he knew it was a serious issue. "And if we lose, it will be someone else's problem."

Duke Rudbek laughed, humorlessly. "Peace talks have gotten nowhere, of course," he said. "The king is making reckless demands, demands we couldn't possibly meet . . . unless he beats the hell out of us, in which case it doesn't matter."

Peter looked at Commodore McElney and frowned as a thought struck him. "Not all of the king's supporters are going to be fully behind him," he said. "We should look for ways to weaken his backing."

"After the coming battle," Duke Rudbek said. "Right now, it isn't a major concern. If the king wins, everyone will flock to him like flies to shit."

"Including most of our families," Duchess Turin said. Her lips curved into a wry smile. "What was the old saying? One to the government, one to the rebellion, one to the church?"

Peter nodded, once she explained. It made a certain kind of sense. Aristocracies didn't survive without being prepared to switch sides, if they found themselves on the losing side. Better to turn one's coat than see the entire family destroyed. He understood . . . but it would have to be timed carefully. If they jumped too quickly, their former allies would destroy them; if they jumped too late, they would have nothing to offer their new masters. And having someone on the other side who would speak for them might be the difference between survival and destruction.

He glanced around the table, wondering who would be first to jump ship. If the battle was lost, there would be a race.

And the hell of it is that it might work out quite well for us, if the king were an honorable man, he thought grimly. *But we know, all too well, that he is not.*

CHAPTER SEVENTEEN

TYRE

"And just what," Admiral Kalian demanded, "did you think you were doing?"

William held himself ramrod straight, torn between a grim awareness that his career, and perhaps even his life, hung by a thread and an insane urge to giggle. He was no schoolboy in need of a whipping, no maggot crewman dreading the wrath of the senior chief; he was an experienced naval officer with nearly forty years of service under his belt. And yet, from one point of view, Kalian was quite within his rights to be angry. William had undercut him in front of his superiors.

But I was ordered to do it, William thought wryly. *What was I supposed to do? Pretend I didn't hear the question?*

He felt a flash of annoyance that had nothing to do with the absurd situation. He'd spent too long watching officers be promoted over his head because of their political connections. He'd watched too many people suffer and die because of decisions taken hundreds of light years behind the lines. He was not going to grit his teeth and remain silent, any longer, when a well-bred superior made a mistake. What was the worst they could do? Fire him? Court-martial him for insubordination? It would be an interesting little court case . . .

"The Duke asked my opinion," he said, with an evenness that would have infuriated him if he'd been on the receiving end. "And I gave it to him."

Admiral Kalian glared. "You undermined me *and* my analysts on the tactical deck."

"The Duke asked my opinion," William repeated. "And my opinion is that the analysts are wrong."

"I see." Admiral Kalian lowered his voice. "A group of high-ranking officers, including your very own commanding officer, have an opinion . . . but that opinion is wrong, because *you* disagree. Because you, and you alone, are right. Right?"

"The majority is not always right," William said. He'd heard horror stories about the Strategy Board. Their exercises were on paper. They had no concept of just how much could go wrong when their ideas were put into practice. And, worst of all, their discussions were led by the senior officers. Very few juniors had the nerve to tell their seniors that they were barking up the wrong tree. "And, in this case, we cannot take the risk of the majority being wrong."

Admiral Kalian took a long breath. "The officers on the board know their stuff."

"Then they should have recognized that Durian is unimportant," William countered. "And that the sole priority is defending Tyre."

"I do not care . . ." Admiral Kalian stopped himself with an effort. "You do *not* undermine me in front of my superiors. In front of the goddamned war cabinet, damn it! You do not!"

Which is what you're really upset about, William thought. He understood Admiral Kalian's reasoning, and his anger, but William found it hard to care. *You're putting your personal prestige ahead of winning this damned war.*

He met his superior's eyes, wondering just which way Admiral Kalian would jump. He had every right to relieve William of duty, if he wished, although *that* might prove politically embarrassing. William did have a very powerful patron. And that connection might prove of inestimable value if the king's forces really did attack. But . . . He wondered, suddenly, why Admiral Kalian had invited him to the meeting. Had someone demanded his presence? Or had the admiral expected him to toe the line? Surely, he knew William better than that.

"I cannot tolerate rank insubordination," Admiral Kalian continued. "And you . . ."

William lifted his eyebrows. "And would you rather I ignored a direct request for my input?"

Admiral Kalian purpled. William concealed his amusement with an effort. How could a lowly commodore, very much the lowest-ranking officer in the meeting, refuse a request for his opinion? How could he? It was a no-win situation. Either he lied to his ultimate superiors, or he undermined his immediate superior. Admiral Kalian should have known better. He should have either given William permission to speak his mind or simply left him out of the meeting. There had been so many high-ranking people attending that William was lower than the coffee boy. Hell, the coffee boy was probably considered more important.

"You knew what the Strategy Board recommended," Admiral Kalian said finally. "You should have merely stated their recommendations and . . ."

"I was asked for my opinion," William said. "And my considered opinion, as I told you, is that the board is wrong."

"You'd better be right." Admiral Kalian's voice rose. "You'd *better* be right. Because if you're wrong, they'll break you. I'll break you. You . . ."

"I understand," William said calmly. A junior who argued with his superior in public was in deep shit, even if he was in the right. A good commanding officer would never put his junior in such a position. Better to have the disagreement in private than risk having to punish the junior officer for the heinous crime of being *right*. "But, if we lose Durian, what does it matter?"

"To you?" Admiral Kalian snorted, rudely. "It doesn't matter. To the corporations that control Durian, that have been turning it into a major industrial node . . . I'd say it matters a great deal. The planet is the jewel in their crown."

"What price the jewel in the crown," William asked quietly, "if the crown itself is lost?"

Admiral Kalian ignored the comment. "It has become clear that you cannot continue as my chief of staff," he said. "The 17th Superdreadnought Squadron is in need of a commanding officer. Commodore Parkhurst has been . . . relieved of command, as you are well aware. You will replace him."

"Yes, sir," William said. He wondered, idly, if there had been some private discussions before Admiral Kalian summoned William for his chewing out. There might have been just enough time for someone to intercede in William's favor. Or, perhaps, Admiral Kalian simply didn't have the nerve to relieve William of duty. The war cabinet would remember if William was *right*. "It will be my pleasure."

Admiral Kalian ground his teeth. "We'll be going with Plan Theta," he continued. "You'll have command of Force Beta. I'm sure I can trust you to carry out the plan."

Particularly as I was the one who devised it, William thought. *Or at least drew out the broad strokes.*

"Turn your post over to Captain Ewing, then arrange transport to your new flagship," Admiral Kalian ordered. "And I don't want to hear from you until after the battle. If, of course, there is a battle."

"There will be," William said. "And we know how to fight it."

Admiral Kalian snorted again. "Out."

William stood to attention and saluted, then turned and marched out of the compartment. He didn't allow himself to relax, even slightly, until he heard the hatch hiss closed behind him. It could have been worse. Perhaps it *should* have been worse. Admiral Kalian had clearly lost confidence in William's ability to support him . . . William contemplated the situation for a moment, then shook his head. Admiral Kalian had many fine qualities, but he didn't have the nerve or the solid resolution to make a good commanding officer. He should have overruled the Strategy Board, if he'd felt the board was making a mistake, or simply sacked William for gross insubordination. Admiral Kalian was neither hot nor cold, but lukewarm. No doubt that was how the Grand Admiral, the *new* Grand Admiral, preferred him.

He took a moment to calm himself, then walked onto the CIC and summoned Captain Ewing, who appeared a moment later. He wasn't a bad choice, William told himself firmly. Captain Ewing was short on imagination, something that had probably ensured he would never see independent command, but he was efficient. William handed the CIC over to him, arranged a flight to *Thunderous*, and downloaded the latest reports from the 17th Superdreadnought Squadron. The formation was, on paper, at full strength, but it had been right at the bottom for supplies and crewmen. Too many of its crewers had been reassigned elsewhere. William rubbed his eyes, feeling a twinge of concern. He had no idea why Commodore Parkhurst had been relieved of his post, but he was pretty sure the reason wasn't good.

"Take care of things here," he told Captain Ewing. "I'll see you on the flip side."

He glanced around the CIC, feeling a moment of regret. He'd turned the admiral's tactical staff into a well-oiled team, even if they probably, privately, detested him. God knew he hadn't gone easy on any slackers. It was almost a shame he wouldn't be taking them into battle . . . He shook his head. He would have been in real trouble if he'd disagreed with the admiral in the middle of a battle.

Dismissing the thought, he turned and headed down to the shuttlebay. It felt wrong, somehow, to be using a shuttle as his own private transport, even though he knew plenty of commanding officers who wouldn't bat an eyelid. It was their *duty* to move from their old post to their new as quickly as possible . . . William sighed as he stepped through the hatch, wishing there were other crewers making the transfer to *Thunderous*. It was *wrong* to tie up an entire shuttle. But what other choice did he have? His lips twitched, humorlessly. Perhaps he should just put on a spacesuit and EVA to his new command.

The shuttle hummed to life. William watched the pilot as she directed the craft out of the shuttlebay, then turned his attention to the shuttle's sensors. Home Fleet had grown over the past two weeks, as more loyalist starships returned to Tyre and others were brought out of the reserves. It was hard to believe that anything could stand up to five squadrons of superdreadnoughts and their escorts, although William knew the fleet wasn't invincible. The king might have a slight advantage in capital ships, and he certainly had a considerable number of escorts under his command.

Which will allow him to do a great deal of raiding, if he wishes, William thought. He wasn't sure *what* that would do to the Commonwealth's economy. *But if he brings the economy crashing down in flames . . .*

He shook his head. That was someone else's problem. Indeed, it would only be a problem if the war lasted for years. William couldn't see that happening, unless the king determined to try to destroy Tyre's industrial base. But if he took out the shipyards and industrial nodes . . . What would he inherit, if he won the war? There would be nothing left. And, perhaps, the colonials would no longer need the king. Who knew what would happen then?

Probably nothing good, William thought grimly. The king was popular. William understood why. But, if he had nothing to offer the colonials, they'd drop him like a hot rock. *The Commonwealth might be ripped apart by infighting.*

He reached for his datapad and brought up the latest news reports. Half of the services he'd subscribed to had been shut down, for one reason or another; the remainder, by and large, seemed to be pumping out bland propaganda rather than anything concrete. William rolled his eyes at one particularly unpleasant hit piece, then turned his attention to the blogs. They seemed a little more unbiased, arguing everything from the king's point of view to positions that were so extreme that neither the king nor his enemies could possibly accept them. A handful even agitated for breaking up the ducal corporations and abolishing the aristocracy.

Which won't make things any better, William thought. He'd seen enough of the universe to know that *every* planet developed an aristocracy, in fact if not in name. *They'll have to change human nature before they can abolish aristocracy completely.*

He put the thought out of his mind as HMS *Thunderous* came into view. She was practically identical to *King Travis*, save for a handful of additional missile tubes that had been slotted into her hull several months before she'd been formally commissioned. The supervisors had clearly drawn the right lessons from the *last* war, William decided. They'd also given her additional point defense weapons, although they'd come at a cost. *Thunderous* had fewer energy weapons than the others of her class.

Which won't matter, if we don't close to energy range, William considered. *The last war was decided by missile salvos.*

He allowed himself a tight smile as the shuttle docked at the upper airlock, feeling *free* for the first time in weeks. Squadron command couldn't compete with *starship* command, the very thought was absurd, and he would still be part of a much greater whole, but he wouldn't have Admiral Kalian breathing down his neck. Indeed, he'd have considerably more independence than perhaps Admiral Kalian had realized. Plan Theta called for Home Fleet to divide into two sections, operating semi-independently. He shrugged. It didn't matter.

And if we lose the coming battle, William thought. *It* really *won't matter.*

His lips twitched as he stepped through the hatch. Captain Georgas was standing by the flag, looking harassed. William saluted the colors, then his new subordinate. She'd taken time out from her busy schedule to come meet him. He hoped that wasn't a bad sign. He simply didn't have the time to deal with a sycophant, particularly one who probably had some political connections. The Royal Navy didn't give its superdreadnoughts to just *anyone.*

"Commodore," Captain Georgas said. "Welcome aboard."

William studied her for a long moment. She was a short, stocky woman with dark hair, tinted skin, and an accent that suggested she'd grown up on an asteroid, probably not too far from Tyre itself. A RockRat from another system would have been a colonial, in the eyes of the Promotions Board. They wouldn't have given her a superdreadnought.

"Thank you," he said, finally. Captain Georgas might have come to greet him, but she hadn't made a production of the gesture. He supposed that was a good sign. "It's an honor to be here."

He fell into step beside her as she ushered him down the corridor. "Status report?"

Captain Georgas didn't hesitate. "We have a full load of missiles and other supplies," she said. "Thankfully, we were finishing up our refit when the shit hit the fan. We're fairly low on crew, but we can fly and fight. We'd just be in some trouble if we took major damage."

"I'll try and get other crew assigned to the ship," William said, calmly. He nodded in approval. Captain Georgas clearly wasn't intimidated by him. She'd give him an accurate assessment. "And the remainder of the squadron?"

"*Havoc* suffered a drive node failure four days ago," Captain Georgas informed him. "We didn't have time for a full refit, so her engineers dismantled the node on the spot and installed a new one, without cutting through the hull. She's doing power trials now. So far, so good."

William had to smile. Removing and replacing a drive node normally required a shipyard, even when the node was beyond repair. Dismantling one in situ, then building up a new node . . . He felt a flicker of admiration for the engineer who'd proposed the plan and the captain who'd approved it. Drive nodes weren't precisely solid-state constructions, but they came pretty close. The captain would have found himself in hot water if the rebuilt drive node had failed to perform.

And it would have been quicker than cutting the hull open to remove the old node and install the new one, he thought. *We don't have time to waste.*

"Good thinking on their part," he said. "As long as it works . . ."

"We were given to understand that speed is of the essence," Captain Georgas said. "And I believe that was their prime consideration."

"And they were right," William said. He made a mental note to ensure that everyone involved got a commendation. Thinking outside the box was a valuable skill. Sure, some ideas didn't work . . . but even *having* them encouraged engineers and technicians to look at problems from a whole new point of view. "There isn't much time before we have to take the squadron into battle."

Captain Georgas nodded as they reached the CIC. "Your new command, sir."

William nodded. A handful of officers were sitting at consoles, murmuring quietly into headsets. They glanced up as he entered but didn't rise. William understood. The staffers didn't have time to salute, not when they were on duty. There were too many issues that had to be handled before they turned into minor nightmares. He'd introduce himself to his new staff when the shift changed.

"I want to be ready for live-fire exercises in two days," he said. It would be a challenge, based on the last set of readiness reports, but one he thought they could meet. If there were problems, the sooner they identified them the better. "And then we'll find out what this squadron can really do."

"We took the King's Gunnery Cup last year," Captain Georgas said. She paused, her expression twisting into an odd little smile. "Or is that politically incorrect, these days?"

William chuckled. "I hardly think we have time to worry about renaming *now*."

"I hope not," Captain Georgas agreed.

"We have a war to win," William said. If someone on Tyre wanted to fret about renaming things that had been named after the king . . . He didn't care. He doubted the war cabinet would care either. They had more important things to do. "And, until the enemy finally arrives, we will be practicing to win the war."

"Yes, sir," Captain Georgas said. "When do you think they'll come?"

"Soon," William said. "Their fleet is already on the way."

CHAPTER EIGHTEEN

Hyperspace

There were people who simply couldn't tolerate hyperspace, Kat knew. She'd met people who had bad reactions, from being unable to watch the ever-shifting lights and energy flows of hyperspace to being unable to tolerate even being *in* hyperspace, feeling queasy even though they were surrounded by millions of tons of metal. It wasn't something *she'd* ever had to worry about, not really. Hyperspace was odd. Something about the realm was utterly inhuman, but it wasn't sickening. There were times when she thought she could stare into the eerie lights of hyperspace for the rest of her life.

She stood in the observation blister, hands clasped behind her back, and watched as the lights danced around her ships. Hyperspace played tricks on the unwary, sometimes suggesting two starships were about to collide or two more were hundreds of thousands of kilometers apart even if they were flying in formation; she felt nothing, apart from grim amusement, as her fleet seemed to spin out of control. In the distance, she could see waves of energy, whirlpools of spinning light . . . luring her onwards, even though she knew she'd never find their source. Her lips twitched. Hyperspace between Caledonia and Tyre was surprisingly placid. She wouldn't want to encounter an energy storm or a hyperspace eddy or one of the few semipermanent *things* in hyperspace. A storm in the wrong place could blow her ships hundreds of light years off course.

Or worse, if we couldn't get out of the way in time, she reminded herself. *A superdreadnought would be ripped apart if she flew right into an energy storm.*

She closed her eyes for a long moment, gathering herself. She'd always felt uneasy before a battle, even when she'd *known* she held the whip hand. There was a chance, always a chance, that one of the enemy missiles would have her name on it, that one of their shots would get through her shields and vaporize the entire superdreadnought. She might not survive the coming encounter, even if her side won. She'd come to terms with the prospect of a violent death, knowing she could die in space, but . . .

It felt odd to be waging war against her own people. Wrong. She'd never had any qualms about fighting the Theocrats, even when their atrocities had been nothing more than rumor; she'd never doubted that they had to be stopped. There had been no way to reason with the Theocrats, no way to convince them to stop . . . save by crushing them. Kat regretted the dead, the men she'd had to kill, but she knew they would have killed her if they'd had the chance. Or worse. She'd known better than to ever let herself fall into enemy hands. The reports from liberated POW camps had been terrifying.

But the people she was about to face were not Theocrats. They were Tyrians.

She'd read the reports carefully. She knew Grand Admiral Rudbek. She knew Admiral Kalian. She knew, of *course* she knew, William. She knew them . . . and she was going to kill them, if they didn't see reason and back down. And yet . . . She knew all too well that they weren't *going* to back down. The dispute between the king and his aristocracy was too entrenched to be ended easily, not without bloodshed. They couldn't stop now. One side might have a reasonable complaint, but the other couldn't give in without feeling as if it had surrendered to bullying, blackmail, or threats. It was astonishing how easy it could be, her father had said once, to back someone into a position where they couldn't give in. The long-term consequences were simply too dire.

This would never have happened if father had survived, she thought, grimly. Her father had been old and experienced enough to bridge the gap between the two sides. She was sure he could have honored the king's obligations to his people and the Commonwealth's debt of honor to the liberated worlds while balancing the books. *He would never have let this get to war.*

She opened her eyes, watching the flickering lights as they seemed to dart closer. They promised answers, if only she abandoned her mortal shackles and joined them. Kat smiled, tiredly. There were entire *religions* based around things people had seen in hyperspace. They even claimed that a person might achieve enlightenment if they flew into a hyperspace storm or simply stepped out of an airlock while the ship was in transit. Kat knew better than to believe them—funny how none of the enlightened ever came back to spread the word—but, in hyperspace, the temptation was there. Suicide would solve so many of her problems . . .

And that would be nothing more than moral cowardice, Kat told herself, firmly. She'd known too many officers who'd dithered for hours, rather than making a decision. *You made your choice. Stick with it.*

The hatch hissed open behind her. Kat turned. "Kitty?"

"Admiral," Lieutenant Kitty Patterson said. "You asked to be informed when we reached the first waypoint."

Kat nodded, turning back to the lights of hyperspace. "Have we been detected?"

"Unclear," Kitty said. "They *should* have pickets this far out . . ."

"But nothing can be said for sure," Kat finished. "And we won't know until we open a vortex and enter the system."

She let out a long breath. She knew the score. A picket could have picked up their ships as they approached Tyre. Or a hundred pickets might have *missed* them completely, their crews convinced that whatever they detected were nothing more than the endless vagaries of hyperspace. Hyperspace around Tyre was monitored closely, the slightest flickering change catalogued in hopes of predicting the next change . . . It was quite possible that *something* had been detected as the fleet approached the planet. But no one had succeeded in predicting the eddies and flows of hyperspace. She rather hoped no one ever would. There was something delightfully *random* about the realm.

"Yes, Admiral," Kitty said.

Kat nodded. "Contact *Merlin*," she ordered. "She's to break formation and execute Plan Eyeball."

"Aye, Admiral." Kitty lifted her wristcom to her mouth and muttered brief orders. "She'll be on her way momentarily."

"Good." Kat lifted her eyes, searching for *Merlin* among the fleet. A handful of heavy cruisers were within eyesight, but she couldn't tell which one was *Merlin*. "It may buy us some time."

She'd given considerable thought to the problem of actually taking and *holding* Tyre. It wouldn't be easy. The network of orbital fortresses would have deterred any sane attacker, particularly one who didn't need to take the planet to win. The ground-based defenses were merely the icing on the cake. And yet, she had to take the high orbitals without letting Home Fleet get in the way. If she could divert the fleet's attention, so much the better.

And we will plan on the assumption that Eyeball fails completely, she thought. She knew better than to devise a plan that relied on everything working perfectly. That was just setting herself up to fail. *We'll hope for the best and plan for the worst.*

"*Merlin* is on her way," Kitty said. "She should be in position to begin Eyeball in seven hours."

Kat took one last look into hyperspace, then turned away. "Then ensure that the alpha crews are all well rested," she ordered. It was time to take a nap herself, even though she didn't want to sleep.

"We'll give them a *little* time to become aware of Eyeball, then we'll move."

And we'll move anyway, she added silently. *We won't know if Eyeball is working or not until after we're committed.*

"Aye, Admiral," Kitty said. She paused as her datapad bleeped. "Commodore Ruben also wishes to speak to you."

"Inform him that we have gone over the plan *quite* enough," Kat said. She didn't fault her subordinates for trying to determine what could go wrong and then planning how best to counter each potential disaster, but there were limits. She had the nasty feeling that Commodore Ruben was trying to forge a paper trail he could use to avoid blame if the engagement went badly wrong. "And that he should get some rest too."

"Aye, Admiral," Kitty said. "And yourself?"

Kat's lips twitched. "I'll get some rest too," she said. "Dismissed."

She watched Kitty go, then turned and walked down the corridor to her ready room. Technically, she should head to her cabin, but she wanted to be close to the CIC. It probably wouldn't matter—if the fleet *was* suddenly plunged into an engagement, her crews knew what to do—but it was a habit she'd never been able to overcome. She wondered, idly, why the captain's cabin wasn't simply attached to the ready room. A *decent* captain didn't spend most of her time in the cabin, did she?

Kat walked through the corridors. They were quiet. The alpha and beta crews were already napping, or praying, or doing whatever they did in the grim knowledge that they might not survive the coming battle. Some of them would be seeking release, in the privacy tubes; some of them would be watching the holovid or playing games or doing whatever they needed to do to relax. The officers would turn a blind eye, as long as it didn't render the crew unfit for duty. They understood. They'd been junior crewmen, once upon a time.

Back when dinosaurs ruled the planet, Kat thought wryly. She'd been amused and horrified to hear crewmen call her the "Old Woman." It was a title of respect, one she could never have *demanded* from her crews . . . yet she didn't feel old. She was hardly the oldest person on the ship, let alone the Commonwealth. *My father always made me feel like a little girl.*

She shook her head as she stepped into the ready room and sat down on the sofa, which was surprisingly small for something an admiral would have to use as a makeshift bed. The cynic in her wondered if the designers had feared the admiral bringing company into the ready room . . . It was not, she admitted privately, an absurd concern. She'd known quite a few admirals who'd traveled with their partners . . . No one had cared, as long as the admirals were discreet—and didn't allow their partners to interfere with their duties.

And it doesn't matter, she thought as she closed her eyes. *I'm alone.*

The thought cost her a pang. She'd had few friends on Tyre, even before the civil war. Most of the people she knew were her subordinates. She couldn't be friendly around them, not without blowing discipline straight to hell. Pat was dead, William was on the wrong side . . .

She was alone. And she would always be alone.

I have my duty. She didn't have time for self-pity. *And that will have to be enough.*

♦ ♦ ♦

"I'm picking up a trio of freighters heading away from Durian, Captain," Lieutenant Honshu reported. "There's no hint they've seen us."

"They won't, as long as they're using civilian-grade sensors," Captain Sarah Henderson said, calmly. She was no sensor expert, but she'd served a term in the sensor department. Military sensors had advanced by leaps and bounds during the war; civilian tech was still lagging behind, despite frantic lobbying by various merchant guilds. "But they might have been refitted in a hurry."

She leaned forward, quietly assessing the situation. *Merlin* was approaching Durian from above the system plane, limiting their chances of being detected . . . although she was grimly certain that they would be detected the moment they opened a vortex and slipped into the system itself. Durian was a major fleet base, only a hop, skip, and jump from Tyre itself. The Royal Navy had felt a certain inclination to make sure that nothing *bad* happened to the system . . . The files suggested that the defense planners had intended to rely on Home Fleet to supply mobile units if all hell broke loose, but Sarah found it a little optimistic. It was far more likely that at least *some* mobile units were within the system itself.

"Alter course to evade," she ordered. "And then take us out at Point Alpha."

"Aye, Captain," Lieutenant Commander Rubes said. "ETA fifteen minutes."

Sarah sat back, wondering, again, how Captain Saul had managed to project an aura of calm as his starship hurtled towards her destination. The old man had never seemed concerned, even when a fleet of enemy starships seemed to have singled him out for special attention; he'd never even given a *hint* of panic. Perhaps he'd been panicking on the inside, Sarah reflected. He'd certainly never been stupid enough to believe that missiles would take note of his exalted rank and pass him by.

And they certainly won't pass me by, Sarah thought. *My ship will be the number one target as soon as we leave hyperspace.*

"We'll reach Point Alpha in five minutes," Lieutenant Commander Rubes said.

"Take us out as planned," Sarah ordered. "Tactical, commence deploying drones the moment we're outside the vortex."

"Aye, Captain," Lieutenant Commander Singh said.

Sarah braced herself as the vortex blossomed to life on the display, a whirlpool of shimmering energy that seemed to reach out and yank her ship into realspace. There was a brief unpleasant sensation, as if she were on the verge of unbalancing and falling flat on her face, followed by a faint shudder as her starship passed though the gravitational eddies and left the vortex behind. The display blanked, then hastily came back to life. Durian lay in front of her, a yellow star surrounded by asteroids and a single rocky world. It wouldn't have attracted any interest, she thought, if it hadn't been so close to Tyre. Even so, the controlling corporations had had to offer *vast* concessions to convince anyone to settle on Durian-I.

And they're skimping on the terraforming, she thought, wryly. *It isn't as if anyone wants to live there.*

New icons flashed to life on the display. "They're launching gunboats, Captain," Lieutenant Commander Rubes reported. "They'll be on us in thirty minutes."

"They may not send them after us," Sarah said. The old-timers had questioned the value of gunboats before the last war. No one doubted that gunboats were dangerous now. Both sides had used them to great effect, relying on swarms of gunboats to bring down capital ships and weaken planetary defenses. "We'll have plenty of time to return to hyperspace before they reach us."

She smiled, thinly. Gunboats couldn't enter hyperspace without assistance. It was their one great limitation. If the enemy CO sent the gunboats after *Merlin*, Sarah could avoid them simply by returning to hyperspace and coming out closer to the fleet base. It was almost a shame that she had strict orders *not* to tangle with the fixed defenses. Admiral Falcone had made that very clear. Nothing would be gained by punching her way into the fleet base . . . assuming, of course, that she could. The base might punch her out instead.

"Captain, the last of the drones have been deployed," Lieutenant Commander Rubes informed her. She could hear the excitement in his voice. "They're ready to go active."

Sarah glanced at the timer. They were on schedule, barely. Admiral Falcone had crafted a great deal of leeway into the plan, but she'd insisted that they had to stick as close to the schedule as possible. If they failed, or even if they succeeded at the wrong time, the entire concept would be worse than useless. She turned her attention back to the display. The gunboats were milling around the fixed defenses, waiting for her. She had no intention of obliging them.

"On my mark, activate the drones," she ordered. *"Mark!"*

"Drones powering up . . . now." Lieutenant Commander Rubes worked his console, fingers dancing over the touch-screen display. "Going active . . . now."

Sarah allowed herself a tight smile as ghostly images—superdreadnoughts, gunboat carriers, heavy cruisers—shimmered into life, as if an entire fleet were decloaking around her. She *knew* the sensor images were faked, she knew they were nothing more than sensor ghosts . . . and yet, even her top-of-the-range military-grade sensors were having trouble seeing through the illusions. The fleet base's sensors wouldn't stand a chance. They'd be sounding the alert, warning their masters that the king's entire fleet was bearing down on Durian. They'd be congratulating themselves for not sending their gunboats after *Merlin* . . .

Which, ironically, would have given them the chance to see through the illusion earlier, Sarah thought. The gunboats wouldn't stand a chance against the king's fleet, but the sensor ghosts were harmless. They'd know they were being conned the moment they weren't blown out of space. *Right now, they'll be trying to decide if they should risk throwing the gunboats away or not.*

She leaned back in her chair. "Send the drones towards the fleet base," she said. By now, the fleet base would be screaming for help.

Home Fleet would have to respond, unless they wanted to take the risk of writing off the entire base. She knew the corporate mindset well enough to know they wouldn't want to risk it. "And hold us at the rear."

"Aye, Captain."

"Keep the vortex generator at the ready," Sarah added. "I want to be out of here the moment Home Fleet arrives."

"Aye, Captain," Lieutenant Polish said. "We'll be ready."

And now we wait, Sarah thought. They'd done their part. Now everything depended on Admiral Falcone. *Now we wait and see.*

CHAPTER NINETEEN

Tyre

"Commodore! Wake up!"

William started, one hand reaching for the pistol that wasn't under his pillow. He hadn't slept with a weapon for years, not since he'd joined the navy; he hadn't even kept a weapon near him on *Uncanny*, with a crew that had turned out to be literally mutinous. There had generally been no reason to keep a pistol under his bed. The only real threat to his life was enemy starships, who wouldn't have been deterred by a handheld weapon.

"I'm awake," he grumbled. Commodore Parkhurst's former steward was bending over his bed, holding out a steaming mug of coffee. "What's happening?"

"Priority signal from the flag, sir," the steward said. "Admiral Kalian would like to speak to you."

William stood and took the coffee, silently grateful he hadn't bothered to get undressed before climbing into bed. He'd spent the last two weeks exploring his ships, meeting his senior officers, and drilling his crews relentlessly. Interesting and necessary, very necessary, but also tiring. He supposed he should be glad his commanding officer had been in a snit. There had been quite a few things a watchful admiral could criticize if he wanted to be unpleasant. But then, Admiral Kalian had had too many other things to worry about.

"Put him through," he ordered.

The steward nodded and departed. William took a quick swig of coffee, then strode over to his desk and checked the terminal. There was no fleet-wide alert, suggesting that the enemy fleet hadn't yet come into view. The admiral had put out a hundred pickets, reinforcing the long-range scansats, but it was quite possible that a *thousand* pickets wouldn't catch a sniff of the enemy fleet before it opened a vortex and dropped out of hyperspace. Kat was smart enough to stay off the beaten path. She could minimize her chances of being detected simply by staying above or below the system plane.

Admiral Kalian's face appeared on the display. "Commodore."

"Admiral," William said. The admiral's voice was cool but professional. William kept his voice likewise. "What can I do for you?"

"We just received a FLASH message from Durian," Admiral Kalian said. An infodump box appeared on William's screen. "The enemy fleet has arrived."

William straightened instinctively. "They're attacking Durian?"

"They're advancing on the system's defenses," Admiral Kalian said. "And they will open fire at any moment."

William's fingers tapped the box. It opened, displaying the latest update from Durian. He felt his eyes narrow as he saw the enemy fleet, which was behaving . . . oddly. If Kat had wanted to take the system, why had she dropped out of hyperspace so far from her target? She should have come out a lot closer, giving her a perfect chance to land a solid blow before the defenses could react. The defenders *were* on alert, William knew, but they wouldn't have been ready. Kat had thrown away the advantage of surprise . . . for nothing.

Or had she?

His lips quirked.

It was a bluff.

"She's trying to draw ships away from Tyre," he said with a certainty he didn't entirely feel. Kat was devious. She might just *want* him to think she was trying to lure his ships out of position. "And then she'll lower the boom here."

His fingers danced over the terminal. It made sense. Kat had nothing to gain by fucking around when she should be coming in for the kill. If she wanted Durian, and if she had the king's entire fleet under her command, she would have brought her ships out of hyperspace right next to the defenses and blown them into rubble before they had a chance to react. She wouldn't have given Admiral Kalian a chance to deploy his fleet and take her from the rear.

No, she was bluffing. William would bet half his savings that the ships on the display were nothing more than sensor ghosts.

"Are you sure?" Admiral Kalian looked pale. "The Durian Consortium is already making a fuss."

"Declare a system-wide emergency and cut all nonessential communications," William suggested. It wouldn't please anyone, particularly the king's spies. Right now, theirs were the only opinions that mattered. "And then order every civilian ship in the system to power down."

"There'll be outrage," Admiral Kalian protested. "And . . ."

"If we win, we will be untouchable," William pointed out smoothly. "And if we lose, we're screwed anyway."

A ghost of a smile wafted across the admiral's face. "Very true, Commodore."

William brought up the in-system display. Hundreds of thousands of ships were crisscrossing the system, from warships on patrol to merchant vessels and asteroid miners plying their trade. Even now, Tyre was easily the busiest system in the Commonwealth . . . perhaps the busiest in all explored space. William would bet good money that one or more of the ships were spying for the king, keeping an eye on the fleet as it gathered itself for war. And the spy might even be able to get a message back home . . .

If Kat has a StarCom with her fleet, he mused, *she might be able to get a warning if we don't take her bait.*

He leaned forward. "I propose we execute Contingency Three," he said. "She . . . the enemy will be waiting for us to move. And then we can slip back into position if things go wrong."

"Make it so," Admiral Kalian said. "And good luck."

"And to you, Admiral." William tapped a command into the console. Moments later, the GQ alarms began to howl. "I'll see you on the other side."

He keyed his terminal as the admiral's face vanished. "Commander Zeeland," he said, formally. "We'll proceed with Contingency Three. The fleet is to execute the contingency in"—he glanced at the chronometer—"ten minutes."

"Aye, Commodore."

"And tell everyone not to panic," William added. "We have time to get ready *and* beat the enemy too."

He found himself grinning like an idiot as he pulled on his jacket and headed for the hatch. There was no time for a shower, no time even to change his clothes, but it didn't matter. Not now. They were about to go into battle. He calculated, carefully, just how much time they'd have before the main body of the fleet arrived. Where would *he* position the fleet, he asked himself, if *he* were in charge? Somewhere close to Tyre, of course, but not *too* close. The odds of being detected might be low, there was really no *might* about it, yet they couldn't be discounted completely. And Kat really hadn't had time to pre-position her forces as she might have wished. She'd practically been forced to adopt a least-time course to the engagement.

The CIC hummed with activity as he hurried inside and took his seat. Icons, green and blue, floated within the vast display. Admiral Kalian had declared a state of emergency, he noted, but it would take time for *every* starship to power down their drives and go ballistic. He hoped the independent skippers would be smart enough to either follow orders or jump into hyperspace before the system defenders took note of them. He could imagine innocent crews being blown into dust because they'd been mistaken for the king's spies.

And the king might have deployed a handful of stealthed platforms within the system instead, he mused. He'd never really understood just how much power the king had until he'd found himself helping to clean up the mess. Hadrian had controlled effectively limitless resources, once upon a time; he'd had a small army of loyalists who'd do practically anything for him. *He was planning for civil war long before anyone else realized that things were getting out of control.*

"Commodore," Commander Zeeland said. She was young, practically untried; she had, William had decided after they'd first met, less to unlearn. "The task force is ready to execute Contingency Three on your command."

William glanced at the console, then nodded. "Signal the task force," he ordered. "Execute Contingency Three."

♦ ♦ ♦

Kat kept her face under tight control as the alarms howled through the superdreadnought, bringing *Violence* to battlestations. She could imagine hundreds of crewmen hurrying through the corridors to their combat stations, praying under their breaths that they'd survive, that they'd do well, that they wouldn't screw up in the face of the enemy. She could practically feel them running, even though she knew it was her imagination. The dull thrumming pervading the ship was nothing more than the pulse of the drives.

"Admiral," Kitty said. "The fleet datanet has been established. All ships are at full combat readiness."

"Good," Kat said. "Time to egress?"

"Seven minutes," Kitty said. "There's no sign we've been detected."

Kat had always assumed that Home Fleet would be ready for them. There was no way to be sure they hadn't been detected, particularly if whoever detected them held their nerve and sneaked around to rush to Tyre and sound the alert. No matter. She'd planned on the assumption that they wouldn't have the advantage of surprise.

She sucked in her breath. They were on a timetable now. If Home Fleet was going to react to her feint, it would have reacted by now. A shame there was no way to be sure Home Fleet had jumped . . . She'd considered a handful of possible schemes to track the fleet as it left Tyre, but none were really workable. They wouldn't have worked in the simulator. They certainly wouldn't have worked in real life.

"Update the fleet," she ordered. "Take us out, as planned."

She felt the last seconds ticking away, an uncomfortable churning sensation in her gut. She hadn't felt so nervous when the fleet had neared Ahura Mazda, readying itself for what she'd hoped would be the last major engagement of the war. She'd known, back then, that the Theocracy couldn't replenish its losses. She'd known that, if her fleet had been destroyed, the next one would have won. But now . . . Everything rested on a knife-edge. The difference between victory and defeat might be as little as a single starship held in reserve.

And let us hope we didn't need Merlin *after all*, she mused. *There's no way we can call her back until the engagement is over.*

The final seconds ticked down to zero. She braced herself as the vortexes flared into existence on the display, sucking her ships back into realspace. The display updated rapidly, red and blue icons flickering into life. She frowned at how *few* blue icons there were—surely interplanetary and interstellar transport couldn't have come to a halt—before realizing that whoever was in command had had the sense to order the civilians to go dark. It wasn't a bad thought. They'd probably decided to make damn sure that any watchful eyes couldn't give away their secrets.

"The fleet is deploying now," Kitty reported. "Long-range probes are being launched."

"Good," Kat said.

She felt her heart begin to race as new icons flashed to life in front of her. The age-old division of labor between the Royal Navy, represented by Home Fleet, and Planetary Defense seemed to have been closed. Home Fleet was holding station close to the planet, its datanet clearly intermeshed with the planetary defense network. Kat wondered, idly, just how well the structure was holding up. They were, in theory, compatible . . . but the king and the House of Lords had worked hard to keep them separate.

The House of Lords is in full control of both Home Fleet and Planetary Defense, she reminded herself. *They don't need to maintain an artificial gap any longer.*

Her eyes narrowed. Home Fleet looked weaker than it should, four squadrons of superdreadnoughts compared to the seven it was supposed to possess. She eyed it narrowly, wondering if they'd been fooled by her feint after all. Ice trickled down her spine. She distrusted it when the enemy did what she *wanted* the enemy to do. Admiral Kalian was not known for being imaginative, and so close to Tyre, it was quite likely he had the Grand Admiral and his political superiors breathing down his neck, but *she* wouldn't have been fooled by the feint. She might even have quietly decided to write Durian off from the start.

But that wouldn't go down well, she reminded herself dryly. *And not every officer has the political clout to avoid career disaster.*

She put the thought to one side. "Signal the fleet," she ordered. "Prepare to advance."

"Aye, Admiral." Kitty's fingers danced over her console. "The fleet is ready."

"Transmit the king's message," Kat said. "And then . . . commence Operation Homecoming."

"Aye, Admiral."

♦ ♦ ♦

Peter sat on his chair, feeling oddly disconnected from the world around him. An enemy fleet had entered the system, a battle was about to take place . . . and he could do nothing but sit in his comfortable armchair and watch. The bunker was astonishingly luxurious for what was—for all intents and purposes—a glorified bomb shelter; he'd been assured that, if the worst happened, he, his family, and his closest retainers could ride out the horror in style. The designers hadn't bothered to say what would happen to them afterwards, if the entire planetary biosphere was destroyed. Peter had watched enough horror movies set on Dead Earth to believe that suicide might be the wisest course. There would be no rescue if no one even knew where to look.

Yasmeena sat next to him, her fingers flying over her datapad. Peter was tempted to tell her to stop, but he held his tongue. Work was her way of coping with the threat of imminent death or—perhaps worse—being buried alive. She had nothing to do. None of them had anything to do but wait. Peter was one of the most powerful men on Tyre, perhaps one of the most powerful in the explored galaxy, yet . . . Right now, his fate rested in someone else's hands. He glanced at Grand Admiral Rudbek's holoimage and felt an odd pang of sympathy. The Grand Admiral too was watching helplessly as his fate was decided elsewhere.

"The stock market has been frozen," Yasmeena said. "But the underground market is showing signs of collapse."

"Joy," Peter muttered. He cleared his throat. "It won't be a problem . . ."

Grand Admiral Rudbek's image suddenly flickered into life. "Your Graces, we are receiving a message from the enemy fleet." He paused, significantly. "The message headers are inserting it into the datanet."

Peter cursed. "Lock it out!"

"We can't, not without bringing down the whole datanet," the Grand Admiral said. "The entire planet will hear the message."

"Shit," Peter said. He glanced at Yasmeena, then shrugged. "Let's hear it."

The king's holoimage appeared in front of him. Peter felt a flash of pure hatred, an urge to reach out and wrap his hands around the king's neck. Useless, he knew; his hands would pass harmlessly through the holoimage. And yet . . . He wanted to *hurt* the king. The youthful fool had plunged his kingdom into a nightmare. How could *anyone* have imagined that he would take them to the brink of civil war . . . and then jump?

Simple, his thoughts answered, mockingly. *We couldn't have imagined it until it was too late.*

The king looked strikingly handsome in his formal robes of office. Peter allowed himself to hope that the king had left something useful behind, in his mad rush to pack his robes before leaving the planet for good, before realizing that he'd probably found spare robes on Caledonia. Peter took a long breath to calm himself as the message began to play.

"I have returned," the king said. "I have returned with a fleet under my command and the winds of justice at my back. I have returned to remove the scourge of partisan politics and burn out the cancer of self-interested politicians. I have returned to prove myself, once again, the father of my people."

Peter snorted. He'd been born and raised an aristocrat. He'd spent his entire life in rarefied circles, dealing with everything from ass-kissing sycophants to people who truly believed that an accident of breeding made them genetically superior to the common rabble. And yet, he'd never heard anything so deluded. Who wrote that . . . that *drivel*?

He glanced at Yasmeena. "The king is overpaying his scriptwriter."

"But I am a king of mercy, as well as justice," the king continued. "I am not blind to the fact that many opposed me through a sincere belief that they were in the right. To them, I hold out my hand. I invite them to join me, to put the past where it belongs—in the past—and work with me to build a better future for us all. And even to my enemies, to the irredeemable who plunged our great union into civil war, I offer mercy. Surrender now, and you will be sent into comfortable exile. I pledge my word of honor as the rightful king of Tyre and the Commonwealth. You will lack for nothing.

"But if you refuse my offer, there will be nothing for you but fire and sword."

There was a pause. "That's the end of the message," Grand Admiral Rudbek said. "It's repeating itself, on all channels. The entire planet will have heard it." His face darkened. "Will there be a reply?"

Peter shook his head. "No reply," he said. He doubted he could come up with something so pompous, particularly on short notice. He paid his speechwriters too well. "Let silence be our answer."

CHAPTER TWENTY

TYRE

"There's been no reply, Admiral."

Kat wasn't surprised. The king had expected his opponents to roll on their backs and surrender the moment they saw his fleet, but Kat knew better. The House of Lords had too much at stake. They wouldn't give up without a fight. She would have been astonished if they'd simply offered their surrender. She would have suspected a trick. She would have thought it far more likely that the House of Lords was trying to stall for as long as it took to recall their forces from nearby naval bases and concentrate them against her fleet.

Diplomacy is the art of saying "nice doggy" while you find a big stick, she thought, feeling a twinge of bitter regret. Her father had said that, time and time again. *And once they get into position to use a big stick, they won't have any incentive to come to the negotiation table.*

She studied the display thoughtfully. Home Fleet was gradually falling back on the planetary defenses, clearly hoping to combine their forces. She would have to go after them, smashing the enemy super-dreadnoughts before they had a chance to slip into hyperspace or simply prevent her from taking control of the high orbitals. But going closer would bring her far too close to the massive orbital battle stations . . . She'd known Tyre was heavily defended, she'd seen the defenses, but she hadn't really grasped their sheer immensity until she'd set out to attack them. Ahura Mazda's defenses had been paper-thin compared to Tyre's.

"Admiral," Kitty said, "I'm picking up hints of turbulence surrounding enemy forces. The analysts think they cloaked half their fleet."

Kat's eyes narrowed. The House of Lords had somewhere between seven and eight squadrons of superdreadnoughts under its direct control, although two of them were supposed to be positioned along the borders and therefore unable to intervene for several weeks even if they'd been summoned back at once. And yet, she could only see four squadrons. Were the others under cloak? She could imagine several reasons for the enemy to wish to hide their formations. It might give them a chance to surprise her if she thought she was only going to engage four squadrons . . .

And yet, we have a chance to surprise them instead, she thought. *Do they know we can see them?*

She felt her frown deepen. There was no way to know. The Royal Navy knew its technology intimately. There were sensor crews who'd spent their careers trying to crack modern-day cloaking devices, cloaking devices they understood perfectly. They possibly expected her to see the cloaked ships, simply because her sensor crews knew what to look for. And that meant . . . what?

"Signal from Commodore Ruben, Admiral," Kitty said. "He's requesting permission to advance."

Kat kept her face under tight control. "Signal the fleet," she ordered. "We will approach along Vector Four."

"Aye, Admiral," Kitty said.

Kat felt a dull thrumming echoing through the deck as the superdreadnought picked up speed. Vector Four offered them their best chance to engage Home Fleet before it could get too close to Planetary Defense, but it also offered them a straight line of retreat if the shit hit the fan. Commodore Ruben would probably be making formal complaints—Home Fleet would also have a line of retreat—but she found it hard to care. Her tutors had taught her that it was better to always have somewhere to run, even if it turned out to be unnecessary. Prior planning made it easier to extract the fleet if things went badly wrong.

She leaned back in her chair, watching as the range steadily narrowed. They were already within extreme missile range, but both sides held their fire. Kat wasn't too surprised. The defenders knew she could simply jump into hyperspace and escape if they were confronted with an onrushing tidal wave of missiles; the attackers knew there was too great a risk of slamming a missile into the planet at an appreciable fraction of the speed of light. Kat allowed herself a moment of relief, even though she knew which side would be assuming the risk of hitting the homeworld. It was good to know that the war would be relatively civilized.

As civilized as war ever becomes, she reminded herself. *There's plenty of room for something to happen before the conflict comes to an end.*

She kept her face impassive. The REMFs and bean counters might expect strict adherence to the laws of war, as if a battle were nothing more than a game of soccer or chess, but she knew better. None of the laws of war had lasted longer than the ability and willingness to enforce them . . . The Theocracy, of course, had never bothered to honor the laws in the first place. She supposed there was something honest about that. The Theocracy had never really understood that the Commonwealth had to care about public opinions either. If they had . . .

"The enemy fleet is holding position," Kitty reported. "They're locking targeting sensors on our hulls."

Kat shrugged. It wasn't as if the defenders *hadn't* been tracking her ships. They could have aimed and fired without ever needing to power up their active sensors. No, it was a final warning. They were trying to deter her from closing the range. And she didn't really blame them either. They might think she had orders to retreat if it looked as if there was going to be a fight. She understood, better than she cared to admit. She was about to fire on her former comrades . . .

She felt her heart twist. It had been easy, earlier, to act without thinking. She had saved the king, she'd transported him to Caledonia . . . She hadn't had a choice, not if she wanted to remain true to herself. But now . . . She was on the verge of killing men and women who had been her friends and allies, once upon a time. She wanted to order her fleet to turn and run, to throw away the king's best chance of victory to save lives. But she knew the battle had to be fought. The House of Lords had to be stopped. Their petty politicking had cost millions of lives.

"Lock missiles on their hulls," she ordered. She sucked in her breath. "Prepare to engage."

"Aye, Admiral," Kitty said.

Kat watched the final seconds tick away. Home Fleet had stopped now, silently drawing a line and daring her to cross. They were close to the planet, too close to jump into hyperspace safely . . . Normally, very few ships would risk opening a vortex so close to a massive gravity well. She'd done it once, when she'd been desperate; she knew she would have been dishonorably discharged if she'd done it in peacetime. The advantage of coming out of hyperspace so close to the planet would have been meaningless, if her ships had been lost in the attempt . . .

"Weapons locked," Kitty said.

"Prepare to fire," Kat ordered.

♦ ♦ ♦

Admiral Greg Kalian felt sweat trickling down his back as he watched the enemy fleet closing the range. He had strict orders to let Hadrian's forces open fire first, to make sure that the blame for starting the war rested solidly with the king, but . . . He knew, all too well, that letting the enemy fire the first shot meant that they would land the first blow. His superdreadnoughts were tough, yet . . . He had no illusions. They were going to take a battering, perhaps more of a battering than the enemy realized. If they knew the truth . . .

His throat was dry. He had no illusions about himself either. He hadn't been promoted for tactical skill but family connections and loyalty. He knew how to serve his superiors . . . and he wasn't a bad naval officer, really. Or so he told himself. A few more years of seasoning might have helped, if he'd had the time . . . He shook his head, keeping his hands firmly clasped behind his back to keep them from shaking. He had his orders. He had to carry them out. And yet . . .

He gritted his teeth. The enemy fleet was getting closer. They would soon enter sprint-mode range. Once they did . . . They could tear his fleet to ribbons before he could fall back on the planet or escape into hyperspace. And, worse, they would see through the deception. The plan, which had been put together so quickly that there had been no time to counter its weaknesses, would collapse, and the engagement would turn into a slugging match. And that, Greg knew, he might not be able to win.

His eyes swept the compartment. His people were working their consoles, readying themselves for the engagement. He wished, suddenly, that he hadn't sent Commodore Sir William McElney away. The man *had* undermined him in front of his superiors, but . . . He *did* have a fine tactical mind. Greg had no particular qualms about letting someone else run the battle, then stealing the credit afterwards. And yet . . . He felt an odd flash of envy, mingling uncomfortably with the churning sensation in his stomach. McElney hadn't hesitated to give his opinion when asked, even though he hadn't told his audience what they wanted to hear. He hadn't cared about his career, he hadn't cared about his life or his freedom . . . He'd just told them the truth, as he'd seen it.

Greg wished he could be that brave. But he couldn't bear the thought of throwing away his career. Where would he go?

Red light washed across the display. "Admiral," Captain Ewing said. "The enemy fleet is targeting us. They're preparing to fire!"

And they'll land the first blow, Greg thought, again. *They can't . . .*

He sucked in his breath. "Signal the fleet," he ordered. "Open fire."

♦ ♦ ♦

"Admiral," Kitty said, as red icons flashed into existence. "The enemy fleet has opened fire."

Kat nodded, feeling an odd twinge of relief. History would record that *she* hadn't fired the first shot, for better or worse. She took a moment to assess the situation, silently noting that the enemy superdreadnoughts had unloaded their external racks in the first volley, then nodded to herself. It was hard to be sure—the enemy ships had racked up their ECM almost as soon as they opened fire—but it looked as if she'd been right. There were at least two squadrons of cloaked superdreadnoughts within the enemy fleet.

"Return fire," she ordered. "And order the gunboats to follow the first strike."

"Aye, Admiral."

Kat calmed herself, grimly, as the wall of red icons rushed towards her ships. The enemy knew *everything* about her fleet, the strengths and weaknesses of her point defense . . . She wondered just how they'd reprogrammed their warheads to take advantage of their knowledge. She couldn't think of any naval force that had known its enemy so intimately, not since the American Civil War. And even *those* naval fleets had rapidly diverged as the two sides sought to expand their fleets and devise new weapons. Her lips quirked. Her tactical staff had sought ways to take advantage of their knowledge too. She wondered, idly, which side had come out ahead.

It might not matter, she thought. She'd seen the plans, everything from improved missiles to newer and better starships. *Given time, we'll diverge too.*

She leaned forward as the enemy missiles tore into her point defense network. They did have an advantage, she noted grimly; they knew precisely how to fool her sensors, how to trick them into firing on illusionary targets. But that wasn't enough. Her ships had trained together for weeks, exercised together until they were practically a single weapon under her command. Thousands of missiles entered the point defense envelope. Only a handful survived long enough to slam into her ships.

"*Hammer* took four direct hits, antimatter warheads," Kitty reported. "She's streaming plasma."

Kat glanced at the display. The enemy had chosen to concentrate on her superdreadnoughts, rather than try to strip away her escorts first. In the short term, it gave her an edge; her escorts could protect the superdreadnoughts without worrying about protecting themselves. But, in the long run, it was dangerous. If the king lost his superdreadnoughts, he'd lose his chance of outright victory too. A fleet of smaller ships wouldn't last long if their enemies were prepared to devote the time and resources to hunting them down and blasting them out of space.

She watched, grimly, as her missiles plunged into the teeth of the enemy formation. Alerts flashed up in front of her, suggesting that there was less point defense fire than she'd expected. Kat felt a surge of alarm, even though it seemed to work in her favor. The enemy couldn't be so incompetent as to let her have a free shot at its hulls. Why weren't they trying to protect themselves? No, why weren't they devoting *every* point defense weapon they had to protecting themselves? There was something half-assed about the whole display.

The enemy fleet fired again, fewer missiles this time. Kat nodded, despite the looming sense of unease. The enemy fleet had already expended its external racks. Cold logic told her that there were hard limits to how many missiles the enemy ships could fire during each successive salvo. Her ships had the same limits. And yet . . . There was something odd about their firing pattern. It was hard to be sure. The enemy fleet was practically lost behind a haze of ECM, made worse by antimatter explosions . . . but *something* was wrong.

Kitty looked up. "Commodore Ruben is requesting permission to close with the enemy."

Kat considered it, briefly. It *was* the right thing to do, based on what she could see. The chance to crush the enemy fleet before it could fall back on the planetary defenses was not to be missed. The enemy fleet had already taken a considerable amount of damage. She could overrun the crippled ships before their crews could make repairs and rejoin their fellows. She could destroy the fleet and then turn her attention to the planetary defenses . . . She could. She knew she could. And yet, something was wrong.

"Permission denied," she said coolly. A shudder ran through the giant superdreadnought as she unleashed another salvo of missiles. "We'll keep the range open."

"Aye, Admiral."

♦ ♦ ♦

"The enemy fleet is firing again, sir," Captain Ewing reported. "I . . ."

"I can see that," Greg snapped.

He regretted it instantly. It was his aide's *job* to make sure he knew what was happening, even if it meant telling him something he already knew. The enemy fleet was belching missiles, vomiting wave after wave of death towards his fleet . . . He clasped his hands tightly, trying not to panic. His career would be made if he survived the battle. No one could question his competence after he won . . . He'd finally have the freedom he'd always wanted, the influence to build a power base of his own . . .

His ship shook, violently. Greg felt his heart skip a beat. The enemy seemed to have singled out *King Travis* for special attention, although it wasn't clear if they knew she was the flagship. They probably did, he thought, as another missile slammed into his vessel. He tried not to look at the status display as alarms began to howl. The king knew everything about his navy. Hadrian had practically *controlled* the Royal Navy, damn him. He probably had spies and saboteurs on every command deck. Greg had placed marines on guard duty, but could the marines be trusted? He didn't know if anyone could be trusted.

"Incoming," an officer shouted. "They're targeting us!"

Greg lost his footing as the hammer of an angry god slammed into his ship. A dozen consoles blanked, the lights flickering and dimming as main power failed. The entire compartment went dark, just for a second. Emergency power came on a moment later, but the consoles remained blank. The status reports were gone.

He was no longer in command. Another missile slammed home . . .

Alarms howled. The lights dimmed again. The gravity started to fade. The captain's voice echoed through the compartment. "Abandon ship! All hands, abandon ship!"

Greg forced himself to stand, to snap orders for an orderly evacuation, but it was already too late. The entire compartment seemed to blaze with light . . .

. . . And then there was nothing.

♦ ♦ ♦

"Another enemy superdreadnought has been destroyed," Kitty reported. "Their datanet has been disrupted."

"We must have hit the flagship," Kat mused. She wondered, with a pang of guilt and grief, if William was dead. He might well have been on the enemy flagship when it died. She forced the thought aside savagely, promising herself that she would mourn later. Right now, she had to take advantage of the opportunity. The enemy datanet wouldn't be down for long. "Order the fleet to push the offensive. We have to take advantage . . ."

Red icons flashed into existence, *behind* her. "Admiral," Kitty said. Alarm ran through her voice. "We have new contacts!"

Kat felt her blood run cold.

They'd been tricked. She'd been too focused on the planet, and the visible enemy fleet, to notice the cloaked fleet sneaking into position behind her. And now . . .

"Designate the new enemy fleet as Enemy Two," she ordered, allowing her training to assert itself. No time to panic. "Recall the gunboats. And prepare . . ."

"Admiral," Kitty snapped. More red icons appeared on the display. "Enemy Two is opening fire!"

CHAPTER TWENTY-ONE

TYRE

"Open fire," William ordered.

He allowed none of his inner turmoil to show on his face as Task Force Two opened fire, two squadrons of superdreadnoughts flushing both their external racks and internal tubes and launching a solid volley of missiles towards the enemy ships. He hadn't liked the thought of leaving Admiral Kalian to stand alone, luring the enemy towards Tyre while William lurked under cloak, but he had to admit that the plan had worked. The king's ships were now caught between two fires.

The enemy ships seemed to flinch—he knew he was imagining it—as his missiles roared towards their positions. Their escorts had been deployed forward, perfectly positioned to intercept missiles from Task Force One; they were badly out of position to intercept missiles from Task Force Two. Kat Falcone, or whoever was *really* in command of the fleet, was trying desperately to reposition her escorts, but they'd been caught with their pants down. She might have the reactions of a cat, she might have given the right orders without a second's hesitation, yet there were limits on how quickly her ships could alter course and adjust their positions. She couldn't hope to reestablish her point defense in time . . .

"Commodore," Commander Tobias said. "The enemy superdreadnoughts are accelerating."

William had to smile. *That* was quick thinking on Kat's part. If the escorts couldn't be repositioned in time, and they couldn't, then have the superdreadnoughts move past the escorts so the escorts found themselves at the rear . . . Good thinking, he conceded, but not quick enough to save her ships. His missiles were already entering her point defense envelope, targeting the superdreadnoughts specifically. Admiral Kalian had been clear on that point, and for once, William had agreed. A handful of smaller ships might be able to wreak havoc for years, the Theocratic remnants had proved *that*, but they wouldn't be able to put the king back on his throne. The war could be ended now, if the enemy fleet was smashed beyond repair.

"Continue firing," he ordered. The enemy ships hadn't returned fire yet, not towards his ships. That would change in a hurry. "Don't give them a chance to recover."

"Aye, Commodore," Commander Tobias said. He paused as a new alert flashed up on the display. "Sir, Admiral Kalian is dead. Commodore Barton has assumed command of Task Force One."

William winced. He'd never really liked Admiral Kalian, but he had to admit the man had died bravely . . . He shook his head. There would be time to mourn later, if there was a later.

"Commodore Barton is requesting permission to activate Fire Plan Charlie," Commander Tobias said. "Commodore?"

"Permission granted." William allowed himself a moment of relief that Commodore Barton was not arguing over who was in overall command. It would be difficult for anyone to exercise command in real time, even though the range was closing rapidly. "And order him to go to rapid fire."

"Aye, Commodore."

William leaned forward, feeling a grim determination to simply *finish* it. Kat was caught between two fires, both of which could do immense damage to her fleet. And she was badly out of position . . . She could try to charge forward and take control of the high orbitals, but the planetary defenses would tear her fleet to ribbons. She could rotate her ships and try to close the range with William instead, yet . . . She might crush Task Force Two, at the price of having Task Force One crush her. William almost hoped she would. The move would be costly, and he would probably be among the dead, but at least it would end the war.

The king's supporters won't stick with him if he loses his fleet, he thought grimly. *They'll sell him out for the best terms they can get.*

♦ ♦ ♦

"Admiral, the planetary defenses have opened fire," Kitty snapped.

Kat bit down a sharp response. Enemy Two's missiles were coming up from the rear . . . and now the planetary defenses were coming at her from the front. She was caught between two fires, unable to deal with one without being crushed by the other. She'd done what she could to reorganize her defenses, but she was grimly aware that the effort hadn't been enough. Her fleet was about to take a beating.

"Alter course," she said. She traced out a line on her console. Her ships would have to alter course anyway, just to open fire on Enemy Two. She could fire on the planetary defenses, but the risk of accidentally hitting Tyre itself hadn't gone away. "Deploy ECM drones to cover our maneuvers."

"Aye, Admiral." Kitty paused, significantly. "Enemy missiles entering engagement range . . ."

Kat gritted her teeth as the missiles slammed into her formation. The enemy had timed it well, very well. Hundreds of missiles fell to her point defense, but hundreds more made it through the wall of fire and threw themselves on her ships. A handful were decoyed away, expending themselves uselessly on drones; the remainder found their targets and slammed home. She watched the damage starting to mount, cursing under her breath as three superdreadnoughts exploded in quick succession. Two more were badly damaged, one spewing out lifepods as it fell out of formation. She silently prayed the House of Lords was in a forgiving mood. If they chose to mistreat prisoners . . .

They won't, she told herself. *They know we would mistreat prisoners in response.*

She squeezed her fists in frustration as she conceded the battle was lost. She'd been tricked, she'd been outthought . . . and now she was on the verge of being outfought too. There *was* a slight chance of taking the high orbitals, but it would come at an immense cost. She might be able to blow her way through the planetary defenses at the price of losing nearly every ship under her command. And then Enemy Two would blow its way through the remaining ships and recapture the high orbitals. She might win the engagement but lose the war. Hell, she might not last long enough to win the engagement.

"Signal all ships," she ordered. "Prepare to retreat."

Kitty looked up, sharply. "Admiral?"

"You heard me." Kat's voice was icy cold. "Prepare to retreat."

The superdreadnought shuddered as it disgorged another salvo of missiles. Kat watched them lance into the teeth of the enemy defenses, dozens of them falling to enemy fire before the remainder struck home. Their target's shields flickered and flared but held firm. Kat scowled, unsurprised. The intelligence reports had insisted that Home Fleet had been badly disorganized, but Grand Admiral Rudbek and Admiral Kalian had had more than enough time to deal with the major problems. They'd certainly had enough time to fix the cracks in the point defense. If she'd insisted on her crews drilling till they dropped, Home Fleet could have done the same.

An enemy missile slammed into her ship. Kat glanced at the display. The shields had held and damage had been minimal, but she knew it was just a matter of time before their luck ran out. In hindsight, she should have transferred her flag to a different ship. Home Fleet *knew* which ship had been her flagship, back when the universe had made sense. She was surprised they hadn't already singled *Violence* out for special attention. It wasn't as if killing her would kill the only person who could surrender.

She felt her heart sink as she calculated possible escape vectors. There was no hope of getting clear of the planet's gravity well and the shadow the planet cast in hyperspace before her fleet was blasted to rubble. Enemy Two had the edge. Given time, it could block her escape, forcing her into a close-range engagement before she could open a vortex and escape. She could still lose the war as well as the battle itself . . .

"Contact the fleet," she said sharply. "The fleet will open vortexes from this point"—she tapped her console—"and escape into hyperspace."

"Aye, Admiral." Kitty sounded shaken. "And then . . ."

Her console chimed. "Commodore Ruben is . . . ah, *requesting* permission to speak with you."

Demanding, more like, Kat thought. She was tempted to ignore the call, but she knew that would cause problems later. "Put him through."

Ruben's face appeared in front of her, looking grim. "Admiral, we can still win this . . ."

"The best we can hope for, right now, is taking the high orbitals with a handful of ships left and hoping they don't call our bluff," Kat snapped. Another shudder ran through her vessel as a missile struck her shields. "The engagement is lost, Commodore. I will not throw good money after bad trying to change what cannot be changed. Prepare your ships for retreat."

"Admiral," Commodore Ruben insisted. His image loomed forward, as if he were trying to tower over her. "I . . ."

Kat allowed her voice to harden. "Those are your orders, Commodore, which you can have in writing if you wish. Prepare your ships for retreat, or I will summarily relieve you of command."

She waited, silently readying herself to issue orders directly to Commodore Ruben's ships. It would be a breach of naval etiquette, but . . . if he was disobeying orders in the face of the enemy, she would have no choice. And she'd have to order his flag captain to relieve him of duty . . . under normal circumstances, a terrible mess. Now . . . She had no idea what would happen. The Admiralty, which would normally stand in judgment, was in enemy hands. She certainly didn't have time to order the marines to board Commodore Ruben's flagship. Doing *that* under fire would test their skills to the limit.

"Yes, Admiral," Commodore Ruben said. "But I must register . . ."

"Later," Kat snapped.

She cut the communications channel with a wave of her hand, putting him out of her mind as she studied the status display. Her datanet was fracturing, although, thankfully, she'd worked enough redundancies into the system that it wasn't on the verge of coming apart completely. But she was still caught between two fires.

"Signal the cripples," she ordered. "If they can make it into the vortexes, we'll tow them home. If not"—she took a breath—"they have permission to surrender once the remainder of the fleet escapes."

"Aye, Admiral," Kitty said.

Kat ran through a handful of possible options. "And then signal the rest of the fleet," she added. There was no time to lose. "They are to open vortexes in five minutes."

"Aye, Admiral."

♦ ♦ ♦

"The enemy fleet is turning away," Commander Tobias reported. A hint of dark amusement ran through his voice. "They're aiming for open space."

"Adjust our course to compensate," William ordered. The tactical manuals insisted that he should close the range, but . . . He had a better idea. He needed to keep the enemy fleet from escaping. As long as it was trapped in realspace, it could be battered to pieces at leisure. He didn't need to risk his ships and crews in a desperate bid to finish them before they could escape. "Order the gunboats to move in and finish the . . ."

New icons flared up on the display. "Commodore, they're opening vortexes," Commander Tobias snapped. "They're trying to escape!"

William blinked. He shouldn't have been surprised. The dangers of opening a vortex—no, several vortexes—so close to a planet were minimal, compared to the certainty of being battered into rubble if they tried to continue the engagement in realspace. And Kat had fought in the Battle of Cadiz. She knew it could be done, even in the midst of an engagement . . . She would take the risk, instead of allowing her fleet to be destroyed. He should have known.

"Launch missiles," he ordered, although it was already too late. The vortexes were open now, inviting the enemy ships to make their escape. "Tell the gunboats to pull back . . ."

He let out a breath as the majority of the enemy ships slid into the vortexes, a handful of cripples remaining behind. They were still spitting fire in all directions, trying to buy time for their fellows to escape . . . William gritted his teeth, wondering what the king had done to deserve such loyalty. But then, it might not have been Hadrian. It might just have been a determination to help their fellows before all was lost . . .

"Gravity sensors are picking up distortions within hyperspace," Commander Tobias reported, calmly. New alerts appeared as the vortexes shimmered on the display. "Sensor Deck suggests they're dropping mines."

Trying to make it difficult for us to follow them, William thought. Only an idiot would risk a major fleet engagement within hyperspace, potentially triggering an energy storm that would scatter or destroy both fleets. *And they've probably succeeded.*

He watched the vortexes snap out of existence and sighed. The battle was over, for all intents and purposes. He'd won. But the king's fleet had managed to escape, and dozens of loyalist ships had been battered . . . He glanced at the tally. It would take weeks to repair the damage, at the very least. And then . . . He shook his head. He'd won the engagement. He would be dealing with the problems of victory. The king and his people would be grappling with the problems of defeat.

And then the rats will start looking for ways to jump ship, he thought. *Will the war cabinet be smart enough to give them a way out?*

"Signal the enemy cripples," he ordered. "Invite them to surrender."

"Aye, Commodore," Commander Tobias said.

William forced himself to relax and let out a sigh of relief as the enemy ships dropped their remaining shields and surrendered. They'd wipe their datacores and destroy them, of course . . . William smiled. The intelligence staff would throw a fit, but no matter. It was easier to convince someone to surrender if they knew their surrender wouldn't cause any further harm to their fellows.

"Send the marines to secure the enemy ships, then prepare their crews for transfer to the POW camps," he ordered. Their ultimate fate was a political decision, but, for the moment at least, they would be treated with respect. "And then signal the fleet. Well done."

"Aye, sir," Commander Tobias said.

♦ ♦ ♦

"The mines have detonated," Kitty reported. "We're clear."

Kat nodded, stiffly. She'd doubted that anyone would chase them into hyperspace, but . . . The mines would make it harder for anyone who wanted to track her fleet. Not, she supposed, that it mattered. It wouldn't take a genius to guess her destination. Where could she go, but Caledonia? She'd have to make a stop somewhere, just to signal ahead . . .

"Order the fleet to set course for the RV point," she said. She'd hoped for victory. Instead, she would have to live with the consequences of defeat. "We'll take stock once we get there."

"Aye, Admiral."

Kat turned her attention to the preliminary reports. They were grim, as preliminary reports were always pessimistic, but she forced herself to read them anyway. Nine superdreadnoughts—a whole squadron—had been blown out of space, and three more had been left behind . . . She told herself, again, that the House of Lords would take prisoners. It couldn't hope to conceal an atrocity if it murdered surrendering crewmen in cold blood . . . Could it? And the remainder of the fleet had taken varying levels of damage. The only real mercy was that most of the escorts had been untouched. Only a handful had been destroyed.

How lucky for us, she thought sourly. *And how fucking clever of them.*

She looked down at her hands, fearing the future. She'd been beaten. There was no point in trying to hide the fact that she'd been beaten. And that meant . . . what? She'd given as good as she'd got, she thought, and made a mental note to go through the post-battle assessments very carefully, but the enemy still controlled most of the industrial base. The House of Lords could replace its lost starships fairly quickly, if it wished. And then . . . The king would be crushed by superior force.

"We'll reach the RV point in fifteen hours." Kitty sounded concerned. "Admiral?"

"Understood," Kat said tiredly.

She considered, briefly, not signaling ahead. They could fly straight to Caledonia . . . She shook her head. There was no way in hell that the House of Lords wouldn't be gloating over its victory. They'd claim that they wiped out her entire fleet for minimal losses; they'd insist that the king's cause was thoroughly doomed . . . They'd be right too if she didn't get word home before it was too late. It might already be too late. The messages might already be on their way to Caledonia, effortlessly outpacing her fleet. How long would it be before the entire Commonwealth knew who'd won and lost?

Not long, she thought sourly. *And no one will be in any doubt which one is which.*

Kat leaned back in her chair, trying to look into the future. The war wasn't over yet. There were still options, weren't there? She could see them. Right?

But, if she was honest with herself, all she saw was darkness.

CHAPTER TWENTY-TWO

TYRE

It wasn't the first time William had flown over Tyre in the course of his career, but it was certainly the oddest. The shuttle was escorted by a pair of assault shuttles, brimming with weaponry; his sensors picked up a handful of police aircars and a pair of media craft holding position at the edge of the secure zone. The streets below were disconcertingly empty, as if the entire planet were in hiding. He knew a state of emergency had been declared as soon as the attackers had been detected, but still . . . He shook his head. The general population might not care who emerged victorious, not really. They had no reason to think their lives would change if the wrong side won the war.

Which may be a mistake on their part, William thought, as the shuttle dropped towards the landing pad. *Whoever wins the war will definitely be trying to change things.*

He stood as soon as the shuttle landed neatly on the pad. A pair of guards in powered combat armor stood outside, their faces hidden behind solid visors. William frowned as he stepped through the hatch. *Something* had clearly happened, but what? The guards motioned for him to stand between them, then ran scanners over his body. William kept his irritation under tight control as they inspected his wristcom and confiscated his service pistol. Didn't they know he had permission to be armed at all times?

"Commodore," a voice said. William looked up to see Yasmeena Delacroix standing by the door. "If you'll come with me . . . ?"

"Of course," William said. He allowed Duke Peter's assistant to lead him into the complex. "Security seems to have been tightened."

"There were a handful of . . . attacks during the main body of the fighting," Yasmeena informed him. "Mostly minor, really. We clamped down on public transport as soon as we sounded the alert, but a couple could have been deadly. We had to tighten security just about everywhere."

Which probably explains why the streets were so empty, William thought. *You're telling everyone to stay in their homes while you try to round up the king's supporters.*

He glanced at her back. "Insurgents? Or just people who support the king?"

"We're uncertain as yet," Yasmeena said. "I daresay we'll find out sooner or later."

She stopped outside an open door and motioned for him to enter. William did, somehow unsurprised to see Duke Peter sitting behind a desk. Another office? William couldn't help wondering just how many offices the man had. The Falcone Corporation was vast, easily one of the largest interstellar corporations to exist. Duke Peter might have a hundred offices on Tyre alone.

"Commodore," Duke Peter said. "Thank you for coming."

William saluted, briskly. He'd had the impression he hadn't had a choice. Grand Admiral Rudbek had passed on the order, once the captured ships had been cleared and the battle declared officially over. William barely had time to shower and grab a change of clothes before he'd boarded the shuttle. He supposed he should be glad they'd given him time to wash. He would have made an impression if he'd shown up without taking a shower, but it wouldn't have been one he wanted to make.

"We just heard from Durian," Duke Peter said. "You were right. The fleet that attacked Durian was nothing more than sensor ghosts and ECM drones."

"Yes, sir," William said. "I assume the system remains in our hands."

Duke Peter smiled humorlessly. "No one was panicked into surrender."

William nodded. "Thank God."

"Take a seat," Duke Peter said. "Admiral Kalian's death leaves an unexpected gap in our ranks."

"Yes, sir." William wondered, grimly, just who would take Kalian's place. "He died well."

"He died," Duke Peter said. "We'll be giving him a hero's funeral, of course, but that isn't the point. The point is that he died."

"Yes, Your Grace," William agreed.

"I have spoken with the other dukes," Duke Peter continued. "We have agreed to offer you the post of fleet commander, under Grand Admiral Rudbek. Will you accept the post?"

William couldn't hide his surprise. Client of the Falcones or not, he was a colonial with a checkered past and dubious relations. Hebrides hadn't declared for either side—the planet itself was dead, while the survivors were too few to have any real impact on the war—but he was hardly a well-connected aristocrat. Dozens of prospective candidates could take Admiral Kalian's place. Hell, he'd expected Commodore Barton to be kicked upstairs once the dust settled. He had the connections, the experience . . . and he looked strikingly photogenic to boot. Commodore Barton was practically the very model of a space navy's admiral.

But . . . His mind raced. He'd never dared dream of anything above command rank. He would never have been promoted to commodore if he hadn't had powerful friends. An admiral's rank? He wanted it. Oh yes, he wanted it. But he wasn't blind to the dangers. He could be used, praised, and discarded once the war was over. Or sooner, if he screwed up. It was quite possible that the next engagement would go the other way.

His mouth was suddenly dry. "I will," he said. "If you're offering it to me . . ."

Duke Peter smiled, thinly. "We are," he said. "We'll make it official later today. We've arranged a brief ceremony . . . But, from this moment on, you are fleet commander."

He leaned back in his chair. "Would you like a drink?"

William couldn't speak for a moment. "Yes, Your Grace."

Duke Peter tapped a command into his terminal, then leaned forward. "There will be a formal discussion after the ceremony," he said. "But, for the moment, how do you propose we win the war?"

Yasmeena entered, carrying a tray with a bottle and two transparent glasses. William nodded his thanks as she poured him a generous measure of something purple, then retreated as silently as she'd come. He took advantage of the pause, as Duke Peter lifted his glass, to consider his options. He'd assumed he would be briefing his new commanding officer, not assuming the rank himself. He hadn't had time to consider how *he* would take the offensive.

"The king's forces took a beating," he said finally. "We've barely started post-battle assessments, Your Grace, but we know he lost an entire squadron of superdreadnoughts outright. A handful of other ships surrendered. The remainder . . . will need to be repaired before they can be flung back into battle."

"Good," Duke Peter said.

William took a sip of his drink. It tasted like . . . He wasn't sure *what* it tasted like. It didn't feel as if it were liquid. He felt more like he was inhaling mist, strangely flavored mist. He'd never tasted anything like it.

"It comes from the vineyards on Mars," Duke Peter said, answering William's unspoken question. "The grapes themselves were a side effect,

I have been told, of attempts to produce plants that could grow and thrive within the planet's atmosphere. They're quite expensive."

Even by your standards, William thought. Shipping a crate of bottles from Mars to Tyre would cost . . . He didn't want to *think* how much it would cost. More than he'd earn in a year, he was sure. *Are you drinking it now to celebrate the victory, Your Grace, or are you making a subtle point?*

William took another sip. "I think it is a little too fancy for me," he said. "And there isn't much of it."

Duke Peter smiled. "There never is. That's why the price is so high."

William shrugged—he'd never bothered to develop expensive tastes—then returned to discussing the war. "The downside is that our forces took a battering too. Admiral Kalian's task force was badly beaten, while mine was hit hard during the closing moments of the engagement. I mixed and matched superdreadnoughts after the battle, in a bid to reorganize Home Fleet before the enemy could resume the offensive, but none of those units have actually trained together. It will take time to iron out the problems."

The duke seemed displeased. "I seem to hear that a lot, Admiral."

William felt an odd rush of pride. Admiral. He was an admiral. But he also had to answer the unspoken question.

"A military force must train, constantly, when it is not engaged with the enemy," he said calmly. "It is important that problems are exposed, and fixed, before the fleet goes into a real battle; it is vital that crews learn their strengths and weaknesses, that any personality conflicts are resolved, that we . . . that we are *ready* before the balloon goes up. An officer who neglects training will be in trouble when he takes his ship to war."

"I see," Duke Peter said. "And you can never rest?"

"Not in the sense you mean," William said. "A naval unit that is not training, Your Grace, is one that is starting to decay."

He eyed his drink, wondering if he should take another sip. "On paper, we should launch an immediate attack on Caledonia. In theory, we should be able to crush the king's remaining ships, occupy the planet, and hopefully capture the king himself. If that happened, we would win the war. However . . . in practice, it might be a great deal harder."

Duke Peter lifted his eyebrows. "How so?"

"Our task force could, at most, consist of five squadrons of superdreadnoughts," William explained. "Less, of course, if we declined to leave Tyre uncovered or take the damaged ships with us. Realistically, I think we'd be looking at three squadrons at most. The king's forces would give them a very hard time. It might end up as a rerun of the *last* battle, with the roles reversed."

"You wouldn't let them catch you by surprise," Duke Peter said.

"Not that way," William conceded. "They might find other ways to surprise me. They will be desperate, Your Grace, and desperate men are often prepared to gamble." He took a breath. "A failed raid on Caledonia might still cost them the war, in the long run," he said. "But can we afford a major failure?"

"Perhaps." Duke Peter looked as if he'd bitten into something sour. "What do you propose instead?"

William wished, suddenly, for a starchart. Or even a few hours to consider how best to make his case. If he'd known . . .

"A number of worlds have declared for the king," William said. He felt an odd little pang as he picked his next words. "I think we should harass them, which will push the enemy to either defend or abandon them, while building up our forces for the final battle. A handful of raids will make life difficult for the king. Military logic will indicate that most of the worlds we'll target are worthless, by and large; political logic will suggest otherwise."

"He cannot abandon them without being abandoned in return," Duke Peter said. He looked, just for a moment, strikingly like Kat. If William hadn't already known they were siblings, he would have deduced it from just how much they had in common. "And if we were to reach out to his allies . . . would they switch sides?"

William hesitated. "That is a political issue . . ."

Duke Peter laughed, harshly. "The higher you climb, *Admiral*, the more you have to take politics into account."

"So I've been told." William braced himself, wondering if he was about to be summarily demoted. Again. "You're treating the colonials as a unified political force, with a single hive mind. That isn't particularly true. The only thing that unites the colonials is resistance to you. They weren't opposed to joining the Commonwealth, Your Grace. They were resistant, very resistant, to being exploited."

"I am aware of the political background," Duke Peter said. "I am *also* aware that none of us planned for all-out war on an interstellar scale."

"Yes." William met his eyes, evenly. "But that doesn't absolve you of having to deal with the consequences. Tyre . . . Whether you care to admit it or not, Tyre was almost overbearingly powerful. The colonies, which were never really colonies, not *your* colonies, didn't stand a chance. Whenever there was a dispute, Tyre came out ahead. Colonials faced discrimination at every turn. I am the highest-ranking colonial in the navy, Your Grace, and before this war I was a captain. My promotion to commodore came when I retired. I don't think anyone actually expected me to do more than claim a commodore's pension."

"There were political issues here," Duke Peter reminded him. "If a well-connected officer was passed over in favor of a colonial, Admiral, what do you think that officer's patrons did? Calmly accept it? Or make one hell of a fuss?"

"I'm not disputing that," William said. He remembered some of the disputes he'd had to mediate when he'd been Admiral Kalian's chief of staff. "But that doesn't stop you from having to deal with the consequences."

"No," Duke Peter said. He didn't sound pleased, but at least he wasn't denying what he was being told. "What would you suggest?"

William bit his lip. There were dozens of possibilities, but most of them . . . There was no way the House of Lords would go for them, even if they weren't in the middle of a civil war. It would be too much like giving in to threats and blackmail.

"I don't think there's much you could *realistically* offer," he said. "Like you say, there would be political opposition to almost any concession you could make. I'd suggest opening up the navy, perhaps by expanding the patronage networks, but even then . . . You'd be gambling the newcomers would be better than the long-established families."

"A risky gamble," Duke Peter noted. "And not one many of my fellows would take."

"Yes," William said. "To be honest, Your Grace, I'd suggest offering to speed up the prewar integration plans. You'd have to take a short-term loss, making sure not to exploit the locals, but in the long term you would come out ahead."

"Which wouldn't be easy," Duke Peter said.

"No," William said. He didn't pretend to understand the economic problems facing Tyre and the Commonwealth, but he knew there was a cash flow problem. "But how could the king position himself as the protector of the colonials if there was nothing they needed to be protected *from*?"

"That's something I'll discuss with my fellows," Duke Peter suggested. "Do you have anything else in mind?"

"Very little," William admitted. "You could offer to accept any world that wishes to switch sides, again, but that might not go down very well either. Turncoats are rarely popular. Their former allies will seek revenge, while their new allies won't be able to trust them."

"Unfortunately so," Duke Peter agreed. His face twisted. "And we don't want to encourage grumbling among the planets that stayed loyal."

He finished his drink. "You'll have some time to put your plans together," he said. "If we're lucky, the diplomatic approach will work now the king's military offensive has been rebuffed. His supporters might just switch sides in a body, bringing us his head." He stopped, thoughtfully. "You don't think so?"

"I don't know anything about the aristocrats who've supported the king," William said. He thought it would probably be best if he didn't mention Kat to her brother. "But I do understand the colonial mindset . . ."

"Go on," Duke Peter said. "Speak your mind."

William took a breath. "Tyre is a very wealthy world," he said. "In many ways, you skipped the early stages of development. Your ancestors poured so much wealth and resources into the colonization process that you practically jumped to stage-four overnight. Your society is so wealthy that you can afford to provide the bare essentials for everyone, from food and drink to medical care and education. Your people have a level of comfort, a base level of comfort, that is . . . Well, compared to my homeworld, it's unbelievable. They can . . . they do . . . trust the government. You don't set out to screw your own people.

"A colonial world doesn't have those luxuries. Even places like Caledonia are orders of magnitude poorer than Tyre. Hebrides . . . We rarely had the resources to take care of our population. And Hebrides was one of the lucky worlds. There are places in the Jorlem Sector with governments that are poor, corrupt, oppressive, or all three. The experience breeds a very different mindset. A colonial can endure more . . . discomfort than a Tyrian. They also know that they have to keep their word, because no one will enforce contracts and suchlike; they know they have to honor their obligations, even ones made to the king. It would take a great deal to make the king's allies switch sides."

"If he betrayed them," Duke Peter said. "And he will. You know he will."

"Yes," William said. He'd never thought the king was particularly impressive. He had shown an admirable degree of resolution during the last war, but he'd had very little choice. Now . . . Who knew? "But he would *have* to make a very explicit betrayal. A colonial . . ."

He paused, choosing his next words carefully. "A colonial knows, Your Grace, that things can go wrong. A colonial knows there are always teething problems. And a colonial will not *stop* if things look to be going wrong. He will not be deterred by minor setbacks. He isn't raised to expect immediate success."

"You make it sound as if they're unstoppable." A slight smile curved around Duke Peter's lips. "Can they be beaten?"

"Of course, Your Grace." William shrugged, irritated. "But don't expect them to jump ship or abandon their commitments immediately. They know, better than you, that something going wrong isn't the end of the world."

And something going right is no guarantee of continued success, he added in the privacy of his own mind. *The war isn't over yet.*

CHAPTER TWENTY-THREE

CALEDONIA

Kat was in disgrace.

She stood outside the heavy wooden door, feeling, to her mingled amusement and irritation, like a little girl who had been summoned before her father to account for her misdeeds. She'd been called to the surface almost as soon as the fleet had entered orbit, with strict orders to proceed directly to the palace, but now . . .

They're playing petty power games, she thought, feeling a twinge of annoyance. She knew the score, and she knew what her father had to *say* about the score, the few times he'd taught her personally. *Anyone who plays petty power games is inherently insecure in his power.*

She ignored the churning sensation in her chest, reminding herself that she was an admiral in command of one of the most powerful fleets in the known universe . . . even if that fleet had taken a beating in its previous engagement. She'd lost the battle, no point in pretending otherwise, but she *had* gotten the fleet out of a trap that would otherwise have destroyed it, sending the king's ambitions falling down in flames. And she'd battered the enemy fleet badly enough to ensure it couldn't launch an immediate counterattack. Not a complete disaster.

No, her thoughts mocked her. *But it looks like a complete disaster.*

She straightened up as the door opened. Sir Grantham appeared, motioning for her to enter the compartment. She pasted a calm expression on her face, as if she were merely paying a courtesy call on a station commander, and walked into the chamber. It had been rearranged to look like a military courtroom. The king and his inner council sat on one side of the table, their faces schooled to immobility. She was apparently expected to sit on the other, as if she were on trial. Perhaps she was. Her lips twitched. They shouldn't have given her a chair if they'd wanted her to feel *really* vulnerable.

"Your Majesty," she said. She didn't take the chair. Instead, she stood at parade rest, her hands clasped behind her back. "You requested my presence?"

The king looked flustered, as if she'd already deviated from the script. Perhaps she had. She had faced two Boards of Inquiry after the mission to Jorlem, where *Lightning* had been lost and *Uncanny* had fallen to mutineers. Even then, the judges had political agendas of their own. Now . . . She allowed her eyes to wander along the table. The king's supporters sat to the left of their monarch, their eyes silently accusing her of heinous crimes; the colonials sat to the right, their faces so impassive that they might as well have been carved from stone. She had the nasty feeling that the discussions before the fleet's return had been acrimonious. A victory would have a thousand fathers, and smooth over the cracks in the alliance; defeat was an orphan, one that would widen the fractures to their breaking point.

"Yes, I did." The king sounded tired. Tired and worn. "What happened?"

Kat felt a stab of sympathy, mingled with irritation. "It's all in my report, Your Majesty."

"But we are asking *you*," Governor Rogan snarled. "What happened, *Admiral*?"

"We lost," Lord Gleneden said. He sounded punch-drunk, as if he was too badly shocked to offer advice. "We lost the war."

"Enough," the king said. "Admiral?"

Kat took a moment, then outlined the brief engagement. She left nothing out, including her failure to recognize the trap before it was too late. The enemy CO had played her like a fiddle . . . Guilt gnawed at her, a mocking reminder that thousands of men and women were dead because they'd followed her into battle. She couldn't deny it. The superdreadnought crews could easily have gone home, or into internment camps, if they hadn't wanted to fight for the king. Or her.

"We lost the battle," she concluded. "But we haven't lost the war."

"Oh yes?" Governor Rogan sounded furious. "Do you know how many planets are threatening to backslide in the wake of *your* defeat?" His eyes bored into Kat's. "Did you *mean* to lose?"

Kat met his eyes, as evenly as she could. "Are you accusing me of treason, sir?"

"I . . ."

The king cut Governor Rogan off. "No one is accusing anyone of anything," he said. "We just want to get the facts."

"The *facts* are that we are about to lose the war," Governor Rogan said. "Their fleet remains intact!"

"Their fleet took a beating," Kat said. "We made sure they were in no state to launch a counterattack."

"And how long will that last?" Governor Rogan glared at the king's supporters. "Your determination to recover your homeworld has led to disaster!"

"Tyre is the *center* of the Commonwealth," Earl Antony said. "Whoever holds Tyre holds the Commonwealth."

"Aye, and who *does* hold Tyre?" Governor Rogan was unfazed. "We should have concentrated on defending our positions!"

"Which would have let them take the offensive," Earl Antony countered. "And given them the edge."

"Perhaps we should consider the latest offers of talks," Lord Gleneden offered. "They *might* be inclined to be reasonable."

"Hah," Governor Rogan said. "Why should they be reasonable? They kicked our asses! They are winning the war!"

"It is true that we may face personal sanctions," Lord Gleneden said calmly. "But they will be relieved to end the war without further bloodshed."

You mean you *won't have to face further bloodshed*, Kat thought. Lord Gleneden was an aristocrat, with strong family connections to the other side. *You might be disgraced, if we lose the war, but you won't be killed. The worst that can happen is that you'll be sent into exile and told never to come home.*

The argument threatened to grow out of hand. The room stank with fear—fear of defeat . . . fear of losing everything. The aristocrats could afford, perhaps, to consider peace talks. Their relatives would make sure that any punishments were relatively mild, certainly in comparison to what their colonial allies would receive. Kat doubted that Governor Rogan and his people would be let off so lightly. It was rather more possible that they'd suffer punitive sanctions, at the very least.

The king slapped the table. "Enough," he said. "We lost one battle. But the war is far from over!"

"The war might be over," Lord Gleneden said. "They have a chance, now, to take the war to us."

"We certainly can't attack Tyre again," Governor Rogan snapped. "Or can we?"

Kat frowned. Governor Rogan was looking at Admiral Lord Garstang.

"My staff have been considering our options," Admiral Lord Garstang said, awkwardly. "It is unlikely that we can mount a second attack on Tyre within the next few months. But we can go on the offensive elsewhere."

"Under someone else's command," Earl Antony demanded. "Admiral Falcone lost the battle!"

"She handled herself well," Admiral Lord Garstang said. He carefully didn't look at Kat. "And post-battle assessment makes it clear that . . ."

"Admiral Falcone chose not to press the offensive," Earl Antony said. "I have it on good authority that she could have won, if she'd closed with the fortresses . . ."

"And lost my entire fleet," Kat snapped.

Her mind raced. Good authority? Which armchair admiral had been spouting nonsense? It was easy for someone with no real experience to pontificate on subjects about which he knew nothing, but Earl Antony should know better than to take them seriously. Or . . . Commodore Henri Ruben? He'd pushed for closing the range, then argued against a retreat . . . He'd had weeks to plan how best to use the defeat to undermine Kat's position. Or perhaps she was just being paranoid. She had no way to know for sure. Ruben certainly wouldn't *admit* to briefing against his superior if she asked. She'd beach him for breaking ranks, and he knew it.

"You gave up our best chance for victory," Governor Rogan said. "If you had taken the high orbitals . . ."

"The fleet coming up behind me would"—she bit down the urge to make a scatological joke—"have destroyed *my* fleet before I could force the planet to surrender. Our entire fleet, our entire cause, would have been lost. It would have been the end."

"You don't know that," Earl Antony said. "They were already considering surrender."

"Sure, just as *some* people were considering surrender after the Battle of Cadiz." Kat resisted the urge to ask him what *he'd* been doing when she'd led the breakout. "They wouldn't have surrendered so quickly. And there was nothing we could have done, up to and including planetary bombardment, to force their hand. It would have been the end!"

She hated repeating herself. But Earl Antony didn't seem to notice. Or care.

"We could have won," he insisted. "I . . ."

"Or we could have lost everything," Lord Gleneden said. "Under the circumstances, I believe that Admiral Falcone made the right decision. She knew that the fleet had to be preserved as a bargaining chip . . ."

"A chip that is of no value to us!" Governor Rogan reddened. "Are you considering selling us out for the best terms you can get?" A rustle of anger ran through the colonials as he repeated his question. "Are you . . . ?"

The king raised his voice. "We are all in this together," he said. His words echoed in the air. "And there will be no separate peace with the House of Lords. We swore oaths."

Oaths can be broken, Kat thought grimly. Joel Gibson and his mutineers had broken *their* oaths, damn them. She wondered how many of the king's supporters were looking for a chance to abandon his cause and join the House of Lords. The defeat might not be as bad as the news broadcasts from Tyre made it sound, particularly the ones that subtly implied the entire fleet had been destroyed, but it was still pretty bad. She was sure that *some* people would be planning for the worst. *Which of you is going to jump first?*

She studied the councilors as the argument raged on and on. The king himself had nowhere to go, no hope of retaining *any* power if he lost the war. The colonials could expect trials for treason and death sentences, at the very least. Their homeworlds would suffer for their crimes. But the others? There weren't many among the king's councilors who didn't have family on the other side. They might well jump, trusting in their families to ensure that they received little more than a slap on the wrist. And they might be right. Their families might not be happy when the black sheep returned, but they'd still have to protect them. To do otherwise would weaken the bonds holding their families together.

The king glanced from face to face, his expression starting to sag. Kat felt another flicker of sympathy for him. It was easy to handle victory, even when victory brought another series of challenges in its wake; defeat, on the other hand, was *never* easy. The king would have to hold his people together, somehow, or risk watching helplessly as his supporters fragmented into a dozen little groups, warring incessantly while the House of Lords tightened the noose. A major falling-out might be enough to utterly shatter the king's cause without his enemies lifting a finger . . .

She stared at Governor Rogan, who was arguing loudly with Lord Gleneden. *With friends like that, the poor bastard doesn't need enemies.*

The king stood. "Enough," he said. "Things have not gone to plan. But, like I said, it is not the end of the war. We have options. And we will play our cards as best as we can."

"We can still win," Earl Antony agreed.

"Quite," the king said. "We will therefore consider our next step . . ."

"But not under Admiral Falcone's command." Governor Rogan looked at Kat, then at the king. "I will not send my people to fight and die under a failure."

Kat felt a hot flush of anger. "With all due respect . . ."

"Your father jumped you up the ranks, time and time again," Governor Rogan pointed out coldly. "And now you have reached the level of your incompetence."

"With all due respect," Kat repeated as she tried not to clench her fists, "I would like to see you do better."

"Commodore Ruben has formally stated that you passed up an opportunity to crush the enemy fortresses before the second enemy fleet showed itself," Earl Antony said.

So it was him, Kat thought. She privately vowed to make sure that Ruben paid a high price for trying to stick a knife in her back. *And he wasn't the one in command of the battle, was he?*

"It is easy to pretend to be wise, after the fact." Kat kept her voice even, somehow. "I might point out, if I was interested in refighting the battle, that the second enemy fleet was *there* all along. They would simply have accelerated their timetable if we'd closed with the first enemy fleet. Indeed, that might even have worked out better for them. They would have had more surviving missile launchers on their side when they sprang their trap."

She met his eyes. "But I am not interested in arguing over what might have been. There is nothing that can be done to change the past. We lost the engagement. We were forced to break off and retreat. Right now, our priority is to repair the damage and resume the offensive before the House of Lords launches its own offensive."

"And before some of the doubters start switching sides," Governor Rogan muttered.

Earl Antony gave Kat a long look, then switched his attention to the king. "I think I speak for everyone, Your Majesty, when I say that Admiral Falcone has lost my confidence."

Kat felt her cheeks heat. *Did I ever have his confidence?*

"Admiral Falcone enjoys my confidence," the king said flatly.

"But she led our fleet into a trap," Governor Rogan said. "I must agree with Antony . . ."

"*Earl* Antony," Earl Antony snapped.

". . . And say that Admiral Falcone can no longer be trusted to command the striking force," Governor Rogan continued, ignoring the interruption. "She may or she may not have thrown away a chance to actually *win*. We do not know. Regardless, we *do* know that she lost a battle. She no longer enjoys my confidence."

"Or mine," Lord Streford said. "A new commanding officer will improve morale and allow us to draw a line under recent unfortunate events."

"Perhaps we should organize a Board of Inquiry," Sir Grantham said quickly. "It would allow us to determine the truth . . ."

"A transparent attempt to delay matters until the truth can be buried." Governor Rogan sneered. "The truth is that Admiral Falcone, for whatever reason, lost the battle."

Kat felt her temper begin to fray. "Are you suggesting that I *deliberately* lost the battle?"

"I'm saying that you *lost* the battle," Governor Rogan said. "And, as someone with . . . divided loyalties . . . you might have hesitated at the wrong moment."

"A Board of Inquiry would settle the issue," Sir Grantham said. "Admiral Garstang can put one together quickly, I'm sure, and . . ."

"And come up with whatever answer is politically convenient," Governor Rogan said. "Did another Board of Inquiry not try to blame us colonials for the mutiny on HMS *Unlucky*?"

"*Uncanny*," Kat corrected quietly. "And the *final* version of the report placed the blame on the mutineers themselves."

"Because it was the convenient answer," Governor Rogan said. His eyes swept the room until they came to rest on Sir Grantham. "And what answer will prove politically convenient now?"

"The truth," Sir Grantham said. He sounded as if he were trying to pour oil on troubled waters. "And the Board would establish . . ."

"Not in time," Governor Rogan said. He wasn't trying to be conciliatory. "We need to act now."

He gave Kat a sharp look. "I demand your resignation."

Kat felt her temper snap. "No."

Governor Rogan blinked. "No?"

"I mean *no*," Kat said. "I will not resign, not now. Not after snide suggestions that I chose to betray the cause. If I'd *wanted* to betray the king, or even sit on my hands until the decision was taken out of my hands, I would not have taken him aboard my ship when he fled Tyre. Or perhaps I would have seized him, when he docked, and handed him over to the House of Lords. I have had plenty of opportunities to betray him and you, *Governor*, and I have taken none of them. If that isn't enough to convince you that I am on your side . . ."

She held his gaze, daring him to look away. "I will not offer my resignation. I will not admit guilt for something I didn't do. If His Majesty has lost confidence in me, he may fire me; if he fires me, I will turn my command over to my successor and find something else to do with my time. But I will not listen to insinuations, and I will *not* submit to an inquest that will rapidly become a witch hunt.

"Right now, I have work to do. My ships need to be repaired. My crews need shore leave. I need to go back to my flagship and *work*. If the king wants to fire me, he can fire me. Until then, I will do my duty to the best of my ability. And I *suggest*"—she allowed her voice to harden—"that you remember that we have to hang together or hang separately. The House of Lords will eagerly exploit any division in our ranks. Do *not* give them the chance."

She saluted, then turned and marched out of the chamber, half expecting someone to block her way.

No one tried to stop her.

CHAPTER TWENTY-FOUR

Caledonia

"I've been at more lively funerals," Lieutenant Maxwell Jones muttered as he sipped his beer. "I thought this was meant to be *shore leave*."

Lieutenant Samantha Brisket was inclined to agree. She'd seen plenty of spaceport strips—the cluster of overpriced shops, bars, and brothels surrounding the planetary spaceports—in her career, but Caledonia's struck her as unbelievably gloomy. Everyone seemed disheartened. The bars were crammed with drinkers, unsurprisingly, but the brothels didn't seem to be doing a roaring trade, and the shops looked as if their owners were considering shutting down for the night. *That* was unusual, at least in her experience. Spaceport strips were generally open twenty-four seven.

Of course everyone's depressed, she thought as she took a sip of her beer. *We lost a battle. We might have lost the war.*

She looked around the bar, a dark and dingy mess. The walls were covered in posters and stained with something she didn't want to think about, the air stinking of tobacco and flavored vapors. Clusters of drinkers huddled together as they drank overpriced beer. It wasn't, she decided, the sort of place she *wanted* to spend her two days of shore leave. She would have preferred to explore the planet itself, to leave the spaceport strip and visit the capital . . . It wasn't possible. They'd been warned not to go too far afield. They might be called back to their ship at any time.

"It could be worse," Jones said. "I mean . . . We could be attending a *real* funeral."

Samantha gave him a rude gesture. They weren't *precisely* friends, although, as they were in the same department, they weren't exactly passing strangers either. It wasn't the first time she'd gone planet-side with an acquaintance if only because *smart* spacers knew better than to be alone the first time they visited a new world. Spaceport strips were full of people trying to relieve a spacer of his paycheck, by means fair and foul. The beer was overpriced, the gaming tables were rigged, the prostitutes were trained to service their customers as quickly as possible . . . She shook her head. Officers, even junior officers, were discouraged from using brothels. There were upmarket escort services for them.

"I suppose," she said. She'd had a brief look up and down the street, but there was nothing *special* about Caledonia. She could have been on any planet. "Is there *anything* to do here?"

Jones pulled his datapad off his belt and took a look. "Nothing much," he said. "There's a VR suite, if you want to have a treat. A gaming complex . . . They're bragging about games imported from the other side of the known universe. And a couple of *really* high-priced hotels." He grinned toothily. "I figure that if we pool our resources, we *might* be able to stay at one of them for half an hour or so."

Samantha had to laugh. "If we were going to be planet-side for a week, I'd want a hotel *outside* the spaceport strip."

"If we could get out," Jones said, suddenly serious. "I heard from Tommy. He said there were guards on the gates, checking everyone who went in and out. No one leaves the spaceport without authorization."

"Odd." Samantha considered it for a moment. "They're not letting us explore the planet?"

"So it seems," Jones said. "Pity, that."

Samantha nodded, slowly. The spaceports and their surrounding facilities were not, as she understood it, governed by planet-side law. The planetary governments were obliged to allow the spaceports to exist, but not to let anyone who landed *out* of the spaceport. And yet, there were exceptions made for naval personnel. They could explore the planets they were supposed to defend without visas . . . She wondered, sourly, why Caledonia had changed the rules. Were they concerned about deserters? Or defeatists? Or . . .

She looked up as a handful of gunboat crewers entered the bar. They looked to have been drinking, two of them barely standing upright. They would have collapsed if their companions hadn't been holding them up. Samantha frowned as the crewers shoved their semicomatose comrades into a booth, then shouted for beer. The waitress, a pale girl in a dress that looked like rags, tottered over, carrying a tray of full glasses. Samantha was mildly surprised that she didn't trip and fall over.

Jones cleared his throat. "There are other places we could go," he said. "Where do you want to sleep?"

"God knows," Samantha said. They had access to the barracks, but she'd rather hoped to sleep somewhere that wasn't controlled by the navy. "I wonder . . ."

"Fucking officers," someone said. "Fucking Tyrians!"

Samantha looked up, alarmed. A half-drunk crewman was looming over her, swaying from side to side. His uniform was stained with beer, his breath reeking . . . She forced herself to stay still, despite an understandable urge to lean backwards. The crewman was huge, easily the largest man she'd ever seen in naval uniform. And he was a colonial. His voice was slurred, but she could still hear his accent . . .

"You abandoned us," he said. He waved the glass in his hand. Beer slopped in all directions, splashing to the sodden floor. "You left us to die!"

Jones half stood. "You're drunk," he said. "Sit down and . . ."

The man bellowed like a bull. "You left us behind," he thundered. "All the gunboats, left behind to die when you turned and fled like . . ."

Samantha gritted her teeth, suddenly aware that the entire bar was watching them. The nasty atmosphere had somehow congealed . . . She could *sense* drinkers exchanging threatening looks, as if they were preparing for a fight. She tried hard to think of something, anything, she could do, but nothing came to mind. She cursed herself for not having armed herself before coming down to the planet. She was an officer. She had a legal right to carry a firearm at all times.

"You fled!" The crewman lumbered forward. "You fled and . . ."

He poured his beer over Samantha's head. For a moment, she couldn't grasp what had happened. Warm liquid was dripping through her hair, trickling down her face, and staining her uniform. The crewman laughed and pushed forward. She couldn't move. She couldn't do anything. She was frozen.

Jones jumped up. "Get back," he snapped. "I . . ."

Samantha didn't see who threw the first punch. One moment, the entire bar was hanging on a knife-edge; the next, everyone was fighting everyone else. Jones hit the crewman who'd drenched her in beer, but the lumbering mass of flesh didn't seem fazed; he merely drew back and punched Jones in the face. Samantha stumbled, shocked out of her paralysis, and grabbed a bottle as Jones fell to the floor. The crewman started to turn, his expression darkening rapidly; she hit him on the head and watched him waver before finally crashing to his knees. And then someone crashed into her. She hit the ground hard enough to hurt, her head barely missing the chair.

Fuck, she thought, through a haze of pain. Someone else had grabbed her attacker, throwing him away from her. She could hear glasses breaking as they were turned into weapons and thrown in all directions. It was all she could do to crawl towards Jones. *How do we get out of here?*

♦ ♦ ♦

There was something nasty in the air.

Sergeant Jerry Spellman could *feel* it as he led the small patrol down the street, weaving in and out of the roadside stalls and unsteady spacers as they tried to drown their sorrows in drink. The spaceport strip had always had an edge to it, a sense that it could explode into violence at any moment, but now . . . He was convinced that something was going to happen. The news of the defeat had been bad enough, when it had leaked out two weeks ago, but now the defeated spacers had returned home. There had already been a handful of men arrested for brawling. He was grimly certain that it was just the tip of the iceberg.

And it won't be long before it all goes to hell, he thought. If it had been up to him, the spacers would not have been given shore leave in the first place. There were just too many of them, crammed into the spaceport strip. *It's going to explode soon . . .*

He glanced up, sharply, as he heard the sound of fighting in the distance. There was a cluster of seedy bars in that direction, if he recalled correctly; he glanced at his patrol, then led them down the street. Dozens of people were running in all directions, some trying to get away from the fighting and others trying to join it. He cursed as he saw a herd of merchant spacers rushing into the morass. *They should have been sent elsewhere*, he told himself. They would just make the aftermath more complicated. He wasn't sure he could handle a budding riot. God knew he'd probably get the blame for anyone who got killed in the fighting.

It was so much easier when the marines handled security, he told himself, not for the first time. The planetary police had lobbied hard to take back security duties at the spaceport . . . It hadn't taken long for Jerry, at least, to realize that they'd claimed a poisoned chalice. *The marines were feared and respected even by the worst of the spacers.*

He turned the corner and swore out loud. The riot had spread onto the streets, sucking in people from all nine bars. He couldn't tell if there were two sides, or ten sides, or indeed any order at all. He tapped his communicator, requesting all available support, then raised his stunner. He honestly wasn't sure where to begin.

"Deploy," he snapped. He saw a young man fall, blood pouring from a gash on his face. "Stun them all!"

He triggered his stunner, firing a stun pulse at the nearest rioter. The man staggered, but didn't fall. Jerry blinked in astonishment, then remembered that naval uniforms were designed to absorb shocks. He lifted his stunner and shot the man in the face. He crumpled and hit the ground as Jerry turned his attention to the next rioter. His platoon opened fire at the same moment, aiming to scatter people. If they wanted to run and escape, he'd let them go. There was no time to set up barriers to pen them in the strip.

"Aim for bare skin," he snapped. He glanced at his communicator and saw no reply to his demand for reinforcements. He hoped that didn't mean there were other riots . . . The strip wasn't *that* large, surely? "Take them all down!"

A pair of naked women ran past him, screaming. He blinked in surprise, then remembered there was a brothel farther down the road. A trio of rioters was chasing them, calling out crude suggestions; Jerry stunned them all and watched, dispassionately, as they hit the ground. They'd be put on trial later, if the government didn't decide to sweep the whole incident under the rug. No one was entirely sure just who was responsible for governing the spaceport strip these days. It could get nasty if the king wanted to pardon his men or . . .

Jerry groaned. It was going to be a horrific mess . . .

"Bastards," someone shouted. "Get them!"

Jerry turned just in time to see a wall of men emerge from the nearest bar and charge the police line. He stunned the first two, but their comrades held them upright and used them as human shields while they closed the range. Jerry glanced at his men, then signaled a retreat . . .

too late. The rioters crashed into the policemen, sending them to the ground. One wrenched the stunner out of Jerry's hand, throwing it away as if it were a piece of junk; another drew back a fist and punched Jerry right in the helmet. The impact would have knocked him out, or worse, if his head had been unprotected. As it was, the blow had been so hard that Jerry felt it through the helmet. And then he felt fingers pulling at the buckles. An instant later, his head was unprotected and the rioters were all around him . . .

Shit.

♦ ♦ ♦

"I do need to know what happened," Governor Rogan said. He sat on one side of the desk, watching her. "And you might be able to tell me."

Captain Sarah Henderson hesitated. She'd thought twice before accepting the invitation to the spaceport hotel. On one hand, Governor Rogan was a colonial. He wasn't a prissy aristocrat who thought he was smart simply because he'd won the birthright lottery. But, on the other hand, asking her for her opinion about her superior officers was a gross breach of military etiquette. She'd heard too many rumors over the last few days—plots and counterplots, betrayals and counterbetrayals—to feel particularly comfortable doing anything that might feed them.

"I wasn't there," she said. "My part of the operation was elsewhere."

And was a total success, she added, in the privacy of her own mind. *I did everything I was asked to do.*

Governor Rogan let out a sigh. "Do you believe, in hindsight, that Admiral Falcone betrayed us?"

Sarah looked down at her hands. She didn't *know* Admiral Falcone, not really. She'd never even met the admiral until the civil war had begun . . . and their meeting had been brief, little more than a confirmation that Sarah would remain in command of her ship. They weren't best buddies, for sure. And yet . . . She knew of Admiral Falcone. The woman had earned her reputation.

"I don't think so," she said, finally. "There are . . . there would have been . . . easier and more effective ways to betray the entire fleet if she wanted. She could have ordered a surrender, after sailing into a trap, or simply collapsed the datanet."

"But she *did* sail into a trap," Governor Rogan said. "Did she see the trap coming?"

"I don't think so," Sarah repeated. She rose and walked over to the window. "Governor, with all due respect, what do you want from me?"

Her eyes narrowed as she peered over the spaceport strip. Were those *flames* in the distance?

"We cannot afford to lose the war," Governor Rogan said. "And we cannot afford to lose trust in our leaders."

"I agree," Sarah said. She glanced at him. "But you cannot afford to go looking for scapegoats right now."

"No," Governor Rogan said. "But we *do* need to show people that we are taking . . ."

Sarah's wristcom bleeped, urgently. She lifted it to her lips. "Henderson."

"Captain," Lieutenant Miscall said. "We've received an urgent request from the planetary police for a marine deployment. There's a riot in the spaceport, and the local policemen are overwhelmed."

"What?" Sarah looked into the darkness. Those *were* flames in the distance. "Why aren't they taking it to the flag?"

"I don't know, Captain," Lieutenant Miscall said.

Sarah's mind raced. A riot in the spaceport strip might be more than the local cops could handle, but they had riot control squads . . . Didn't they? At worst, they could call in the planetary militia or the army. They didn't need the marines, unless . . . She shivered, remembering some of the rumors she'd heard. Governor Rogan wasn't the only one looking for someone to blame. A dispute between a group of Tyrians and a group of Colonials could easily have led to violence.

Her mind raced. No planetary government would have called the marines unless the situation was urgent. It defied belief that any bureaucratic underling would have made the call without his superior's full support. And yet . . .

"Put the marines on alert, ready them for a quick insertion," she ordered. She knew she could order her marines to deploy, but it might only make things worse. "And then contact the flagship. Admiral Falcone will have to make the final call."

"Aye, Captain," Lieutenant Miscall said.

Governor Rogan stood and paced over to the window. "Trouble?"

"A riot," Sarah said as she closed the connection. "Could get nasty."

She frowned, trying to gauge how far they were from the fighting. The hotel was meant to be upmarket, according to the brochure she'd downloaded during the flight from her ship, but . . . Was it defended? Did it have a security team? Could the team keep the rioters out if they wanted in? Or . . . She shrugged, dismissing the thoughts as pointless. She doubted the rioters would get far, with or without her marines joining the fray.

And they asked me for help, she thought. *Why didn't they take it straight to the admiral?*

"I have to get back to my ship," she said. "I'm sorry I couldn't be more helpful."

"It's quite all right," Governor Rogan said. "But I'd like you to think about something, while you're on your way. Which side are you on?"

Sarah allowed herself a moment of irritation. "Ours."

"But if it came to a choice between supporting the king and supporting us, the colonials," Governor Rogan pressed. "Which side would you take?"

"I am a colonial," Sarah said, although she knew that wasn't an answer. "What do you mean, sir? Do you think there will be a split?"

"There are people who can go home, reasonably safely," Governor Rogan said. "And people who cannot hope for mercy, if they lose. Think about it."

He nodded, then turned away. "Good luck with your next mission, whatever it is," he added. "And watch your back. You never know who might try to put a knife in it."

Yeah, Sarah thought. *And are you one of them?*

CHAPTER TWENTY-FIVE

CALEDONIA

Kat wasn't sure what she'd expected after she'd walked out of the council chambers. She knew how she would have reacted if a junior officer had turned his back on her without permission; she was fairly sure she knew how her father would have reacted, although he would have known better than to try to turn someone into the scapegoat for a disaster that had been largely out of their control. She'd waited for two days, concentrating her efforts on repairing and reorganizing the fleet, before the king's office got in touch with her. Hadrian had invited her to a private dinner.

She had no idea, either, if that was a good or bad sign. A quicker summons might have indicated a decision made in haste, but . . . Two days should have been more than long enough for the king to consult with his councilors and make a final decision that satisfied everyone, if that was even possible. But then, she supposed too much had happened over the last two days for anyone to care about her. The handful of riots had put everyone on edge. Fifty-seven officers and crewmen were in the morgue, a further two hundred seventy in sickbay. She couldn't help thinking that she'd taken fewer casualties when she'd pitted her fleet against the Theocracy.

And then we knew who the enemy was, she reminded herself. *We weren't surprised when the Theocrats tried to kill us.*

She put the thought out of her mind as the shuttle landed neatly on the palace's landing pad, allowing her to disembark. There were four guards on duty now, the latter two wearing heavy armor . . . as if they expected a full-scale invasion to materialize out of nowhere at any moment. Kat frowned as they scanned and searched her, wondering grimly if the show had been laid on for her personally or if the king was feeling paranoid. Her intelligence staff had warned her of hundreds of threats made against the king's life. She would be surprised if some of his supporters weren't considering what sort of deals they could make if the king were to be removed from power or simply killed.

Sir Grantham met her as soon as she was ushered through the security door. "Right this way, Your Ladyship."

He's not calling me Admiral, Kat thought. A bad sign? Or a reminder that she was a noblewoman as well as a naval officer. *Things must have changed.*

She ignored Sir Grantham's attempts at making conversation as she followed him through a maze of corridors. There were more guards at every level, suggesting that the king didn't trust his own people any longer. Kat wondered, sourly, if he feared threats from his nearest and dearest . . . or if someone was merely engaging in a bit of empire building. Admiral Lord Garstang had built his own little empire while her back had been turned, re-creating the Admiralty with himself at the top. She wasn't sure if she should be impressed or horrified. The real test of the system would come when its creator retired . . . or died. If it couldn't outlast him, it was doomed.

Sir Grantham opened a pair of wooden doors. "Admiral Lady Falcone, Your Majesty."

Kat stepped past him and walked into the chamber. It was surprisingly small, for royal apartments. Small, but comfortable. A single table stood in the center of the room, with a pair of covered bowls and a bottle in the middle; two simple chairs sat on each side. The king sat on a sofa, drinking a glass of wine. Kat saluted him formally, then took the seat at the table he offered. She didn't relax. The king might have insisted that it was a private dinner, but there was no way it was *not* business. She had the feeling she wasn't going to like what she was about to hear.

The king stood. "I asked the kitchens to prepare something you liked, but they didn't know your tastes," he said. "They had to fall back on the old standbys."

Kat kept her face expressionless. On Tyre, the kitchen staffers were meant to keep track of who liked what . . . and serve it, upon demand. The king's kitchens had been reckoned second to none, once upon a time. He'd always been able to give his guests a good dinner. But now . . . She wondered, grimly, just how badly it had struck him. He was no longer even master of his house, not on Tyre. He was a king in exile.

"I had to eat naval rations," she said wryly. "I think I can cope."

The king smiled as he sat down, placing his glass beside his seat. The smile didn't quite touch his eyes.

"Yes. Yes, you can," he said. "Still . . ." He took another sip of wine. "Would you like a drink? There's some pretty good . . ."

"No, thank you," Kat said. She cocked her head. "Should *you* be drinking?"

"You sound like my governess." The king smiled, as one does at a joke that isn't particularly funny. "It's a bloody good thing you don't *look* like her."

"I suppose not." Kat eyed Hadrian, concerned. "How much *have* you been drinking?"

The king shrugged. "Does it matter?"

It might, Kat thought.

"It hasn't been a good week," the king said as he opened the nearest bowl. The smell of fish stew wafted across the table. "First the defeats . . . and then the riots. The brawls, I should say. I . . . I shouldn't be surprised, should I?"

"I'm afraid not," Kat said. "You've welded two different groups together, Your Majesty, groups that are not natural allies. The defeat widened the cracks between them."

"And accusations of treachery only made the cracks wider," the king said. "It isn't just *you*, you know. There are others . . ."

"I read the reports," Kat said. It would be weeks before the investigations into the riots reached any conclusions, but the general picture was already clear. The rioters had been angry at Tyrians, and Tyrian officers in particular. "Has anyone else been mentioned by name?"

"No one in the navy," the king said. "But there are all sorts of accusations being hurled about. Someone, sooner or later, is going to get hurt."

"People have already been hurt," Kat said bluntly. The reports had noted that the highest-ranking officer to be injured during the rioting had been a lieutenant commander. He'd hardly been a commanding officer, let alone a flag officer. "And it will only get worse if you don't act fast."

"I don't know what to do." His words were almost a cry for help. "Whatever I do, I'll lose *something*."

"There are very few perfect choices." Kat picked up her spoon and tried her stew. It was stronger than she'd expected, but definitely tasty. "All you can do is pick the best possible option and cope with it unflinchingly."

The king shook his head, wordlessly, and took another swig from his glass. "If I do one thing, I anger the noblemen in my camp; if I do the other, I anger the colonials. And I can't afford to lose either of them."

You could probably do without two-thirds of the noblemen, Kat thought. Her lips twitched in grim amusement. *But what would that imply for your future rule?*

"We've had offers of help from the outside," the king added, after a moment. "But they'll come with a price."

Kat felt her eyes narrow. "From the outside?"

"A couple of the other Great Powers," the king said. "The Star Union of Marseilles has expressed particular interest. They're going to be dispatching an ambassador in the next few weeks, according to their last message. And there are others."

"Perhaps," Kat mused.

She considered it, doubtfully. The Theocratic War had left the Commonwealth with a pronounced edge over the other Great Powers, both in number of hulls and military-grade technology. Even the peacetime establishment had been strong enough to give any combination of interstellar powers a very hard time, if they wished to attack the Commonwealth. She had no doubt that the Star Union of Marseilles and the other Great Powers were working frantically to duplicate the Commonwealth's technology as well as build up their fleets before the Commonwealth turned expansionist, but . . . She frowned as a nasty thought occurred to her. Marseilles could close the gap very quickly if it acquired actual *specimens* of Commonwealth tech.

And the king could give them everything from pieces of technology to detailed plans and specifications, she thought. *They would demand nothing less if they took sides during our civil war.*

"It would be risky," she said. "We might win one war, only to find ourselves facing another."

The king shook his head. "The Frogs won't pick a fight with us," he said. "They were happy to sit back and watch as *we* fought the Theocracy to a standstill, then carried the war into their space and crushed them in their lair."

"They were some distance from the Theocracy," Kat reminded him. "And I'm sure they used the time well."

"Quite." The king glanced down at his empty glass, then poured himself another. He hadn't even touched his stew. "My ambassadors will discuss all such matters with them."

"Please don't make any hasty decisions," Kat said. "If the House of Lords hears about it . . ."

"The bastards would sell their own grandmothers if they thought it would make them a handful of crowns," the king snapped. "And you know it."

Kat put her spoon down and *looked* at him. "Why did you call me here?"

The king looked back at her, then turned away. Kat felt her heart sink. She was to be fired, then. She supposed she shouldn't be surprised. She'd always had enemies, but the defeat had given them teeth and a cause. Earl Antony and Governor Rogan made strange bedfellows, yet . . . They had something in common. No doubt they'd agreed to work together long enough to get rid of her, then resume their scheming and intriguing around the king. She wondered, idly, who'd supported her. She didn't have a network of friends and allies, not outside the navy. Hell, very few naval officers were loyal to her personally.

"It has been decided that you cannot continue to serve as the commander of our principle naval unit," the king said. "I have, reluctantly, been forced to agree."

Kat felt numb. "I see."

"Accordingly, you will be given command of a battlecruiser squadron and sent off on an inspection voyage," the king continued. "You will, of course, continue to hold your seat on my privy council, but your position in our war council will be held by Admiral Garstang."

"I'm sure he will do a good job," Kat said, struggling to keep anger out of her voice. She had served the king faithfully. She didn't deserve to have her command taken from her, not like this. And yet, if they'd lost faith in her, they might have no choice. They couldn't afford to keep her in place if they didn't trust her. "And I assume Commodore Higgins will take over the superdreadnoughts?"

"No," the king said. "Commodore Ruben will take command."

He'll get a lot of people killed, Kat thought. "Your Majesty . . ."

"I had to fight hard to convince everyone to accept Commodore Ruben as the commanding officer," the king said. "They wanted it to go to a colonial."

Not all of them, Kat guessed. She couldn't see any of the king's aristocratic supporters being keen on a colonial candidate. But then, there weren't any reasonable colonial candidates for the post. She wondered, sourly, just how much horse trading had been going on behind the scenes. *What did Governor Rogan demand in exchange for supporting Commodore Ruben's promotion to Admiral?*

Kat leaned back in her chair. "It is a mistake, Your Majesty," she said flatly. "Commodore Ruben's . . . aggression is more suited to a heavy cruiser squadron, not the line of battle. He will be unable to resist the temptation to . . ."

The king held up his hand. "The decision has been made," he said coolly. "And I would *appreciate* it if you refrained from undermining your successor."

Kat felt a hot flash of pure anger. Commodore Ruben had undermined *her*! She wanted to take a shuttle over to his flagship and wring his scrawny neck. She wanted . . . She told herself, sharply, not to be silly. Nothing would be gained by undermining her successor, not now.

"If that is your command, Your Majesty, I will obey," Kat told him. "But I feel that it is a serious mistake."

"So you have said," the king commented. "And, over the last two weeks, there have been quite a few people telling me that *your* appointment was a serious mistake. They feel that you can go home at any moment."

Kat resisted the urge to roll her eyes. Her eldest brother wouldn't welcome her home. And Peter might find it impossible to plead for leniency for her, even though she *was* his sister. She'd simply done too much. She would be lucky if she was simply given her trust fund and told to fornicate off. The thought gave her a bitter pang. If Pat had lived, if they'd purchased their freighter and set out to explore . . . She wouldn't have fought in the civil war on either side.

But Pat was dead.

"I think my brother isn't going to be happy to see me," she said dryly. "And that goes for you too."

"They've probably already found some distant relative who can take the crown," the king agreed. "I'm surprised they haven't formally dethroned me yet."

"That would make negotiations difficult," Kat pointed out. Technically, a king couldn't be dethroned without a chance to defend himself; practically, it was unlikely that the king, any king, would agree to return to a world controlled by his enemies to make a speech hardly anyone would heed. "It would be nailing their colors to the mast, would it not?"

"Perhaps," the king said. "Which makes it all the more important that we find a way to take the offensive, as soon as possible. The House of Lords is not going to sit on its hands and fiddle while we repair the fleet."

"Yes, sir," Kat said. She considered a handful of possibilities, then shrugged. Admiral Lord Garstang and Commodore—Admiral—Ruben were in command now. She'd send them her suggestions, and they could do what they liked with them. She had a more important problem. "Your Majesty . . . Hadrian . . . are you well?"

"I never realized just how hard it would be to hold the coalition together," the king said. He lifted his wineglass and seemed surprised to find it empty. "Everyone wants something, everyone wants something *now* . . . and if they don't get it, they'll pick up their toys and go home. And, no matter what I do, I can't satisfy *everyone.* There will be people who will be disappointed and . . . they'll betray me. The only person who seems to be fully on my side is Drusilla."

"And me," Kat said. "You wouldn't be the first person to have doubts."

"She's always telling me to be strong, that people will fall into line if I make it clear that I am in charge," the king said, as if Kat hadn't spoken. "But they don't fall into line, no matter how hard I press. I have to keep promising things and . . ."

Just like a junior officer. Kat felt cold. William had commented, once, that the king was a junior officer well out of his depth. *And there are no seniors he can ask for help.*

"Things will be easier soon," she said finally. "There are always teething troubles."

The king looked up. "Really?"

"Always." Kat smiled, as reassuringly as she could. "Everything has teething troubles, from a simple raid on an enemy convoy to an all-out attack on the enemy homeworld. Pieces of tech don't work as well in the field as they do in the lab, trained but inexperienced crew waver at their first taste of real combat . . . ships and crews have to be worked up before they can be taken into battle. Even the early years of settlement, on Tyre, had problems that stemmed from the rules not being tested. It takes time for things to settle down."

"I hope you're right," the king said. "I just get . . ." He shook his head. "I'm sorry, Kat. You deserve better."

It was a dismissal, Kat recognized. "I'm sure you did your best," she said, although she wasn't remotely convinced. "And I will continue to serve you on the battlecruisers."

"Sir Grantham will take you to your shuttle," the king added. "You'll be taken to your next command."

"Indeed." Kat wasn't pleased. She didn't have *much* on the super-dreadnought—she'd never had the time to *really* personalize the cabin—but she wasn't pleased with the thought of leaving packing to the orderlies. "I suggest you advise Commodore Ruben to keep my staff in place. They are trained and experienced, *and* they've worked together for the last year or so."

"I'll make sure of it," the king said. "And thank you. For everything."

Kat said nothing as she was ushered out of the chamber, her mind racing. A battlecruiser command was hardly a dismissal, let alone a court-martial with only one possible sentence, but still . . . The demotion felt like a slap across the face. For all she'd done for him . . . but then, he probably hadn't had a choice. She had too many enemies for him to defend her easily, too many people who suspected her, who wanted her gone . . .

I could go, Kat thought. *It would be easy to simply leave.*

She considered the idea briefly, then shook her head. She'd given the king her oath. And it would take a great deal to make her break her word.

CHAPTER TWENTY-SIX

Tyre

The Royal Palace felt . . . *eerie.*

Peter walked through the empty halls, trying not to notice the handful of close-protection agents who surrounded him. They'd advised him not to visit the palace, pointing out that the royal family had had secrets and the king might have left booby traps in his wake when he fled the planet. Peter had scoffed, insisting that the king hadn't had *time* to leave any unpleasant surprises behind for anyone who invaded his home, but now he wasn't so sure. There was a sense of pregnant anticipation in the air, as if the palace were just waiting for something to happen. He felt almost as if he were walking through a haunted house.

And you're letting your imagination run away with you, he told himself. He'd always kept his imagination under tight control, if only because his younger siblings would have mercilessly mocked any hint of childishness in their oldest brother, but there were times when it just wanted to run free. *The palace is empty. The staff have been taken away and interned. Any surprises have long since been uncovered.*

He reached a stairwell and started down, heading towards the lower levels. It hadn't surprised him to discover that the monarch had a secret underground complex, one under the underground complex everyone knew about. The palace was a center of government as much as it was a home to the king and his family. Falcone Manor had its own secrets, some of which would never be shared with anyone outside the family. But he *was* surprised by the sheer scale of the king's complex. It beggared belief that he'd managed to hide his command center from the aristocracy. But then, the king had commanded vast resources. Disguising extension work as sewer repairs or something equally innocuous wouldn't have been that hard.

And he had passageways leading to the sewers, just like something from a bad movie, Peter thought. He didn't laugh. His properties had their own set of secret entrances and exits. It wouldn't do to have the media follow his every move if he wanted to maintain certain secrets. *He could have slipped in and out of the palace whenever he wanted.*

He reached the bottom of the stairs and frowned. The wooden paneling was gone. The walls were plain concrete, unmarked save for a single sigil placed by the blast doors. Peter stepped through, marveling at their construction. He'd been told that the bunker would survive anything, save perhaps for shaped antimatter charges. And no one would risk using such weaponry on a planetary surface unless he wanted to render the entire planet uninhabitable. The king could have simply retreated to his bunker and waited.

But we wouldn't stop watching for him to come out, Peter thought, as he walked through the inner blast doors and into a giant situation room. *We wouldn't be able to get to him, but he wouldn't be able to harm us either.*

He looked around the chamber, feeling a chill running down his spine. There were dozens of consoles, all unmanned. The screens were dark. The holographic displays were switched off. The giant table, clearly designed for the king and his staff, was empty. The space felt abandoned, as if the king wasn't coming back any time soon. And yet, something was eerie about the setup. He heard a clattering sound in the distance and almost jumped despite himself. It was a relief when

Investigator Niles came into view. He snapped to attention as soon as he saw Peter.

"Your Grace," he said. He was a tall, dark man, dressed in an unmarked uniform that clearly identified him as an intelligence officer. "I didn't know you were coming."

"I came incognito," Peter said. He was mildly surprised someone at counterintelligence hadn't warned the investigator. Heads were going to roll when Niles got back to the office, hopefully metaphorically. "I wanted to see the complex for myself."

"It's pretty extensive," Niles said. He waved a hand at the floor. "There's an entire cluster of bedrooms, barracks, and supply chambers under our feet. Power generators, recyclers . . . I daresay this place could hold out forever, as long as the planet itself survived."

"It is impressive," Peter conceded. He glanced around the chamber, again. "Did the king leave any surprises behind?"

Niles looked pained. "The complex's datacores were wiped shortly before the king boarded his shuttle. I'm surprised they weren't physically destroyed, afterwards. He might have hoped the complex would remain undiscovered until his return to the planet."

"Maybe," Peter said. "Have you discovered anything interesting?"

"We're still digging our way through the datafiles," Niles said. "We *have* been able to recover traces of the wiped data, but most of it is a little . . . *jumbled.* I don't expect a *real* breakthrough, not in a hurry. That said . . ."

He paused. "We knew, of course, that the king had a private intelligence service as well as everything else. It's possible that this service was engaged in black-ops. There are hints in the files, many of which are tantalizingly incomplete. We may be barking up the wrong tree, Your Grace, but . . . the king may have been engaged in subversive operations for far longer than we realized. Perhaps even before he took the throne."

"Someone would have had to handle the dirty jobs," Peter mused. It was hard to find someone capable of handling the sensitive work, the work that simply couldn't be entrusted to anyone outside the family. "I take it the king was engaged in more than just industrial espionage?"

"We fear so, Your Grace." Niles leaned forward. "For one thing, we found a stash of compromising material. The king had blackmail material on at least two MPs . . . probably more. We just haven't recovered anything further yet."

"Ouch." Peter cursed under his breath. "What sort of blackmail material?"

"One MP was engaged in fraud," Niles said. "And the other was involved in . . . ah . . . sexual deviancy."

Peter could imagine. "What now?"

"So far, we haven't done anything with the material," Niles said. "But that will have to change, sooner rather than later. I have an obligation to report certain criminal offenses to my superiors."

"Sit on it for the moment," Peter said. "I'll discuss it with the war cabinet."

And see if we can turn the situation to our advantage, he added silently. He felt no pity for the MPs—they wouldn't have been compromised if they hadn't compromised themselves—but it would be a shame to throw away the opportunity to do *something* with the discovery before it was too late. *We might be able to feed the king false information.*

Niles nodded towards the dark consoles. "We're still trying to track down the remainder of the king's servants, Your Grace. We don't think they will all have fled to Caledonia, not when they could be more useful here. However, it won't be easy. The king didn't *have* to forge documents for them"—he shrugged—"and any documents they do have will pass inspection because they're real. We may find it impossible to get a lead on their locations."

Peter frowned. "What are they doing?"

"I don't know," Niles said. "Not yet. We're still trying to recover pieces of data from the wiped datacores. And the king could easily have created a whole web of fake companies and suchlike to hide just about anything. We could have a breakthrough this afternoon, Your Grace. Or it might be sometime in the next decade."

"They could be doing anything," Peter mused. "If, of course, they exist at all."

"We have to assume they do," Niles said. "The king didn't miss a trick."

"So it would seem," Peter said. "I assume you interrogated the servants?"

Niles looked as if he'd bitten into something sour. "The majority of the palace staff knew nothing, Your Grace. They were domestics and largely kept away from the restricted areas. The ones who might know something were given security implants. It was part of the price of their jobs."

"And so you can't learn anything from them," Peter said.

"No, Your Grace." Niles made a face. "The implants will react to everything from truth drugs and subtle conditioning to outright torture. If they think the bearer is being interrogated, they will kill the . . . ah, the bearer. We're reluctant to risk ending their lives by trying to outwit the implants. The king could afford the best."

He paused, then changed the subject. "Would you like a tour of the bunker?"

"Yes, please," Peter said.

He spent the next hour being shown around the massive complex before finally giving in to the demands of his office and returning to the aircar. The king had clearly been planning for something long before anyone else had realized that open conflict was looming on the horizon, although Peter wasn't sure what. Civil war? Or had the king assumed that he could simply take power in a bloodless coup or . . . He shook his head. Nothing to be gained by worrying about it now. He skimmed the latest report as the aircar came to rest on the landing pad on the roof of Falcone Tower. They'd just have to wait and see what the king had been hiding.

Yasmeena met him as he entered the building. "Your Grace, Masterly and Masterly have requested an urgent meeting."

It couldn't have been that urgent, or you would have called me directly, Peter thought. *But they wouldn't have risked asking for a meeting if* they *didn't think it was urgent.*

"I'll see them in my office," he said. "And ask the staff to bring tea and coffee."

"Yes, Your Grace," Yasmeena said.

Peter put his concerns to one side as he walked down to his office. The two accountants were waiting outside, looking deeply worried. Peter felt cold, wondering just what they were going to tell him now. He didn't want more problems. There were times when he wondered how his father had made it look so easy. He'd juggled being on the war cabinet with being the CEO of the Falcone Corporation and . . . Peter shook his head. Perhaps the old man *hadn't* found it easy. He'd just been skillful enough to hide his problems beneath an urbane veneer.

He took his seat and motioned for the accountants to sit on the other side of the desk. "I assume this is urgent," he said. "Let us skip the formalities."

"Yes, Your Grace." Alex Masterly slotted a datachip into the projector. A holographic image appeared above the desk. "As you know, we have been assessing the economic situation and . . ."

"I had *better* know that," Peter said, sarcastically. The corporation might be too big for him to be aware of everything that was going on, let alone micromanage every last aspect of its operations, but he kept a close eye on the important details. "What do you have?"

"A potential headache," Alex Masterly said. "I believe . . ."

"Get to the point," Peter snapped. He could feel a *real* headache starting to build behind his temples. "Now."

Alex Masterly looked shocked. "We have a looming supply problem, Your Grace. And one that cannot be solved in a hurry."

Peter leaned forward. "Explain."

The two accountants exchanged glances. "The long and short of it, Your Grace, is that we were . . . *encouraged* . . . to purchase various components from factories located outside the system. The king was keen to encourage industrial development across the Commonwealth, and he pushed hard for us to source basic components from newly built factories, with the intention of creating a demand that those factories would fill. This would allow the factories to pay for themselves, then start responding to demand from their homeworlds and shape indigenous starship construction . . ."

"And boost the overall economy," Peter finished. "I am familiar with the program."

Alex Masterly's face was so impassive that Peter *knew* he was nervous. "You may not be familiar with the implications, Your Grace. Our facilities for producing such components ourselves were . . . repurposed during the wartime years. Ah, the *last* wartime years. We assumed that we would continue to receive supplies from factories that are now behind enemy lines and . . . and have no interest in supplying us in any case. It will not be long before the lack of certain components starts to bite."

Peter bit off a curse. "Are you telling me that our navy is going to grind to a halt because we can no longer produce components we *need*?"

"Not exactly, Your Grace," Alex Masterly said. "The components are very basic, after all. We can repurpose our industrial nodes to produce them. But this will obviously limit our production of other components. We might wind up with a surplus of basic . . . well, *something* starships need and a shortage of . . . missile warheads or something. I'm not a military man."

"I'll have to discuss it with the Grand Admiral," Peter said. He sucked in his breath. "How the hell did we get blindsided by this?"

Clive Masterly looked embarrassed. "Technically, Your Grace, we own the factories," he said. "And, as such, they were incorporated into our economic projections. But . . ."

"The factories are now in enemy territory," Peter snapped. "And they aren't going to send us *anything.*" He straightened up. "Does this give the king any advantage?"

"I'm not a military man, Your Grace," Alex Masterly repeated. "My opinions of such matters . . ."

"Speculate," Peter snapped.

Alex Masterly took a breath. "The original project included a considerable number of tech transfers," he said. "However, nearly everything that was transferred to the colonies was civilian grade. The working assumption, prior to the war, was that the colonies would continue to purchase their military gear from us. That, of course, was blown out of the water by the war itself. However . . ."

He looked down at his hands. "My belief is that this doesn't give them any additional military punch. But I am not a military man. I may be wrong."

"Duly noted," Peter said. He rubbed his temples. "How did we get into this mess?"

"The king was insistent that we assist the colonies in developing their economies," Alex Masterly said. "There was a demand for industrial capacity, Your Grace, but a shortage of funds for its development. The king solved two problems at once. No one anticipated civil war."

Of course not, Peter thought. *No one apart from the king, who was laying the groundwork to ensure a victory . . .*

"I'll consult with the war cabinet," he said. "How long until the shortage becomes serious?"

"It's hard to determine, as it depends on what assumptions are fed into the simulators," Clive Masterly said. "The worst case suggests that we will start to feel the pinch within two to three months, while the best case hints that it will be at least nine months . . . perhaps longer. We really don't have any good figures regarding usage rates . . ."

"Too many variables," Peter mused.

"Yes, Your Grace." Alex Masterly nodded, too quickly. "The real problem is that we are bringing the naval reserve online. That creates a demand for components of all shapes and sizes, one that is inherently unpredictable. It might be considerably higher than I suggest, and then . . . the crunch would come all the sooner."

"I see," Peter said. "I want you to start planning to shift production as quickly as possible. Get projections to me by the end of the day. I'll discuss the matter with the war cabinet, and then we can get moving."

"Yes, Your Grace," Alex Masterly said. "I would also suggest that we shift back to a wartime economy. If we had a unified economy . . ."

"Might be practical." Peter cut him off. "But it is politically impossible, particularly now."

"Understood," Clive Masterly said. "Thank you for your time, Your Grace."

Peter dismissed them with a nod, then studied the holographic report. The accountants were right, damn them. How the hell had they missed the simple fact that a number of their factories were now behind enemy lines? The king really hadn't missed a trick. It was a neat way of weakening his prospective enemies, something that wouldn't cause any problems unless civil war broke out. Peter wondered, sourly, if the king had done it deliberately, or if it had merely been a happy accident. It was quite possible that the king had had a vague plan for civil war all along.

He isn't that good, Peter told himself. The king wasn't *stupid*, but he lacked experience. Peter had been working for the family since he'd graduated, moving from position to position until he could truthfully say he knew the corporation intimately. And if Peter had failed, or proved himself unworthy, he would have been sidelined long ago. The king's father hadn't been able to discard his son. *He's too clever by half.*

His terminal bleeped. "Your Grace, Investigator Niles is calling," Yasmeena said. "Should I put him through?"

"Please," Peter said. Niles wouldn't be calling unless it was urgent. "I'll speak to him here."

"Your Grace," Niles said. There was no visual, just audio. "I'm sorry for disturbing you."

"Don't worry about it," Peter said, curtly. "What is it?"

"We cracked another section of the king's files," Niles said. "It turned out that he effectively owned and operated the Falkirk Island complex."

Peter felt his eyes narrow. He'd heard of the complex. But where?

"It was done through cutouts," Niles added. "We wouldn't have put it together if the king's files hadn't told us where to go."

"And so?" Peter rubbed his forehead. "What does it mean?"

"Admiral Morrison died on Falkirk Island," Niles said. "There was an accident with the mindprobe. It was speculated that he'd been assassinated, but no one found proof . . ."

"I remember," Peter said. His father had insisted that Admiral Morrison's mystery patrons had murdered the admiral when he'd outlived his usefulness. "And that means . . . ?" The pieces fell into place. "Are you suggesting that the *king* was Admiral Morrison's patron? And his murderer?"

"Yes, Your Grace," Niles said. "That is *precisely* what I'm suggesting."

CHAPTER TWENTY-SEVEN

CALEDONIA

Under other circumstances, Kat thought, she would have loved her new command. A battlecruiser squadron was the perfect mix of speed and firepower, a cluster of ships capable of either outfighting or outrunning anything it might encounter. She might not be in the command chair, she might not be sole mistress of a ship, but . . . It was as close as she'd get for the remainder of her career. A battlecruiser squadron was every officer's dream.

But it was tainted, she knew, by the king's lack of faith in her. It hurt, even though she knew he'd had little choice; it felt as if she'd been betrayed, as if she'd been cast out. She walked the decks, inspecting her ships and whipping her new command staff into shape, all the while trying to keep her emotions in check. She'd done so much and yet . . . She'd been pushed to one side. It was galling to look at the system display and know that Commodore Ruben, now Admiral Ruben, was sitting in her chair, commanding her ships. Even the grim awareness that the superdreadnoughts weren't likely to see any action didn't console her.

And if the system is attacked, she reminded herself, *the superdreadnoughts will see more action than they might like.*

She sat in her ready room and read the latest set of reports. The news was grim. There hadn't been any more full-scale riots, thank the gods, but there *had* been an endless series of clashes between the king's supporters and the colonials. Accusations of treachery and betrayal had been thrown around like hand grenades, threatening to tear apart the fragile government before it could solidify into something permanent. And morale was threatening to go down the tubes. A starship that hadn't returned had been assumed to have defected to the enemy, a handful of commanding officers had requested relief . . . She shook her head, feeling a stab of pity for Admiral Lord Garstang. He was going to have to figure out a way to balance the competing factions, somehow. Kat suspected such a feat wasn't possible.

Her wristcom bleeped. "Admiral, I just heard from Supply," Commander Katie Hamada said. She was almost painfully young for her post, a colonial officer who'd been on the verge of seeking employment in the civilian sector before the civil war had broken out. "The missile loads we were expecting will be delivered this afternoon."

"Have them loaded aboard ship as soon as they arrive," Kat ordered. She couldn't wait to get away. She'd never liked hanging around in orbit when she wanted to take her ships into interstellar space and see what they could do, but right now she just wanted to leave Caledonia and the warring factions far behind. "And inform the crew that we will be leaving this evening. Anyone who doesn't make it back to the ship will be left behind."

"Aye, Admiral," Katie said.

Kat smiled, rather wanly. She hadn't really wanted to allow her crew to go on shore leave, but . . . She knew it would be weeks, if not months, before they had the chance to leave the vessel again. Her concerns about sending her crew planet-side didn't justify keeping them cooped up aboard ship. Besides, the spaceport strip was supposed to be *safe*. Martial law had been declared, with the marines and planetary militia patrolling heavily. It wasn't as if she were deliberately sending them into a trap.

And it might be their last chance to see home, she reminded herself. A quarter of her crew came from Caledonia. *We might not come back alive.*

She pushed the thought aside as she turned her attention to the shipboard reports. *Relentless* and her sisters were ready for battle, save for the missile shortage. Kat had the feeling that was going to bite, sooner or later. The colonials had started mass production of missiles and had actually been churning out a surprising amount during the last war, but the current supply wasn't enough. A lone superdreadnought could fire off a sizable percentage of their monthly production in a single engagement. *Relentless* had fewer tubes, but she was designed for rapid fire.

Her intercom bleeped again. "Admiral, we were just pinged by *John Galt*," Katie said, slowly. "Her commander is requesting permission to come aboard."

Kat frowned. *John Galt?* The name meant nothing to her. A colonial vessel? Or . . . or what?

"Is he?" She tapped her terminal, trying to pull up the file. "And who *is* he?"

"He said you'd know him." Katie sounded embarrassed. "He had the right codes and everything. I . . . His ship's IFF includes a pair of prewar intelligence codes. I don't know . . . Ah, should I call security?"

Kat glanced at the codes, then shook her head. "No," she said. She knew who was on that ship. She knew who it had to be. "Allow him to board, then have the marines search him before escorting him to my ready room."

"Aye, Admiral," Katie said. The relief in her voice was almost palatable. "I . . . I thought . . ."

"Don't worry about it," Kat said. "If it's who I think it is, we might have something to talk about."

She glanced around her ready room, making sure that anything classified was firmly out of sight, then waited. If her guess was correct, the marines would have to strip her guest of everything that might prove dangerous, directly or indirectly, before escorting him to her quarters. And if she was wrong . . . She shook her head, again. She'd welcome the diversion.

The hatch hissed open. A tall man wearing a basic shipsuit was shown into the compartment. Kat rose in welcome. "Commodore McElney," she said. "It's a pleasure to meet you at last."

"Lady Falcone," Scott McElney boomed. William's brother smiled at Kat. "You're truly as beautiful as they say."

"It's astonishing what the media will say if you give them a great deal of money," Kat said. She knew she was beautiful, she'd been specifically engineered to be beautiful, but that was far from uncommon among the aristocracy. Her looks weren't anything *special*, not on Tyre. "Or what people will say if they think it'll flatter you."

"And smart too," Scott said. He took the seat she indicated. His body seemed to flop slightly, as if he were too big for the real world. "You'll make someone very happy one day."

Kat felt a flicker of pain, which she ignored. William had told her, years ago, that his brother had a habit of trying to annoy people. He'd developed it as a young man, back when his family had gone through hell . . . Kat understood, although she found it more amusing than annoying. She'd heard a great deal worse from people who were supposed to be on her side.

She sat behind the desk. "I'm surprised you kept the codes. I would have thought you'd have scrapped them."

"Ah, you never know what will come in handy until it does." Scott crossed his legs, leaning back in his chair with an air of studied casualness. "And then, if you're unlucky, you'll have time to realize what you had . . . too late to actually make any use of it."

Kat nodded, curtly. "I'd like to chat for longer," she lied, smoothly. William had said that his brother was only tolerable in small doses. Five minutes after meeting Scott for the first time, Kat understood precisely what he'd meant. "But time is not on my side."

"Of course." Scott rested his hands in his lap. "Your boss has put out a call for supplies. I rather thought I might inquire as to terms."

"The king put out a call," Kat agreed. "Why not go to him directly?"

Scott leered cheerfully. "You think a lowly shipping agent such as myself could speak directly to the king?"

Kat felt her cheeks heat. "Point," she conceded ruefully. She'd grown too used to being able to speak to Hadrian at any moment. She doubted she could do *that* now, even though she was still on the privy council. "But he does have agents."

"I thought it might be better to make a low-key approach to you," Scott said. He waved at her, cheekily. "Hi."

"Hi." Kat felt her patience begin to fray. "What are you offering?"

"You might be surprised," Scott said. "We have sources everywhere. Supply depots, factories, hidden installations . . . We can get you just about anything you might want, given time."

"Really." Kat had her doubts. The House of Lords had been tightening security at weapon and supply depots even before the civil war had broken out. *Someone* had emptied one of the depots, after all. "You're saying you can get *anything*?"

"Pretty much," Scott said. He leaned forward. "Of course, we would require something in return."

"Of course," Kat echoed.

She studied Scott for a long moment. Strange. He looked very much like his brother, but different . . . bigger and bulkier, without ever crossing the line into being fat. And there was an edge to him that William lacked. Scott had endured a harder life, one that had left its mark. The bonhomie couldn't disguise the fact that he could and would sell everything and everyone, if it ensured that he would come out ahead. William had once commented that his brother would happily take money from the Theocracy, or join the slave trade, or do anything . . . as long as it paid. Kat rather feared William was right.

"I may not be able to bargain with you," she said shortly. "What do you want?"

"We want to go legal," Scott said, simply. "But, at the same time, we want to maintain our own rules. We want to buy and sell freely, without having to worry about planetary tariffs or corporate monopolies or anything that might impede free trade. We want to be legitimate traders."

"Whatever you are actually carrying in your holds," Kat mused. She understood, better than she cared to admit. Free traders and independent spacers kept prices down, irritating the larger shipping combines. They retaliated by establishing semilegal monopolies, locking out the independents. "It might be a hard sell."

"Even though we're offering something the king wants," Scott commented. "There will never be a better chance to win the war outright."

"No," Kat agreed. The king might like the idea, and the colonials might go for it, but some of his supporters would be horrified. She doubted the ones who envisaged themselves returning in triumph and taking control of their family corporations would be inclined to cut their own throats. "It's something you'll have to ask the king himself."

She studied her fingertips for a moment. "I can put you in touch with one of the king's . . . assistants. He'll see that your offer gets considered."

"The offer won't be open forever," Scott said. "There are factions that think we should dicker with the corporations instead."

And those factions might include you, Kat thought. The smugglers might prefer to deal with the king, Hadrian needed them more than they needed him, but they weren't dependent on coming to terms with him. *You have no intention of being on the wrong side of this war.*

"That's something you will have to mention to the king's assistant," she said. She'd call Sir Grantham. He'd be able to handle the matter, which might keep him from scheming for a few hours too. "On the record, I wish you luck."

Scott arched an eyebrow. "And off the record?"

Kat's lips twitched. "Off the record, do *not* try to pressure the king into making a decision. He hates that. He will happily cut off his nose to spite his face if he thinks it's . . . giving him laws. He's too mulish to react well to any sort of pressure."

And he bitterly resents it when someone does *manage to give him laws*, she added in the privacy of her own mind. Her father had said that, years ago. *And that isn't good for anyone.*

"I'll bear that in mind," Scott said. "But we're not supplicants. We're striking a bargain."

"Quite," Kat agreed.

She met his eyes, just for a moment. "Have you heard from your brother?"

"Not since he left Asher Dales," Scott said. "I've run a handful of trading missions up there over the last couple of months. Not much to buy and sell, not now, but you never know what'll happen if you get in on the ground floor. I'm hoping to leverage my contacts into something new, particularly if the interstellar corporations stay out for the next few years."

"They might," Kat said. The House of Lords had been withdrawing from the region over the last year, and after the civil war had started, they'd effectively pulled out the remainder of their forces. "I don't think they'll want to return until they've solved their current economic crisis."

"We shall see," Scott said. He looked back at her, evenly. "Do you want me to take a message? One perhaps that you can't send through the StarCom? You never know who might be listening."

Kat hesitated. She was tempted, but . . . but what could she say?

"I could also have one passed to your brother," Scott added. "Or someone else on Tyre. Just say the word."

"No," Kat said. "But thank you."

She tapped her console, sending a brief message to Sir Grantham. It would be interesting to see how quickly he responded and arranged a meeting. It would show just how much influence she had left, with both the king and his courtiers. And if Sir Grantham blew Scott off . . . She made a mental note to check on progress before she departed. It would be a shame if the opportunity to strike a deal was missed just because Sir Grantham was putting politics ahead of practicality.

"You can go down to the surface and take a room in the spaceport strip," she said when she'd finished. "You'll be contacted there."

"Good," Scott said. He stood. "I thank you."

He studied her thoughtfully, an unreadable expression on his face. "And the offer remains open, whatever happens. I'll be happy to relay a message to Tyre if you wish."

"We'll see," Kat said.

She called the marines, gave orders for Scott to be escorted back to his shuttlecraft, and watched as he left her ready room. It was hard to think badly of him, if only because he looked so much like his brother. She *thought* the offer was sincere, but . . . She wasn't sure. William would have meant it. His brother—the smuggler, the mercenary—wouldn't be so keen to risk himself for a cause. Or even for his closest friend. He'd been betrayed by his homeworld, and now . . . Now he cared for no one.

And his homeworld is a radioactive nightmare, Kat thought. *No one will ever live there again.*

She glanced at her inbox as she sat down, then rested her head in her hands. She was alone. Pat was dead. Her father was dead. William . . . was hundreds of light years away and on the wrong side. She didn't have any real friends on *Violence*, let alone *Relentless*. There was no one she could talk to, no one she could trust . . . She couldn't even talk to the king. She wondered, morbidly, just how different things would have been if Pat had lived. He would have come with her, she was sure. She could have shared her doubts and concerns with him, and he would have offered her good advice.

William would have advised me not to support the king, she mused. *But he would have been wrong.*

She sighed, bitterly. She'd never really understood why her father had cherished his few real friendships, not until she'd reached flag rank. The people she met were either her subordinates, people who couldn't befriend her, or people who wanted something from her. And her father had the same problem . . . Peter had it now, she assumed. She was pretty sure he was surrounded by supplicants, doing whatever it took to attract his attention. His wife was going to *love* it . . .

And I am alone, she thought. A grim thought. She'd never had many friends. Even the small armies of sycophants who'd surrounded her older siblings had ignored her as much as possible, beyond a handful known more for flattery than common sense. Everyone had known she wouldn't inherit unless something went very wrong. *I don't have anyone to talk to.*

She allowed herself a moment of self-pity, then sat upright and tapped the terminal. A starchart snapped into existence, displaying their planned schedule. She'd chosen it personally, ensuring that they'd visit a number of wavering worlds in hopes of keeping them loyal to the king. She was grimly aware that some worlds might switch sides if they saw *anyone's* warships enter their system, but it would have to do. She and her ships would be needed back at Caledonia eventually. By then, the king might have decided on his next course of action.

And the House of Lords might mount its own offensive. She had no doubt William wouldn't allow the grass to grow under his feet. He'd want to take the offensive as soon as possible. And Grand Admiral Rudbek—no fool, for all his political connections—would probably listen to William's advice. *We might be called back at any moment.*

Shaking her head, she stood. There was no point in worrying, not now. All she could do was hope for the best . . .

. . . And prepare, as best as she could, for the worst.

CHAPTER TWENTY-EIGHT

TARLETON

"Admiral," Captain Lucy Cavendish said as she stepped into William's ready room. "Do you have a moment?"

William glanced at the display. The fleet was nearing its target—he'd picked Tarleton, after some careful consideration—but they had nearly an hour before they had to go to battlestations. He could take some time off, if he wanted. They'd been in transit for nearly two weeks, and he was a little surprised that his flag captain hadn't talked to him before, but it didn't matter. *Something* always demanded immediate attention.

"I do," he said gravely. "What can I do for you?"

He felt an odd flicker of fondness for his flag captain, even though they'd met for the first time only three weeks ago. Lucy Cavendish reminded him of Kat, right down to the family connections pushing her up the ladder, even if she didn't want to climb so rapidly; indeed, in many ways, they could almost be sisters. Lucy had long, dark hair—no one had dared to tell her she needed to cut it short, just like Kat—but otherwise they were very similar. The only real difference was that the Cavendish Corporation was in serious trouble, barely kept alive through emergency loans and other financial shenanigans William didn't pretend to understand. Lucy might discover, if she hadn't already, that the family name wouldn't be enough to protect her from a real screwup.

And I need to keep an eye on her, he thought as he motioned her to a chair. *She needs experience before she's ready to take command.*

He felt a flash of déjà vu as Lucy sat, resting her hands in her lap. She *was* very much like Kat, except . . . This time, *he* was the commanding officer. He was her superior. He could . . . He smiled, inwardly. He might be the admiral, but there were limits to his power. He could issue orders to her, yet he *couldn't* issue orders to her crew. *She* had to rely his commands, and technically she could refuse . . . if, of course, she wanted to find herself in front of a Board of Inquiry. He shrugged, dismissing the thought. He knew better than to put someone in such a position. He'd known commanding officers who hadn't.

"I was wondering . . . ," Lucy said. She clasped her hands together, tightly. "We're about to attack a colony world. And *you're* a colonial."

"I am," William confirmed.

Lucy looked at her pale hands. "Are you *comfortable* with it? With . . . attacking your own people?"

"I was born on Hebrides," William reminded her. "And Hebrides is *gone*."

"But Tarleton is still a colony world," Lucy insisted. "Doesn't it bother you?"

William studied her for a long moment. "There are more than forty colonies, depending on how you count," he said. The handful of worlds settled directly from Tyre hadn't even considered joining the king. "And that means there are forty different *types* of colonial."

"Who are currently united against us," Lucy said. "Are you really not bothered?"

"No one who has seen war is enthusiastic about war," William said carefully. "And I am dismayed at the speed with which both sides plunged towards igniting a second war. I feel that there were still grounds for compromise, before the shooting started."

He held up a hand before she could speak. "Yes, there is a part of me that feels that I am doing the wrong thing. That I am waging war on my people, on the Commonwealth, rather than on our shared enemies. But we have no choice. The king has to be stopped."

"You might be killing your fellow colonials," Lucy pointed out.

"The fact *has* crossed my mind," William said. "There are—there *were*—other officers and crewmen from Hebrides. But that doesn't change the simple fact that the king has to be stopped.

"There's no such thing as the *perfect* choice," he added, carefully. "Everything you do, whatever you choose, will bring costs as well as benefits. If we'd stood up to the Theocracy earlier, before it took control of the Gap, we might have stopped its expansion before it could threaten our inner worlds. But if we'd done so, it would have, relatively speaking, cost us far more. Here . . ."

He shrugged. "I'm not keen on waging war. But this war has to be ended as soon as possible. And that means gritting our teeth and getting on with it."

"Yes, sir," Lucy said.

"It's like going to the dentist and having a rotten tooth removed," William commented. "It hurts like hell to have it taken out, but you feel better afterwards."

Lucy looked blank. Tooth decay was rare, almost unknown, on Tyre. There were genetic tweaks and vaccines that countered it, ensuring that the population had perfect teeth from birth to death. On Hebrides, on the other hand . . . He shuddered. He would sooner be scourged by a Theocratic Inquisitor than visit his childhood dentist again. The man had been a sadist of the highest order.

William met her eyes. "Will that be all?"

"I understand, I think," Lucy said. "And thank you."

She stood. William watched her go, feeling old. Lucy would probably outlive him . . . *Kat* and her family would outlive him. Peter Falcone was pretty much the same age as William, and yet . . . His genetic heritage would ensure a life span of nearly two hundred years, assuming he didn't meet a violent end. William had to smile at the thought. There would be hundreds of ambitious young noblemen waiting in the wings for their parents to die . . . It wouldn't be long before one of them decided to take matters into their own hands. And God alone knew what would happen then.

I won't live to see it, he thought, as he turned back to his work. *And Kat may not live long enough either.*

He worked patiently until the GQ alarm started to ring, at which point he rose and walked calmly into the CIC. HMS *Belfast* had been designed as a command ship, unlike *Lightning* and *Uncanny*; she'd had no trouble hosting William and the two staffers he'd brought with him. He'd hoped to bring an entire fleet, instead of just two squadrons of heavy cruisers, but Grand Admiral Rudbek had overruled him. The war cabinet had flatly refused to allow any superdreadnoughts to be released for service elsewhere until the reserves were finally brought online. William understood their logic, but the decision was irritating. They'd passed up their best chance to win the war in a single blow.

"Admiral," Commander Isa Yagami said. "We will leave hyperspace in twenty minutes."

William took his seat, concentrating on projecting an image of calm. "Establish the datanet, then establish secondary and tertiary networks. I do *not* want any breakage in the command and control system."

"Aye, Admiral," Yagami said. He looked as if he wanted to ask *why*, but didn't quite dare. "Primary network going online . . . now."

"*Belfast* is a known command ship," William said, taking pity on the younger man. He'd always disliked not knowing the reasoning behind his orders too. "The enemy will have no trouble picking us out of the squadron. And then they'll throw everything at us. We don't want them to break the network if they take us out."

He leaned back in his chair, choosing to ignore the waves of uncertainty and fear running around the compartment. They'd known they would fly straight into the teeth of enemy fire, of course, but it hadn't quite dawned on them they would be targeted personally. William understood. It had been hard—not impossible, but very difficult—for command ships to be identified and destroyed during the war. The Theocracy had found such acts almost impossible. But the king's forces had access to naval databases. They'd *know* that *Belfast* was a command ship.

And I couldn't change ships without putting our schedule even further back, William thought. *In hindsight, that might have been a mistake.*

"We'll be leaving hyperspace in five minutes," Yagami reported. "Captain Cavendish is bringing the ship to battlestations."

William nodded, bracing himself as the final seconds ticked away. It was customary for a fleet to pause in hyperspace, gathering itself for the attack before it entered the target system, but he hadn't bothered. They'd wasted too much time getting the squadron ready to go. Besides, the analysts insisted Tarleton should be an easy target. The colony's defense force couldn't stand up to them . . . he thought. If they were smart, they'd retreat at once.

It isn't as if we're going to scorch the planet clean of life, he thought. He'd made it absolutely clear that there would be no atrocities. He'd told his subordinates that he'd personally kill anyone who committed a crime against the planet's population. And he'd meant it. *There's nothing to be gained by trying to stop an unstoppable force.*

Belfast shuddered as she plunged through the vortex, returning to normal space. William glanced around, silently noting who looked queasy. He'd grown used to the sensation over the decades he'd spent in naval service, but most of his subordinates were young. It was a shame that more staffers couldn't be drawn from experienced officers, yet . . . He shook his head. A staff job was often seen as a death sentence, at least for an officer's career, something he intended to correct if he ever had the chance.

"Deploy recon drones," he ordered as the display started to fill with icons. "And transmit the surrender demand."

"Aye, Admiral," Yagami said.

William barely heard him. He was too busy studying the display. Tarleton was more developed than he'd realized, with dozens of large settlements scattered across the surface and a handful of industrial nodes and settled asteroids floating in orbit. The planetary defense force was rushing to the alert, gunboats already launching as the remainder of the ships came to life. William allowed himself a moment of relief as the enemy icons came into view. They'd caught the defenders by surprise. He'd feared the king's agents would have provided some warning.

"Admiral, some of the freighters are running," Yagami said. On the display, a handful of freighters opened vortexes and vanished into hyperspace. "They're ignoring our message."

"Ignore them, as long as they don't pose a threat." William's eyes found the StarCom, floating defiantly in orbit. "They're not going to surrender as long as there's a chance they can escape."

He felt a flicker of sympathy for the independent spacers. They'd hate to be grounded, they'd hate to have their ships confiscated . . . Even if the courts ruled in their favor, it would still be years before they saw their ships again. Nothing would be gained by chasing the freighters down, not as far as he could see. He wouldn't waste his time. As long as they fled as far as they could, he wouldn't pay any attention to them.

"The enemy fleet is forming up, sir," Yagami said. "They're taking up position in front of the planet."

William's eyes narrowed. Someone had been busy. Nineteen ships, including three relatively modern heavy cruisers and an outdated battlecruiser . . . probably of UN design, he decided, although the ship's weapons and sensors would be modern enough. He wondered, idly, who'd sold the ship to Tarleton. She'd make a good training ship, outdated or not, but he doubted the planet could afford to crew her.

"Still no response to our signals," Lieutenant Elsa said. "They're not responding at all."

"So it would seem," William said. The range was closing rapidly. "Signal the fleet. Prepare to engage."

"Aye, Admiral," Yagami said. "We'll enter primary engagement range in three minutes."

"Hold fire," William ordered. "We'll engage when we enter secondary range."

"Aye, sir," Yagami said. If he thought it was an odd order, he kept it to himself. "We will enter secondary range in five minutes."

"Understood," William said.

He sucked in his breath as the range closed. Whoever was in charge on the other side was a cool customer, he decided, although his opponent didn't have many options. William found himself wishing that the enemy CO would just run, even though it meant he'd probably face the same ships at a later date. There was no need to kill thousands of men for a point of honor. Even if the ships were being run by skeleton crews, hundreds of men were still going to die.

"Entering secondary engagement range," Yagami said. "Admiral?"

"Fire," William ordered.

The command chair vibrated as *Belfast* unleashed a spread of missiles. The display updated rapidly, showing a wave of missiles, pitifully weak compared to a superdreadnought's broadside, as they raced towards their targets. The enemy fleet twitched, then returned fire. William's eyes narrowed as their missiles were launched. There were more incoming missiles than he would have expected, even with external racks. They must have bolted missile pods to their hulls, just to double and even triple their opening broadsides. They'd gambled everything on giving him a bloody nose with their opening salvo.

"Point defense is standing by, ready to engage," Yagami said.

"Good," William answered.

Another shudder ran through the ship as she fired her second salvo. William allowed his staff to handle the details as he watched the display, silently tracing the steady evolution of the engagement. The enemy point defense network *looked* tough, but clearly their datanet was somewhat lacking. His probes were already making progress on locating command and control nodes. If they were lucky, they would even pick out the enemy command ship.

"Their point defense is based on civilian gear," Yagami said. "Why . . . ?"

"It might have been all they had," William commented. His missiles were slamming home now, antimatter blasts knocking down shields and smashing armor. A handful of enemy ships were blown out of space before their crews could begin to evacuate. "And they were desperate."

He watched as the enemy missiles tried to slip through his point defense and slam into his shields. There were a *lot* of them, but they were trying to break through his defenses through sheer weight of numbers. The missiles were more advanced than anything the Theocracy had thrown at him, yet they weren't being used to their best advantage. He wondered, grimly, what had happened to the planet's spacers. The king might have called them away to serve in his fleet, leaving reservists in their place. That seemed about right.

The enemy battlecruiser fell out of formation, leaking plasma from a drive structure that had been outdated before the Breakdown. It had been a good design in her day, William recalled, but that day was long gone. He tapped a command into his console, ordering the gunners to spare the battlecruiser now she'd stopped firing. Her crew were trying desperately to escape, lifepods shooting out in all directions. William intended to pick them up as soon as the fighting was over. They wouldn't have much hope of survival otherwise. Planetary defenses might consider them hostile and blow them out of space if they tried to land.

At least the lifepods won't be used for target practice, not here, William thought. The Theocracy had done that, years ago. In hindsight,

Theocrats had clearly been trying hard to make sure that their population could expect no mercy from the Commonwealth. *They'll have the best chance to survive that we can give.*

He smiled as the remnants of the enemy fleet stopped firing. A handful of ships had survived, but they'd been pounded into scrap. He doubted there was anything to be gained from salvage, even if he tried to take the ships home. There certainly wouldn't be any prize money. The Admiralty had stopped offering more than the bare minimum of prize money for Theocratic warships after learning that most of them were held together with spit and baling wire. William hadn't really been able to disagree with the logic. There had been little gained by capturing enemy warships. It simply hadn't been worth the risk.

And none of these ships are worth anything, he thought tartly. *Not now.*

"Admiral, the orbital defenses are continuing to fire," Yagami reported. "But a number of habitable asteroids have stopped firing."

"Silence the ones that keep firing, then ready marine parties to board the orbital installations and recover drifting lifepods," William ordered. "Send a demand for their surrender directly to the asteroids. Don't give them time to check with the government. They can make that decision for themselves."

He took a breath. "And then signal the planetary government. Inform them that we are in possession of the high orbitals and call on them, once again, to surrender."

"Aye, Admiral."

William gritted his teeth. The planet was now defenseless, unless they were harboring a secret weapon out of a science-fantasy flick. They had to know it too. And they had to surrender . . . Didn't they? There was little hope of successful resistance once an enemy fleet held the high orbitals. Only Tyre and a handful of other worlds had the kind of planetary defense installations that might allow them to stand off an enemy fleet.

And if they don't surrender, William thought grimly, *I'll have no choice but to destroy them.*

CHAPTER TWENTY-NINE

TARLETON

"What the fuck do we do now?" Castellan Dalton's voice echoed around the conference chamber. "We can't just surrender!"

Premier Alistair Lipitor rubbed his temples with both hands. He'd had few qualms about joining Hadrian, although he was more interested in planetary issues and concerns than the king's right to rule his subjects. Tarleton owed the Commonwealth money, money they were quite unable to pay; he knew, all too well, that the economic crunch meant that the money would be demanded back sooner rather than later. The king had promised debt forgiveness to planets that joined his side . . . It had seemed like a good idea at the time. Alistair shuddered as he eyed the orbital display. Taking out the loans had *also* seemed like a good idea at the time.

"Let them land," Dalton snapped. "We will defy them!"

General Mulligan shook his head. "They control the high orbitals," he said. "There is no way we can fight a guerrilla campaign and drive them back to orbit. They can just drop KEWs on our people when they try to fight. There's no point in trying to resist . . ."

"And you call yourself a military man!" Dalton yelled. "Why did we spend so much money on the militia if it's fucking useless?"

Mulligan stared back at him, evenly. "We designed the militia for local defense, not for all-out war. We assumed that we'd have no choice but to fight if the Theocrats landed. Their occupation would be unbearable. Now"—he waved a hand at the map hanging on a concrete wall—"they can land wherever they want, they can prevent us from rushing reinforcements to the landing sites, and if we decide to be stubborn, they can systematically tear the planetary infrastructure apart. They have no obligation to give us a fair chance by putting their forces within shooting range."

He took a long breath. "Mr. Premier, my considered opinion is that we should sue for terms."

"They'll ruin us," Dalton insisted.

"We were in a better place to negotiate *before* they killed our fleet," Mulligan pointed out, coldly. "Did the fleet even scratch their paint?"

"It showed them our resolution," Dalton thundered. "They have no stomach for a long war . . ."

"They don't *need* a long war," Mulligan said. "The Theocracy wanted to convert us. The Commonwealth, Tyre, merely wants to bring us back under their control. Hell, they don't need us. They can just hold the high orbitals and wait until the war is over before turning their attention back to us."

"Some planets drove the Theocrats back into space," Dalton pointed out. "They . . ."

"They had outside help," Mulligan countered. "And how much of the planet survived the war?"

"Enough," Alistair said. He shook his head. "The king isn't coming to our rescue."

"He will," Dalton said. "We just have to hold out. We sent a message . . ."

"It's a minimum of nine days from Caledonia to here." Mulligan cut him off again. "And that assumes that the king can dispatch a sizable force at once. It may take hours, perhaps even a day, for them to set out."

"We can survive ten days," Dalton said. "Can't we?"

"We don't even know there *is* a rescue force coming," Alistair said tiredly. "And the Tyrians could simply bombard everything of value on the planetary surface, then retreat if the king showed up. They don't have to land."

"They wouldn't *dare*," Dalton insisted. "There would be vengeance."

Alistair held up a hand. He understood Dalton's point, and the fear hiding behind his words. Dalton had built his political career on defiance. He'd run for office on a platform of debt repudiation, claiming, with the support of a number of well-paid economists, that the loans were actually designed to keep Tarleton from reaching her full potential. And the arguments had seemed convincing to enough voters to win him the second place in the government, only one step from the premiership itself. He couldn't back down now, even at gunpoint. The voters would kick him out of office in the next election cycle.

If there is a next election cycle, he thought. *The occupation government may not feel inclined to hold elections.*

He sighed. Dalton's position was more precarious than he might realize—no, he probably *had* realized. Technically, he could be prosecuted under Commonwealth law for urging Tarleton to repudiate its debts. The case would be judged by the Supreme Court on Tyre, hardly the most . . . unbiased place in the universe. Dalton could have the best case possible and still lose. The hell of it was that the corporations, under the law, would have the far better case.

"I think we have to face facts," he said. "The king is not coming. And even if he does . . ."

"If you surrender, I'll push for your impeachment," Dalton snapped. "The Chamber will not allow . . ."

"At least they'll be alive to impeach me," Alistair snapped back. He looked at Mulligan, ignoring his deputy. "Connect me to the enemy commander."

"Yes, Mr. Premier," Mulligan said. He didn't show any annoyance at being ordered around like a mere flunky. "I'll do so at once."

Alistair nodded, trying to paste a calm expression on his face as he waited for the link to be established. He hoped the terms wouldn't be too high, too high for him to meet without compromising himself completely. He'd met Tyrians who seemed to believe they were the absolute masters of the universe, talking down to the lowly colonials as they built their castles in the sky. He wasn't sure he could handle someone who demanded craven capitulation, complete surrender; someone who would delight in rubbing the planet's nose in its humiliation. And yet, he had no choice. Mulligan was right. Further resistance was pointless. It would merely get a lot of people, his people, killed.

He braced himself as a face popped into view on the display. The enemy CO looked oddly *old*, for a Tyrian. The combination of genetic engineering and advanced medical care ensured that *most* Tyrians looked to be in their midtwenties right up until their dying day. But *this* Tyrian looked worn . . . if he'd been born on Tarleton, Alistair would have assumed he was in his sixties. Tarleton's population had yet to reap the benefits of modern medical technology.

"Mr. Premier," he said.

Alistair took a breath. The enemy CO hadn't identified himself. He hoped that wasn't a bad sign. "What are your terms?"

The enemy CO looked a little relieved. "My terms are very simple. You will order the remainder of your forces to stand down. My troops will occupy the remaining orbital and interplanetary installations, as well as the planetary spaceports. Anyone who wishes to remain in the occupied zones may do so, on the understanding that the zones will be under martial law and attacks on my forces will be punished harshly. Outside the zones, your government will remain in control. We expect you to do everything in your power to discourage pointless acts of resistance."

"I understand," Alistair said.

"You will hand over every scrap of intelligence you have on the king's forces, his government, and his ultimate intentions. Your people will cooperate fully with my intelligence staff. Beyond that . . . as long as you behave yourselves, I see no reason to tighten my grip."

As long as we behave ourselves, Alistair's thoughts echoed. The king wasn't going to be happy. Not, he supposed, that it mattered. *We don't know anything that might cost him the war.*

He heard Dalton snort and sighed inwardly. "And after the war?"

"That's out of my hands," the enemy CO said. "But, as long as you behave yourselves, I suspect the postwar terms will not be too onerous."

Dalton snorted again. "They just want to fatten us up for the kill."

"Be *quiet,*" Alistair snapped. The enemy CO could hear the idiot. He cleared his throat. "I accept your terms."

"Good," the enemy CO said. "My forces will begin landing in an hour. You have that long to remove your forces from the spaceports."

Alistair nodded tiredly. The terms were better than he'd expected, although . . . They weren't *final.* The end of the war might see punitive taxes leveled on his homeworld, as punishment for siding with the king . . . He shook his head. They had no choice.

Sure, he thought. Shame boiled at the back of his mind. Part of him wanted to fight. *Keep telling yourself that, why don't you?*

♦ ♦ ♦

"They surrendered," Yagami said. He sounded surprised. "Sir, they surrendered."

"The smart thing to do," William said curtly. "Pass the word. The marines are to begin landing, as planned, in an hour. The intelligence staff can go with them."

"Yes, sir."

♦ ♦ ♦

Commander Stacy Benson braced herself as the shuttle dived into the atmosphere, trying not to show her fear in front of the marines. They were tough, confident men; she was grimly determined to show them that she could handle a drop into enemy territory. And yet, it wasn't quite a *real* combat drop. The planet had surrendered. They had no reason to expect resistance as they landed on the surface. She wasn't exactly falling into the teeth of enemy fire.

Be grateful, she told herself, as the shuttle lurched violently. She had to swallow hard to keep from being sick. *It could be a great deal worse.*

She stared at the deck, trying to ignore the shaking . . . and the handful of curses from the marines. If they were worried . . . She told herself, again and again, that there was nothing to fear. The briefing officer had made it clear that the planet had surrendered. She had no reason to expect anything but a simple mission. And yet . . . She closed her eyes as the shuttle lurched again. She wished she hadn't eaten that ration bar before joining the marines in their craft. Right now, it was threatening to come up and spew all over the floor.

"Gus thinks he's making an assault on a stinker world," someone muttered. "Can we duff him up after the landing?"

"No," Sergeant Tombs said. His voice was sharp, cutting through the air like a knife through butter. "Grab your kit and get ready."

A dull *bang* echoed through the shuttle. For a horrific moment, Stacy thought they'd been hit. And then the hatches slammed open . . . It took her several seconds to realize that they'd landed, that the marines were scrambling out of the hatch and dropping down to the tarmac below. Sergeant Tombs caught her shoulder, hauled her to her feet, and thrust her towards the hatch. Stacy forced herself to run. The briefer had *also* made it clear that, if there *was* resistance, the shuttles would draw fire.

The air outside was hot, muggy. Stacy felt water droplets splashing against her face. She kept her head down and ran, following the marines as they jogged towards a giant spaceport building. Sergeant

Tombs barked orders, each one completely incomprehensible. She glanced from side to side, noting that seven or eight shuttles had arrived simultaneously. Lines of marines flowed in all directions, weapons at the ready. Apparently there was no resistance. She hoped that was true.

"Sit there and wait," Sergeant Tombs snapped.

He pushed her towards a corner and hurried onwards, barking orders to his men. Stacy felt a flash of anger, mingled with a grim awareness that Sergeant Tombs was trying to keep her alive. Technically, she outranked him; practically, she'd been told—in no uncertain terms—that the sergeant was in charge, and if he told her to sit on her ass and wait, then she damn well had to sit on her ass and wait. She certainly *didn't* want to mess up her big chance to make a career for herself. A negative report from the marines would probably see her relegated to a desk job back on Tyre.

It felt like hours before Sergeant Tombs returned. Stacy had plenty of time to watch the marines establish command posts, take control of the spaceport facilities, and begin copying everything in their computers. Laymen wouldn't understand why the intelligence staff wanted everything, but *Stacy* did. Something as simple as a list of shuttles and starships that had passed through the system could become the key to a greater puzzle, if they managed to slot it into place. She had few qualms about doing whatever it took to gather intelligence. If she found something good, it would make her career.

"The car is ready," he said. "Are you?"

Stacy nodded. This was it. She would be the first intelligence officer to get a look at the king's diplomatic correspondence. She would learn what lies he'd told to swing the colonials to his side. And what she'd find would change the war. They'd name classified awards after her, awards that were never openly acknowledged outside the intelligence community. She would be famous, at least to the people who mattered. Worth any risk . . .

Her mouth was suddenly dry. "Yes, Sergeant."

She felt her heart start to race as the sergeant led her through the spaceport and out onto the parking lot. It was empty, save for a trio of armored vehicles. Stacy clambered into the middle groundcar, bracing herself as the engine hummed to life. The driver followed the lead car as it drove down the road, through a gatehouse—now occupied by the marines—and onto a street leading towards the city. She kept her eyes open as they joined a main road, which was heaving with traffic. It looked as if the entire population was trying to leave the city. She supposed she should be grateful that they weren't driving on the wrong side of the road. The city already looked chaotic enough.

Her eyes narrowed as they made their way into the city. Tarleton City was larger than she'd expected, a cluster of skyscrapers and residential blocks surrounded by cookie-cutter houses and, less pleasantly, makeshift housing and slums. The planet had quite a high population, if she recalled correctly, and had been doing quite well for itself, at least until the war had ended and the postwar recession began. And the ungrateful bastards had . . .

That's not helpful, she told herself, firmly. Her training had taught her to look at things from the other side's point of view, even if she thought the other side was so wrong that there was no need to put together an objective explanation of why it was wrong. Just because she thought someone was dumb didn't mean that they were being willfully dumb. *You have to remember that these people were caught in a jam.*

The car turned the corner. Stacy let out a breath as she saw the howling crowd, shouting and screaming obscenities she could hear through the heavy armor. The driver slowed as objects began bouncing off the cover: glass bottles, pieces of brick, even something mushy she didn't care to look at too closely. She saw children among the crowd, shaking their little fists and making rude gestures. Her heart twisted at the thought of them being killed or injured, if they were pushed under the treads by their older comrades. What sort of bastard would bring their children to a violent protest? Grown adults wouldn't be safe if all hell broke loose . . .

"They don't have any heavy weapons," the driver called back. She thought he was trying to be reassuring. It wasn't working. "The worst they can do is poop on us."

"Joy," Stacy said. In the distance, she could see someone burning a Tyrian flag. Another flag, she assumed of local design, was being waved enthusiastically by a bare-breasted woman, her lips framing words Stacy couldn't hear. "What do we do?"

"Well, if we're lucky, the planetary police will clear the crowd before too long," the driver said. "And, if we're unlucky, the protesters will be used as cover for a *real* attack. A shitload of them will be killed in the crossfire."

Stacy groaned. "I'm sorry I asked."

♦ ♦ ♦

"The marines have secured the principal locations," Yagami reported. "There's been some trouble getting the lead intelligence staff to their destinations, and Colonel Nobunaga has ordered the legate to remain at the spaceport until the roads are cleared, but otherwise the deployments are completed."

"Very good," William said. "Pass system control to Captain Harris. His squadron will remain here. We will return home once we have received the preliminary intelligence assessment."

"Aye, sir," Yagami said. He grinned, suddenly. "We could stay here, couldn't we?"

"No," William said. "Tarleton isn't *that* important. There's nothing to be gained by trying to hold it, not now. If the king wants it back, he can have it."

He shrugged. Captain Harris's ships would give anything smaller than a battlecruiser squadron a very hard time. William had given the younger man strict orders to retreat, after firing a salvo for the honor of the flag, if he *was* confronted by equal or even slightly inferior force . . . but the king wouldn't know it. He'd have to dispatch a sizable fleet if he wanted to recover Tarleton. And, in that time, William could be knocking out *another* colonial world.

And if he chooses to ignore our little jaunt, he thought grimly, *and tell the colonial worlds that they will be abandoned, his followers will start to desert him. His entire government could come crashing down.*

"And we will go somewhere else, soon enough," he added. He'd seen the pattern, back during the war. Hadrian would have to be very lucky to catch his fleet, let alone catch it with enough force to guarantee victory. "And while the king is trying to smash us, the rest of the fleet can ready itself for the final offensive."

CHAPTER THIRTY

DARIUS

"It is a great honor to have you among us," President Maxine Bryant said. "You are more than welcome here."

"Thank you," Kat managed. She'd never liked formal dinner parties, even though most of her peers had loved them. Far too easy to make a mistake that would get one shunned, even if it was a pointless and minor breach of etiquette rather than something serious. But attending *this* party seemed to be part of her duties now. "His Majesty is grateful for your support."

"We have faith that His Majesty will recognize the justice of our claims," Maxine said calmly. "Do you intend to hold the hearing now?"

Kat winced inwardly. There were two worlds within the system, Romulus and Darius, and they'd been bickering for decades over who had mining and exploitation rights to the rest of the system. The conflict struck her as thoroughly pointless—there were two gas giants and uncountable thousands of asteroids, providing enough fuel and raw materials to keep both planets going for hundreds of years—but that hadn't stopped them from preparing for war. Even Commonwealth membership hadn't been enough to dampen the fires. The case had been sent to the Supreme Court on Tyre, but the judiciary hadn't come to a decision by the time war broke out.

"His Majesty will appoint a special judge," she said carefully. Diplomacy was not her forte. "I will not be involved."

"But you *are* one of his closest advisers," Maxine pressed. "I'm sure you could swing things in our favor."

Kat resisted the urge to groan openly. She really *wasn't* one of the king's closest advisers, not any longer. She'd spent the last two weeks cruising from world to world instead of sitting at the council table and offering her advice. Admiral Lord Garstang and Admiral Ruben had usurped her position. She didn't think the king would bother to read any missive she sent, even if she marked it urgent. The local dispute was purely local and . . . Hell, the king would be better off not taking sides. The world he ruled against would promptly declare for the House of Lords.

And if the House of Lords wins the war, their supporter would get the mining rights, Kat thought. *What do they have to lose?*

"I am purely a military adviser," she said. "And, right now, the king has to focus on winning the war."

"Of course, of course," Maxine said. "And what are the odds of the king winning?"

"Very good," Kat said. "He is certain of victory."

She allowed her gaze to wander the massive chamber, wondering at the sheer number of people who'd attended the dinner. She'd had her hand pressed and her cheek kissed more times than she cared to remember over the last few hours; she'd had countless requests for private discussions, some from the planetary president's closest allies. It made her blood boil to think that she was *here*, wasting time, while the war raged on. She and her ships should be on the front lines . . .

And the resources that were expended on this banquet could have been used on starships instead, she thought. She knew that wasn't entirely true, but she didn't care. *And, instead of trying to coax me into helping, they could simply ask for what they want.*

She sighed to herself as the dinner wore on. God, she *hated* diplomacy. Everyone was two-faced, making sly insinuations rather than talking plainly and telling her what they actually wanted. She knew enough about diplomacy to understand that the politicians were giving themselves plausible deniability, ensuring they had room to retreat if their suggestions fell on hostile ears; she knew it and hated it. She missed the military. A starship officer who didn't speak plainly, particularly when discussing the objective facts of shipboard life, would find himself being mercilessly mocked. If, of course, he didn't get himself into trouble first.

No room for talking around the subject when the fusion core is on the verge of melting down, she reminded herself. *People have to* know *it's an emergency.*

"I hope you'll have time to see the sights," Maxine said. "We used to have quite a few tourists who visited our world. Not now, alas."

"The economy has been contracting since the war," Kat agreed. She had no particular interest in tourism for the sake of tourism, not since Pat's death. "I'm sure it will recover soon."

"I can arrange a tour," Maxine pressed. "You'll enjoy it."

And you'll have a chance to speak to me alone, Kat noted. She'd declined all requests for private meetings. It wasn't as if any of the requesters had anything to offer her. *What do you want from me?*

Her lips twitched as the toastmaster went to work, praising the king and his followers in a resounding voice before launching into a speech that managed to say nothing in a great many words. She was tempted, very tempted, to ask bluntly what Maxine actually *wanted.* Kat assumed she wanted the interplanetary dispute resolved in her homeworld's favor, but . . . Why couldn't she just *say* it? Politicians were allergic to straight talking. Kat wondered what Maxine would say if she *did* ask. Perhaps she'd faint. Or die of shock. Or . . . She put the thought aside as the toastmaster finished his speech to resounding applause. The cynical part of her mind rather suspected that the audience was just relieved that it was over.

"It's common for the seniors to gather in a private room," Maxine told her as the tables started to empty. "You are, of course, welcome to join us."

"That's very kind of you," Kat lied. "I'll be happy to . . ."

Her wristcom bleeped. "Excuse me."

She tapped the wristcom, feeling cold. She'd been tempted to arrange an emergency call, something that would have gotten her out of the banquet before it killed her, but she'd resisted. Instead, she'd told her staff to contact her *only* if it was an emergency. If an enemy fleet had arrived . . . She cursed under her breath. She was planet-side. It would take too long, far too long, for her to return to orbit before battle was joined. If the enemy had had a stroke of good luck . . .

"Admiral," Commander Katie Hamada said. "We have just received an urgent message from Caledonia. Priority-one. It's encoded to your personal seal."

Kat thought, fast. It was unlikely to be *that* urgent. If the House of Lords had attacked Caledonia, the message would have said so. Admiral Lord Garstang wouldn't have tried to hide the truth, if only to ensure that Kat's staff knew the missive was urgent. But then, he'd also know that there was no way Kat could make it back in time. The battle would be decided, one way or the other, before her ships could get anywhere near Caledonia.

But it *would* get her out of the after-party . . .

"I'll be back as soon as possible," she said. "Thank you."

She closed the connection, then looked at Maxine. "Duty calls," she said. "I have to get back to the ship."

"I quite understand," Maxine said. "And the offer of a private tour remains open."

Kat saluted, shook her hand, and headed to the shuttlepad before someone else could try to catch her eye. The presidential house seemed crammed with strangers, as if there were no private apartments for Maxine's family or secure sections for private discussions. She reminded herself, rather dryly, that there probably were quite a few private chambers under the building itself. Falcone Manor had a dozen sections that weren't marked on any of the building's plans. Her mother had been fond of giving visitors tours that suggested they'd seen the entire mansion, while concealing almost everything of importance.

And she blew a fuse when she discovered me roaming through the secret passageways, Kat recalled. The mansion had been a wonderful playground when she'd been alone. *Whoever designed the building must have been a child at heart.*

She boarded her shuttlecraft and took her seat. Her console blinked, informing her that she had a dozen messages marked urgent. She waited for the shuttle to take off, then glanced at her inbox. *All* the messages came from planet-side, from politicians who were trying to buy her favor. Kat skimmed the messages, shaking her head in disbelief. Perhaps her father would have handled them better. But then, her father had also had the power to give the petitioners what they wanted. The best *she* could do was take their concerns to the king.

"Admiral, we'll be docking in a couple of minutes," the pilot called. "Do you want to connect to the upper hatch?"

"No need," Kat said. The maneuver would shave a few minutes off her flight, she supposed, but would otherwise be pointless. "Land at the shuttlebay."

She leaned back in her chair and took a long breath, centering herself as the gravity field rippled over her. If the king had sent her a private message . . . She wondered, for a moment, what it might be, then put the thought aside. She'd know soon enough. Instead, she stood, nodded her thanks to the pilot, and hurried through the hatch. There was no welcoming committee. Her flag captain, thankfully, had realized she didn't *want* to be greeted by her subordinates when she returned to the ship.

I can worry about that when I board a ship for the first time, she thought as she walked to the CIC. *Right now, not a problem.*

She glanced at the system display—there were no red icons, although she knew that meant nothing—before stepping into her ready room. Her terminal was blinking silently, alerting her to a priority-one message. Kat sat down and pressed her palm against the scanner, allowing it to check her DNA. There was a long pause, just long enough for her to start to wonder if something had gone wrong, then the message started to decrypt itself. The king had done everything in his power to ensure that it would be read only by Kat herself.

Which may not stop it from being decrypted, if it was intercepted somewhere along the way, Kat reminded herself. There was no such thing as completely unbreakable codes. The steady advance of technology practically guaranteed that yesterday's encrypted message might as well have been sent in plain text. *And we can bet everything we own that the House of Lords is trying to decrypt the king's messages.*

A small holographic image of the king appeared in front of her. "Kat," he said. "I'll keep this short. Twelve hours ago"—the image glanced at a watch—"the enemy attacked Tarleton and defeated the planetary defense force. As of the last message, the planet had surrendered, and the enemy troops were landing."

Kat felt her eyes narrow. Tarleton? It wasn't a stage-one colony world, a planet incapable of offering help to either side, but it wasn't Caledonia either. It was . . . She didn't see any real *value* in the House of Lords attacking Tarleton. The planet's small industrial base was hardly worth the effort. And they'd have to garrison the planet, tying down some of their ships . . .

"We cannot let this go unanswered," the king's image continued. "You are therefore ordered to abandon your current mission and proceed at once to Tarleton. Once there, you are to recover the high orbitals, liberate the planet, and take their treacherous government into custody. They will be put on trial for betraying their planet, and the cause, to the enemy."

Shit, Kat thought. She was delighted at the prospect of heading into danger again—there was no reason to think that her inspection tour of the colonies was actually accomplishing anything useful—but . . . arresting a planetary government? If they'd lost control of the high orbitals, surrender was the only logical option. It wasn't as if they were facing the Theocracy. *We can't blame them for conceding defeat.*

"I want you to make it clear that selling out will not be tolerated," the king said. "I'll dispatch a justicar once the system has been liberated. He will consider the case and render judgment appropriately."

"We have to recover the system first," Kat muttered. "Better to leave the government in place until we know what actually happened."

There was no response. She hadn't expected one. The recording could hardly hear her, let alone respond.

"I've attached the final messages and tactical updates to this recording," the king finished. "Good luck. Give them hell."

His image froze. Kat studied it for a long moment. Hadrian looked haggard, as if he was being henpecked to death. She dismissed the image with a wave of her hand. She had no doubt she *could* recover the system, unless the House of Lords had decided it merited a superdreadnought squadron . . . She doubted it. Tarleton had probably been chosen because it was an easy target, not because of any special value. She wondered, sourly, why the invaders had even bothered to land troops. Did they intend to loot the entire planet?

Probably not, she told herself.

She keyed her terminal. "Commander Hamada, signal the squadron," she ordered. "We will depart for Tarleton in two hours."

"Aye, Admiral," Katie said.

Kat scowled. The crew hadn't been given shore leave, which had been judged too dangerous in the wake of the riots on Caledonia, and her ships had held their drives at standby. But they weren't ready to depart in a hurry. They'd planned to stay three more days before they lit out for their next port of call. *That* would have to be changed, she told herself sharply. But if they put so much wear and tear on the drive systems . . . They wouldn't *need* the enemy to damage their ships. Sooner or later, fragile components would start to fail and need to be replaced.

Later, she thought, grimly.

She opened the reports buried within the encrypted packet and forwarded them to the tactical staff, then scanned them herself. Two squadrons of heavy cruisers—she felt a pang as she remembered *Lightning*, lost in the Jorlem Sector—had attacked Tarleton, blowing their way through the planet's defense fleet with frightening ease. She wasn't surprised. The planet's ships had been mostly outdated, even by prewar standards, but it was still worrying. Governor Rogan and his ilk would be pointing out that what had happened to Tarleton could easily happen to one of their worlds . . . and he'd be right. Most colonial worlds couldn't stand off against two squadrons of heavy cruisers.

And the ones that can will receive visits from superdreadnoughts instead, she mused. *And be trashed too.*

She tapped her terminal, bringing up the starchart. Tarleton was fourteen days from her current position, even if she pushed her drives to the max. A lot could happen in fourteen days. There were no less than seven other possible targets near Tarleton, some of which were strikingly vulnerable. She dreaded to think what would happen if the enemy decided to continue the offensive—sweeping in, blowing the hell out of the orbital defenses, and simply retreating back into deep space. It wouldn't do much practical damage to the king's ability to wage war—she thought—but it would send morale straight into the gutter. They would have to find a way to strike back.

And, ideally, a way to lure the House of Lords into a battle on uneven terms, she thought slowly. *We'll have to bait a trap. But how?*

She contemplated a handful of possibilities as her squadron prepared to depart. Perhaps if she were to set a trap . . . She turned the ideas over and over in her head, wondering if she could talk the king into trying them. He'd placed his faith in Admiral Ruben . . . She wondered, grimly, if she could talk Admiral Ruben into trying them. He wasn't very subtle, but . . .

The intercom bleeped. "Admiral," Katie said. "The squadron is ready to depart."

"I'm on my way," Kat said.

She stood, putting the plans aside for the moment. She'd consider her ideas in transit, then direct her tactical staff to study the concepts and determine if there was something *workable* in them, something she could turn into a reality. And then . . . She'd have to take it to the king. And hope that he'd listen to her, instead of either the hawks or the doves. She stepped into the CIC, silently relieved that the display was still clear. She wouldn't put it past the House of Lords to mount an attack on Romulus and Darius if they knew she was there, in hopes of catching her with her pants down. The chance to take out a battlecruiser squadron at minimal cost could hardly be ignored.

"Admiral," Katie said.

Kat took her seat. "Take us out of orbit," she ordered. "And straight into hyperspace as soon as we are clear of the gravity well."

"Aye, Admiral," Katie said.

A low hum echoed through the ship as the battlecruiser slowly slid out of orbit, followed by the remainder of the squadron. Kat leaned back in her chair, thinking hard. She'd told the crew it was urgent, but . . . fourteen days. Her mind ran in circles. A lot could happen in fourteen days. By the time she reached Tarleton, it might be too late to do more than chase the occupation fleet out of the system. The planet's industrial base, such as it was, might already have been destroyed.

But the king is right, she told herself. She watched the vortex opening up in front of her fleet, then swallowed hard as her ship plunged into hyperspace. *We can't let this go unanswered either. We have to find a way to make them pay.*

CHAPTER THIRTY-ONE

TYRE

"Hail the conquering hero," Duke Peter said as William was escorted into the conference room. "Congratulations on your stunning victory."

"It wasn't a stunning victory, Your Grace," William said bluntly. "Whoever wrote the press releases should be shot."

He tried hard not to show his disgust on his face. The battle had been brief and completely one-sided. That hadn't stopped the media from portraying it as a great and glorious victory against overwhelming force. They'd practically credited him with defeating the enemy fleet single-handedly, as if he hadn't had two squadrons of heavy cruisers under his command, and called the enemy commander every name under the sun. And what they'd said about Kat Falcone . . . William ground his teeth in silent rage. If he ever got his hands on the muckrakers who'd written those pieces of crap, he'd snap their necks with his bare hands. He wouldn't even lower himself to use their newspapers to wipe his ass.

"They haven't had much to celebrate," Duke Peter said. He motioned to a chair. "The conference is about to begin."

William sat, wondering if the duke knew what the media had been saying about his youngest sister. He could have stopped them in their tracks with a single word. Had he decided to let them slander Kat without repercussion, on the grounds that Kat had joined the wrong side?

Or had no one dared to tell him? William rather suspected the latter. Aristocrats always protected their own, whatever side they were on. Kat wouldn't even be shot for treason, if the king lost the war; she certainly wouldn't be slandered by a reporter too foolish to know which end of the missile was the *dangerous* end.

He accepted a cup of coffee from the duke's secretary, then watched as holographic images started to blink into existence. Something was oddly imperfect about them, something that made it impossible to believe they were *real.* He puzzled over it for a moment—there was certainly no *technical* barrier to projecting perfect holograms—and then decided that the imperfection must have something to do with etiquette. A too-perfect hologram might lead to some embarrassment if it fooled the wrong person.

"The meeting is now in session," Prime Minister Israel Harrison said calmly. "First, the House of Commons has formally issued a vote of thanks to Admiral Sir William McElney, in recognition of his victory."

I'd prefer a few more ships, William thought coldly. *You can't stop enemy missiles with a vote of thanks.*

He nodded, silently accepting the honor. It meant *something*, even if it wasn't another knighthood or a hereditary peerage. The House of Commons didn't have anything like the clout of the House of Lords, and patronage networks ensured that the MPs never united against the aristocracy, but it still had a certain level of independence, even now. They'd probably meant well. He resolved to accept the recognition in the spirit it was given.

"Second, Investigator Niles has a formal report," Harrison continued. "I believe you will find it of interest."

He raised a hand. Another holographic image, a black man wearing an unmarked uniform, appeared out of nowhere. An intelligence officer, William noted. And, quite probably, one with strong ties to the House of Lords. He wondered, as the newcomer stepped forward, just who had picked him as a client. It could be any of the dukes.

"Your Graces," Investigator Niles said. He didn't spare a glance for the others. "My team and myself have continued our investigation into the king's connection to the Falkirk Island Detention Center. On paper, the complex was owned and operated by Planetary Security; in practice, it is clear that the king's nominees were practically the sole operators of the complex. We think it is fairly clear, therefore, that Admiral Morrison's death was no accident. The king or one of his trusted agents may well have ordered it personally."

We knew it wasn't an accident, William thought. He'd been too low-ranking to hear the full story, at the time, but he'd heard enough to be fairly sure that Admiral Morrison had been murdered. *We just wondered who wanted to shut his mouth permanently.*

Investigator Niles continued, remorselessly. "The investigation into the death was conducted by the Special Security Force, which reported directly to the king. All four of the agents who handled the matter have vanished, their ultimate fates unknown. We believe they had orders to ensure that Admiral Morrison's death was buried as quickly as possible. In this, they were successful. They were apparently unable to link any of the possible suspects to the murder."

"So the king ordered the murderers to investigate themselves and prove their own innocence," Duke Tolliver muttered. "The investigation, which was supposed to be conducted by outsiders, wasn't anything of the sort?"

"Yes, Your Grace," Investigator Niles said. "From what we have been able to determine, they made no *real* attempt to uncover the truth. They just . . . published a report that suggested the full truth would never be known."

"So Admiral Morrison was the king's client," Duchess Zangaria said. "Why? And how did this remain undiscovered?"

"It was handled through cutouts and disposable agents," Investigator Niles said. "The king's nominees would have followed orders without ever really being aware of the big picture, ensuring that Admiral

Morrison was put in command of Cadiz before the Theocratic War began. They may not have realized that they, unintentionally, helped contribute to a disaster."

William swallowed, hard. The king had known that war was coming. William would give the young bastard *that* much credit, at least. He'd known there was no way the Commonwealth could delay war indefinitely. And he'd done his best to prepare his people for war.

And yet, he gave Admiral Morrison orders to do nothing to provoke the Theocracy, he thought coldly. *It makes no sense . . .*

His blood ran cold. It *did* make sense. The king could not declare war on his own. The Houses of Parliament would have to vote to declare war. And a series of skirmishes might not lead to war, if they were far enough from Tyre not to impinge on the political battleground. But if the Theocracy could be lured into committing an outright act of war by crossing the border in force and attacking Cadiz . . . Anything was possible. Admiral Morrison might have had orders, secret orders, from his hidden patron, to ensure that Cadiz looked like a very tempting target. The Theocracy had come very close to smashing the fleet in a single blow.

He might not even have had such orders, William thought. *The king might have known him well enough to know what he'd do, if he'd been placed in such a position . . .*

Duke Falcone appeared to be having similar thoughts. "Do you know what you're saying? Do you have any idea at all?"

"Yes, Your Grace," Investigator Niles said. "Admiral Morrison was a tool, used to trigger the war. And when he became a liability, he was unceremoniously killed."

"But you don't have *proof*." Duchess Zangaria sounded stunned. "You don't *know*."

"No, Your Grace," Investigator Niles said. "All I have is a string of coincidences that might, or might not, be tied together. Sir Reginald Grantham, one of the king's . . . ah, *assistants*, appears to have played a major role in the whole affair. He may well have pulled strings to ensure that Admiral Morrison was placed in command of the fleet base; he certainly made two visits to Falkirk, before and after Admiral Morrison's untimely death. And now he's gone too. The last verified sighting was shortly before the king fled the planet. I assume he took Sir Grantham with him."

His eyes swept the room. "Nothing was ever written down, as far as we can determine. I don't think we'll ever find an order, written in the king's own handwriting, directing his people to commit treason on a colossal scale. It's quite possible that we are drawing the wrong conclusions. But . . . we don't think so. There are just too many coincidences."

Like Admiral Christian and his fleet being moved to the border, William thought. In hindsight, it had been a very wise move. But if the king had known that war was coming . . . He might have intended to limit the damage. *Or* . . .

He clasped his hands behind his back, trying to keep his thoughts under control. The war had killed millions of people. An entire planet had been rendered uninhabitable, while dozens of others had been bombarded heavily. The Theocrats hadn't even spared their own people. He shuddered to think how many of their subjects had worked themselves to death, trying to support a war machine that had been threatening to fall apart at the seams even before the war had begun. And if the king had deliberately *started* the war . . .

His mind raced. The Theocrats had *had* to be stopped. He had no doubt of it. But . . . The king had sacrificed uncounted millions of his own subjects to do it. Why? He could have . . . William felt his heart sink. Power. In peacetime, the king's powers were limited; in wartime, they were extensive. Very extensive. And, when the peace had finally been signed, he had been reluctant to give them up. Instead, he'd fought tooth and nail to keep them.

"So he was planning the war all along," Duke Falcone said. "Shit."

William dragged his attention back to the duke as he kept speaking. "And was he responsible for supplying the Theocrats with weapons, just to prolong the occupation?"

"We believe so," Investigator Niles said. "But, again, we have no solid proof."

"Treason." Duchess Zangaria sounded shaken. "Treason. Real treason."

"We have no proof," Duke Rudbek said.

"We don't *need* proof, Your Grace," Harrison said. "We have more than enough evidence to impeach the king."

William bit his lip to keep from snorting. He knew little about impeachment law, but . . . The king was hardly going to submit to impeachment. The Houses of Parliament could formally impeach Hadrian, if they wished, yet . . . It made no difference. The king wasn't going to surrender, and his followers weren't going to desert him even if he *was* impeached. The mice might as well vote to bell the cat! Who was going to be the poor sucker who had to put the bell *on* the cat?

Us, William thought. *We'll have to beat the king's forces into submission.*

"We can impeach the king," Duke Falcone said. "But legally . . ."

"To hell with legality," Duke Tolliver snapped. "Impeach him!"

"And then . . . what?" Duke Falcone looked very much like his youngest sister when he was angry . . . and trying to hide it. "From a legal point of view, anyone threatened with impeachment has a right to put his case before the Houses of Parliament. If we impeach the king without giving him the chance to explain himself, he can claim the proceedings are illegal and thus invalid. And even if we ignore the requirement and impeach him anyway, what then? His people will not abandon him. They've gone too far."

His eyes swept the room. "We'll look like fools."

"Perhaps we could offer blanket amnesty," Duchess Turin suggested. "We can promise no punishments, no retaliation . . . if they abandon the king. The slate will be wiped clean. We can even offer debt forgiveness if they end the war now."

"There will be banking houses that will kick up a fuss," Duke Rudbek sharply predicted.

"And you own half of them," Duchess Turin said. "Come on! Do you think we're ever going to see that money again?"

"It's the principle of the thing," Duke Rudbek said.

"To hell with principle," Duke Tolliver said. "We have to end this war before it kills us in the moment of our victory!"

Duke Falcone slapped the table, making everyone jump. "We can try to impeach the king, if we wish, but there's no way we could convince everyone to accept the sentence. And yes, we can tell his people what we've discovered"—he shrugged—"but most of them won't believe it. So much crap has been hurled around over the last few months that this is practically unnoticeable. They may wonder, but . . . They may only believe it because it is *convenient* to believe it."

"We can share the evidence," Duke Tolliver pointed out.

"Your Grace, the evidence is flimsy at best," Investigator Niles said. "Yes, we have enough to open a full investigation—if this were a routine matter—but not enough, now, to pass muster. We don't even have enough, under peacetime laws, to interrogate his followers."

"We're not at peace," Duke Tolliver growled.

"And, even now, we might not be *able* to interrogate the king's followers," Niles continued, calmly. "They all have implants. Interrogating them may be impossible."

"And, in any case, we'd need to lay hands on them first," Duke Falcone pointed out. "How do you intend to do that, may I ask?"

He looked from face to face. No answer.

"Grand Admiral Rudbek," Duke Falcone said. "Can we capture the king and his followers?"

"We *could* launch an attack on Caledonia," Grand Admiral Rudbek said. "However, we would need to concentrate most of the fleet to be fairly sure of success . . . and in doing so, we would leave Tyre itself uncovered."

"So the basic equation hasn't changed," Duke Falcone said. He looked at William. "Do *you* have any thoughts?"

William tried to keep the dismay off his face. Admiral Kalian had been *furious* when William had been asked for his opinion. Grand Admiral Rudbek might feel the same . . . even though William largely agreed with him. But it couldn't be helped.

"Uncovering Tyre would be a considerable risk," he said, carefully. "We could and would attempt to pretend that the superdreadnoughts were still here, defending the planet against all threats. However, if they realized what we were doing, they might launch an attack themselves. They'll be reluctant to tangle with the orbital defenses again, I think, but . . . Well, we might end up swapping planets."

A low chuckle ran around the room. "That would be amusing," Duke Rudbek commented dryly.

"That would be disastrous for both of us," Grand Admiral Rudbek corrected. "It might ruin us *and* the king."

William gathered himself. "Right now, we would be better off raiding another world. If we can keep them on the hop, and thus unable to launch an offensive of their own, we can prepare our forces and advance on Caledonia. Or we can simply raid Caledonia; jump in, shoot off a few missiles, and jump out again. It would make it difficult for them to react without weakening themselves."

"You make it sound as though we both have fleets of superdreadnoughts that we cannot use," Duke Tolliver grumbled.

"That's essentially true, Your Grace," William confirmed. "We cannot afford to uncover Tyre. They cannot afford to uncover Caledonia. We will be messing around with whatever squadrons can be spared, at least until one of us gathers the force to smash the other in pitched battle. It may take some time."

"Yes," Duke Falcone said. "Put together a plan for another raid. I think we can all agree we need to press our advantage."

There was a mutter of assent. "And we need to prove the king guilty," Harrison added. "If nothing else, it will provide a fig leaf of respectability for anyone who wants to abandon him."

"Quite," Duke Falcone said. "We'll meet again after lunch?"

William sat back as the holographic images faded into nothingness, feeling his head spinning uncomfortably. It was easy to forget that they *weren't* in a crowded conference room, even if the holograms weren't entirely perfect. They had all the disadvantages of VR simulations, without any of the advantages. He sipped his coffee, which had cooled while he'd been talking, and waited for Duke Falcone to dismiss him.

"The king came up with a mad plan," Duke Falcone said. It sounded more like he was talking to himself, rather than William. "What was he trying to do?"

"Be clever," William said flatly. He'd warned more junior officers than he cared to remember that trying to be clever was asking for trouble. The more moving pieces a plan had, the more the planner *needed* to go right for the plan to work, the greater the chance of a spectacular failure. Boring but practical was better than awesome but *impractical.* "He was trying to be clever, and it worked better than it should have."

"But why?" Duke Falcone shook his head. "My father would never have gone along with a plan to *start* a war."

"Or at least tempt the Theocracy into starting one," William said, deciding not to point out just how many "police actions" had taken place before the first *actual* war. Lucas Falcone had signed off on more "asset recovery" missions than his son had realized. "He wanted the war to start on his terms."

"Madness," Duke Falcone said. He let out a sound that *might* have been a giggle. "And we can't even *prove* it."

William nodded, slowly. "No one would believe us, not without proof."

Duke Falcone met his eyes. "Do you know that you have a sibling on the other side too?"

"Pardon?" William blinked, trying not to let the sudden shift blindside him. "My brother?"

"Your smuggler brother has been making eyes at the king, if the latest report is to be believed," Duke Falcone said. "Now you have a sibling on the other side too."

"My brother always puts himself first and foremost," William said tersely. "But it might be useful to have a link to the other side that can't be cut, not easily. You never know when we might want to send a message."

"True," Duke Falcone agreed. "This war is going to be the end of us, isn't it?"

"I hope not," William said. "But nothing will be the same when the shooting finally stops."

CHAPTER THIRTY-TWO

TARLETON

"The squadron is at full alert," Commander Katie Hamada said. "We will drop out of hyperspace in five minutes."

Kat nodded. She'd considered a handful of possible approaches to the system, but there hadn't seemed much point in trying to be clever. She simply didn't have *time* to sneak into the system and open fire before her opponents realized she was there. Better to get the engagement finished as quickly as possible than risk running into something she couldn't handle.

Two heavy cruiser squadrons hit the system, she thought as the timer continued its steady countdown towards zero. *Did they stay in the system?*

She studied the empty display, her thoughts spinning in circles. Objectively speaking, Tarleton wasn't *that* important. Its entire defense force was little more than a petty nuisance, designed more to deal with pirates and raiders than a full-scale attack from a modern navy. The best units had been stripped out weeks ago to join the king's fleet. But subjectively, losing Tarleton was a serious blow. Planets that had declared for the king would be demanding protection, protection the king could not afford to give. And if they couldn't be protected, their leaders would be considering switching sides. Again. Kat disliked politics, but she wasn't blind to the implications. Tarleton had to be liberated as quickly as possible.

Which means we could be flying into a trap, she mused. She'd been considering a dozen different ways to lure the enemy into a trap. The House of Lords might have had the same idea. *They have to know we'll respond in force.*

"Vortex opening, Admiral," Katie said. "Here we go . . ."

Kat leaned forward, gripping her armrests as the battlecruiser plunged back into realspace. The vessel shuddered once, the drive field fluctuating for a long second; Kat felt a chilling vibration running through the hull, a grim reminder that they'd redlined their drives in a desperate bid to reach the occupied world as quickly as possible. She keyed her console, bringing up the live feed from engineering. They hadn't lost any drive rooms, thank all the gods, but at least one drive node was showing signs of wear and tear. It would have to be pulled and replaced sooner rather than later.

She shook her head in frustration and turned her attention to the main display. She'd never visited Tarleton, but she'd studied the files carefully during their headlong rush to the planet. The orbital weapons platforms were gone. The planetary defense force was gone. In their place, nine heavy cruisers held position in geostationary orbit over the capital city. A very unsubtle threat, she noted, although the effect was slightly spoiled by the simple fact that no one on the ground would be able to *see* the ships with the naked eye. They'd need a pair of binoculars to see more than points of light.

"Admiral, sensors have located one cruiser squadron," Katie reported. "There's no sign of the other."

"Deploy recon probes," Kat ordered curtly. They no longer had an unlimited supply—another shortage, more irritating than most—but she had no choice. "If those ships are still within the system, I want to find them."

"Aye, Admiral."

Kat watched the display update rapidly. The enemy ships were rushing to battlestations, bringing up their drives and weapons with commendable speed. They must have kept themselves at readiness, even if they hadn't been permanently at red alert. Kat nodded in grim understanding. The House of Lords had to be having problems with putting undue wear and tear on their ships too, but could probably solve the problem more quickly than their opponents.

Given time, we can do it too, Kat thought. The king had launched an ambitious program of industrial expansion, building on the infrastructure he already had. It would keep his fleet supplied . . . if, of course, he had time to complete the program. *Will they give us the time?*

"There's no sign of the other enemy squadron," Katie reported. "I'm not picking up any hints of cloaked or sensor-masked ships."

They might have powered everything down, Kat thought. A powered-down starship might as well have been an asteroid, for all the betraying emissions it would emit. *But they'd never be able to power up in time if we did stumble across them.*

She turned the idea over and over again, considering all the angles before dismissing it. There was no *reason* to hide a second heavy cruiser squadron, not here. If they'd hoped to catch the relief fleet on the hop . . . She shook her head. They'd gone fishing for minnows, not sharks. An entire battlecruiser squadron was too much for two heavy cruiser squadrons to handle. They would give her a hard time, she thought, but she'd come out ahead.

But not for long, she reminded herself. *Are they ruthless enough to sacrifice two heavy cruiser squadrons merely to wear us down?*

"Signal the enemy ships," she ordered. "Demand their surrender."

"Aye, Admiral."

Kat leaned forward, putting her doubts aside as the range closed. In hindsight, perhaps she should have tried to come out of hyperspace closer to the planet . . . although she'd had no way to know where the enemy ships actually *were*. That sort of trick worked only in bad novels and worse movies. It was better to have some maneuvering room, rather than risk either running into enemy fire or literally ramming an entire *planet*. The enemy might think she'd done it deliberately.

If they ever figured out what happened, she thought. *They might never realize what actually hit the planet.*

"There's no reply, Admiral," Katie said. "They're moving away from the planet."

"Adjust our course to intercept," Kat ordered. Battlecruisers were fast, but, given time, heavy cruisers could outrun them. Their acceleration curves were steeper than hers, although she did have the advantage of coming out of hyperspace at speed. "Prepare to engage as soon as we enter range."

She watched the icons on the display as they moved farther away from the planet. The enemy CO had to know that he was badly outgunned, but . . . What would he do? Who *was* he? Kat knew officers who weren't too proud to admit defeat and back off, choosing to preserve their ships and crews to fight another day, and officers who would sooner die in hopeless battle than risk being mocked as cowards. There was always *someone* who would say that he could have won, if he'd fought. It had always amused her that that *someone* was always hundreds of light years from the front lines.

The House of Lords isn't stupid enough to start shooting officers for conceding defeat, she told herself. *Or has that changed?*

It didn't seem likely, although . . . She wasn't sure. Peter wasn't that stupid, her *father* hadn't been that stupid, but what about the others? Kat knew, all too well, just how much power the ducal families wielded. It was easy to forget that the sheer concentration of wealth and power under their control wasn't enough to buy *everything*. It was easy to believe that one cold have anything, even victory, just for the taking. And if one believed that, it was easy to start thinking that the defeated officer *could* have won, if only he'd fought.

It depends on who's calling the shots, she mused. *They can't be having an easy time holding their government together, not without the king.*

"The enemy ships are locking weapons on our hulls," Katie reported. "They're preparing to . . ."

She broke off as the display sparkled with red icons. "Correction, Admiral. The enemy ships have opened fire."

Kat nodded. "Return fire."

The battlecruiser shuddered. Kat checked the feed from the weapons rooms—the battlecruiser had emptied her external racks as well as her missile tubes—and then turned her attention to the enemy salvo. The heavy cruisers had fired everything they could, but their salvo looked pitifully weak compared to the tidal wave of destruction raging towards them. Kat had no doubt they were a well-drilled formation—she hadn't seen any of the hesitation that would have suggested the ships had been thrown together only a few short days ago—but there was no way they could stand up to her fire. She'd crush their point defense through sheer weight of numbers . . .

"Admiral, they're opening a vortex," Katie reported. On the display, the enemy ships blinked and vanished. The vortex itself vanished a second later. "They're gone."

"Signal the missiles to power down," Kat ordered sharply. Someone was going to complain about the missiles she'd fired off, even if most of them could be recovered, refurbished, and pressed back into service. A handful would be beyond recovery. They'd have to be scrapped or detonated, if indeed they were recovered at all. "And prepare to swing about to the planet . . ."

Her eyes narrowed as the enemy missiles tore into her point defense. They were *modern* missiles, with the latest penetration aids; she silently blessed her foresight in making her point defense crews practice against simulated missiles that were faster, smaller, and simply *better* than anything they would face in real life. And yet . . . Her eyes narrowed as five missiles slipped through her defenses and slammed into a battlecruiser's shields. They'd come far too close to doing *real* damage.

"*Valiant* reports minor damage," Katie said. "But not enough to knock her out of formation."

Kat allowed herself a moment of relief. Battlecruisers were fast and highly maneuverable—designed to get in, land a blow, and get out before the enemy could respond—but they paid a steep price for their speed. They were *fragile*, certainly when compared to a superdreadnought. A blow that a superdreadnought could shrug off would break a battlecruiser's spine. And she knew she couldn't afford to take heavy damage. It would take far too long to repair.

"Take us back towards the planet," she ordered. "And attempt to open communications with whoever was in charge."

She glanced at the live feed from the intelligence department, but, not remotely to her surprise, they couldn't tell her anything *useful*. Tarleton's StarCom had been shut down as soon as the planet had fallen, depriving her of actionable intelligence. She had no way of knowing if the planet had been garrisoned, if the enemy had landed troops on the surface, or if they'd settled for occupying the high orbitals. Kat wasn't sure what *she'd* have done, if she'd been the enemy CO. Tarleton was in financial debt to Tyre, but there was no point in trying to collect it at gunpoint. Tarleton simply didn't *have* the money. And the occupiers hadn't had time to dismantle and steal the industrial nodes.

Which doesn't mean they won't try to destroy them, Kat mused. *They won't have left the orbital stations alone, even if they never landed on the surface.*

"We're being hailed," Katie said, "by a General Falk."

Kat frowned. She didn't know him.

"Put him through," she ordered.

Her terminal bleeped. The intelligence staff had located Falk's file and forwarded it to her. She glanced at it, briefly. General Falk was Planetary Defense, not Royal Marines or Commonwealth Army. She winced. That could be either good or bad. A planetary defense officer would have powerful patrons, patrons he'd be reluctant to disappoint, but ideally he'd have the sense to know his position was hopeless. She hoped the latter would outweigh the former.

General Falk's image appeared in front of her. He was a rough-looking man who would have been handsome, in a rugged kind of way, if he hadn't been looking at her as if she were something he'd scraped off his shoe. His file made it clear that he'd never seen *real* action, beyond a handful of enemy raids . . . She rather suspected, from his expression alone, that he regarded her as an outright traitor. It made her want to wince, again. He might find the idea of surrendering to *her* worse than surrendering to a random officer in the king's service.

"Admiral." Falk bit off the word, making it an insult. "This system is under occupation . . ."

Kat cut him off. "Your ships have departed," she said, resisting the urge to tell him that his ships had *fled*. It was the smart move, but it wouldn't sit well with a pencil pusher. "Your positions are entirely at my mercy."

Falk glowered at her. "What are your terms?"

"You will surrender your positions, both in orbit and on the surface," Kat said. "If you are holding planetary officials captive, you will release them at once. In return, you and your men will be taken into my custody and treated well, at least until we can organize a prisoner exchange."

She braced herself, unsure what to expect. Falk's position was hopeless, but . . . if he feared the consequences of surrender more than the consequences of defeat . . . She leaned forward, trying to convey trustworthiness. She hoped, prayed, that his forces hadn't committed any atrocities down on the surface. That would make it much harder to convince him to surrender without a fight.

"Fine," Falk growled. "I surrender."

Kat allowed herself a moment of relief. "What do you *have* on the surface?"

"Garrisons in all the major spaceports and a single large garrison in the capital," Falk said. "I can order the latter to withdraw to the nearest spaceport, if you would prefer."

"Please," Kat said. "I'll dispatch my marines to the surface in an hour. By then, I want your people back to the spaceports, ready for departure."

She felt her relief deepen. If Falk had made a fight of it, with his forces in the middle of a civilian sea, the death toll would have been staggering. Her marines were well trained, but there was no way they could have prevented civilians from being caught in the crossfire. Only a politician or a reporter could be stupid enough to believe the military could prevent civilians from dying.

"It might take longer," Falk said. "Two hours . . ."

"Two hours," Kat conceded. "No longer."

She met his eyes. "And I'm dispatching marines to the orbital installations now," she added sternly. "I want them handed over without delay. And you are *not* to engage in any sabotage."

Falk's face didn't change, but she thought she saw *something* flicker across his face. The Board of Inquiry would find it easy to blame him for not disabling the industrial nodes before Kat arrived. Falk would make an ideal scapegoat, if the House of Lords wanted one. She wondered, idly, why he hadn't disabled the nodes before she'd arrived, when he could have done it without violating any surrender terms. Perhaps he'd thought he could hold the system indefinitely. Afterwards . . . Tarleton would need the industrial nodes if it was to have any hope of repaying its debt.

"As you wish," Falk said. "I'll make ready to receive your men."

His image vanished. Kat leaned back in her chair. The end of an occupation was always fraught, even when the occupiers had been relatively civilized. Soon the planet-side population would realize that they'd been liberated, if they hadn't realized already. And then they'd turn on the occupation forces. It would be difficult, if not impossible, to prevent a bloodbath if the penny dropped before the occupation forces were out of the city.

She looked at Katie. "Signal Colonel Hammond," she ordered. "His men are to take possession of the orbital facilities, then prepare for planetary landings. The enemy troops are to be transferred to makeshift detention camps until they can be repatriated or exchanged."

"Aye, Admiral." Katie's face twisted into a brilliant smile. "We won!"

". . . I suppose we did," Kat said. She had no illusions. The brief engagement had no real significance, not in the short term. Tarleton wasn't worth *that* much to either side. But in the long term . . . She'd placed significant strain on her ships and expended thousands of missiles for no real return. The war wasn't going to be decided by a single great battle. It was going to be decided by the cold hand of economics. "But this isn't the end."

"No, Admiral," Katie agreed. She sounded as if she had no doubt of their ultimate victory. Kat envied her. "We still have to land on Tyre."

Kat shook her head, then watched as the marine assault shuttles headed towards the orbital nodes. She didn't expect trouble. General Falk wasn't stupid enough to throw lives away for nothing . . . She hoped. It was the *planet* that was going to be a problem. And then . . . She wondered, absently, if General Falk could be induced to defect. A person with powerful political connections might know something useful. It was almost a shame he couldn't be interrogated. But he wouldn't have been sent out without his superiors taking precautions against him falling into enemy hands.

He'd have to join us willingly, she thought. *And, given his prior connections, that seems unlikely.*

She brought up the starchart, considering the possibilities. They couldn't stay at Tarleton for more than a few days. It wouldn't take *that* long for Tyre to dispatch a superdreadnought squadron, if they wished to catch her before she could head back into interstellar space. And then . . . There might even be a superdreadnought squadron far closer, lurking in hyperspace. The whole system could be a trap.

And that gives me an idea, she mused. *If, of course, we survive the next few days.*

CHAPTER THIRTY-THREE

TARLETON

"They were quite well behaved, for occupiers," Premier Alistair Lipitor spat as they walked around the edge of the spaceport. "But they were . . . occupiers."

Kat nodded in understanding. Tarleton hadn't *enjoyed* the brief period of occupation, but compared to the worlds that had been occupied by the Theocracy, they'd been very lucky. There had been no mass arrests, no gang rapes, no forced religious instruction . . . The worst that had happened, according to even the bitterest local, was the indignity of having to tolerate the occupation force in the first place. The handful of minor incidents had been handled by the occupation force itself.

I suppose they knew better than to indulge in casual brutality for the sake of it, she thought sourly. The Commonwealth's military had never condoned atrocities. Even after Hebrides, there hadn't been many voices demanding retaliation in kind. *And the House of Lords wouldn't want to give people the impression that they couldn't surrender.*

She looked at the premier. "And how did they treat you?"

"Remarkably well, all things considered," Lipitor said. "They locked me up, but otherwise . . . they treated me well. I don't think they quite knew what to do with me."

"Or they were just waiting until the end of the war before they decided your fate," Kat said. "It wouldn't be easy to negotiate with you *after* they shot you."

Lipitor shrugged. "We're not that important," he said, a hint of bitter tiredness in his tone. "Our fate won't be decided here."

Kat nodded. Tarleton hadn't been particularly important even before the civil war had broken out. The planet would be a prize for the winner, whoever that happened to be. Still, she wondered if anyone would care. Tarleton simply didn't have much to offer, not now. And the planet's population wouldn't work to build up its industrial base if they thought it wouldn't bring them *any* benefits. It might be a long time before the planet recovered from its ordeal.

Her wristcom bleeped. "Admiral," Katie said. "Justicar Montfort has arrived. His shuttle should land in ten minutes."

"Understood." Kat frowned. The justicar had been dispatched well before her ships had liberated Tarleton. It would have been extremely hard for him if he'd reached the planet before she'd driven the enemy ships away. "I look forward to meeting him."

Lipitor glanced at her. "A justicar?"

"The king's personal investigator." Kat felt her frown deepen. Technically, she knew the king had wide-ranging powers to uphold the rule of law; practically, she couldn't remember ever hearing of a justicar doing anything more than rubber-stamping courtroom rulings. It was a check-and-balance that had fallen by the wayside years ago, as the Kingdom of Tyre slowly morphed into the Commonwealth. "I'm not sure why he was sent here."

But I have a nasty idea, her thoughts added silently.

She turned, leading the way back towards the spaceport complex as the shuttle appeared in the distance. The justicar hadn't wasted any time, she reflected. He hadn't even delayed in orbit long enough to make certain that all enemy forces had been neutralized. Instead, he'd headed straight down to the spaceport. She supposed he had nerve, but still . . . She couldn't help feeling cold. It was an ominous development.

"You have my personal thanks, if nothing else," Lipitor said as they stepped into the giant building. "I probably won't survive the next election cycle."

"Tell your people to wait and see who wins the war," Kat said. Her wristcom bleeped, once. The justicar had landed. "You never know who might come out on top."

She allowed him to show her into a small meeting room, feeling a twinge of sympathy. It was hard to blame Lipitor for not wanting to go back to the capital city, not after the planet had been liberated. The occupation force had insisted that he speak to his people, that he tell them to remain calm and not to resist . . . Lipitor hadn't had a choice, of course, but who cared? He would be blamed for everything, from the occupation itself to the decision to side with the king.

"I won't," Lipitor said. "And that is all that matters now."

Kat started to say something but stopped when the door was flung open and Justicar Montfort stepped into the room. He was a statuesque man with a stern face and strong lantern jaw that looked to have been carved from stone . . . the result, Kat was sure, of extensive cosmetic surgery. His face was so unfashionable that there was no way any parent would willingly inflict it on a child. And his eyes were hard, cold . . . *fanatical.* She felt a shiver run down her spine. The last time she'd seen eyes like that had been on a Theocrat who'd been trying to kill her.

"Admiral." Justicar Montfort's voice was as cold as his eyes. "My congratulations on your victory."

"Thank you, Justicar," Kat said. "What is your business here?"

"My orders are to investigate the planet's surrender," Montfort said sternly. "I trust I have your *full* cooperation?"

Kat studied him for a long, cold moment. "My first priority is defending the planet." It was hard not to tell him where he could stick his demand for full cooperation. "You can have everything I can spare, save for what I need."

"As you wish." Montfort bowed, then looked past her. "Premier Lipitor?"

Lipitor nodded. "Yes. Welcome to . . ."

"I would appreciate it if you escorted me to your capital," Montfort said. "My staff and I have much work to do."

Kat frowned. Whatever else he was, Montfort was no diplomat. Talking like *that* to a planetary leader . . . It just wasn't done. Governor Rogan would blow a fuse when he heard about it. The king was likely to pay a price for his servant's attitude. She glanced at Lipitor, who shrugged and motioned to the door. Kat watched them go, feeling troubled. It definitely didn't bode well for the future.

She made a mental note to discuss the issue with the king at the earliest opportunity, then left the room and headed down to the makeshift command center. Colonel Hammond and his staff had already set up shop, although Kat had made it clear that they wouldn't be staying. As soon as the planetary militia was re-formed and put in charge of the detention camps, they'd be on their way. The last thing she wanted was to be pinned against the planet by a squadron of enemy superdreadnoughts. It would end badly.

"Admiral," Hammond said. He seemed surprised that she was wandering around without a close-protection detail. "We've rounded up the last of the occupiers."

"Very good," Kat said. "Any trouble?"

"A handful got beaten up by the locals," Hammond said. "I've taken the liberty of transferring them to sickbay. The remainder . . . They're fine, if a little unsure. A couple of them seem to think they were hung out to dry."

"Their ships had no choice," Kat said. "They *had* to leave."

"Yep." Hammond shrugged. "But they don't know that."

Kat felt her heart ache, just for a second. Hammond reminded her of Pat . . . She turned away, concentrating on the displays until she got her emotions back under tight control. The constant flow of data was interesting, but not particularly helpful. The House of Lords had sent intelligence specialists to Tarleton in the belief that they might be able to find something useful, yet it was hard to tell what, if anything, they'd found. The intelligence officers had departed four days before Kat's squadron had arrived.

They probably didn't find very much, she thought. *They would have stayed for longer otherwise.*

She keyed her wristcom, organizing a flight back to orbit. She'd done all she could on the surface. She'd reassured the planetary government, met the justicar . . . Better to be in orbit if—when—the shit hit the fan. The marines didn't need her while they were busy preparing to pull out . . .

"Admiral," Hammond said. "There is a . . . ah, a *situation* at Government House."

Kat looked up at him sharply. "A situation?"

"A standoff between the security forces and the local militia," Hammond clarified. "They're both asking for our help."

Shit, Kat thought. The security forces . . . Montfort's team? And they were engaged in a standoff with the planetary militia? She felt her blood turn to ice. *That* didn't sound good. What was happening? *Has he uncovered evidence of treason . . . or has he done something stupid?*

She met Hammond's eyes. "I'm going," she said. "Summon my close-protection detail."

Hammond looked as if he wanted to protest. Kat understood. It was his job to keep her out of danger. *Pat* would have used all necessary force to stop her from putting herself in needless danger too. But, at the same time, they might need her. If two allied forces were on the verge of actually *shooting* at each other . . .

"Aye, Admiral," Hammond said. "Be careful."

Kat nodded, then headed towards the door. Her flyer was waiting outside, her close-protection detail holding position around it. Two marine flyers were hovering overhead, crammed with troops in armor. They looked impressive, although Kat recalled Pat grumbling that the flyers were nothing more than death traps. A single HVM could blow the vehicle out of the air, killing the marines inside before they could bail out. Kat checked her service pistol as she took her seat, then sat back as the flyer took off. They'd be there almost before she knew it.

"The planetary militia is going on alert," Captain Akbar Rosslyn said. Her bodyguard sounded as if he wanted to physically drag Kat to the shuttle and send her straight back to orbit. "They're summoning reinforcements from the countryside."

"Understood," Kat said. No actual *shooting*, not yet—she was sure the marines would yank her out the moment all hell broke loose—but it was starting to look bad. Very bad. What the hell had happened? "Let's see if we can calm it down without any real shooting."

She leaned forward as the flyer flew over the city and descended towards Government House. It was a large brown building, far less pretentious than anything she'd seen on Tyre; she couldn't help thinking that the structure promoted humility rather than the arrogance that was so deeply embedded in the aristocracy. Outside, a handful of security troopers, distinctive in their blue-and-red uniforms, faced off against a squad of planetary militia. Kat didn't need to be a marine to pick out the other militiamen lurking nearly, keeping out of sight while remaining close enough to intervene if things went spectacularly wrong. The entire scene looked as if it was going to explode into violence.

"Tell the other flyers to keep back," she ordered. "We don't want anyone doing anything foolish."

Rosslyn gave her a look that said, quite clearly, that he thought *she* was being foolish, but he relayed the order anyway. Kat felt another stab of grief—Pat would have done the same, she was sure—as the flyer dropped to the ground. The hatch clicked open, allowing her to step outside. She kept her face impassive as she surveyed the scene, trying to ignore the hundreds of weapons that weren't *quite* pointed at anyone in particular. It was hardly the first time she'd been in danger, but there was something oddly personal about having a gun aimed at her face. Superdreadnought salvos simply didn't have the same immediacy.

She caught sight of Premier Lipitor and Justicar Montfort glaring at each other. Two more men stood behind Lipitor, their faces impassive masks. Politicians, Kat guessed. They had the air of men who were calculating how best to turn the situation to their advantage. She wondered just how many of them would survive if someone pulled a trigger. The crossfire would probably cut down everyone outside the building.

"Admiral," Montfort said, "Premier Lipitor and his government are under arrest."

Kat blinked. "On what charge?"

"Treason and collaboration," Montfort said. "By surrendering, they provided material aid to the enemy and . . ."

"We had no choice!" Lipitor seemed to have found his missing spark. "If we hadn't surrendered, they would have bombarded our world back into the Stone Age!"

"You didn't even try to destroy your records!" Montfort glared at Lipitor, then looked at Kat. "How many people will die because of him?"

Kat held up a hand. "And what authority do you have to arrest *anyone*?"

"The king gave me full authority to investigate the surrender," Montfort said. "It is my considered belief that Premier Lipitor surrendered when he could have continued the fight and, furthermore, collaborated with the occupation forces during their brief period of residence. It was *his* urging that kept his people from resisting the occupiers and . . ."

"Getting themselves killed," Lipitor snapped.

"You have no authority to arrest anyone, not here," one of the politicians said. "We didn't join the war so the king could walk all over us."

"I have all the authority I need," Montfort insisted. "Admiral, I insist . . ."

Kat lifted her eyebrows. "You *insist*?"

"I *insist*," Montfort repeated. "By order of the king himself, all collaborators are to be tried in a special court . . ."

"We can handle such matters," the other politician said. "And . . ."

". . . And I *demand* you put them all under arrest," Montfort continued. "As a loyal servant of His Majesty, you are required to enforce his word."

Kat thought fast. There would be a bloodbath if Montfort tried to arrest Lipitor and the planetary militia decided to resist. Montfort and his team would probably be killed in the crossfire, along with Kat herself. The marines would put down the uprising, with fire support from orbit if necessary, but then . . . what? A clash between the king's supporters and a colonial government would end badly. Governor Rogan and his faction might break with the king completely.

"No," she said flatly.

Montfort looked shocked. "Admiral . . ."

"I don't know just how much authority the king gave you," Kat said. "I *do* know that *I* have final authority over the system, at least until the king overrules me. And I will not expend time and effort arresting people who can be handled by local authorities."

She met his eyes, silently willing him to give in. She couldn't allow a clash between the two sides. The planetary government might want to put Premier Lipitor on trial for treason, collaboration, or whatever other charges it thought it could make stick, but it couldn't allow an outsider to drag Lipitor off-world for trial. Too many colonial worlds had joined the king to get away from overbearing outsiders. They could hardly submit to the king now. And Lipitor himself hadn't requested an off-world trial.

"Admiral, I have my orders," Montfort protested.

"Consider them overridden," Kat said. She glanced at Rosslyn, who nodded. "You and your men are under arrest. You will be confined to quarters aboard my ship until we return to Caledonia, where you can put your case before the king himself. He can rebuke me if he feels I overstepped *my* authority."

She watched as the marines quickly rounded up the security troops, disarming them before marching them to the flyers. She would have expected Montfort to be relieved—at least they'd avoided bloodshed—but he merely glared at her as he was half pushed towards the shuttle. Kat exhaled. He might feel humiliated, she had no doubt he felt humiliated, but at least he was still alive. And no one could blame him for failing in his mission.

It depends on what the king will make of this, she thought. *He may throw Montfort to the dogs or back him to the hilt.*

"Thank you, Admiral," Lipitor said. "I thought that was going to turn nasty."

"I thought so too," Kat said. She saw the flyers taking off, heading back to the spaceport. "I don't know what he was thinking."

One of the politicians stepped forward. "Admiral, I want you to know that we will not surrender our sovereignty to the king," he said. "We can and we will handle the matter ourselves."

"I'm sure you can," Kat said. She had no reason to think that Lipitor had betrayed anyone, particularly the king. He hadn't really been *able* to betray the king. "I would suggest, however, that you remember that the eyes of posterity are on you."

"We'll see to it that everyone gets a fair trial," the other politician said. He sounded more reasonable, although there was a nasty edge to his tone. Kat guessed he stood to gain if Lipitor was found guilty. "We won't dissuade you from sending observers, if you like . . ."

"I have to return to Caledonia," Kat said. She needed to talk to the king before he managed to alienate everyone. She'd stopped Montfort from starting a civil war within the civil war—*an* uncivil *war*, her thoughts mocked—but the mere fact he'd *tried* to assert himself over the planetary government would upset people. "I'm sure the king will send more observers, in time."

"We'd like it to be you," Lipitor said. "You've earned our respect."

"I can't stay," Kat said. She understood, better than she cared to admit. The next representative might be more inclined to follow orders without question. Who knew *what* orders the king would give him? "I have to leave in two days."

"Then know that you have our thanks," Lipitor said. He shook her hand firmly. "And may God go with you."

Kat saluted, then walked to the flyer. It was time to go.

CHAPTER THIRTY-FOUR

WACO

"It's very quiet," Commander Isa Yagami whispered.

William snorted, loudly enough to make his staff jump. HMS *Belfast* might be sneaking her way into the Waco System, doing everything in her power to ensure that she remained undetected, but there was really no point in whispering. Sound didn't travel through a vacuum. The entire crew could be having a keg party, complete with strippers and really loud music, and no one would hear them. He was more concerned about a tiny flicker of betraying energy than anything else.

"They don't know we're coming," he said, dryly. "Of *course* it's quiet."

He studied the display thoughtfully as *Belfast* and her sisters crept towards their target. Waco was an unusual system, unusual enough to attract a great deal of investment and scientific investigation before the Theocratic War. In realspace, the system was dominated by a massive cluster of asteroids that everyone agreed had *once* been a planet; in hyperspace, the approaches to Waco were half shrouded by giant semi-permanent energy storms. William had read the files carefully, even the ones that suggested that the destroyed planet had once played host to an alien civilization. The writers insisted that there were people in the government who took the prospect very seriously. There was no proof.

No one had discovered so much as a *hint* of alien life since humanity had started to explore the universe, but that hadn't stopped people from insisting that the government had covered everything up.

And there are plenty of stories of weird sightings in hyperspace, William reminded himself. *It's just a shame that none of those sightings are ever recorded.*

He kept his eyes on the display. The asteroids had attracted an unusual number of settlers, who'd brought a considerable amount of investment with them. Thousands of asteroids had been turned into homes, ranging from tiny single-person bubbles to giant settlements that housed hundreds of people in reasonable comfort; thousands more had been mined to provide raw material for a rapidly growing industrial base. The system's government was so weak as to be almost unnoticeable, although that wasn't as much a problem as one might suppose. A society based on asteroids forced its inhabitants to cooperate. Rogues rarely lasted long enough to stand trial.

"We'll be within firing range in twenty minutes, Admiral," Yagami said.

"One would hope so," William said. "Prepare to fire, but do not go active until I give the order."

"Yes, Admiral."

William scowled as the squadron inched closer. Waco should have attracted more attention from the House of Lords, if only because the system had remarkable potential. Instead, its inhabitants had practically built their industrial base from scratch. They'd taken loans from the Commonwealth Central Bank, according to the files, but unusually they'd managed to pay them off well before the debts had come due. And it had worked for them. They owned a cluster of industrial nodes and even a couple of small, civilian-grade shipyards. They'd been planning a major expansion before the war, but the recession had washed over their system like a tidal wave. He couldn't help feeling a little guilty as the timer ticked down to zero. The system might have sided with the king, but they'd built most of what they had without his help. They didn't deserve to watch helplessly as it got smashed.

"Missiles locked, Admiral," Yagami said. "We have their shipyards bang to rights."

William let out a breath as the timer reached zero. There was no point in trying to go closer. The shipyard was surrounded by hundreds of sensors, ranging from military-grade active sensors that pulsed emissions into the inky darkness of space to passive sensors that watched silently for any *hint* of a cloaked ship. The odds of being detected were already too high, even though his ships were protected by the most modern cloaking systems known to man. It was all too likely that the locals, who would have a feel for how local space *felt*, would notice if something was wrong. He would have preferred to keep his distance . . .

"Decloak," he ordered. "And fire!"

The display wavered, slightly, as *Belfast* decloaked. Her active sensors went online a second later, confirming the targeting data before her missiles fired. The enemy shipyard was a glowing mass of possible targets, ranging from full-sized freighters to commercial starships that could easily have passed for destroyers. He felt his eyes narrow as he looked at them, wondering, again, just how long Hadrian had been planning for civil war. Most commercial ships couldn't be turned into warships—they were too slow and ungainly for military use—but a handful of designs could be adapted into warships fairly easily. He'd seen the plans. Given time, the king might be able to add quite a few vessels to his roster . . .

"Missiles away, sir," Yagami confirmed. "The defenses are coming to life."

William nodded. The shipyard was heavily defended. Its tactical sensors were sweeping space, looking for targets; behind them, he knew the point defense platforms would be getting ready to engage his missiles. They were top-of-the-line platforms too, he noted absently. Someone had been bending the rules on weapons and tech transfer . . .

the king, once again? Or someone else? The economic recession had made some people so desperate that they were prepared to bend or even break the rules if it meant keeping their heads above water.

New icons sparkled to life on the display. "They're launching gunboats, Admiral," Yagami warned. "And they're assembling their defense fleet behind the lines."

"Pull us back," William ordered. A lone gunboat wasn't a problem. A swarm of gunboats could bring down a superdreadnought. "Launch the second salvo of missiles with active seeker heads as we go."

"Aye, Admiral." Yagami sounded puzzled. "We're leaving?"

William studied the display for a long moment. The entire system was coming to life. Hundreds of ships were heading towards him, hundreds more were heading away . . . either to jump into hyperspace and flee or simply get out of the firing line before it was too late. It looked as if they were going to be stung to death if they stayed where they were. He'd never planned to occupy the system. It wouldn't cost him anything to retreat.

"Yes," he said. "I think we've outstayed our welcome."

He watched, grimly, as the missiles lanced into the shipyard. Dozens were picked off by the point defense, or gulled into wasting themselves on harmless sensor decoys, but the remainder made it through and slammed into their targets. Antimatter explosions flared briefly in the endless cold of space, each expanding ball on the display marking destroyed structures and vaporized lives. William hoped, despite himself, that the locals had evacuated the shipyard before it was too late. He wanted to deny the system to the king, not commit butchery. He'd never felt such qualms about fighting the Theocracy . . .

But the Theocracy would have killed us all, if we hadn't killed them first, he reminded himself. *Here . . . we're waging war on our former comrades.*

"Seventeen hits detected, Admiral," Yagami reported. "Preliminary assessment suggests that we crippled the shipyard beyond immediate repair."

"Let us hope so." William felt another pang of guilt. "Signal the squadron, Commander. Order them to go to full military power."

"Aye, sir."

William nodded to himself, watching the display as the gunboats closed the range with terrifying speed. They'd be armed with missiles . . . but what *kind* of missiles? If they carried shipkillers, his squadron was about to have a very hard time. No one had managed to design a gunboat that carried more than a single shipkiller, thank the gods, but there were so *many* of them. And they were all going to be launched at sprint-mode range. It was going to be difficult to stop them before they struck home.

"Launch our shipkillers on wide dispersal," he ordered. A dangerous tactic, particularly when there was the prospect of running into enemy capital ships, but it might save their lives. "And detonate them when they're within explosion range."

"Aye, Admiral."

William braced himself as the gunboats closed to sprint-mode range, ducking and weaving to evade his point defense fire. The pilots were good, he acknowledged ruefully; they'd probably been practicing since before the war. And they were firing . . . He cursed under his breath as the missiles roared towards his ships, moving too quickly to be stopped easily. The remaining gunboats broke off, an instant before . . .

Belfast plunged, the gravity field seeming to twist for an instant before snapping back to normal. William heard someone scream behind him, perhaps terrified that the internal compensator had failed. Idiot. If the compensator had failed, the ship would either have crash-stopped, which might well have killed them all, or kept moving, in which case they would *all* be dead before they knew what had hit them. The display flashed red, then calmed down. The shields had taken the brunt of the blast.

"*New Coventry* is gone, sir," Yagami reported. "*Sheffield* has taken heavy damage."

William glanced at the display. All but one of his ships had been damaged. *Sheffield* was too badly wrecked to be salvaged, at least without months in the yards . . . He glanced at the display, watching the tidal wave of ships and gunboats raging towards him. There was no time to evacuate *Sheffield*, no time to get her crew out of the trap . . . He sucked in his breath, bitterly. The only consolation was that the crew wouldn't be mistreated. The king seemed to be doing his best to keep the war as civilized as possible.

Which is a pleasant change, he thought numbly. *Most civil wars turn uncivil very quickly.*

"Contact *Sheffield*," he said. "Order Captain Hocks to . . ."

"Captain Hocks is dead, sir," Yagami informed him. "Lieutenant Purim has assumed command."

William winced. He didn't know Purim, but if he was in command . . . At least three or four senior officers had to be dead. Or out of contact . . . He hoped the latter, but he feared the former. There were so many redundancies built into warships that it was hard for someone to be put out of contact without being killed outright.

"Order Lieutenant Purim to drop his shields, destroy his datacores, and signal surrender," he said. "He is to do everything in his power to keep his crew alive."

Yagami paled. "Yes, sir."

"And we're to enter hyperspace as soon as possible," William added.

"Aye, sir."

William glanced at the icon on the display—*Sheffield* was already falling behind—and schooled his face into immobility. The ships he'd captured during the Battle of Tyre were already being pressed back into service, after a hasty repair job. They'd been built at Tyre, after all; the yarddogs had known how to replace their datacores and repair the battle damage. *Sheffield* might be repaired too and pointed back at her former owners, given time . . . He briefly considered ordering Lieutenant Purim to abandon ship and activate the self-destruct, but there was no time. Besides, it might be misunderstood by the defenders.

He felt space twist around him as the remaining cruisers flew through the vortex and plunged into hyperspace, picking up speed as they raced away from the stricken system. He kept a wary eye on the display, but there were no hints that the enemy intended to give chase. They were probably relieved to have chased the raiders off, he decided. Why risk an engagement in hyperspace that might easily wind up with both sides destroyed?

"Stand down from battlestations," he ordered once it became clear they'd made a clean break. "Damage report?"

He listened to the report with a growing feeling of dissatisfaction. He'd known, of course, just how dangerous gunboats could be, but . . . He shook his head. The colonials had built and deployed more gunboats than he'd expected, that was all. There was no need to worry . . . unless, of course, they had *far* more gunboats than he'd realized. They were a relatively cheap way to defend a system, after all. They'd just proved their value . . .

They wouldn't have done so well if we'd had more escorts, he reminded himself. *They're not silver bullets.*

He stood. "Inform Captain Cavendish that we will proceed to Point Allen, as planned," he ordered. "I'll be in my ready room."

"Aye, Admiral."

William didn't allow himself to relax until he sat down at his desk and scanned the preliminary reports. It definitely *looked* as though the mission had been a success, at least by some standards. They'd damaged, if not destroyed, an enemy shipyard, something that would force the colonials to demand protection from the king. *They will all want superdreadnoughts*, William thought. And yet, there was no way the king could afford to give them superdreadnoughts. He'd have to find a way to protect them without dispersing his fleet.

He could gamble and uncover Caledonia, William thought. The House of Lords had flatly refused to allow Grand Admiral Rudbek and William himself to uncover Tyre. *It wouldn't be that big a risk for him.*

His steward stepped into the compartment, carrying a pot of coffee. William motioned for him to put it on the desk, then turned his attention back to the terminal. His steward poured the coffee before leaving as silently as he'd come. William barely noticed. He was too busy skimming the damage-control reports. He'd have to write his own report before they reached Tyre. He wondered, morbidly, just what had happened while he'd been away.

His doorbell chimed. He looked up. "Come."

Captain Lucy Cavendish stepped into the compartment. "Admiral."

"Captain," William said. He nodded to the nearest chair. "Please, take a seat."

"Thank you," Lucy said. "I wasn't expecting so much resistance."

"This time, we tangled with more modern defenses." William shrugged. "Caledonia itself will be *much* harder to attack."

"And it cost us a cruiser. Two cruisers, really." Lucy sounded as if she didn't think the trade-off was worth it. "And hundreds of men will go into POW camps." She looked up. "They will treat them well, won't they?"

William met her eyes. "The king has treated his POWs well," he said carefully. He thought it would be better not to mention that the POWs might be mistreated well before they were handed over to the king. The most dangerous moments of going into captivity were always the first few hours *after* capture. Angry soldiers could hurt or kill prisoners before someone in authority arrived to take control. "I don't think they'll be in any real danger."

"I hope so," Lucy agreed. "I knew Captain Hocks."

"He was a good man," William agreed. "And he won't be the last friend you'll lose."

Lucy grimaced. "I never liked Captain Wiseman," she added. "But he didn't deserve to die." She shook her head. "It's a strange war, isn't it?

We know the other side almost as well as we know ourselves. We used to work together, fight together. And now . . . we're trying to kill each other. This isn't a football field, where we might be rivals without hating each other. This is . . . This is war."

"Yes. It is." William knew just how she felt. "Brother against brother, fathers against sons . . . Civil wars are always unpleasant."

Lucy snorted, humorlessly. "You've fought in many, Admiral?"

"No." William opened his drawer, looking for the bottle Duke Peter had given him before he left. "But I've studied history. This isn't a battle for independence, when one side wants to leave and the other doesn't want to let them go. This is . . . This is a battle over the same land, a battle that cannot end with one side walking off and leaving the other alone. It's not over getting away from the system, it's over who *controls* the system. We can't solve this problem by deporting vast numbers of people to another world."

He poured two glasses of wine, trying not to think about how much the bottle might have cost. He hadn't dared look it up. Probably more money than he'd seen in his entire life. He honestly wasn't sure if the drink was a bribe or a promise of more to come.

"So we have to fight," he said. "And hope we can win without mass slaughter."

Lucy took the drink he offered her and held it up. "Cheers."

"Cheers," William echoed.

"Those civil wars," Lucy said. "How did they end?"

"Some ended well, with compromises." William took another sip. "Others ended with one side being thoroughly crushed and the other warped by victory. And . . . they didn't end well."

"So I see," Lucy said. "Why didn't they just agree to disagree?"

"They couldn't coexist," William said. "Like here and now. The king wants supreme power; the Houses of Parliament don't want him to have it. And so they have to fight because otherwise . . ."

"They have to surrender," Lucy said. She sipped her drink. "People are the same everywhere, aren't they?"

"Pretty much." William returned the bottle to the drawer. "They live and die, eat and drink, love and hate . . . They're the same underneath, wherever they are. There's nothing new under the stars, not really. Our war is just a reflection of older wars, which were, in turn, reflections of still older wars."

"You're a philosopher as well as a historian, then," Lucy commented. She passed him the empty glass. "How would *you* end the war?"

"This war?" William shrugged. "I don't think the two sides can compromise. And I don't think that one can let the other go. So they have to fight it out and hope for the best."

He grinned tiredly. "And, afterwards, we can think about the future."

CHAPTER THIRTY-FIVE

CALEDONIA

"I object," Earl Antony thundered.

Kat glowered at him. It had been a long flight home, one that she'd spent alternately trying to convince Justicar Montfort to calm down and planning what she'd say to the king when she finally reached Caledonia. She hadn't been too pleased to receive an immediate summons to the war council, even before her ships had entered orbit. She'd had to leave her flag captain in command and head straight for the planet itself. It felt as if she'd abandoned officers who depended upon her.

It was probably a mistake to let Montfort write home, she thought sourly. She hadn't been able to think of a legitimate reason to stop him, worse luck. They'd started powering up the StarCom before she realized that it might be a good idea to keep it inactive for a few days longer. *He had a chance to get his say in first.*

She stood at ease, her eyes sweeping the room. The two factions had been arguing for days, ever since Montfort had been placed in detention. The aristocrats looked outraged that Kat had dared interfere with a justicar, to the point of accusing her of outright treason; the colonials looked furious that Montfort had ever been sent out at all. Kat didn't really blame them. The Commonwealth's interference in their internal affairs had been a major grievance, pushing them into rebellion and open war. They clearly weren't happy that the *king* had also been interfering in their internal affairs.

And the poor bastards on Tarleton didn't have a choice, Kat reminded herself, sharply. One didn't have to be a tactical expert to know the position was hopeless. *It was either surrender, and collaborate as little as possible, or watch helplessly as their planet was bombarded into rubble.*

She looked at the king. He looked distracted, as if he was having problems following the debate. Kat felt her sense of unease deepen as she noticed the princess, sitting next to the king. *She* was paying close attention, her eyes flickering from speaker to speaker as they ranted and raved. Kat met the king's eyes and saw a faint smile flicker across his face, mingled with bitterness. There was nothing he could do that wouldn't upset at least half of his supporters. Trying to weasel his way out would only alienate everyone.

The whole plan has fallen apart, and he doesn't know how to react, she thought. She'd seen it before, time and time again. A junior officer would come up with a brilliant tactical concept, which fell apart the moment the enemy did something unexpected. Someone too impressed with their own brilliance might not bother to think up contingency plans . . . or follow the plan into ruin because they couldn't conceive of it going wrong. *Whatever he does, he's going to have to pay a price.*

"You have no *right* to send a justicar to Tarleton," Governor Rogan snapped. He was looking at the king, even as he addressed his words to Earl Antony. "And you certainly have no right to arrest an entire planetary government!"

"They sold us out," Earl Antony snapped back. "They *need* to be put on trial."

He glared at Kat. "And *you* shouldn't have stopped him."

"I kept him from starting another civil war," Kat said evenly. She'd envisaged having a chance to defend herself formally, if the king and his advisers chose to disapprove of her actions. "The justicar had no authority to arrest anyone on Tarleton."

"He had the king's authority," Earl Antony thundered. "He had all the authority he needed."

Governor Rogan slapped the table, hard. "At no point did we agree to surrender supreme power to the king! We are equals and partners, not subordinates and slaves!"

"And you surrendered," Earl Antony said. "Are you really committed to the cause?"

Kat winced as the shouting grew louder. Earl Antony had crossed a line. Governor Rogan *hadn't* surrendered. Of course he hadn't surrendered. But he was a colonial, and all colonials were the same in aristocratic eyes. Kat was tempted to just pick Earl Antony up, drag him outside, and kick his ass. It could hardly have made the situation worse.

"Perhaps we should form a committee to investigate the incident," Sir Grantham said quickly, trying to pour oil on troubled waters. "It would assess things without anger and . . ."

Governor Rogan cut him off. "Out of the question! We want it understood now! We are not subordinates . . ."

"Perhaps we should ask Admiral Falcone why she saw fit to intervene," Admiral Lord Garstang said. "The whole affair was out of her remit."

Kat kept her face carefully blank as all eyes turned to her. "There is a difference between outright treason and collaboration, *willing* collaboration, and collaboration extracted at the point of a gun. The planetary government had no choice but to surrender. The situation was hopeless. And, during the occupation, it had no choice but to do everything in its power to keep the planet from boiling over. Any uprising would have ended *very* badly for the planet's population. They did not enthusiastically collaborate. They did as little as they could get away with."

"And you think that excuses them?" Earl Antony didn't sound convinced. His voice became mocking. "That's a strange attitude from a military officer, if I may make so bold."

"Being a military officer requires a strong grip on reality." Kat allowed her voice to harden. "They had no way to resist directly, no way to kick the occupiers off their planet. They did as little as they could. There's no sign they rounded up dissidents, provided additional security, or did anything else that might cross the line between enforced collaboration and willing collaboration. They simply had no choice."

"They could have done nothing," Earl Antony snapped.

"And then . . . what?" Kat let out an angry breath. "Yes, sure; they could have forced the occupation force to do a great deal *more* for itself. Yes, they could have done that. But it would have come at a price, a price their people would have paid in blood. I'm not happy they surrendered, nor am I happy they collaborated, but . . . they had no choice."

She met his eyes, daring him to look away. "It's easy to pass judgment from hundreds of light years behind the lines. It's easy to say that you would never surrender, that you would never collaborate, that you would never be a party to your humiliation . . . It's easy to say that, when you're *safe*. I've heard all sorts of people talking tough, telling everyone that they would stand up to bullies and rapists, but when the crunch comes . . . they fold. They surrender. They don't even *try* to fight."

Earl Antony purpled. "I have been in danger . . ."

"No, you haven't." Kat had no idea what Earl Antony had been doing with his life, but she was fairly sure he hadn't faced real danger. "If you had, you would have understood."

"Well said," Governor Rogan said. "I find no fault in Admiral Falcone's actions."

"Well, I do." Earl Antony looked at the king. "She shouldn't have arrested Montfort."

"She *did*, technically, have authority over the system," Admiral Lord Garstang pointed out, smoothly. "The justicar didn't relieve her when he arrived."

"The planetary government simply reclaimed its power," Kat said. She'd made no move to declare herself the planetary governor. She'd seen no need to claim the position for herself. It wasn't as if Tarleton had been genuinely hostile territory. The welcome her ships and crews had received spoke volumes about how much the planet had needed them. "And I'm not convinced that the justicar had any authority over the planetary government."

"He was appointed by the *king*," Earl Antony said. "He outranked . . ."

"No, he didn't," Governor Rogan said. "He had no authority on Tarleton."

Kat rubbed her forehead. The argument was going in circles. She looked at Lord Gleneden, who was keeping a watchful silence. The king's doves, the aristocrats who wanted a peaceful settlement, understood that Montfort had acted badly . . . but they couldn't say it out loud. Of *course* not. That would have been taken as a betrayal. Earl Antony would paint them as subverting the king himself. They'd been pushed into a position where there were no winning moves, where whatever they did would have unpleasant consequences . . .

Just like the king himself, Kat thought. *But if they don't do anything, the whole provisional government will come apart.*

Hadrian straightened, visibly. "It is true that I appointed Justicar Montfort to his position," he said. His voice was very calm, betraying none of his inner turmoil. "It is also true that Montfort overstepped his authority. He had orders to establish the facts and make recommendations, not start arresting people. I believed he could be trusted to handle the matter responsibly. I was clearly wrong."

Kat kept her face carefully impassive. Montfort's orders had been vague to the point of uselessness. She had the feeling that whoever had written them—the king himself, perhaps—had intended to ensure there was plenty of room for ambiguity . . . and plausible deniability, if the whole thing blew up in his face. There would have been a private meeting, she assumed, before the justicar had been sent off . . . but whatever had been said there would remain unknown. The king had neatly ensured that *he* would have an out, whatever happened.

"I will deal with Montfort personally," the king informed them. "I will also write a personal letter of apology to Tarleton's government, informing them that Montfort overstepped his bounds and that they may handle their collaborators however they wish. And I believe we owe Admiral Falcone a vote of thanks for resolving the situation before it got out of hand."

And you just threw one of your servants under the aircar, Kat thought coldly. She wondered what had been said when Montfort met the king before his departure. The king would have had to clarify the written orders . . . Wouldn't he? *Montfort gets kicked out on his ass, and you survive.*

She clasped her hands behind her back as she studied the room. Lord Gleneden looked relieved. Earl Antony looked outraged. Sir Grantham's face was a stone-cold mask. And Governor Rogan looked utterly unconvinced. The king's words were plausible, Kat noted, but the governor had good reason to disbelieve them. Justicar Montfort would not have taken such a big step without feeling reasonably sure his master would back him.

The king looked at her. "I thank you for your service," he said. "And I'm sure everyone else will agree."

Kat nodded, curtly. "Thank you, Your Majesty."

"My staff will take custody of the justicar," the king said. "And now . . . you can give us your report."

And give everyone a chance to forget what happened, Kat thought. She was fairly sure it wasn't going to work. Governor Rogan certainly *wasn't* going to forget the past. Nor was Earl Antony. *It might be better to sort things out now.*

She put the thought aside and stood to attention. "We won."

A low chuckle ran around the room. "At least you're not trying to bore us," the king said, with a flash of his famous smile. "Details?"

Kat smiled back, feeling the councilors start to relax. "We entered the system as planned," she said. "There was a very brief engagement—they fired a salvo for the honor of the flag—before the enemy ships retreated. The remaining occupation forces surrendered without a fight. We landed troops, secured the spaceports, and handed local authority back to the planetary government. A largely meaningless victory."

Earl Antony gave her a sharp look. "Meaningless?"

"Meaningless," Kat repeated. "We recovered the system. Yes, we recovered the system. But they can capture it again, any time they like. The system might change hands a dozen times before the war comes to an end. They know it too. There's no point in trying to tell the universe we accomplished a great victory."

"We did." The king's lips curved into a smile. "We made it clear that we would liberate any worlds they capture."

"A promise we may not be able to keep," Kat pointed out. "If *I* was on the other side . . . next time, I'd bait a trap."

"Then we have to move fast," Admiral Lord Garstang said. "Admiral Ruben and I have been drawing up a plan to take the offensive."

You mean your staff officers have been drawing up a plan, Kat thought wryly. The two senior officers seemed to spend most of their time politicking rather than commanding the king's navy. But they'd been told they couldn't take their ships away from Caledonia, not yet. The defeat had spooked too many of the king's supporters for his peace of mind. *And do you understand just what is at stake?*

"Very good," the king said. "Let's hear it."

A holographic starchart appeared, hovering over the table. "The Granger System, Your Majesty," Admiral Lord Garstang said, as the hologram focused on a single star. "Seven light years from Tyre. Home to a minor naval base and, more importantly from our point of view, a major supply depot. The base was earmarked to be closed during the drawdown, but very little was actually done before the House of Lords made its bid for power."

The king leaned forward. "And you intend to capture the base?"

"No." Admiral Lord Garstang smiled, grimly. "I intend to raid it. We capture the supply depot, we carry off everything we need to continue the war . . . and we pull out, leaving the system empty. They can have whatever's left."

Kat frowned. A workable concept, she supposed, but . . . They wouldn't have *time* to strip the system bare, not before Home Fleet responded to the raid. She tried to calculate just how long it would take to steal everything and drew a blank. Days, at the very least. More like weeks or months. Supply depots were huge. The Royal Navy had plenty of experience at rearming and resupplying starships at speed, but . . . She shook her head. The defenders could simply blow up the supplies rather than let them fall into the king's hands. And *that* assumed that Granger was a soft target.

Governor Rogan seemed to have the same idea. "Are you sure you can *take* the system?"

"Yes," Admiral Lord Garstang said. "Granger is a curious system. There's a planet that has some quite heavy defenses, but the supply depot itself orbits the local gas giant and isn't *that* heavily defended. During the war, there was a powerful flotilla stationed at Granger; afterwards, the ships were withdrawn and decommissioned. Right now, they only have a handful of starships on defense duty."

"So they summon more from Home Fleet," Kat pointed out. "What then?"

"We take out the StarCom first," Admiral Lord Garstang said. "Granger will be unable to signal for help. It will take four days for a courier boat to reach Tyre and a week longer for them to dispatch Home Fleet to recapture the system. That's more than long enough to pillage the supply depot and retreat."

Eleven days, Kat thought. *It* might *be long enough. Even if they dispatch the ships when they lose contact with the planet, without waiting for updates, they'd still need seven days to get them to Granger.*

She frowned. On paper, the plan looked perfect. In practice, she wasn't so sure. Too many things could go wrong. If the enemy failed to react in the manner they expected . . . She considered the plan carefully, feeling her blood turn to ice. There was a very good chance the king's forces wouldn't have the advantage of surprise. Too many people already knew the target. She thought the king's councilors were above suspicion, but what about their aides, advisers, and sycophants? She would be astonished if there were no spies on Caledonia. Too many people were passing through the system and trying to make contact with the provisional government for them all to be vetted. There was probably an entire series of spy rings already active . . .

Just as we have spies back home, she reminded herself. *We can't keep them out completely.*

"Admiral Falcone will conduct the main assault," Admiral Lord Garstang said. "Once she captures the system, we can ship in the freighters and start stripping Granger of anything useful. And then . . ."

"I'd want to see the plans and projections for myself," Kat said bluntly. "And ensure we have a line of retreat if things go badly wrong."

"Of course," Admiral Lord Garstang said. "We would welcome your input."

He nodded to the starchart. "The engagement will be small compared to the Battle of Tyre, but it will have long-lasting repercussions. We will no longer have shortages right across the board. Instead, we can gather ourselves for a second, successful attack on Tyre. We can end the war."

You hope, Kat thought. Sooner or later, they *would* have to assault Tyre again. The thought chilled her, even though, this time, the planet wouldn't be caught by surprise. The House of Lords had had months to improve its defenses. Even if Admiral Lord Garstang was right, the casualties would be staggeringly high. *And what if you're wrong?*

"Very good," the king said. "I think we can approve your plan."

Governor Rogan frowned. "And what happens if we lose another colony while you're mounting your glorified smash-and-grab?"

"We can survive losing another colony," Admiral Lord Garstang told him. "But we cannot survive running out of supplies."

"And our morale won't survive losing another colony," Governor Rogan disagreed.

The king raised his hand. "Enough," he said. "Victory will let us liberate any occupied colony."

And defeat, Kat thought, *will mean the end of everything.*

CHAPTER THIRTY-SIX

CALEDONIA

"There are more guards on duty, I'm afraid," Sir Grantham said as he led Kat towards the king's rooms. "His Majesty is feeling a little paranoid."

Kat scowled at Sir Grantham's back. "Does he have *reason* to be paranoid?"

Sir Grantham turned his head, just enough to give her a look that suggested he thought she was being an idiot. "There have always been death threats leveled at His Majesty, Admiral, but now the threats have become considerably worse. Not everyone is his friend, and some of those who *aren't* have access to modern weapons. We have to do everything in our power to keep him safe."

"True," Kat agreed. Her father had been assassinated on Tyre, supposedly the safest place in the Commonwealth. A lone gunman, in the right place at the right time, might decapitate the king's cause along with the king himself. "I'm glad to know you're taking the threats seriously."

"We are," Sir Grantham said. "But it can be hard to tell just how many of the threats are actually serious."

He fell silent as they approached the guards, who looked as if they expected a regiment of marines to charge their position at any moment. Kat kept her thoughts to herself as they confiscated her pistol, ran scanners over her body, and checked anything that even *looked* suspicious.

They still appeared unhappy when they waved her through, even though they'd surveyed her body right down to the atomic level. They knew as well as she did that there was no such thing as total security. A madman who wanted the king dead might well manage to take him out, even if at the cost of his own life.

And someone who really wanted him dead would use a nuke to blow up the capital, Kat mused grimly. *The buildings aren't* that *strong.*

She stepped through the open door and frowned as she saw Princess Drusilla sitting next to the king. They'd clearly been discussing *something*—the king looking tired and worn—but whatever it was, they didn't seem inclined to continue the discussion in front of a witness. Kat closed the door, curtsied to the king, and took the comfortable armchair he offered. He didn't rise. He looked too tired *to* rise.

"Your Majesty," she said, formally. "You wanted to see me?"

"I wish you hadn't arrested Montfort," the king said. His voice was almost a whisper. "It caused too many problems."

"It would have caused too many problems if I *hadn't* arrested Montfort," Kat pointed out dryly. "He might have started a shooting war with the planetary militia."

She settled back in her chair, trying to keep the disquiet off her face. She'd had too long to think about it. Montfort and his men would have been quickly killed or captured, if the shit had hit the fan, but what then? Kat wasn't sure what she would have done . . . not then. She had a duty to uphold the king's authority, but also a duty to uphold his cause. On one hand, she couldn't let people mistreat his servants; on the other, she couldn't let his servants ruin his cause. It would have been a horrible, ghastly mess. And the House of Lords would have been utterly delighted. It would have been the greatest propaganda coup they could possibly have desired.

"He's a fool," the king agreed. "But it also made me look foolish."

"Some people simply cannot be trusted with power," Kat said. She had relatives who couldn't be trusted to serve as school lunch monitors, let alone corporate CEOs or starship captains. The power would go to their heads within a day. "Why him?"

"I expected him to carry out my orders," the king said. "And I thought I could trust him."

He tapped a switch by his chair. A trio of waiters entered carrying trays of food, which they placed on the table. The king made a show of tasting his dinner, then dismissed the waiters with a wave of his hand. Kat watched them go, then looked at Hadrian. Princess Drusilla was looking back at her, her brown eyes shadowed.

"It isn't easy choosing whom to trust," she said as she sat up and reached for her tray. "Why are we here?"

The king's lips twitched. "Daddy did a bad thing with Mommy, and nine months later . . ."

Kat had to laugh. "I mean, why *here*?" She waved a hand in the air to indicate the sitting room. "Why not a proper dining room?"

"It's harder to have proper dinners with my friends now," the king said. "If I hold a dinner for you, I'll have to invite everyone or insult the people I don't invite. And if I just invite you . . . too many people will demand to know why."

"Ouch," Kat said. Her father had had the same problem. Private dinners with his family had often turned into dinner parties, sometimes without any warning at all. Kat had never really understood why her father had tolerated it. He could surely have banished his distant relatives from the mansion with a single word. "Admiral Lord Garstang will think we're plotting against him?"

"Everyone will think I'm plotting against them," the king said pensively. "It was a great deal easier when everyone knew the rules."

"I suppose," Kat said. She eyed him for a moment as he poured the wine. "How have things been here? For you, I mean?"

The king drained his glass in one gulp, then poured himself another one. "It seems that I am condemned to be permanently misunderstood." He sounded rather more self-pitying than Kat would have expected.

"Whatever I do, there is always someone ready with a pettifogging objection, ready to think the worst of me. If I put forward plans to coordinate our militaries, I'm plotting to become a tyrant; if I propose economic options to rationalize our development, I'm planning to tie down the colonies . . . just like the House of Lords. It seems, sometimes, that I simply can't get anything done. Too many people spend all their time telling me I can't do something rather than figuring out a way to do it."

"They want structure in their lives," Kat said. "My father . . ."

"Your father could get everyone to form an orderly line, just by giving them a snotty look," the king said. "I always envied that in him."

"He was a good man," Princess Drusilla said.

Kat studied her for a long moment. "What do *you* think of the current . . . situation?"

Drusilla lowered her eyes. "It wouldn't be *proper* for me to hold an opinion."

"Really." Kat didn't believe that for a moment. If Princess Drusilla had been the proper model of Theocratic womanhood, she would never have fled the Theocracy in the first place. "But you have an opinion, don't you?"

"I believe my husband should assert himself," Princess Drusilla told her. "But apparently it is not so easy here."

"No." Kat felt disturbed, almost despite herself. She wasn't quite sure why. "There are checks and balances woven into our system."

"Too many checks and balances," the king said. He drained his glass, again. "What do you think of the plan?"

"On paper, it's a good plan." Kat didn't have to ask which plan he meant. "But, in practice, it's going to fail."

The king sat upright so fast he nearly threw himself out of his chair. "You think it's going to *fail*?"

"The plan was discussed openly at a meeting of the war council," Kat told him, surprised at his reaction. He looked as if he wanted to have her hauled off and beheaded for daring to question the plan. "By now, I'd bet that half the planet knows that you're sending me to Granger."

"The council is above suspicion," the king said icily.

"Are they?" Kat met his eyes. "Even if they are, what about the people they'll tell? It doesn't *need* a spy to get word back to the enemy. All it needs is one person with a big mouth and a complete lack of discretion."

The king's face fell. "So they'll be waiting for us."

"I suspect so," Kat said. She closed her eyes for a moment, recalling the starchart. "They'd actually be in a better position to rush reinforcements to Granger than we'd be to get the assault force to Granger in the first place. They would have time to adjust their plans, just in case we were bluffing them. At best, they'd have a chance to mousetrap us and hand out a minor, but significant, defeat; at worst, they'd protect the supply depot and lose nothing. They wouldn't even look like fools if we couldn't prove we'd tricked them."

And that assumes the supply depot is still intact, she thought. The reports claimed it was, but she had her doubts. The House of Lords should have stripped the base bare themselves by now, if they weren't willing to commit ships to its defense. *Even if the base isn't stripped now, they'll start stripping it the moment they hear we're coming.*

"Right." The king took a long breath. "What do you propose?"

Kat met his eyes. "We take steps," she said. "But we cannot let anyone know what we have in mind."

The king frowned. "What do *you* have in mind?"

Kat outlined the idea, silently glad she'd had time to think of possible attack plans during the flight to and from Tarleton. She hadn't considered an attack on Granger, but she'd done a certain amount of staff work that could easily be adapted to support Garstang's plan. A gamble, certainly, but . . . The strategy just might work. And even if it came close to failure, she should be able to cut her losses and retreat.

"I see," the king said when she'd finished. "And you expect me to take the risk?"

"You don't have a choice," Kat pointed out. "Either you take some risks now, Your Majesty, or you lose the war. The House of Lords holds too many cards."

"True." The king smiled wanly. "Start making preparations then. And hope that no one catches wind of what you're doing."

"Quite." Kat didn't bother to hide her dismay. Secrecy was their only chance. "I'll make sure of it."

The king nodded, pouring himself yet another glass of wine. Kat frowned inwardly, trying to remember just how much he'd drunk. Four glasses? Five? She hadn't been keeping count. And she had no idea how much he'd drunk before she'd entered the room. The local alcohol was *strong*. He was possibly already tipsy. Drusilla didn't seem the sort of person to tell him that he'd had too much to drink.

Kat took a bite of her food, barely tasting it. The local chefs were supposed to be good, but many of their offerings *sounded* awful. Perhaps they were trying their hardest to make the king feel at home, she mused. The meal tasted like someone had been trying to create a dinner fit for the aristocracy, with only the vaguest idea of what the aristocracy actually ate. She silently thanked Pat for her decidedly plebeian tastes. The commoners didn't know it, but they ate better than their social superiors.

If only because everyone wants to pretend they're keeping up with the latest and most expensive fashions, she thought. She'd never really understood or cared to understand why her sisters fought so hard to follow what was fashionable when they had the social clout to set trends for themselves. *Maybe they thought they had to take the lead or be trampled from behind.*

"I heard whispers about your . . . discussions with Marseilles," she said. "Did anything come of them?"

"They'll be shipping us weapons and supplies, in exchange for certain technical details." The king started to eat his own meal with every evidence of enjoyment. Beside him, Princess Drusilla barely touched hers. "We won't be giving them everything, of course."

"Of course," Kat echoed. She wasn't so sure. Marseilles had sent observers to the Commonwealth-Theocratic War. They knew what the Commonwealth could do, even if they didn't know *how*. Knowing something was possible was halfway towards figuring out how to do it. "And how long can we stall before we have to give them something dangerous?"

"As long as possible," the king said. His tone turned reflective. "You do know where Marseilles is, don't you?"

Kat nodded, slowly. "Why . . . ?"

"If you visualize the Human Sphere as a *sphere*, Marseilles would be on the inside," the king continued, as if she hadn't spoken at all. "Their borders are solid, locked in place by three other powers . . . including us. They cannot break out. They cannot expand their territory unless they wage war on one of their neighbors. We're the logical target."

"They *could* simply pass through our territory and establish colonies on the far side of the Rim," Kat pointed out. "Or forge links with the Jorlem Sector. Or the former Theocratic worlds. Or . . ."

"We could cut them off at any moment," the king said. "Sure, everyone has freedom of navigation through hyperspace . . . but that wouldn't last a second if a real war broke out. We certainly wouldn't let them pre-position their ships if it looked like there was going to be trouble. They'd need to secure solid lines of communication through our territory . . . and I'm afraid that would mean waging war on us. *We* are the logical target."

"We're the most advanced interstellar power in the Human Sphere," Kat pointed out. "And we *know* war."

"We drew our forces down as soon as the last war ended," the king pointed out. "And now . . . we're fighting a civil war. We're weaker than we seem, on paper."

Kat shook her head slowly. "You think they're going to jump us? Or try to take advantage of the civil war?"

"It's what *I'd* do," the king said. "It is the duty of a monarch to look at the long term, isn't it? And the blunt truth is that Marseilles is in a bind. They must expand or risk losing power and influence . . . and the easiest way to expand is to go through us."

"I hope you're wrong," Kat said. "It will be centuries before they start running out of resources."

"At which point they will find themselves in an even worse bind," the king countered. "By then, there will be fewer stars to take on the far side of our territory."

Kat wasn't so sure. The Human Sphere was unimaginably vast, by human standards, but compared to the sheer size of the Milky Way it was barely a grain of sand on a beach. There were millions of star systems within the galaxy, only a tiny fragment of which had been surveyed, let alone claimed and settled. She had no doubt that it would take millions of years before the entire galaxy was settled . . . unless, of course, humanity ran into aliens. No one had encountered any proof that aliens existed, but the universe was vast. An alien empire on the other side of the galaxy might as well be on the other side of the universe itself. The human race had no way of knowing it was there.

"Then that would probably be a mistake to give Marseilles advanced technology," she said, switching gears. "Do we have anything else to trade?"

"No," the king said. "And they won't have *our* best interests in mind either. That's another reason to win this war quickly. If it lasts for years, Kat, whoever wins will be badly weakened. They'll be in no state to resist an all-out invasion."

"I hope you're being paranoid," Kat said. She took a sip of wine, a drink so strong that she thought, for a moment, that it was meant to be diluted. "And that they aren't considering the possibilities."

"They wouldn't be human if they weren't," the king said. He leaned against Princess Drusilla. She glanced at Kat, as if she expected instant condemnation, before wrapping her arm around his shoulders. "When will you be departing?"

"Two days," Kat said. "I should be able to lay the rest of the plans by then. Hopefully, no one will catch a whiff of what we're doing. A word out of place, and the entire plan will fail. I want it to work."

"Me too," the king said. He looked down at his empty plate, as if he couldn't remember what had happened to the food. His eyes wandered the room before focusing on Kat. "Don't fail me, Kat. Not this time."

Kat frowned. The king was starting to sound . . . tired. Again. "I'll do my best," she promised. "And thank you for the dinner."

"It's always good to see a friend," the king said. "You do know you're one of the few people I can trust? I mean . . . *really* trust?"

Kat felt flattered, and wary. "I know," she said. The last time anyone had spoken to her like that, it had been part of a plan to play a prank on an older cousin. She should have known better than to go along with it. "And I won't let you down."

The king drained his glass. "Too many people have let me down. I won't let it happen again. Too much is riding on my success to risk defeat."

Maybe you expected too much, Kat thought as she stood and left the room. *Maybe you gave them imprecise orders. Or maybe you made the mistake of listening to the ones who told you what you wanted to hear.*

CHAPTER THIRTY-SEVEN

TYRE

"You'll be pleased to hear that your stock is still high," Duke Falcone said once William had been shown into his office. "The . . . *retreat* . . . from Waco drew some sarcastic remarks, I must admit, but you appear to have weathered the storm."

"That's good," William said. He accepted a cup of coffee with a nod. "It does help that we weren't planning to occupy the system."

"Quite," Duke Falcone said. "Our sources on Caledonia haven't had much to say about the whole affair. Timing wise, they should have heard about it five or six days ago. We think there's a reasonable chance the king may be suppressing the information."

"It wasn't a complete victory for him, but it was hardly a defeat either," William pointed out calmly. "I'm sure he could spin it into a victory, if he tried."

"Perhaps," Duke Falcone said. "We're not expecting him to be able to keep quiet for long. There were plenty of witnesses, and most of them aren't going to keep their mouths shut indefinitely. Our general thinking is that he's trying to keep the news under wraps for a few short weeks."

William felt his eyes narrow. Something about the meeting felt . . . off. A duke, even a friendly duke, would hardly be giving him an intelligence briefing. Was he about to be sacked? Or demoted? Or reassigned to Home Fleet while a junior officer took the heavy cruisers on the next raiding mission? The move would certainly *feel* like a demotion, whatever it was in reality. He preferred commanding a heavy cruiser on a mission to a superdreadnought permanently on home defense duty.

"Our sources *have* turned up something interesting, however," Duke Falcone said after a moment. "The king is apparently planning to attack Granger."

William frowned. "Granger? The supply depot?"

"Apparently so," Duke Falcone said. "You're familiar with it, are you not?"

"We've been drawing supplies from Granger for Home Fleet," William said. He'd never liked the concept of a handful of supersized supply depots, even though he had to admit that it had worked out in his favor. "We're not even close to emptying the depot."

"The king has had the same idea, if our sources are to be believed," Duke Falcone informed him. "His fleet intends to attack Granger, steal everything they can carry, and destroy the rest. Our intelligence staff believes that this is solid."

"Are they *really* sure?" William had his doubts. "This isn't a decoy of some kind? A bluff to make us look elsewhere while they lower the boom?"

"Apparently not," Duke Falcone said. There was a pause. "My intelligence staff was keen to point out that our sources could have been misled, even if they weren't actually lying to us, but . . . they appear to think that the information is accurate."

William considered the ploy for a moment. Granger was a logical target. The king had every reason to want to capture the supply depot and steal everything from missiles to starship components and spare parts. But, at the same time, it was too logical a target. The king might intend to attack somewhere else altogether . . . He shook his head. There was no way he could convince the war cabinet of that, particularly when he couldn't think of anywhere else that stood out as a possible target. Tyre was the closest possible target, as far as he could tell, but . . . It wasn't as if they were going to send the entire Home Fleet to Granger. Tyre would not be left undefended.

"It seems logical," he said. "But why did they let the news leak?"

"They didn't exactly put it in a press release," Duke Falcone commented dryly.

"That's not what I meant," William said. "If they wanted to keep something secret, they wouldn't have blabbed about it to anyone. Only a handful of people would know the truth. Everyone else . . . would be told to just shut up and soldier. The odds of a leak would be minimized. Instead . . . it seems to have leaked out."

Duke Falcone met his eyes. "Do you think we're being hoaxed?"

"I don't know," William admitted. God, he *hated* intelligence and counterintelligence work. It was so hard to guess who knew, and who knew they knew, and who knew they knew they knew . . . It was easy, so easy, to start chasing one's own tail. If the king knew who was spying on him, he could easily have leaked false information to them; even if he didn't, he might have organized the leaks anyway, just to see if word got back to Tyre. "Granger is a logical target. And we can't let them get away with raiding the base."

Duke Falcone looked at his fingers. "Can we evacuate the base in time?"

"I doubt it," William said. "It would take weeks to strip the base of *everything* . . . days, even, just to plan how best to remove everything to Tyre. I . . . We might be able to strip the base of missiles and suchlike, but even *that* would be difficult. The logistics experience we built up during the war was allowed to fade away . . ."

And a number of logistics officers went over to the other side, he added silently. Colonial officers had been allowed to rise in logistics units, if only because they weren't as glamorous as combat positions. William didn't fault them for their choice, but it was inconvenient. *We might not be able to rebuild the units in a hurry.*

"And then what?" Duke Falcone looked up. "The staff have been offering me all sorts of plans. Grand Admiral Rudbek believes we can use this to bait a trap. He talks about somewhere called Antietam, somewhere where . . . it happened. Can we use this? Or should we look elsewhere?"

It struck William that, for all they were roughly the same age, Duke Falcone was much less mature. Kat's oldest brother was still unused to the power he wielded, still unaware, subconsciously, that the buck stopped with him. *He doesn't have the arrogance of many of his peers,* William thought, *but he also doesn't have the cold-blooded determination to wield power that his father had either.* Perhaps it had been deliberate on his father's part. Perhaps Lucas Falcone had expected a smooth transfer of power from father to son, instead of a sudden death and succession. Peter Falcone simply hadn't had the time to learn to wield his power, to understand its practical limitations, before it was too late.

"I haven't seen the staff reports," William said. "But it should, in theory, be possible to ambush the enemy fleet."

Duke Falcone frowned. "Like Antietam?"

"I don't know," William said. He vaguely recalled hearing of a place called Antietam, but he couldn't remember why it had been important or understand its relevance to the here and now. "But if we have a chance to catch them by surprise, we should take it."

"Very good," Duke Falcone said. He relaxed, very slightly. "You'll command the operation, of course. Grand Admiral Rudbek has already assigned ships to your command."

"Thank you, Your Grace." William wasn't sure it *was* a good thing, but there was no point in arguing. If something went wrong, he was expendable. "I won't let you down."

"I know." Duke Falcone met his eyes. "You know what is at stake, I believe. The king has to be stopped."

"We need to keep the pressure on," William said. The king wasn't old and wise enough to know that there were times it was better to just grit one's teeth and take it, rather than doing something hasty that would just make matters worse. "And when we have the fleet built up, we can take the war to Caledonia and end it."

"The sooner, the better," Duke Falcone said. He stood and held out a hand. "Good luck, William. Yasmeena will show you out. Your orders will be waiting for you in the shuttle."

William shook his hand firmly. "Thank you, Your Grace."

He bowed, then headed through the door. Yasmeena met him on the far side, looking too demure for his liking. He would have bet good money that she had *some* way of observing events inside the secure room, if only to ensure she was in place to meet William when Duke Falcone dismissed him. Perhaps the aristocrat had access to implant technology that was beyond cutting edge . . . Possible, he supposed. The idea of wiring a starship's crew into a neural net had never quite gone away, even though the technology stubbornly refused to come off the drawing board. He frowned. It wasn't something *he* wanted to do. He'd had enough experience with VR helmets to fear what could happen if someone hacked a neural net.

Yasmeena said nothing as she led him up a flight of stairs and out into the open air. A shuttlecraft was sitting on the landing pad, waiting for him. William frowned, inwardly, as he realized that he was getting launched into orbit without any time to himself. Better he went straight to his new command rather than spending time in the city below. If he said the wrong thing to the wrong person . . .

He picked up the secure datapad as the shuttle rose into the air and pressed his finger against the scanner. There was a brief pause, then a series of datafiles unlocked themselves. He scanned them quickly, feeling his frown begin to deepen. Duke Falcone's aides had the sense to include the raw intelligence data. There was no reason to doubt the information, something that worried him. Long experience had taught him to beware of anything that looked too good to be true. It almost certainly was.

And this is something that we have to take seriously, he thought. *And they have to know it too.*

He gritted his teeth and read the rest of his orders. Grand Admiral Rudbek's staff had apparently been planning the operation for days. William had instructions to assume command of a superdreadnought squadron and attached elements, then take them straight to Granger with orders to lurk under cloak until the enemy arrived. At that point, he was to smash the enemy fleet before it could escape. There was a pleasing lack of *specification* about the orders that suggested they came directly from Grand Admiral Rudbek himself. He wouldn't care about how the orders were carried out, as long as they were.

The shuttle quivered as she turned towards HMS *Thunderous*. "Nearly there, sir," the pilot called. "We'll have you there in a jiffy."

William had to smile. "Not a naval pilot, then?"

"No, sir," the pilot said. "I work for the family."

The Falcones, William thought in amused disbelief. *They have a private fleet of shuttle pilots.*

He shook his head, telling himself not to be stupid. The Falcones had a private fleet. A shuttlecraft, an entire squadron of shuttlecraft, was minor, compared to a fleet. And . . .

I suppose it's a wonder that Peter and Kat came out as normal as they did, he thought wryly. *And why they have so many problems too.*

"Take us in to dock at the upper airlock," he said. "And inform the crew that I don't want any ceremony."

"Yes, sir."

The shuttle docked so smoothly that William barely felt the gravity field flicker. He was morbidly impressed. There weren't many naval pilots who could handle their shuttlecraft so well, although he supposed that the pilots received special training to keep VIPs from feeling even the slightest bit of discomfort. He picked up the datapad, placed it in his belt, and stepped out of the shuttle. Captain Georgas was standing by the flag, not entirely to William's surprise. Orders or no orders, it was a rare captain who *wouldn't* welcome the squadron's commanding officer to her ship.

"Admiral," she said, snapping a salute. "Welcome back."

"It feels as though I never left," William said. "I trust you kept my suite in order?"

Captain Georgas smiled. "It remains untouched, sir," she assured him. "Of course, that *also* means that the dirty linen is still there as you left it."

William grinned, realizing that he was being teased . . . and tested. "Perhaps it would be better to have the steward change the bedding," he said. He allowed her to lead him down the corridor, even though he knew the interior of the ship almost as well as she did. "It is probably a *little* unclean by now."

Captain Georgas suddenly became serious. "I heard you had some trouble with gunboats?"

"Yes," William said. No point in trying to downplay it. "We're going to have to undertake more gunboat defense drills."

"We can handle it." Captain Georgas frowned. "The task force has already assembled, more or less. When do you want to leave?"

William made a mental note to thank Grand Admiral Rudbek. "As soon as possible," he said, slowly. "Do you see any problems in departing within the hour?"

"None." Captain Georgas smiled at his astonished expression. "We recalled our crewmen as soon as we received the warning orders. Our drive nodes are already heated up. I daresay we could lumber out of orbit in fifteen minutes, without putting excessive wear and tear on the drives. We haven't done badly at all."

"Not at all," William agreed, as they reached the CIC. "Inform the crew. We depart in two hours."

"Aye, Admiral," Captain Georgas said. "And our destination?"

"I'll inform you once we are well clear of the system," William said. "Security."

"A positively dirty word," Captain Georgas observed. She didn't sound happy. "I understand, Admiral. And may I say it's good to have you back."

"You may." William wasn't sure if Captain Georgas was being sincere or not, but it didn't matter. "It's good to *be* back."

He spoke briefly to the tactical staff, most of whom he remembered from his previous stint on *Thunderous*, then walked into his ready room. He hadn't had time to pack a bag, or have his possessions sent over from *Belfast*, but the steward had already laid out a fresh uniform and naval-issue underwear. His lips curved into a smile—it wasn't as if he'd ever developed the habit of wearing tailored uniforms—then sat down at the desk. The staff had done a very good job. They didn't know the mission, they didn't know where the task force was going, but they'd made sure he knew everything he needed to know. A far cry from the confusion, from the endless series of tasks he'd needed to do himself, that had plagued the early days of the civil war.

Good, he thought. He keyed his terminal, bringing up the file on Granger. No one had ever seriously envisaged the system being turned into a war zone. *And now . . .*

He tapped his wristcom. "Commander Tobias, inform the senior officers that we will hold a conference once the fleet is underway," he ordered. "We have an operation to plan."

"Aye, sir."

♦ ♦ ♦

"The task force has departed, Your Grace," Grand Admiral Rudbek said once his holoimage had materialized in Peter's office. "You asked to be informed."

"I did," Peter confirmed. He was surprised Grand Admiral Rudbek had informed him in person, although it was quite possible that anyone lesser would have been unable to speak to him without prior orders. "Will they get there in time?"

"They should," Grand Admiral Rudbek said. "We've run a dozen projections. They all say the task force should beat the king's fleet by several days."

Peter frowned at the holoimage. "And if we're wrong? If we're being tricked?"

"It will be embarrassing," Grand Admiral Rudbek admitted. "We're not even sure his fleet has left. Caledonia is under surveillance, but he's been shifting ships around more or less at random. Cloaking some, powering down others . . . It's difficult to be entirely sure of what's going on. I think he's doing it on purpose."

"To disguise the fact he's sent out a fleet?" Peter asked. "Or just to annoy us?"

"It could easily be both," Grand Admiral Rudbek said. "We just don't know."

"There are no certainties," Peter muttered. His father used to tell him that, usually followed by a warning of the dangers of complacency. "And what of the other reports?"

"That the king has come to terms with Marseilles?" Grand Admiral Rudbek gave him a sharp look. "We don't know."

"That's the problem, isn't it?" Peter called up a starchart and indicated the border. If Marseilles dispatched a fleet to the border, Tyre would have to respond . . . or risk tempting Marseilles to launch a smash-and-grab of its own. "Are they going to risk starting an all-out war?"

"Would the *king* risk starting a war?" Grand Admiral Rudbek looked back at him, evenly. "Would your sister go along with it?"

"I don't think so," Peter said. "She's a patriot, not . . ."

"People can make mistakes," Grand Admiral Rudbek said quietly. "And they can find themselves tumbling down the slippery slope without ever realizing what they're doing, at least until it's too late. The longer this war continues, the greater the chance that *someone* will try to take advantage of it."

Peter nodded, slowly. The king wouldn't sell out. He was sure the king would never *willingly* sell out. But if he was desperate, if the offer was sweet enough, if he thought he had no other choice . . . Peter swallowed, hard. The king might do something desperate if he thought he was screwed. And if the odds tipped badly against him . . .

"We have to end this war as quickly as possible," he said. "And if that means we have to take risks, then we'll take them."

"Understood, Your Grace," Grand Admiral Rudbek said. "I'll keep you informed."

CHAPTER THIRTY-EIGHT

GRANGER

"The squadron is at full alert," Commander Katie Hamada said. "We will drop out of hyperspace in ten minutes."

Kat nodded stiffly, unable to hide her growing concern. The strategy had seemed so brilliant when she'd put it together and when she'd briefed the handful of officers who knew the *true* plan, but now, as she was on the verge of putting it into action, she was having second thoughts. It was already clear that half of Caledonia knew the navy intended to attack Granger. She would be astonished if word hadn't already reached Tyre. Their spies wouldn't have to do more than drink in the right bars to hear the rumors from a dozen trustworthy sources.

Unless they've decided we're trying to bluff them, she thought. *She* would certainly have been suspicious if the enemy had obligingly told her where they intended to attack. It was more reasonable to believe that either she was being conned or the operation was going to be canceled, on the assumption that the advantage of surprise had been thoroughly lost. *They might let us attack the system because they think we're trying to lure them out of place.*

She smiled, humorlessly. *That* would be funny, if frustrating. But this wasn't the sort of plan that actually worked, not in the real world. It would depend on the enemy drawing the right conclusion and doing the right thing . . . not a sound basis for anything other than a plan of utter desperation. She would have been given demerits at Piker's Peak for proposing such a ploy when she'd been a cadet; she dreaded to think what her first commanding officers would have said if she'd suggested such a concept. But then, she supposed it did have one advantage. It would be simple enough to compensate if the plan didn't work.

And she was woolgathering. She put the thought out of her mind, as the timer continued its remorseless countdown, and concentrated on studying the status displays. The king had done her proud, she supposed; he'd given her two additional battlecruiser squadrons and nearly fifty support ships, as well as a small armada of freighters. She had more than enough capacity to steal everything they needed from the supply depot, if she managed to capture it intact. She was grimly aware that wasn't going to be easy. The House of Lords would have given orders that supply depots were to be destroyed, rather than surrendered. In this war, neither side would have any trouble using the other side's ammunition.

"Admiral," Katie said. "We're coming up on the exit point now."

"Take us through the vortex," Kat ordered. "And launch recon drones as soon as the entire fleet is out."

She braced herself as the display twisted into a conical vortex, opening and widening as the fleet plunged back into realspace. The star system appeared in front of her; a single yellow star, a handful of rocky planets, and three gas giants, one surrounded by dozens of orbital installations. Granger had been unlucky, in some ways, but very lucky in others. The planet had attracted a great deal of investment from Tyre, even before the Commonwealth had been more than a utopian ideal. There hadn't seemed any real downside to developing the system as a naval base as well as an industrial center.

A set of red icons appeared on the display. She leaned forward, watching with cold interest as the defense force took shape and form. A dozen heavy cruisers, including a handful of outdated designs; two squadrons of destroyers, hastily concentrating their formation in the face of an overwhelming threat. She allowed herself a moment of pity, wondering if—when—the enemy CO would signal a retreat. They could sting her ships, but they wouldn't be able to do any real damage before she crushed them. They simply didn't have enough mobile firepower to scratch her paint.

And if they withdraw into the gravity well, I'll pin them against the gas giant, she mused. The *smart* thing to do, for the enemy CO, would be to retreat at once. But would he prefer to risk an engagement, rather than the anger of his superiors? He might fire a handful of shots before retreating, just for the honor of the flag. *He's running out of time to make his choice.*

She glanced at Katie. "Deploy gunboats," she ordered. "All units with special orders are to carry them out. The remainder of the fleet will advance to engage the enemy."

She felt a dull quiver running through the battlecruiser as she started to pick up speed. Kat allowed herself a tight smile at just how *well* the formation was shaping up, even though it had been flung together at short notice. Admiral Lord Garstang and, she hated to admit, Admiral Ruben had done a good job, putting their crews through constant training exercises while they waited for an attack that had never materialized. There were still some rough edges, unsurprisingly, but they were steadily fading away.

"Admiral, the enemy ships are retreating into the gravity well." Katie sounded astonished. "They're daring us to come after them."

"They know we have to enter the gravity well ourselves," Kat said. She silently cursed the admiral who'd put the supply depot deep within a gravity well. The logic was sound, and her ships would be in serious trouble if the plan misfired. "If they fall back on the supply depot's defenses, we may be in some trouble."

She felt her heart start to pound as the range closed steadily. The enemy ships intended to lure her into a trap, she was sure. It was the only explanation that made sense. And she intended to spring the trap . . . She watched the display, wondering just how the enemy would choose to move. She'd run through hundreds of simulated engagements, but none could tell her *precisely* what the enemy would do. They had a number of possible options . . .

"Admiral, long-range sensors are picking up drive emissions from the supply depot," Katie reported. "They may be evacuating the complex."

"Transmit the prerecorded message," Kat ordered. "And ready the marines to board the station."

She braced herself, feeling as if the entire battle was resting on a knife-edge. The war had been surprisingly civilized, so far . . . Was that about to change? She had no illusions. The supply depot's manager would presumably prefer to blow it up rather than let it fall into her hands. And if he'd had time to make preparations . . . It wouldn't be that difficult. All he *really* had to do was switch off the antimatter containment chambers. The resulting explosion would be visible halfway across the system.

Normally, we store antimatter well away from anything else, she mused. There were enough horror stories about accidents that involved antimatter to make sure that everyone took the dangers seriously. *But that could have changed if the House of Lords was determined to make sure that we couldn't capture the depot . . .*

Another quiver ran through the battlecruiser as she moved deeper into the gas giant's gravity well. It would be dangerous, if not impossible, to open a vortex and escape into hyperspace now. The enemy ships had cut off their sole line of retreat, although . . . She had to admit that a skilled captain could probably evade her vessels long enough to get out of the gravity well and escape. Or simply power down and pretend to be a piece of space junk until reinforcements arrived from Granger or Tyre.

"Two minutes to engagement range," Katie reported. "They're running out of room."

"It looks that way," Kat said. "But . . ."

She glanced up, sharply, as alarms shrilled. Red icons appeared on the display, *behind* her. Katie bit off a curse, a hint of panic in her voice. Kat looked at her sharply, then turned her attention back to the display. An enemy fleet had materialized out of nowhere . . . Kat allowed herself a moment of admiration. The enemy ships had somehow managed to avoid being detected until they dropped their cloaks. But . . . She supposed it made a certain kind of droll sense. They knew her capabilities as well as she did.

"One squadron of superdreadnoughts, two squadrons of heavy cruisers, five squadrons of destroyers," Katie reported. "They're coming up behind us!"

"I noticed," Kat said. She wondered, idly, who was in command of the enemy fleet. They'd timed their ambush very well, making sure that Kat's fleet was mired in the gravity well before they showed themselves. "Signal the fleet. Prepare to alter course."

Katie swallowed visibly. "Aye, Admiral."

♦ ♦ ♦

William had never quite believed the plan would work, even though he'd devised it. Kat—he thought Kat was in command, given the presence of *Relentless* among the king's ships—would have known the danger of heading into the gravity well, certainly before she'd made damn sure that the system was undefended. Indeed, she should have taken the time to survey the system thoroughly . . . even though time was not on her side. She hadn't even bothered to silence the StarCom.

Not that it would have mattered, he thought. *There'll be no point in hanging around the system if she can't force the supply depot to surrender.*

"Order the fleet to advance," he said calmly. "Pin them against the gas giant."

"Aye, Admiral," Commander Tobias said.

"And transmit the surrender demand," William added. "We'll give them a chance to give up."

"Aye, Admiral."

William leaned back in his command chair as the superdreadnought lumbered forward. Kat had trapped herself, but . . . He frowned. Kat would have known the dangers . . . Of *course* she would have known the dangers. Perhaps it wasn't Kat in command. The intelligence staff had claimed that Admiral Lord Garstang and Admiral Ruben were in command of the king's superdreadnoughts, but one of them could easily have transferred to *Relentless*. Admiral Lord Garstang was a solid man but known more for thoroughness and attention to detail than imagination. It might never have occurred to him that Caledonia might be a hotbed of spies as well as a wretched hive of scum and villainy.

He contemplated the possibilities, quickly. Kat had nowhere to hide, nowhere to run. Her ships couldn't evade his sensors long enough to cloak, not when he'd seeded the entire sector with stealthed recon platforms. They couldn't break for high orbit and safety; they couldn't even keep the range open, not when his vessels were armed with long-range missiles. She might as well be at the bottom of a hole with him standing above her, hurling rocks at her head. Sooner or later, she'd run out of luck and die.

"There's no response, Admiral," Commander Tobias said. "I don't think they want to surrender."

William scowled at his aide's back. Commander Tobias sounded pleased, as if he *wanted* to see the enemy ships smashed to atoms. William was much less sanguine. He didn't want to be responsible for the deaths of tens of thousands of people, people he'd probably known before the civil war had divided them.

"Advance to firing range," he ordered. "And fire on my command."

"Aye, Admiral."

Surrender, please, William thought. *I don't want to blast your ships to atoms.*

He waited, resisting the urge to get up and pace as the seconds ticked away. Kat wouldn't *want* to surrender, not even to him. It wasn't in her nature, and she'd known, of course, what her last set of enemies did to prisoners. Even now . . . Even with a guarantee of good treatment, she wouldn't want to surrender. But if she held out, her people were going to be shot to ribbons. There was no escape.

"Entering firing range now," Commander Tobias said. "There's still no response."

William nodded, slowly. Kat's ships were bottoming out, adjusting their formation to stand off fire from above. There was no sign of panic, he noted, no hint that they were coming apart at the seams. Even the freighters were holding formation. But it didn't matter, did it? The end was practically inevitable.

I'm sorry, he thought. *I really am.*

"Fire," he ordered.

♦ ♦ ♦

"Admiral," Katie said. She appeared to have regained control of herself. "The enemy fleet has opened fire."

"Noted," Kat said as the display spangled with red icons. The sight seemed *wrong*, somehow . . . It took her several seconds to understand why. The enemy CO had showed a frightening lack of concern about what his rogue missiles would hit, about the planet under Kat's ships, but . . . no matter. The missiles would slam into a gas giant. There was no real danger to innocent lives. "Point defense is to engage as soon as possible."

"Aye, Admiral," Katie said.

Kat took a moment to assess the situation. The enemy CO—she wondered, suddenly, if it was William in command—had pinned her. Or so it seemed. He'd certainly launched everything he could at her, expending his external racks as he fired his missiles from outside standard missile range. She would have liked to think that his missiles would burn themselves out well before they reached engagement range, but their drive emissions were very clear. They had more than enough range to hit her ships well before their drives burned out.

"Hold fire," she ordered. *Her* ships were carrying standard missiles. There was no point in firing them now. "Let them close the range."

"Aye, Admiral."

Kat kept her face calm as the enemy missiles roared towards her formation. The enemy CO had done a very good job. A single squadron of superdreadnoughts could launch hundreds of missiles in a single salvo, but . . . He'd also launched a handful of ECM drones and penetrator warheads, creating a haze of electromagnetic distortion that would make it difficult for her point defense crews to get a solid lock on the enemy missiles. Her lips quirked. There were definite disadvantages to fighting a civil war. Once again, both sides knew precisely what the other side could do.

At least we're keeping things reasonably civilized, she mused. *But that may not last.*

She tensed, watching the missiles as they sliced through her point defense. The long-range missiles had one solid disadvantage, despite the ECM; her gunners had plenty of time to plan how to take out as many of the missiles as possible, well before they raged into engagement range. But there were so many of them. She gritted her teeth as the damage started to mount, a handful of her smaller ships taking multiple hits and being blown to plasma. The enemy CO wasn't even trying to target the battlecruisers first. She guessed he wanted to force them to surrender instead.

And there's no point in going for the biggest ships when they have us trapped, she reminded herself. *Strip away the defenses first, then kill the big boys.*

"Admiral," Katie said. "They're entering our engagement range now."

"Target the superdreadnoughts," Kat ordered. "Return fire."

"Aye, Admiral," Katie said.

"And send the signal," Kat added. "It's time."

♦ ♦ ♦

"The enemy ships have opened fire," Commander Tobias reported. "They're targeting our superdreadnoughts."

"Their best chance for victory," William noted, although it was a scant chance indeed. The superdreadnoughts mounted vast arrays of point defense weapons. They didn't need their escorts to be formidable. "Continue firing."

He watched, feeling cold, as the engagement continued to develop. The enemy missiles tore into his formation, trying desperately to reach the superdreadnoughts before it was too late. But it was already too late. The enemy ships just couldn't force him to break off, no matter how many missiles they fired . . . and, as long as he held the high ground, he could pound them to scrap from a safe distance. Or a reasonably safe distance, he noted as a missile struck *Thunderous*. The massive superdreadnought barely noticed.

"They must be running out of missiles soon," Commander Tobias said. "Surely . . ."

"Surely," William agreed. The damage was mounting, but . . . It wasn't enough. "Repeat the surrender demand."

"Aye, Admiral."

William wasn't surprised when there was no response, even though Kat, or whoever was in command, had to know the situation was growing increasingly desperate. No escape, no way to hide . . . They were doomed, unless they surrendered. Their point defense was steadily growing weaker, their battlecruisers taking hits as the smaller vessels were steadily wiped from existence. It had been a mistake to allow the battlecruisers to enter the gravity well. Their advantages were useless, so close to the gas giant; their disadvantages were going to get their crews killed. Unless they chose to surrender . . .

Perhaps it isn't Kat in command after all, William thought. *Perhaps it's some inbred moron with more balls than common sense.*

"No response, Admiral," Commander Tobias said. "I . . ."

He stopped, but William could hear the unspoken question as clearly as if it had been spoken aloud. *Why try to urge them to surrender? Why not finish the job?* William understood, even though he knew he wouldn't have been pleased if Tobias had asked the question out loud. There was a time and a place for debate, for understanding the motives behind one's orders . . . and it wasn't in the middle of a battle. They could discuss it later . . .

"Continue firing," William ordered.

Another shudder ran through the giant ship. William glanced at the status board, then at the constantly updating stream of intelligence from the analysts. Tobias was right about one thing. The enemy ships had to be running short of missiles. Battlecruisers simply didn't have the space to carry superdreadnought-sized loads. Perhaps they were just shooting themselves dry before the inevitable surrender . . .

"Admiral!" Commander Tobias practically jumped out of his chair as new icons appeared on the display. "Vortexes opening, right behind us!"

CHAPTER THIRTY-NINE

GRANGER

Admiral Henri Ruben had to admit he didn't like Kat Falcone.

It was galling, all the more so as he knew deep inside that his dislike wasn't really fair. It wasn't her fault that she'd been born to a level of wealth, power, and security that his family couldn't hope to match. It wasn't her fault that she could afford to treat the civil war like a game, in the certain knowledge that she wouldn't face any serious consequences if the House of Lords won the war. Henri didn't have that certainty. His family might have been aristocrats, but they'd been so low on the totem pole that he'd needed the king's patronage to climb the ladder to flag rank. Henri would do anything for the king, his family's only hope of survival. If the king lost the war, Henri's family would lose too.

But she did pull off a pretty good plan, he conceded as he led his superdreadnoughts out of the vortex. *The enemy fleet is right where we want them.*

"Fire," he snapped.

The superdreadnought shuddered as she unleashed a single massive salvo. It had been hard, almost impossible, to convince Admiral Lord Garstang to detach two superdreadnought squadrons and add them to the raiding party, but Kat Falcone had managed it. Henri had worried—he'd heard the rumors that Kat Falcone had the king's ear, as well as another part of his anatomy—yet her connections seemed to have worked in their favor. A squadron of enemy superdreadnoughts was at his mercy, right in front of him. He watched the missiles roaring towards their targets and smiled, coldly. The ambush had worked perfectly.

We're going to ram our missiles right up their asses, he thought. It was the kind of crudity he would never allow himself to *say*, but he could *think* it. Oh yes, he could *think* it. *And there's no way they can block us in time.*

♦ ♦ ♦

William had been a naval officer long enough to know that the only thing one should expect was the unexpected. The enemy always had plans of his own, and when those plans interacted with his plans, the results could be spectacular. Or painful. He felt his heart clench as he saw the enemy ships pouring out of the vortex, already launching their missiles towards his ships. Kat . . . he knew, with a sick certainty, that Kat had devised the plan . . . had lured them into an ambush. And the jaws were starting to close.

They forced us to pin their fleet in place, he thought. *And they knew that would make our position predictable.*

"Roll ships," he snapped. Thankfully, they'd been skulking along the edge of the gravity well rather than plunging straight into it. "And return fire."

He cursed again as the display updated. The enemy in front of them was finally detaching its gunboats, launching them towards his ships . . . He'd wondered why they were keeping them close, and now he knew. They hadn't held the gunboats back to use them as mobile point defense platforms. They'd kept them in reserve for this moment, for the instant when the battle suddenly turned on its head. William had seen victories turn to defeats before, and he'd fought in more battles than he cared to remember, but this was savage. They'd been tricked. And, worst of all, he'd walked right into it.

"Enemy missiles entering engagement range," Commander Tobias warned.

"Retarget the point defense," William ordered. The hell of it was that they were now caught between two fires. Luckily, the enemy battlecruisers had nearly shot themselves dry before the superdreadnoughts appeared. Their salvos were already weakening. They were probably trying to conserve missiles, just in case they had to prolong the engagement. "And recall the escorts. We need more ships between them and us."

He gritted his teeth as the enemy missiles slashed into his defenses. His crews were doing what they could, but they'd been caught flat-footed by the enemy's sudden appearance. And all the escorts were out of position. It would take time to reorient the formation, time they didn't have. Whatever happened, they were about to take a major beating.

"Impact in twenty seconds," Commander Tobias said. "Admiral . . ."

William bit down a curse as the superdreadnought shook violently. He braced himself, half expecting the order to abandon ship before the shaking steadily died away. The display was awash with red lights, blinking out one by one as the automated damage report systems realized that the ship wasn't so badly damaged after all. Five antimatter missiles had struck home . . . He let out a breath he hadn't realized he'd been holding. Superdreadnoughts never ceased to impress him. *Thunderous* had taken one hell of a pounding and survived.

"Admiral, nine of our escorts have been destroyed," Commander Tobias said. "One more is dead in space, apparently drifting."

"Let us hope her crew gets off in time," William said. There was nothing he could do for the stricken ship, not now. Whoever won the battle would have to search the hulk, hopefully before it drifted farther into the gravity well and plunged into the gas giant's atmosphere. "Continue firing."

He studied the display as his missiles slammed into the enemy superdreadnoughts. It *looked* as if the king's ships didn't have the latest in sensor technology—Kat's fleet had been on a long-term deployment when Home Fleet's ships had been refitted—but they made up for it through experience and bloody-minded determination. And there were twenty-four superdreadnoughts. Collectively, they didn't *need* escorts to stand firm against his fire. It looked as if they had more than enough point defense to keep themselves intact long enough to crush his ships like bugs.

And there's no way we can move to take advantage of their deployment, William thought, stiffly. Kat had gambled, for the very highest stakes . . . and won. *We couldn't get Home Fleet to Caledonia in time to put an end to the king's rebellion.*

The vectors steadily developed. Kat's timing hadn't been *perfect* . . . Under the circumstances, there was no way it could have been perfect. She hadn't pinned them against the gas giant, but merely . . . made it difficult for them to break through to clear space. Her ships didn't hold the high ground. They looked as if they were angling to give chase, not trap him. He didn't think they had any choice.

"Order the fleet to accelerate," he said grimly. It was going to be a slugging match now, at least until they broke into clear space. "And prepare to open vortexes as soon as we're clear."

"Aye, Admiral."

♦ ♦ ♦

"It worked, Admiral," Katie said. "Your plan worked!"

Kat nodded, torn between relief and frustration. The plan *had* worked, but it hadn't worked perfectly. Her opponent had reacted with commendable speed, even though he'd been caught by surprise.

He'd returned fire with a rapidity that had surprised her. He certainly wasn't too proud to admit he was losing and order a retreat. *Perhaps it is William on the other side*, she thought. He'd always known the difference between appearance and reality. He was certainly smart enough to retreat, rather than turn a minor setback into a disaster by *not* retreating.

Better to face a court-martial than throw away thousands of lives trying to change something that cannot be changed, she mused. It was how William thought. *And his superiors might realize he'd done the right thing.*

"Order the gunboats to continue their attack," she said, "and bring the fleet about."

"Aye, Admiral."

"And signal the supply depot," she added. "Call on them to surrender."

"Aye, Admiral."

Kat gritted her teeth. The supply depot's staff wouldn't have hit the self-destruct at once, not if they knew the enemy fleet was waiting to ambush her when she showed her face. There was nothing to be gained by destroying supplies the House of Lords could use as easily as she could. But now . . . The battle had shifted, and unless there was a *second* enemy fleet on the way, she was going to win. The supply depot's staff might have already triggered the self-destruct and bugged out before the depot blew up. She hoped, she prayed, that they'd held themselves back long enough for her to win the battle.

And try to talk them into surrendering, she thought. She didn't want to send the marines into what might as well be a death trap. Blowing up a ship to kill the boarding party was a dirty trick. Pirates were the only people who did it regularly, if only because they knew they couldn't expect mercy in any case. *If they refuse to surrender, all this will be for nothing.*

She smiled, grimly. It wasn't *quite* for nothing. They'd won an engagement, even though it had come at a cost. The king could make something of that, she was sure. This triumph might just shut his enemies up long enough for him to win the war. And afterwards . . .

♦ ♦ ♦

"Admiral, we're getting a priority-one message from the supply depot," Commander Tobias said. "The enemy is demanding a surrender, or else."

William frowned. So far, both sides had largely honored surrender conventions. But then, there hadn't been *that* much at stake. Neither side wanted to slaughter purely for the hell of slaughtering. Now . . . There was an entire supply depot at stake. There was no way he could let it fall into the king's hands. At best, it would prolong the war; at worst, it would shorten the conflict in the worst possible way. And yet . . . He scowled. Kat wouldn't execute the staff for carrying out their orders and blowing up the supply depot, he was sure. The king, on the other hand, would be furious. He'd always been a shortsighted man.

"Order them to set the self-destruct, then abandon the base," he said calmly. There was no way to *save* the depot, not now. He'd just have to make sure the supplies were denied to both sides. "They are to attempt to evade capture, if possible. If not, they are to make it clear that they destroyed the base on my orders."

"Aye, sir," Commander Tobias said. He sounded bemused, as if he hadn't quite understood the orders. "Message sent."

"Good." William felt another missile strike *Thunderous*. "And take us into the vortex as soon as we're clear."

He watched as the damage continued to mount. The enemy were firing constantly . . . and they had the advantage. They could match two of their ships against each of his ships, hammering them constantly until their shields started to fail. Thankfully, the range was only closing very slowly. William wouldn't have wanted a close-range energy weapons duel, but his counterpart might have other ideas. He had the numbers to pull off the gambit too.

Although perhaps not as much as he might like, William thought. *The king will find it harder to repair his ships.*

He considered, briefly, reversing course and closing the range as sharply as possible. He dismissed the thought a second later. There was nothing to be gained by throwing away his entire squadron, even if it *did* work out in his side's favor. No, the battle was lost. Better to cut his losses and go home. Besides, they had inflicted terrible damage on the enemy ships. The king would have problems repairing them. A handful were so badly battered that they probably needed to be scrapped. He wondered, idly, if the king would try to repair them anyway. His fleet was very short of hulls.

The display bleeped. "Admiral, the supply depot has been destroyed," Commander Tobias said. "It's gone."

"And so we win a strategic victory, even as we suffer a tactical defeat," William mused. It wouldn't be easy to convince the House of Lords that they'd come out ahead, not when his forces had lost the battle, but he'd have to try. "Are we clear of the gravity well?"

"We'll be well clear of the gravity well in five minutes," Commander Tobias said. "And then we can go home."

William smiled, tiredly, as another missile struck his ship. "Yes. We can go home."

♦ ♦ ♦

"Admiral." Katie's voice was very quiet, as if she feared Kat's anger. "The supply depot has been destroyed."

Kat nodded slowly, clenching her fists in rage. They'd won the engagement, but they'd also lost . . . They'd lost their one chance to capture the supplies that would have allowed them to win the war quickly. Without them . . . She let out a long, slow breath. At best, the war was going to be prolonged; at worst, they were going to lose. She silently congratulated her opponent as the display continued to update, confirming that the entire depot had been destroyed. Nothing left but atoms.

"Order the fleet to pull out of the gravity well," she said. She briefly considered an attack on Granger itself, then dismissed it as pointless spite. It wouldn't help the king's cause and might well do a great deal of harm. Besides, the planet was heavily defended. "And order Admiral Ruben to press the offensive. I want those superdreadnoughts crippled and destroyed before they can escape."

"Aye, Admiral."

♦ ♦ ♦

"Signal from the flag, Admiral," Lieutenant Sallie called. "Admiral Falcone's compliments, sir, and you're to press the offensive as hard as possible."

Henri's lips twitched. What did Admiral Falcone think he was doing? Sitting on his command deck, playing with himself while the battle went to hell? His ships were trying to catch the enemy, but superdreadnoughts were lumbering brutes, better suited to massive assaults on targets the enemy *had* to defend instead of chasing down fleeter foes. The enemy superdreadnoughts had the same acceleration curves, worse luck. The only way he'd be able to overrun their ships was through sheer bloody luck.

"Continue firing," he ordered. It was a shame they couldn't fire missiles in sprint mode, but that would be worse than useless unless the range closed sharply. The missiles would burn themselves out hundreds of kilometers from their targets. "And continue to deploy ECM drones."

He allowed his smile to widen as he sat back, keeping his thoughts to himself. Oh, it had been a victory . . . unless the enemy had another surprise of their own. But it had also been a defeat, a defeat for which Kat Falcone would get the blame. Henri was surprised to discover that he didn't dislike her that much, not anymore, but still . . . His career came first. She would get the credit for the victory and the blame for the defeat, and *he* would be in a good position to take advantage of it. He'd be promoted into her shoes, while she . . . She'd go somewhere else. He didn't care where.

And it doesn't matter either, he told himself firmly. *She's just not committed to the cause.*

♦ ♦ ♦

"*Tyrant* has suffered extensive damage," Commander Tobias reported. "I . . ."

An icon vanished. "Sir, *Tyrant* is gone."

Destroyed, William thought grimly. There would be time to mourn later. *They're trying to make up for the lost supplies.*

He watched the timer ticking down as more and more enemy missiles sliced into his defenses. The damage was starting to mount rapidly, threatening to put half of his ships in the repair yard even if he *did* manage to get them out of the firing line. His superiors were not going to be happy about that . . . but the trap had worked perfectly. They'd just not anticipated the enemy finding a way to take advantage of it . . .

There'll be plenty of recriminations to go around, he thought, dryly. The intelligence services had clearly made a mistake, somewhere. Had they been tricked? Or had the information leaked, accidentally giving the enemy a chance to stage an ambush of their own? He didn't know. No one would know, at least until the war was over. *We'll have a chance to study their files afterwards . . .*

"Admiral," Commander Tobias said. "We are clear to jump into hyperspace."

"Open the vortex," William ordered. "And take us home."

♦ ♦ ♦

"Admiral," Katie said. "The enemy fleet has escaped."

Kat let out a breath she hadn't realized she'd been holding. On one hand, she'd wanted to destroy the enemy fleet; on the other, she'd been all too aware that destroying the fleet would mean killing people she knew, people who had been, only a few short months ago, on the same side as herself. And there had been a serious risk of crippling her own fleet in the process. The king could not afford heavy losses. She knew that wasn't entirely true of his enemies.

"Order the fleet to regroup at Point Alpha, then prepare to depart," she said. They'd won. Partly. They'd lost the supply depot, but they'd won the engagement and forced the enemy to retreat. That would be enough, she hoped. The king might not have won, but he hadn't lost either. "We'll fly straight back to Caledonia."

"Aye, Admiral."

Kat nodded, then glanced at the damage report. The price had been high. Seventeen ships destroyed outright, a further twelve badly damaged. Two of her cruisers would have to be towed home . . . Normally, she would have considered abandoning them on the spot. But she couldn't afford to discard hulls she desperately needed. If they could be repaired . . .

If, she thought. She glanced through the report, silently tallying how much work would be required to make the damaged ships spaceworthy again. *But we may just be wasting our time.*

She sighed. Her father had commented that everything came with a price, but at least they *had* it. The people who didn't would be feeling a great deal worse. Right?

Right, she told herself. She knew it had been, at best, a costly victory. *If only I believed we'd truly won.*

CHAPTER FORTY

Caledonia/Tyre

The king didn't seem to be in good shape when Kat was finally shown into his sitting room. He looked as if he needed a few good hours of sleep, followed perhaps by a long holiday somewhere well away from any trouble and strife. Kat knew that wasn't going to happen. It had been sheer luck she'd been able to arrange an appointment with him before the council met, once she'd returned to Caledonia. Naturally, news of the engagement had raced ahead of her. She had no doubt that everyone who thought they were important had already formed their own opinion of the inconclusive engagement.

"You didn't capture the supplies," the king said. He sat up and poured himself a stiff drink. "Frustrating."

"You knew the odds of taking the supply depot intact were low," Kat said. She was too tired to hide her annoyance. She'd already heard rumors that she'd deliberately botched the mission, for some absurd reason of her own. No one with any experience in naval affairs would have agreed, of course, but the ones who didn't have any experience seemed to be the loudest voices. "They had too many chances to destroy it."

"And they did," the king said. He drained his glass and poured another one. "You lost."

"On the other hand, we gave Home Fleet a battering," Kat said. "They'll be a lot more careful in future."

The king assayed a humorless smile. "My spin doctors are already making that clear," he said. "They're playing up the angle of you luring them into a trap."

"And let's hope they believe the message," Kat said. Anything that made the House of Lords question its spies was a good thing. As useful as it had proved, the simple fact that Home Fleet had been able to stage an ambush was not a good thing. The next time, it might not work out in their favor. They'd have to be much more careful about security in the future. "They may think their spies lied to them."

She shook her head. There were just too many people passing through Caledonia, from colonials and mercenaries offering their services to the king to smugglers and foreign observers. There was no way they could clamp down hard, not without causing all kinds of diplomatic problems. Kat would have suggested moving operations elsewhere, but she knew the king wouldn't agree. He had to be somewhere public, somewhere where he could see and be seen. She was tempted to point out the danger—one man with a gun could put an end to the entire war—but she understood. Hadrian had to show that he was sharing the dangers.

"We have to keep fighting," the king said. "Admiral Ruben has plans for a second attack on Tyre."

Kat shook her head. "We're not ready," she said. "Not yet."

"He thinks otherwise." The king drained his glass. "And he might be right."

He reached for the bottle. Kat picked it up and moved it out of reach. He blinked, as if he was having trouble processing what had happened, then glared at her.

"Give that back," he ordered. "Now."

Kat shook her head. "You've already had too much to drink," she said. The king was . . . Well, the king was the king, but she knew what she'd say to a midshipman who'd had a little too much. And she'd have to be restrained from *killing* an officer who turned up roaring drunk. "You need to keep your wits about you."

The king's glare grew darker. "I can have you shot."

"You have to be sober to sign an execution warrant," Kat said, trying not to show how much the comment had disturbed her. Normally, no one, not even the king, could order someone shot out of hand. The death penalty could be handed out only after a fair and very careful trial. But now . . . She realized just how many conventions had fallen by the wayside. The structure she'd taken for granted for most of her life was gone. "You shouldn't be drinking at all."

She felt a sudden stab of guilt, mingled with bitter amusement. Had *she* acted like that, when she'd talked to her older siblings? She'd had the excuse of being a child, but still . . . She shook her head, telling herself it didn't matter. She couldn't change the past. The future, however, was constantly in motion.

And we won't have a future if the king drinks himself to death, she mused. *The entire cause will come crashing down.*

"I can handle it," the king insisted. "Give me the bottle."

Kat shook her head, firmly. "You need to go to bed and sleep it off," she said. She glanced towards the bedroom. Was there a sober-up in the medicine cabinet? Normally, sober-ups and contraceptives were included as a matter of course, but here . . . The palace wasn't a hotel. Who knew what the king would have in his bedroom? "Come on."

"I have appointments," the king mumbled. "Important appointments . . ."

"They'll just have to wait," Kat said. She helped him to his feet and steered him towards the bedroom. He was surprisingly heavy for a man of his slight build. "I'll deal with them."

She pushed the door open and blinked in surprise. The bedroom was immense and stunningly ornate, as if someone had deliberately tried to cram as many expensive pieces of artwork into the space as they possibly could. There was a complete lack of taste, Kat noted numbly; she saw solid gold candlesticks positioned next to expensive furniture that looked to date all the way back to Old Earth. The effect was more like a hoarder's den than a bedroom someone actually *used.* Kat had gone through a stage of redecorating her room every so often, like any other teenager with money to burn, but she'd never come up with something like this . . .

A shape stirred in the bed. "Hadrian?"

Kat felt herself flush as Princess Drusilla sat upright, her sheet falling away to reveal her form. The princess glared at her, then let out a little yelp and dived back under the covers.

Kat shook her head, torn between amusement and embarrassment. "He needs a nap," she said. She helped the king into bed, trying not to think about how the whole situation could be misinterpreted. "I'll see him in the morning."

She turned and left the bedroom, resisting the urge to giggle as soon as she was back in the living room. The situation was funny, but . . . It was a distraction from the real problem. The war had stalemated—she admitted that, at least to herself—but that wouldn't last. It wouldn't be long before one side tried something to tip the balance in its favor.

And if we don't win quickly, she thought as she headed out in search of Sir Grantham, *we might not win at all.*

♦ ♦ ♦

"A more inconclusive battle than we might have hoped," Grand Admiral Rudbek observed. "You were defeated."

"No." William met his superior's eyes evenly. "We may have conceded the battlefield, sir, but we did not lose the battle. We achieved two of our objectives and would have achieved a third if the second enemy fleet hadn't arrived."

Grand Admiral Rudbek looked cross. "You are sure?"

"Yes, sir," William said. "The engagement took out a considerable number of enemy ships and damaged several more. It also prevented the enemy from capturing supplies that would have allowed them to prolong the war, if not win it outright. We *were* caught by surprise, denying us the chance to win a complete victory, but we did accomplish our goals."

"You missed your calling," Grand Admiral Rudbek said. "You should have been a lawyer."

William said nothing. He knew it wasn't a compliment.

"We will, of course, be talking up your successes as much as possible," Grand Admiral Rudbek said. "It's unfortunate that your ships were damaged, of course, but we will definitely point out that you inflicted considerably more damage on the enemy. The general public, fortunately, doesn't really understand the difference between a superdreadnought and a destroyer . . ."

He shrugged. "Unfortunately, I was not able to convince the House of Lords to authorize an immediate attack on Caledonia."

"Unfortunate." William looked down at his hands. "That might have been our best chance to put an end to this."

"Probably," Grand Admiral Rudbek agreed. "For the moment, there is going to be a pause in the storm. Your ships will be repaired, we'll continue to build up our fleet . . . and then we will take the offensive. You will, of course, be a part of the mission."

"Yes, sir," William said. He was mildly surprised he hadn't been made into a scapegoat for the inconclusive engagement. "What do you want me to do?"

"When the time comes, we'll start *crushing* the king and his followers." Grand Admiral Rudbek held up his hand, then squeezed his fingers into a fist. "And that will be the end."

William nodded, feeling a twinge of regret.

"Enjoy a couple of days of leave, Admiral," Grand Admiral Rudbek said. "Report back to your command station on Monday."

"Yes, sir." William rose. "I just have to check in with my staff, then I can go on leave."

"Have fun," Grand Admiral Rudbek said. "It's sometimes good to know what you're fighting for."

♦ ♦ ♦

"Your Grace," Yasmeena said. "Investigator Niles is requesting an urgent meeting."

Peter frowned as he looked up from his work. He'd made it clear he wasn't to be disturbed unless the world was coming to an end. The meeting to lay the groundwork for economic rebirth after the war was important. But Yasmeena wouldn't have interrupted him unless it truly *was* urgent. He hoped Investigator Niles hadn't snowballed her. Peter would make sure his superior gave him a thick ear if he had.

"Have him shown into the blue room." He stood, nodding his apologies to the other attendees. It was a mark of how important the meeting actually was that so many other high-ranking figures had attended instead of sending their assistants. "I'm on my way."

He gritted his teeth as he strode down the corridor, feeling his head starting to pound. It simply wasn't *possible* to fine-tune the economy, no matter how much wealth and power you possessed. Economies were like farms; they had to be planted, maintained . . . and, sometimes, the crop you grew wasn't the crop you expected. The best they could reasonably do was let the air out of the bubble before it could explode, then take steps to make it easy for newcomers to make money. It made him sick, sometimes, to realize how much damage the Theocratic War had done to the system. Too many of his fellows had their eye on short-term advantage instead of long-term stability. The king's flight had only made things worse.

"Your Grace." Investigator Niles was standing by the table instead of taking a chair. "Thank you for coming."

"Sit down," Peter ordered. He took a chair himself and flopped into it. It wasn't a very ducal pose, but, for the moment, he didn't want to be a duke. "What can I do for you?"

Investigator Niles sat, with all the care of a man who suspects that his children have done *something* to the chair. Peter watched, feeling ice starting to crawl down his spine. Something was wrong. The investigator wouldn't have come so quickly unless something was very wrong . . .

"As you know, my team and I have been studying the records left behind by the king," Investigator Niles said. "It has been a complicated task . . ."

"I know," Peter said sharply. In his experience, people who told him things he already knew—people who *knew* they were telling him things he already knew—were trying to delay the moment when they had to come to the point. "Investigator, I'm a very busy man. Please, would you spit it out?"

"Yes, Your Grace," Investigator Niles said. "We were running through files concerning the king's secret black-ops units. It was complex, until we managed to start linking files and dates together. The king's people were evidently quite active during the war, from what we have been able to discover. We don't have all the details . . ."

"Of course not," Peter said. "What did he do?"

"One operation was carried out shortly before the end of the war," Investigator Niles told him. "On the surface, a black-ops team was ordered to shoot a particular aircar out of the sky . . ."

Peter felt the bottom fall out of his stomach as he put the pieces together. "My father . . ."

"We believe so." Investigator Niles continued, remorselessly. "Judging from context, it is clear that the team was authorized to shoot your father's aircar with a military-grade HVM. If they hit the target, and they did, there would have been no hope for any of the passengers. They would have died before they knew they were in danger."

". . . Fuck," Peter said. "Do you know . . . do you understand . . . what you're saying?"

"Yes, Your Grace," Investigator Niles said. "Duke Lucas Falcone, your father, was assassinated on the direct orders of the king."

To Be Concluded

ABOUT THE AUTHOR

Christopher G. Nuttall is the author of more than a dozen series, including the bestselling Ark Royal books, as well as the Embers of War, Angel in the Whirlwind, Royal Sorceress, Bookworm, Schooled in Magic, Twilight of the Gods, and Zero Enigma series. Born and raised in Edinburgh, Scotland, Christopher studied history, which inspired him to imagine new worlds and create an alternate-history website. Those imaginings provided a solid base for storytelling and eventually led him to publish more than one hundred works, including novels, short stories, and one novella. He still resides in Edinburgh with his partner, muse, and critic, Aisha. For more information, visit his blog at www.chrishanger.wordpress.com and his website at www.chrishanger.net.